THORNWOOD ACADEMY: LIVE TO TELL

BOOK FOUR

LJ SWALLOW

CHAPTER I

VIOLET

"You can't take the tiara. The item belongs to me," I say coolly, keeping a lid on the collection of insolent words waiting to follow.

Mrs. Lorcan sits behind the desk in her office, immaculate in a gray skirt suit offset by an eye-wateringly lime green shirt. I meet the pleasant smile painted onto her lineless face with a glare.

"You know, Violet, it can be difficult to tell if you're scowling at me considering you're usually sullen and miserable."

"And it can be difficult to tell whether you're untrustworthy or merely stupid," I reply as that lid flies off.

"Watch your tongue, young lady. You're on thin ice already after your performance at the Spring Ball."

Ah. I received a not-unexpected demand to meet the headmistress first thing this morning, and I'd prepared myself with basic facts to share, ready to give assurances my father would investigate, before retrieving the tiara.

Now, I am sharing nothing as there's no tiara to retrieve.

I'm already annoyed that nobody allowed me to visit Sienna

last night, Mrs. Lorcan even going as far as to ward the infirmary in case I invited myself in. I sat outside that room for hours, constantly refused entry. Rowan waited with me the whole time, occasionally attempting—and failing—to persuade me to leave. Sometime around 4AM, I gave up my vigil and stormed away, ready to begin investigations without speaking to Sienna first.

Now, Mrs. Lorcan informs me she's locked away the tiara and won't tell me where.

The headmistress stands. "If your claim is true and the tiara is yours, Violet, you're implicated in harming another student with magic."

"Excuse me?"

"A magical attack on Sienna using the tiara. Perfectly plausible since the Darwin House residents do treat you unkindly."

I choke. "I have no ill intent towards anybody at this academy and nor would I ruin the Spring Ball for Holly. You're *perfectly* aware of my disdain for other students and I wouldn't waste energy on trivial spells."

"Trivial?" Mrs. Lorcan's brows tug together. "The poor girl's traumatized. I've the unpleasant task of dealing with Sienna's parents, who're demanding answers."

I'd like to demand answers.

Still, at least the tiara is no longer stuck to Sienna's head by a curse and therefore recoverable. Somehow.

"Tell me where you've hidden the tiara," I demand.

"Secured safely, not hidden," she corrects.

"At the academy?" She gives a tight smile. "And where is Sienna?"

"I haven't hidden her." I grit my teeth at Mrs. Lorcan's light laugh. "Although I believe she's leaving the academy."

What? "When? Not before my father's people can interview her."

Mrs. Lorcan trains a steady gaze on me. "There's no reason for Dorian to involve himself. There're no lasting effects on the girl."

"How can you know?" I protest. "The incident happened less than twelve hours ago!"

"Sienna has no memory of the incident, nor is she suffering ill effects from her experience." The headmistress lifts her chin. "If not magic, how would 'your' tiara do such a thing to a girl?"

"Well, technically, it's my father's tiara," I correct.

She smiles. "Now that is a sight I can't imagine."

"Not one he wears." I take a calming breath. "I borrowed the tiara for the dance." *Technically*.

"Hmm. Your story is changing, Violet."

I narrow my eyes and swerve. "Who's Madison? A pupil from the academy?"

"A figment of Sienna's imagination caused by the magic," says Mrs. Lorcan. "Mrs. Riverside delicately swept Sienna's mind last night while she rested, and there's no sign of a 'Madison' inside."

The second-rate witch who teaches divination? Hardly conclusive. "No memories? Humans shouldn't touch valuable or potent witch artifacts and not expect consequences," I say. "The tiara could hold strong energy imprints—images of the past to explain why Sienna would daub bloodied words on a mirror!"

"Energy imprints? Did psychometry spells *work* on the tiara?" she asks. "I'm sure you and Rowan would've tried already if you believe the item's significant. You evidently *do*, since you're making such a fuss."

Over the last few days, my and Rowan's attempts to locate an image of the tiara online or in a library book proved futile, as did identifying the couple in the photograph. Therefore, we need the item to continue our investigation—if I can't locate the tiara, I shall locate Sienna and ask what happened.

"If you won't give the tiara to me, then you should hand the item to Dorian to investigate further. This is a supernatural occurrence and a supernatural object."

Her brow raises again. "Perhaps, but if the item were important to him, Dorian wouldn't allow his daughter to use it as *costume jewelry*. The tiara will be held safe from interfering fingers until I decide what to do."

"Interfering fingers may exist at the academy."

"Yes, they do, Violet," she says pointedly. "And that is why I have secured the item, and only I know where."

Secured. Where's secure? Because if someone hid the tiara in a box beneath a human factory floor, it wasn't 'secure' before.

"Why do *you* get to decide what to do with the tiara?" I demand. "Why can't I keep hold until my father retrieves it?"

"Because the item has caused injury in my academy. If your father has genuine concerns, he may contact me. However, word and images of the debacle have spread thanks to social media." The woman's face grows sourer.

I straighten. "Images? Of what? Bloodied words?"

"Everything, Violet," she says through clenched teeth.

Hmm. A task for Rowan. Social media still makes no sense to me; he can search the quagmire for clues.

"Where *did* the item come from, Violet?" she asks.

"Don't bother trying to read my mind," I tell her stiffly.

"Does the object have any connection to the murders?"

"I'm not permitted to share any information about the ongoing investigations with you or anybody else who isn't involved," I inform her. "But I am sure Dorian won't be happy if you interfere with the tiara."

The woman's face sours, although as usual her skin doesn't crease. "And tell me, is your father extending his investigations to the academy?"

"Has he told you such?"

"Everybody apart from the humans accepts there's more to these murders, and I will not be impressed if my academy comes under scrutiny."

My academy. "Are you seeking a replacement for Mr. Willis in order to share the burden of leadership?"

"Well, we all know that your father has the final word on who's employed at Thornwood." Her voice is as displeased as her expression. "Perhaps someone could take the vacant position next semester. I can manage currently."

"And I'm sure my father will keep a close eye on the academy in case you do need help," I say casually.

She sucks on her teeth while I bite my lip hard to prevent myself from using the silence to pick through her thoughts—Mrs. Lorcan would sense the invasion, and I'd face more trouble.

This continued meeting is pointless. If the tiara isn't here, I need to locate the item before somebody else does. Social media has a habit of spreading images far and wide—somebody will recognize the tiara and attempt to remove it from the wild.

What is Mrs. Lorcan hiding? Either she's worried about the reputation the incident will give her academy, or she knows something about the item's history.

"Just to confirm, you will not return the tiara to me?" I ask.

"No, Violet, I will not."

"Or tell me where it's located?"

She narrows her eyes as I give in to temptation and casually throw a spell her way. "Violet Blackwood. Mind reading is illegal and ill advised against your headmistress. Especially if you'd like to remain at Thornwood, which you now apparently do."

"Fine. I'll find the answer elsewhere." I straighten my blazer sleeves.

"Do not approach Sienna and use your 'skills' on her either," warns Mrs. Lorcan.

"I have no intention of doing such." I cross my arms over my chest. "Besides, I'm lacking in the social skills I'd need to use."

"That isn't the skill I mean."

"I know."

More silence. No answers. Stalemate. I turn to leave.

Correct. I don't have social skills or any level of acceptance amongst my peers, but I know a girl who does.

CHAPTER 2

VIOLET

I RETURN TO MY ROOM, and change into the academy uniform, ready to start as I mean to go along now—a fully participating member of the student body. I've barely used the uniform until today, and I slide my fingers between the stiff shirt's choking collar and my neck. Rowan's refusal to button his makes more sense now—he's seeking comfort rather than attempting non-conformity. Grimacing, I slip on the yellow-striped blazer and avert my eyes from the mirror.

How unusual that I'm the one preparing for class, when usually Holly's readying herself with unnecessarily bright excitement while I plan how to *not* go to lessons. She wasn't in bed this morning before I left to see Mrs. Lorcan. As Holly never returned to our room, she must've attended the impromptu party that replaced the Spring Ball. The loud one inside Darwin House that interfered with my concentration while I figured out events of the night.

If Holly returned before I left to visit Mrs. Lorcan in order to find my tiara, I would've endured pointed comments about

Rowan's presence in my bed. Annoyingly, the fully clothed guy fell asleep midway through an important conversation about tiaras. Rowan's help in combing through the night's events would've been more useful than his snoring. Apparently sitting outside the infirmary with me until 4AM sapped all Rowan's energy, although I suspect the beer that Leif brought him didn't aid in his remaining awake.

Rowan looks quite different when he sleeps, his face softer and the usual pinch to his brow absent. The unconscious guy had a gentler, calmer aura, the tension he carries lost somewhere else. Thus, I left Rowan alone to sleep—I'm sure he wouldn't appreciate me climbing into bed and disturbing him.

I stayed awake—less sleep requirement is a boon for a detective—and spent a frustrating time on my laptop looking for any connections between supes, the town, academy, and a 'Madison'. Nothing.

When I headed to meet Mrs. Lorcan, I left the sleeping Rowan a note instructing him to gather the others and meet before class starts. We must discuss our next move. He'll grumble about that —Rowan dislikes my notes and once teased that I need more practice at writing love letters. Then he smirked just as I opened my mouth to retort. Of course.

My meeting with Mrs. Lorcan wasted time. Brushing my hair hard in frustration, I again frown at where I've scrawled new names and timelines on my notepad because none seem to link. A knock distracts me. Didn't I tell Rowan we'd meet in the library as usual?

I open the door and tip my head back in order to meet Leif's eyes, that're partly hidden beneath his curls as usual. Dressed in uniform, he's paler this morning, eyes rimmed with shadows— possibly because his is one of the voices I heard late into the night.

Leif doesn't speak, and my gaze drops to the object in his hands. "What's that?"

His lips purse. "Flowers. Obviously."

Crinkling silver paper wraps around the small purple flowers in the bouquet, and I'm au fait enough with courtship rituals to know what this is. I glance over my shoulder to the blood-stained toy dog, which I placed prominently on my nightstand in an attempt to atone for my less than grateful response to the gift. I won't make that mistake again.

"I presume these are for me and not Holly." I step back and open the door wider for Leif to join me in the room.

"Why would I buy Holly flowers?" Leif's grip crushes the paper.

"Is there a reason for your gesture?"

"Will you just take them?" he asks, the same irritation around him as the 'dog incident' as he holds the flowers out.

"Apologies. I'm merely taken aback as you've never brought me flowers before. Thank you, Leif."

He shrugs, a rather odd reaction considering his tense demeanor.

"The ritual suggests these are either a token of your affection or an apology for something." I take the gift. "Chase bought Holly an ostentatiously large bouquet last week after one of their many disagreements. I could barely breathe over the stench for days. We haven't argued, so this is an affectionate gift?"

Leif sighs. "You always have to analyze everything. I wanted to buy you flowers and they're also kind of a sorry."

"Why? What did you do?" I ask.

"Kissed you without asking," he says quietly and his cheeks tinge pink. "That's wrong."

"Oh." I frown at the flowers, considering a response. "I didn't break your fingers. Does that not suggest I didn't mind?"

"But still." He runs a hand through his hair, fingers snagging. "I hope I didn't mess up completely."

"Omigod, that's so cute!" comes a familiar voice from the doorway.

Holly stands, rainbow shoes in hand, the dress from last night now sporting a couple of stains from the alcohol I can smell, and

THORNWOOD ACADEMY: LIVE TO TELL

her hair has returned to its wilder state. I'm unable to ascertain whether the dark beneath her eyes is tiredness or smudged eyeliner.

Leif moves further into the room to allow Holly inside, chewing on his lip as he avoids her eyes. Holly's face lights up when she takes a closer look. "Oh! *Violets.*"

"Yes, I am aware," I reply.

"That is *so* sweet, Leif," she exclaims, as if he'd bought the bouquet for her. "I'll find a vase! You can put them on your desk."

Before I can respond, Holly disappears into her cavernous closet. I gesture at Leif with the bouquet in my hand. "Although my response lacked the enthusiasm of Holly's, I do appreciate the gesture, Leif. Nobody brought me flowers before."

"Really? Not even Rowan?" His wary eyes brighten.

"Rowan once brought me chocolate, not flowers. Although I believe he worried I might be hungry due to blood loss and attack a student. And Grayson..." I can't ever imagine him doing something like this. "I don't think he's a gift-giver."

Holly returns and relieves me of the bouquet, which she sets about arranging in a small teardrop glass vase. "We need to talk, Violet," she says, her tone suddenly terser.

Oh. No. "But Leif is visiting me. Perhaps later?"

She turns from my desk. "Not only talk to you. Leif and the others might know more about what you did, so I want answers from them too."

"What *I* did?" I frown. "You don't think I'm responsible for events last night. Surely."

Holly tips her chin. "I'm fed up with you telling me half a story all the time, Violet. I'm your friend and you should trust me. You *know* I want to help, and I have skills you don't."

"Social skills?" asks Leif and I slice him a look.

"I'm involved in everything. I see and hear things," she continues.

"Such as?" I ask, now curious.

"*Such as*, I can talk to Sienna, who would never speak to you."

Her expression grows smug. "And I'll tell you everything she says *if* you tell me the truth."

"Is that sensible? I've expressed concern for your safety before, Holly," I reply. "*You've* expressed concern and taken an extended stay with Marci in case somebody murdered you in your sleep."

"Well, I'm connected to you so I'm in danger anyway, right?" She rubs her nose. "I know your father's asked questions about me and my family, which is rather rude considering we're *friends*. Ask Dorian if he found anything, because there's nothing *to* find."

I glance at Leif, who looks at her in bemusement. "Holly wants in, Violet."

"In what?" I ask.

"Your secret gang or whatever you are." She tips her chin. "I want to get involved."

I watch her impassively, carefully considering my response. "I would need to approve this with Rowan and Grayson."

Leif coughs in amusement and Holly chuckles. "Violet, everybody knows you're in charge. I need to shower and change for class. Let me know where you're meeting later, and I'll tell you what I know."

I watch Holly wander to the bathroom, and grimace. "First the Spring Ball, now this. The girl has the persuasive skills of a whole room of pneuma vampires."

"Which probably makes her useful," comments Leif. "I should go if Holly's changing."

"Right. We're meeting at the library in an hour."

"Of course," he says. "Day one of your new case, Detective Blackwood."

I know Leif's teasing, but there's still the buzz that runs through me when I consider how *I'm* the one capable of solving these things.

With help.

"Thank you for the violets," I say.

For a guy who says he's leaving, Leif hasn't moved any closer to the door. I'm not in tune with people, but my tangling with the three guys means I can read them based on their past actions.

And I can read what's in Leif's eyes, and why he's paused.

"Are you considering grabbing my backside again, Leif?" I ask.

"Uh. No." He wriggles his large fingers at me. "I've an art assignment to finish and need these intact."

Although I didn't respond with the semi-shriek and hug that Chase received from Holly, I *am* touched by his gesture. I close the gap between us, the scent of violets from before replaced with his familiar earthiness. Holding his cheeks in both hands, I press my mouth to Leif's and our lips stay together for a few seconds.

Did the shock at my action prevent the eager response I expected? Because Leif doesn't do anything. I edge back and smile at him. Leif touches my lips with a rough index finger.

"You know what, Violet? Your smile's worth more than a kiss," he says softly, pupils darker.

"Both are scarce commodities."

He chuckles. "Yeah."

"Well, you make me smile, Leif." I straighten my blazer sleeves. "Now. Could you find Rowan and Grayson if possible? Then I'll bring Holly to the library."

Leif returns my smile and tugs me into one of his semi-suffocating hugs. "You're hilarious."

This guy really does like hugging. And bringing me gifts.

Perhaps I need to find a gift for Leif?

CHAPTER 3

VIOLET

HOLLY's sunny personality is decidedly cool today, despite my generous invite to our meeting. I'd even say as icy as I often am. Does Holly truly blame me in some way? I definitely saw Marci's explosive side when the dance came to a halt mere hours into the event, as Mrs. Lorcan closed down activities. Some people moved on to hastily arranged parties in the different houses, including Leif, who I encouraged to rejoin his human friends. Grayson? I'm unsure where he went.

Rowan doesn't look any more refreshed after his sleep as he props his head on one hand, elbow on the desk beside his laptop. Leif sits on a chair also looking rather tired and complains about a headache. Grayson remains at a distance—from the desk and me —slumped in a chair at another desk close by, hands in pockets and face also containing less color than usual.

"Did you speak to Sienna?" I ask Holly.

Holly's definitely less sparkly eyed than usual but still immaculately uniformed and groomed, unlike the rest of our half-hearted efforts. "I didn't need to. The haunted tiara was the sole topic of conversation at breakfast."

"Haunted?" I scoff. "Cursed, perhaps, but the spirit world does not exist outside of human imagination."

"'Haunted' by who?" asks Rowan.

"A girl who died," replies Holly.

Grayson snorts. "Well, *obviously,* if the humans believe the tiara's possessed by evil spirits."

"Which girl?" I throw Grayson a look; the last thing I need is him upsetting Holly.

"As you know, the spirit's name is Madison, and—"

"Not a spirit, Holly," I interrupt.

"Someone murdered her—maybe at the academy—and now there're all kinds of stories about mysterious happenings over the years."

"Good grief," I mutter. "It's a supernatural academy, of course there's 'mysterious happenings'. Who murdered Madison? When? How?"

"Violet," whispers Rowan. "Put your pen and paper away."

I glance at where I've already begun my notes.

"I only spoke to Cassie because Sienna's too upset, and her parents are collecting her later. Cassie *did* tell me Sienna freaked out and screamed that she couldn't breathe or see anything."

I tap the pen on the notepad. "Perhaps Madison was asphyxiated? Buried alive or some such? Although, if Sienna couldn't *see* anything either, that's rather annoying. Without a visual, there're no helpful clues to where and when this occurred."

A familiar silence draws over the group and I frown at Rowan, who inclines his head to Holly. The girl's face drains of color, but her expression sharpens with disgust.

"How can you be so cold and cruel?" she asks.

"What? The girl is likely deceased. I'm investigating circumstances around her death and merely stating facts."

Holly clutches the neck of her blazer. "But still. To say Madison died horribly—and in such a matter of fact tone."

"And that's all you found out, Holly?" interrupts Leif.

"That's it. A girl called Madison died and her ghost possessed the tiara, which tried to suffocate Sienna." I roll my eyes at Holly's explanation. "Sienna stopped breathing, Violet!"

"How long for?" I ask.

"Again, matter of fact!" snaps Holly.

"Not long otherwise she'd be clinically brain dead." Oh. I look up, a sudden lurching in my stomach. "Sienna *does* still have a functional body? You've seen her?"

"No. But others have." Holly scoffs and adds sarcastically, "Maybe she died and a *necromancer* brought her back. Did you sneak into the infirmary, Violet?"

Both my brows shoot up. "What do you mean by necromancers? Has Marci mentioned one?"

"Uh." Holly stares. "I know one. And I was joking, but now I'm unsure if I am. Are there other necromancers beside you and your mother, Violet?"

"This isn't necromancy," says Grayson laconically. "I saw Sienna last night, and I caught enough of her thoughts to know her mind hasn't changed."

"Saw her where?" I demand. "Why didn't you tell me?"

Grayson flicks his tongue against his top teeth, the eyes I avoid looking into glinting as they meet mine. "I spent time at a human party and as I left the room, Sienna passed on the way back from the infirmary."

"The nurse told me Sienna wasn't leaving the infirmary until the morning."

"In the hope you'd eventually go away," mutters Rowan, and I huff.

"The party was in the common room, the opposite end of Darwin House to Sienna's room," says Holly. "Why were you in that part of the building?"

Grayson pushes a strand of hair from his cheek. "I spent time at a different party, not one in the common room."

"Omigod!" breathes out Holly. "Were you one of the hemia who took—" Her eyes slide to me.

"Who *what*?" asks Rowan sharply.

Blood? I shake away the thought, remembering the day I assisted Holly in locating water, when a nurse mentioned students 'experimenting' with blood play.

"Can we return to what's important?" I say and glance at Grayson, who's now examining his nails. "Holly. You have no information apart from a theory that the girl who cursed the tiara possibly died of suffocation?"

"Yes, and Sienna's fine, thanks for asking."

"I didn't ask." Holly's eyes narrow. *Oh. This again.* "I am happy to hear Sienna's suffering no ill effects and remains alive."

"Luckily for you," says Holly. "What *is* that tiara? Does it really belong to your family?"

Holly asked me this several times last night, albeit a little more hysterically. "I've a greater concern—*where* is the tiara?" I reply. "And why is my father not interfering yet? It's his favorite pastime."

"Dorian might be distracted by the other things," says Leif wearily. "The shifters and witches are more important than a 'haunted tiara'."

And Josef. "Cursed. We need to stop people from calling it haunted." I wrinkle my nose. "But you're right. The tiara hasn't killed anyone. I suppose this must become *my* investigation until I have a chance to speak to Dorian and request his help."

"What if Madison was a witch... are there any records of the old academy pupils?" asks Holly. "Photographs?"

"Nothing online, and the librarian told us there're no records held in the library. Dorian's council doesn't have anything either —fire destroyed most Nightworld Academy documents or pictures," says Rowan.

"There'll be records somewhere, surely," says Holly.

"We have a name for the victim. We'll comb through supe registration documents held by the supernatural council since the Reveal," I tell her. "Madison existed and likely was a supe."

Holly falls quiet. "I really hope that she didn't die horribly."

"*I* really hope that she's still alive," says Leif and Rowan looks at him doubtfully. "What? Maybe Madison is out there and hidden?"

I sink back in my chair and cross my arms. "A vague possibility. Unfortunately, we can research everything we want, but until I have that tiara again, we'll get nowhere."

CHAPTER 4

I BARELY NOTICE the afternoon lesson end, lost in my own time and place, ignoring the students learning around me. Yes, I indicated that I intend to become a Thornwood pupil rather than just a resident, and so I'm in a classroom. But I've more important things on my mind than Chemistry/Potions lessons.

Such as the tiara.

The longer my father's people take to arrive and retrieve the item, the greater the chance it'll fall into the wrong hands again. Not human ones—I doubt another would touch 'the haunted tiara'—but instead someone in the academy who's curious. Or even knows what spells and secrets cover the tiara.

Spells and secrets the tiara did *not* reveal to me or Rowan.

My distraction isn't helping me assist with Holly's experiments, as I process the meeting with Mrs. Lorcan and my subsequent annoyed phone call with Dorian. He sees no urgency and refuses to rush over here or send his minions. Leif's correct— Dorian's focus is elsewhere.

Leif doesn't attend this class, and Rowan's focused on his

17

work, including the 'more advanced tasks' he happily and smugly allows others to hear that he's performing. The humans grow small blue crystals on threads of cotton; Rowan transforms matter into precious gems.

Grayson's absent, not unusual, but there're few hemia around today, period. I must discover more gossip about last night's events. If Grayson involved himself in blood play, I do hope he was sensible. Something in his response to Holly revealing said gossip earlier had a double effect on me—confusion about why Grayson chose such risky behavior and an uncomfortable feeling spreading through my chest. Not because he took blood—if he did—but that his attitude in the library almost seemed as if he *wanted* a reaction from me.

Holly shoves a text book and pink notebook into her fancy black bag, in a rather violent fashion, then focuses on the zip without looking up.

"I detect you're annoyed with me still," I say as she climbs from the stool.

She shakes curls from her face. "Not everything is about *you*, Violet. I've arranged to meet Marci and don't want to be late." She pauses. "You could come too; I'm sure she'll be overjoyed to see you."

That was a definite hint of sarcasm. I look to Rowan, still in conversation with Mr. Woodside. "Marci's absent from class? Therefore, she must remain upset about last night's events. Events I'm confused why you blame on me."

"That wasn't an ordinary tiara, and you *knew* that. I thought you didn't waste time on people, yet you played a cruel trick," she snaps. "Your behavior ruined the whole evening. Mrs. Lorcan shut down the dance."

Well, this is quite vitriolic compared to our library meeting earlier. Is Marci feeding her these possibilities?

"Holly. You know me well enough. The chances I'd waste breath, let alone magic, on vapid human girls rank below zero." I shake my head. "The incident that halted the dance was not my doing."

"Hmm." Holly hauls the bag onto one shoulder, dwarfing her diminutive figure. Then her lips press together, and eyes take on a recognizable weirdness—she's debating whether to tell me something.

"Yes, Holly?" I ask.

"A couple of other girls are in the infirmary today."

I straighten. More tiara shenanigans? "What happened?"

"Blood loss," she whispers. "I didn't want to go into details with Grayson around earlier."

That's what I needed to do to gain entry into the infirmary last night? Offer a vein to a hemia? As if that's even a possibility—or desire. *Grayson could've helped.* I shake away the thought. We've well-established the unlikelihood of *that.*

"And this is what you referenced at the library—a party inside Darwin house. Humans and hemia?"

"Does that bother you?" asks Holly.

"I've no desire for an invite to a bloodfest. I don't consume blood, remember?"

"I mean, Grayson taking a girl's—or girls'—blood," she says cautiously.

"If he did so, Grayson chose unwise behavior. Although, better a human than a witch, as he has poor self-control."

Poor self-control. Like I have around him. I'm beginning to learn the term hypocrisy and when to apply it. Like now. To myself. But still...

"No. Grayson didn't partake."

Holly frowns. "How do you know?"

"I just do."

And that's the problem. I know Grayson's body didn't contain human blood this morning, and I know he's worried that I believe he took part.

Is Grayson aware *how* aware I am?

"He appeared too pale for a recently gorged hemia," I add.

Grayson *wasn't* stupid. I hope.

Finally, the over-studious Rowan joins us, and Holly's conversation topic abruptly ends. "I'm late," she says and dashes away.

"Huh?" Rowan digs hands into his trouser pockets and watches her go. "What have I done?"

"Recently? Nothing untoward in your behavior has bothered me."

He laughs. "No. What have I done to upset Holly?"

"Oh. No idea." I pull my phone from a pocket and mutter. No response from my last message to Dorian. As I stab another to him, Rowan takes the phone from me with warm fingers. "What?"

I'm irritated by the beginnings of a smirk.

"I know something that you don't know, Violet."

"Are you five years old?" I retort. "And there's little that you do, hence I had no need to pay attention to Mr. Woodside's class today."

Human students file from the classroom and we follow. There was less chatter and activity in this lesson compared to the last one I attended. I'd presumed due to their late night party but are some paler for other reasons?

Outside, I rest against the painted wall as Rowan stands over me, his magical and physical proximity sparking a different awareness. I don't avoid closeness to Rowan any longer— obviously—but I'm perturbed by how his effect grows. Rowan doesn't touch me, but he's already imprinted on my skin from the times he has, my dislike of contact confusingly absent with Rowan.

"Occasionally, teachers confiscate magic items," he says.

"I imagine so, since this is a magic school for teenagers who're likely to commit delinquent acts due to age and immaturity."

He laughs. "Like me?"

20

"Oh? And when did someone last confiscate an item from you?"

"A week before you arrived. A lodestone infused with Willowbrook magic taken for 'safe-keeping' until my parents find the time to collect the item. I'm sure Mrs. Lorcan would store the tiara in the same place—hidden and warded."

"Hidden and warded? Then how is your information advantageous?"

"Violet." He runs a finger along my nose before kissing the tip, and I give him a warning look. *Public.* "I'm strongly attuned to the Willowbrook energy, which is one reason the teachers removed the stone from me. When I looked for it, I couldn't detect anything in the admin area of the academy. Confiscated items must be kept somewhere surrounded by intense magical energy, which would overwhelm any magic that's attached to stored objects and make them harder to detect."

"You now know where the confiscated items are kept?" I whisper, eyeing the two girls walking by the pair, who're also whispering as they fix me with unpleasant looks.

"Yes, I do." He hands back the phone and places a hand on the wall above my head.

"And?" Rowan arches a brow. "I hope this isn't another of your 'if you kiss me, I'll tell you' moments," I say. "Because that never works."

His eyes drop to my lips. "Violet, I said that once as a joke." He pauses. "But I won't say no."

"Good grief," I mutter at him. "I've told you numerous times I will not make a public display of myself."

"Oh? Like with Leif at the dance?" he asks, his arched brow moving higher.

"That was different."

"Uh huh." He drops his hand from the wall and steps back. "I know better than to blackmail you, Violet Blackwood."

"Precisely."

"And I don't need to."

Our eyes meet, his gleaming with the challenge at me to deny the times I've shoved him against a wall and kissed him. Me. The girl who hated touch, with a personal space boundary a mile wide, now enjoys Rowan's attention.

I no longer avoid the guy who I'd looked at with mild irritation much of the time. Rowan understands me and curiously when he isn't around Rowan's still with me. Although Rowan does still irritate me at times—something definitely mutual— and that's what usually leads to the wall shoving.

I'm beginning to suspect he likes to clash with me for that very reason.

CHAPTER 5

ROWAN

I'M aware of the stone's location as I've attempted to reclaim the object once before. I haven't bothered since Violet arrived, as there's less urgency in perfecting the protective spell around Leif and myself. I don't need the additional energy source the stone would give me.

Besides, I've a greater source now—Violet.

Shortly after the academy took the stone from me, I located the room hidden in an older part of the campus, but struggled to break and pass the wards. The area containing the room is out of bounds to students, therefore anybody seen around the place would arouse suspicion.

There's no guarantee we'll get past the wards anyway, but it's worth a try with the potency from both our magic. I totally agree with Violet—we need to get the tiara in ours or Dorian's hands asap before somebody else gets hold. Even though I couldn't find anything with the psychometry, I'm positive there's a magic block on the item. Did Sienna somehow accidentally and unpleasantly remove that? Because if she did, psychometry could work next time, and somebody may not want us to read the energy imprint.

The fire that destroyed the old academy never touched this area on the edge of the building. Some wanted the whole place pulled down afterwards, but others wanted to preserve the magic infused in the stone from years of students passing through. And so, the peeling painted walls and scuffed floorboards became a museum of sorts—a snapshot in time of a different world, with the new academy built around the magical center.

Violet wanders beside me, occasionally touching the flaking walls. "I don't sense anything different."

"The old library was over there." I indicate a set of stone steps towards the end of the hallway. "Above the place magic converges."

She perks up. "Any books left inside?"

"No. Long gone. There were witches' study rooms beneath, and I tried to sneak in there once but again, heavy wards." I rub my cheek. "That's where the academy stores all the confiscated items now."

Violet's face brightens. "Perfect. We may find other things."

"Um. No. We should only take the tiara."

She frowns. "Not your stone?"

"Only if I want to shout from the rooftops 'I stole something from a room I'm banned from entering'."

"Why on earth would you do such a thing?" Violet's inability to differentiate what's literal or not amuses me still, but she gets pissed if I show that amusement, and usually wait for her to catch up nowadays. "Oh. Figure of speech?"

"Yeah. I meant, the stone's easily detectable, and whoever stores items will know I've taken it."

"But you do stand on the rooftop on occasion. Once with Wesley, when you threatened to throw him off with magic." Violet edges towards the stone steps and pauses, head slanted as she listens for movement or voices before we step into the heart of the forbidden area.

24

Oh, yes. I've a clear memory of that day. I would never wish the arsehole dead, and I know 'don't speak ill' of him, but Wes was a vicious bastard who got off on the power his father's position gave him.

Leif found me on the cusp of acting on impulses created by angry magic—one of the first times he interrupted when I lost my shit. I would've terrified Wes into thinking I'd force him to jump, but not finished the spell.

Or would I? There's something in me I can't trust, and Wes tapped into that darker side Violet now encourages. Wes assaulted a witch girl and justice wasn't served—Lucia forced to leave the academy rather than implicate him in a crime. Yeah, privileged bastard thought he could take what he wanted from anybody.

That's what led to his near-death, pissing himself, experience. Still, added benefit—he never bullied me again.

I startle as Violet touches my hand. "Rowan. What's wrong? Your energy shifted weirdly. Is this area influencing you?"

The growing burn in my chest now spreads through my limbs and is more than the heat of anger prompted by my thoughts. *Magic.* I quickly glance at my hands. No shadows—at least a memory can't do that. Yet.

Memories of Wes's actions against that girl prompt other images. "You never told me what happened with Wes's friends at the party," I say quietly as we sneak up the stairs. "Did they touch you?"

"Strange of you to ask now," she comments. "And yes, you know that. Grayson prevented me from pulling them apart for the audacity."

"They're lucky Grayson didn't remove their organs."

She sneers. "I saw into their heads. I would've removed their dicks if they'd tried anything."

Violet's matter of fact tone never switches when she's joking, and in this case I uncomfortably believe that she isn't. "Grayson. Why was he there?"

She pauses and looks back, her eyes gleaming in the dim moonlight cast through a window at the top of the steps. "At the party? Kai invited him."

"No. In the bedroom, as if he knew you'd be there."

"He likely followed me. Grayson possesses stalker tendencies; something not unusual for hemia."

"Right." I arrived on the scene upstairs at the party because I sensed a shift in Violet's magic, even from a distance. Maybe Grayson did follow—or maybe he experienced the same thing as me, but through his weird connection to her blood?

I'm unsure how or why some vamps get hung up on each other's blood. Is that to create a deeper connection with each other? Or are they looking for an extra high? I asked Violet if she felt any different now that Grayson's blood flowed inside her. She became so quiet and still that I kicked myself for asking the question.

Then she kissed me. Despite her protests earlier, Violet soon figured out that's the best way to shut me up.

And Violet really *doesn't* like talking about Grayson. The pair behave as normally towards each other as Grayson and Violet could ever manage, guarded like the early days, but friendlier. Although there's no way anybody can miss the undercurrent that'll drag them down—and together—sooner rather than later.

"Is that the library?" Violet points at where one of the double doors remains, and when I nod she scurries forward.

Violet shares the disappointment I had the first time I snuck into the circular room—no books, only empty shelves on the intact parts of the four floors. The old librarian's desk remains too —a semi-circle close to the front of the library. Even the magic contained beneath the academy mostly drained after the disaster, and left the library an empty shell. Still, that energy must've been bloody strong if these remnants exist.

Violet stands in the library's center and tips her head to the high ceiling where the shelves stretch up and around us. The place absorbed the smell of the wood that smoldered in the fire that missed this room and has a cool mustiness from disuse. I would've loved this place and the opportunity that magic offered.

"Did your parents attend the old academy?" asks Violet.

"Probably."

She looks back to me. "Probably. How do you not know? Aren't yours founding families?"

"My parents are amongst those who don't talk about life before the supes revealed themselves to humans." Why? I've researched, terrified my family had links to the old terrorist Dominion, but found nothing. Dad says he refuses to look backwards and then clams up. Did my family lose people or are there skeletons in closets that I haven't found yet?

"My parents never attended," Violet remarks and wanders across the cracked tiled floor towards spiraled stairs leading to a lower level. "Obviously."

Yeah. Another past that's best not spoken about. "No. This way." I lead Violet towards a back corner and a rectangular, handle-less door that matches the dark wood shelves on either side, almost blending in. The entrance to the old study rooms. "The first wards are here."

Violet chews her lip and places a hand on the frame, causing runes to spring up and glow faintly white. She scoffs to herself, and flames appear at her fingertips as they did in the factory. Easily breaking the runes by scorching them, Violet opens the door to a small set of stone steps.

At the bottom, two other doors, these with silver lever handles, are sealed and with visible runes this time.

"This is as far as I've gotten," I say and conjure a witch light into my palm. "The room with the artifacts is on the left and wards impossible for me to pass."

Violet finds obliterating *these* runes with fire impossible and mutters with frustration after several minutes trying to break them. She reaches back for my hand and our fingers curl together.

Sometimes, the intimacy from the spell energy passing between us surpasses the type of touch that comes from the desire for something more physical. When we link, Violet's magic begins as a gentle stroke along my arm, and if we're connected long enough, that magic beats through me into something more arousing. A different arousal to when we kiss—I'm enmeshed with Violet on a level that's different to sex, as there's a part within that I can only reach in moments like these.

Connecting this way overwhelms me as Violet becomes the center of who I am—through the breaths that synchronize, her soul meeting mine, shared energy running through my blood. Violet always falls silent at these times and it's another of her 'discuss this later' topics. I can't figure out if she feels everything as intensely as I do, but as Violet avoids discussing the situation, I'm positive she does.

However and whatever Violet feels, the magic potency created by joining means she won't avoid the act itself.

My vision refocuses when Violet's grip drops. The runes have faded and with a triumphant glance at me, she pushes down the carved silver handle. The energy firing inside fades, but the desire for Violet doesn't as we step into another unlit, sparsely furnished room.

Residual magic from past spells seeps from the walls and floor, as if we've broken into somewhere hermetically sealed. If I touched anything, I'd lose myself in the time of witches studying in the room.

"I'm not using magic in here." I snuff out my witch light and point to a half-melted blood red candle, then flick a flame of my own at the wick. "I don't want to leave any imprints behind."

The small light reveals chairs stacked in a corner and several solid wood shelves containing jars and boxes. I cross to examine items closer; most contain ingredients that can be used for dangerous spells—including belladonna. If I'd succeeded in breaking into this place before, I wouldn't need to steal from Violet's room that night. *Attempt* to steal. The first time we magically met head to head. I smile at the memory. Who would've thought we'd be here now?

I peek inside a carved walnut box—a variety of precious stones in varying sizes, some set in signet rings, and necklaces with talismans humming with energy. Setting the box down, I run fingers along a row of leather books. Most have no names on the side, but again, the magic and imprints hit me. I pull my hand away, not wanting the distraction. One thing's sure—I'm glad I hid my family's grimoire in the current library before someone found the book. If that's happened, the book would've ended up here alongside the Willowbrook stone.

"How boring," comments Violet as she takes hold of what appears to be a rabbit's foot on a black ribbon, before pulling a disgusted face and dropping it into a basket of white runestones.

She roughly rummages through drawers, occasionally examining the contents of small boxes before climbing on wobbly stacked chairs to inspect the tops of a higher bookcase. "Where's the tiara?" she grumbles as a small book falls onto the moldy rug.

I shake my head and turn away, searching for my own item. I easily locate the Willowbrook stone, tucked inside a charmed velvet pouch inside an iron box. The black stone fits into my palm, and I squeeze tight. Instantly, the object sharpens my Willowbrook magic, squeezing my chest, and my fingers curl tighter. *Don't let go.* I'm pulled in two directions—leave the item here for my parents to collect or pocket it.

Another book flies from the shelf as Violet's frustration increases.

"Can't you sense the tiara at all?" I ask.

"No. If this is a ploy for me to aid you in stealing back your item, I shall be most unimpressed," she informs me.

"Yeah, because making you pissed is *always* such a great idea, Violet." I shake my head. "Your silent treatment when you don't get your own way is childish and boring."

Her lips press together. "Sometimes silence is better than sharing my thoughts."

"Mmm." I toss the stone in my palm and step towards her. "Want to know *why* the academy removed *this* from me?"

She blows hair from her face, cheeks reddening with her exasperation. "More attempts at mystery, Rowan?"

I hold the object up between my thumb and forefinger. "The stone channels people's thoughts and allows the Willowbrook holding it to manipulate them."

"Right." *Unimpressed?* "So, mental magic? Hardly unique."

"Mind control. Like the day with Wesley," I add.

Violet studies but doesn't touch the stone. "Then my theory that you manipulated Leif could've been correct."

"Not possible, because I didn't have the stone at the time."

"You have influenced Leif before?"

"No. I would *never* do that to a friend." I step back in disgust. "And I only used the stone for protection."

"Apart from Wesley on the rooftop?" She looks pointedly at me, then turns her back and crouches down to open a brown leather trunk on the floor. "Your stone—I find *that* type of magical item always leads to trouble."

"In the wrong hands, maybe."

She looks over her shoulder. "And you think yours are the right hands, Rowan?"

Her words slap me, almost an accusation that I'd use magic to further my aims. We've discussed this numerous times—that's no longer my desire, and in the past I only wanted to protect myself through gathered power. Now I'm bonded to one of the strongest supernatural creatures in existence and possess shadow magic. Magic I'm keen to explore.

Alright. I see Violet's point.

"Would you please explain why you've broken into this room?" comes a terse woman's voice from the doorway.

Panic hitting, I turn and swiftly pocket the stone. If anybody notices this missing from the room, the academy will obviously know who took the item, and that'll lead to trouble. But, now I've the stone in my hand I can't let go, as if clinging on and begging me not to leave it behind.

Despite the lack of decent light, I recognize the short woman

30

with her black hair in a severe bob-styled hair, wearing one of her oversized shirts over leggings. The librarian, Mrs. Eldridge, stands, hands on hips. "This room is out of bounds to everybody. Do you understand the trouble you could be in?"

"Everybody? Then why are *you* here?" replies Violet.

"As librarian and historian, I'm custodian of the magical artifacts stored within the academy," she replies.

"Still, rather unusual that you choose to visit this particular room the day the tiara's placed here," continues Violet.

"Mrs. Lorcan warned me this might happen and I'm keeping a closer eye on the place."

"So, you followed us?" accuses Violet.

I've a good relationship with Mrs. Eldridge, the woman always helpful if I need to locate anything in the library and we'd often chat since—until recently—I'd visit alone. She assisted me and Violet in finding history books as we attempted to discover more about the old academy in the hope of finding names or more photographs, or the origins of the tiara. We found little. With the old library destroyed and the old Confederacy's decision to stay in the Dark Ages and not keep electronic copies, the only books available are modern accounts of the past—and no help.

"I'd expect better from you, Rowan," Mrs. Eldridge says, and I grit my teeth at her condescension. "Have you found what you're looking for?" The question's directed at me, not Violet. Does she know I have the stone in my hand? "The tiara?"

"No," mutters Violet. "But I intend to find it."

"You're not taking anything from this room," she warns.

"The tiara belongs to me."

"No. It does not."

"You sound rather convinced, yet you couldn't find us a picture, nor did you recognize the tiara when I asked in the past," retorts Violet. "If not me, who *does* this belong to?"

"Following yesterday's incident, I now *know* the tiara is a powerful artifact—as does everybody else within the academy. The tiara remains in this room until we find the rightful owner."

"You're avoiding my question and lying," says Violet. "You came here to take the tiara."

"Violet, shush," I urge.

Tutting, Violet turns away to investigate more boxes. As she pries open the lid on an oak chest, Violet's knocked backwards across the room, smacking her head on a table leg. Her eyes flash with anger when Mrs. Eldridge chuckles.

"Do you think wards only prevent people from getting into the room, Violet, and not into the boxes?"

She hops to her feet and glares, unflustered by the knock on her head. "Where's the tiara?"

Something else catches my eye as Violet and Mrs. Eldridge face off. One of the bottles crowded onto a nearby shelf stands out from the rest. Most are either clear or brown glass and some are labelled. This one belongs on a store shelf—plastic, labelled but as make-up remover not a potion, and containing a clear liquid. I sidle in front of the shelf, facing the others, and reach behind for the imposter while Violet continues to argue with the librarian.

"Go on. Touch another box or drawer," says Mrs. Eldridge smugly.

"Stop pushing me," snaps Violet. "Or you'll regret the decision."

"You'd attack a staff member? I thought you wanted to remain at Thornwood."

"I'm not leaving this room for *you* to take the tiara!" she snaps again.

"And I'm not leaving here until you do. If you go now, I won't report you."

"Why not?" Violet replies.

Mrs. Eldridge's brow tugs. "You *want* me to report you?"

"No. Because I bet *you're* not supposed to be here. I don't believe Mrs. Lorcan would tell you the tiara is in here, because she told me nobody knows where she placed it apart from her. I'll report *you* if the tiara is missing tomorrow." Violet jabs a finger at her. "I'm onto you, Mrs. Eldridge."

Sighing, I take Violet's hand and squeeze. "Random accusations never help, Violet."

"This woman knows what the tiara is and wants to steal it!"

The more agitated Violet becomes, the less likely I can keep her mouth or attitude in check. "I'd rather nobody knew I'd snuck in here, Violet," I tell her. "Let's go before Mrs. Eldridge changes her mind."

"I have no intention of taking the tiara," says Mrs. Eldridge. "I *protect* artifacts and have respect for them; I have no desire to possess a dangerous one. If the tiara is missing tomorrow, there'll be one culprit. You."

"Violet doesn't have the item," I say. "And we're leaving now." No response from the light of my life. "Violet?"

"This is wrong!" says Violet tersely and walks towards where Mrs. Eldridge still stands in the doorway. "Mark my words, I will bring you to justice if you steal the tiara."

"Dear me, such melodrama. Justice for what?"

"The murder." Violet reins back in her control and watches for Mrs. Eldridge's reaction.

"Sienna isn't dead, you silly girl."

Uh oh. Violet's pissed energy spikes at the woman's continuing condescension, but at least Violet has the sense and self-control not to divulge anything else about the tiara and her suspicions.

Straightening her shoulders, Violet edges by the librarian. "Well, Dorian will no doubt arrive to retrieve this tomorrow."

"Interesting. You'd risk stealing the tiara if you think your father's coming to collect it?" she replies.

I give Mrs. Eldridge a tight smile, the stone and bottle in my pockets weighing heavier as she looks at me. "Violet's concerned, that's all. We'll leave now."

"Concerned? There are many words I'd use to describe the girl, and that isn't the one I'd pick."

"Good grief," mutters Violet as I maneuver her towards the doorway.

"Go before she changes her mind," I repeat.

"Of course, she won't change her mind," says Violet. "The woman isn't supposed to be sneaking around down here either."

Throwing an unimpressed look over her shoulder, Violet stalks away towards the stone steps.

We might not have the tiara, but I have something Violet will be extremely interested in. And something else I'm unsure why I took.

CHAPTER 6

VIOLET

I sit on Rowan's bed and unscrew the lid from the small plastic bottle, then sniff. Unmistakably the aniseed scent that I could barely stomach the first few times I took this potion. "You found the bottle on a shelf in the artifacts room?"

He nods. I take a sip.

Definitely my missing potion. I screw the lid back, jaw tight, losing the calm that I'd managed to instill in myself after our encounter with Mrs. Eldridge. A clue. "Who has access to that room apart from the librarian? Mrs. Lorcan? Anybody else?"

"I don't know. Very few people and only important ones."

"Well, now I have a culprit for stealing this." I shake the bottle at him. "The same person who drew the runes in Wesley's room."

But who? Why would Mrs. Lorcan take my potion? The last thing she'd want is bloodshed at her academy—the hemia cause enough problems without adding in a feral hybrid. The librarian? She would need a key to *my* room too. I place the bottle in a pocket. "I hope somebody notices that it's missing. I want to see what happens—who behaves suspiciously."

35

Rowan sits beside me. "Yeah. I hope somebody doesn't notice *this* is missing."

He pulls a familiar stone from his jacket pocket. The only light in the room comes from Rowan's desk lamp, but the black object now glows a soft white as if its own light source.

This time, I hold out a hand to take hold, but Rowan curls his into a fist around the stone. "This belongs to me."

"Like the library book when we first met?"

"That was Willowbrook spells. This is Willowbrook power."

I blink at him, not liking the harsh way he said 'power'. "As I said earlier, power that's dangerous in the wrong hands, Rowan."

"Best not give the stone to you then," he teases.

"I only want to take a look. Is that a problem?" I ask.

Something odd crosses his face—a pinch of distrust to his brow before he shoves the stone back into his jacket. "Later. Let's talk about tonight."

"This *is* like the library book." I say with suspicion.

"Figuring out what happened tonight is important. It's late. Let's come up with some theories and plan our next move before you go. I thought that would be your immediate aim. We've a clue."

Go? The guy often stalls to keep me in his room as long as I'm prepared to stay. "Rowan. What's wrong with me examining your stone?"

He drags a hand through his hair. "Other witches aren't supposed to touch this, okay?"

"Not even the witch you're bonded to?"

"Just leave it, Violet," he snaps. "I wouldn't have shown you if I'd known you'd get weird about it."

Heat flares on my cheeks. "*Me* weird about it?"

"Anyway, we need to look into the librarian further," he continues. "I didn't find any information about the tiara in library books—what if Mrs. Eldridge hid something?"

"Yes. If she takes the tiara, I'll be extremely annoyed."

Understatement. "Stop changing the subject. You're behaving like the irritating witch I met in the library the day I arrived. What are you deflecting?"

"Where's my thanks for finding your potion?" he bats back.

"Thank you. Now tell me why you're so possessive of the stone—or is it possessive of *you*?"

"Don't be ridiculous."

"Then why the sudden personality change?" His eyes narrow. "Show me the stone or I won't believe you." They become slits. "I won't touch."

Just when I think he'll ignore me, Rowan pulls the stone from his pocket.

I lied.

Lurching towards him on the bed, I grab at the stone, my reflexes faster than his, but Rowan's grip of the object is tight. "What the hell, Violet?"

"Let me look."

Rowan holds the stone above his head, and I reach out again, shoving him back until he almost falls from the bed. I climb onto him and pry at his fingers, but he keeps tight hold, looking up at me as I straddle him. My hair falls into his face as I lean across to reach his outstretched hand.

"What is your problem, Rowan?" I say through clenched teeth.

"Don't you think *you're* overreacting?" he says and blows my hair from his face.

But I need to see this stone. Touch, even for a moment. *Need*, as if it would satiate a hunger I'm unaware I had. I move again, frustrated and on the verge of digging sharp nails into his fingers.

"I *want* the stone."

"What the hell has gotten into you?" I shift positions against his body as I try to move myself upwards and closer to taking hold, and Rowan swears beneath his breath before attempting to get out from under me.

I'm so focused on the stone, he blindsides me when I'm flipped on my back across his bed, my wrists pinned above my head by one of his hands in a sudden grip, the stone in his other. "Rowan," I snarl and pull at his hold.

"You don't steal this."

"I'm not stealing your stone! Don't be ridiculous."

Why can't I move my hands? I've twice as much physical strength as this guy. I tip my head up and my heart jolts. Small tendrils of shadows bind my wrists to his fingers, their clammy cool spreading across my skin.

Shadows? If I moved now, I wouldn't get far—I'm literally bound to him.

"Good grief, Rowan. What's happening with you?" I say and buck against him.

He moves to sit on me, stone in one hand as he leans forward to keep my wrists trapped in the other. My breathing grows ragged, Rowan's weight on my hips isn't as big an issue to me as his decision to bind me with magic. That he *can* bind me. His lips are slightly parted as he looks down, and although I'm transfixed by him, I'm uneasy at the intensity in his expression.

My focus snaps to the stone and logic hits my mind. *The stone wants my magic.* That's the desperation taking hold of me. I draw in a shaky breath. "You should take that thing back to the room and not touch it again," I say. The glow spreads from the stone to Rowan's hand and his heart beats louder, as if outside his body and audible in the room.

Magically stronger; physically weaker.

Taking a deep breath, I gather the vamp energy that's my defense against his magic and buck again. The shadows drag like blades across my skin, painful as I tear my hands from his shadow magic hold, and I shove him hard in the chest.

"Fuck!" The word comes from Rowan along with his winded breath, as he's pushed from me, almost whacking his head on the side of his bed as he falls to the floor, onto his back.

I rub my wrists, examining them for magic or injuries. No

shadows on me—but they're still on Rowan. He's lying against the hard floor, catching the breath I knocked from him, stone still firmly glowing in his fist.

As the shadows crawl along his arm towards the glowing stone, a sick dread spreads from the depths of my soul. No. Whatever magic the stone contains, shadows shouldn't touch it. Look at the effect the object's having on him. Me.

How potent *is* Willowbrook magic?

In a heartbeat, I throw myself at Rowan again, pinning the tendril wrapped arm out straight against the floor. He won't let go of the stone, and the shadows sneak closer. "Let go, Rowan!"

"Get off me, Violet!" As I try to loosen his fingers, they become vice-like, unnaturally strong for Rowan.

The shadows don't slow in their aim, and my dread morphs into panic. *Stop them. Now.* "Sorry, Rowan," I say, then lift his fingers, and bite.

He shouts out, releasing the stone, which I grab and hurl into the corner of the room, beneath his dresser. Rowan doesn't try to move, completely still, staring at his grazed fingers instead.

"You bit me!" he says hoarsely.

I wipe the small amount of his blood from my lips, too scared to taste. "Only a little bite."

He chokes a half laugh.

"The shadows wanted to join whatever magic your stone holds, Rowan," I say hoarsely. "Or the other way around." I'm still lying on him, refusing to move—if I'm here, he can't escape, and there's no way I'm allowing that stone back in Rowan's possession.

I cast a glance to where the object glows beneath his dresser, and fight my own gnawing need to take hold. Why this reaction now? I was fine in the artifact room. Because I wasn't as close? The further I am from the object, the less I want to take hold. Or is this because Rowan and his magic aren't attached to the stone now?

"Didn't you see?" I ask him. "The shadows aimed for the stone. I've told you to never use shadow magic."

"You triggered me by fighting," he retorts and rubs at his fingers, mumbling about me biting him.

"The stone knew I'd stop the shadows you possess from touching it and influenced you against me."

"That's not true."

I scoff, heart still thumping, but with fear of what I just witnessed. "And if I took the stone and hid it?"

"No!" His eyes go wider.

"That response tells me you can't keep that item, Rowan." The time he attempted to blackmail me with Holly's coat, he wanted help from someone 'with Blackwood magic running through their veins'. There must be something already inside Rowan for me to prompt them easily.

Could this Willowbrook stone absorb and amplify the Blackwood magic I gave him too?

"I can't believe you bit me—and not in a good way," he complains.

"How could I ever bite you in a good way?"

"I won't answer that." He half-smiles.

"Honestly, Rowan," I mutter. "Have some common sense."

His hand sneaks into the back of my hair, and he brushes a thumb across the nape. "Should I trust you now you've tasted my blood and have me pinned to the floor?"

"I barely tasted you," I retort. "Grazes produce little blood."

"Mmm. But you're still holding me down." Fingers digging into my neck, he lifts his head and pulls my bottom lip into his mouth.

Taking advantage of my surprise for the second time this evening, Rowan flips me back over, pressing his mouth and body hard against mine. I could easily send him careening halfway across the room and ensure he does hit his head this time.

But I don't.

Rowan's kissed me like this before, the craving he suppresses escaping as his tongue tangles with mine, devouring, wanting more. My preference for hard kisses recently moved away from just a preference, and towards our shared yearning for more than kisses.

So when Rowan slips his hand beneath my shirt, and runs fingers along my side, the touch ignites desire rather than affront. I delve my hands beneath his T-shirt, Rowan's skin softer than I imagined, the muscles beneath taut against my fingertips. His fingers don't move anywhere else, instead lightly stroking the skin he's found, and I dig my nails into his side as the kiss continues, our limbs entwining.

For the first time ever, I'm shaking because everything about this situation creates a girl who's a million miles from the one in careful, total control of her body and mind. I've experienced a lot of change since I arrived at Thornwood and *this* I'm struggling to deal with most.

Rowan pulls his mouth away, an invitation for me to move, but I don't want to escape from under him or lose his touch on my skin. Flames can never touch me, but the heat licking every inch of my skin burns arousal, and I'm aching in places I never thought I'd ache, the heat from our fight now pooling low in my belly.

Rowan's magic forged with mine many times, and a desire for a more intimate connection surges between us as that happens, but this is different. Rowan's magic isn't what's pulling us towards joining physically, nor is mine.

Neither of us speak, our breaths mingling, as his hand moves further up my side, but he stops as my own hand tenses against his back.

"I don't like this," I say hoarsely.

His eyes widen. "Really?"

"What's happening?" Rowan side-eyes where the stone rolled beneath his dresser as his heart thrums against mine. "What magic is *in* that?" I ask.

He runs his fingers along my lips, swollen from his harsh kiss. "I told you. Power."

"I don't understand. I've never wanted something that badly," I say. "My *magic* wanted it. Whatever the power your stone holds, I don't think Blackwood magic should merge with it."

Rowan slowly pulls his hand from beneath my shirt, the trail of sensation shivering along my skin. He pushes himself up, caging me with his arms, palms on the floor behind me as I look up at him.

Don't say it.

The small voice in my mind. The one from the warehouse.

Rowan's.

Don't say it.

I frown. "Don't say what?"

His mouth parts. "What?"

"Yes. What? I hear your thoughts recently, which is another worry."

He takes a ragged breath, lips hovering closer to mine again. "Something dumb." His chest presses to me, lips softer in a ticklish way as they touch briefly.

"Nothing unusual there," I say hoarsely. "Say what you want."

"Fine," he says quietly. "Violet, I have never wanted anything as badly as you."

I take a sharp breath. This definitely isn't only magic flowing between us—not the bond *or* whatever that stone is doing. "You *have* me."

"All of you." His weight leaves, and he sits on his haunches, as I lie back watching him, still struggling to breathe as if he's still on me.

Rowan's eyes are dark, breaths rapid. Has the stone done this? Pushed us into another place we avoid? "You don't understand how much I love you, Violet."

"I do."

"How?"

I swallow. "I've learned from the way you look at me. The finding excuses to be around me—ensuring we spend time together as much as possible, like Holly does with Chase." And other things I see with Holly and Chase. "Touches. Kisses. Everything that emanates from you when we're together, and not only magic." I prop myself up on my elbows. "Is that what I should understand is you loving me?"

"That isn't the response I expected, Violet," he says quietly. "You're not claiming the bond causes how I feel. Are you beginning to understand that what we are together is more than magic?"

I prop myself up on my elbows. "I didn't understand why people crave to be together so much that they would make illogical choices in life."

He laughs softly. "And you're one big illogical choice."

"Yet here we are." I sit forward and kneel opposite him. "You're with the girl you swore you'd never choose because she 'didn't give a shit about anybody but herself.'"

"But I'd already started falling in love with that girl before the bond. You're a force of nature that nobody can constrain, and I loved that. Everything about you pulled me in. I'd met my match, and I loved *her* from the first time she opened her beautiful, snarky mouth."

"But the fighting? Like now—what was that? Something in this room wanted to swallow us. That... thing affected our minds and came between us."

"Uh. Not when you tangled yourself with me, Violet."

The flaming in my veins flares again. "You know what happens when we fight."

"Yeah. I always wish we fought harder." He rubs a thumb across my lips.

I fall silent, listening to my heart thudding in my ears. "I don't want to cross a line, Rowan."

"The one you crossed with Grayson?" he asks, suddenly wary.

"You worry the potion won't work against my blood if we get too intimate?"

"Do you?" I ask.

"Never," he whispers and reaches out a hand. "What line do you mean?"

I shake my head, and his mouth parts. "Violet." He runs fingers through my tangled hair, then the back of his hand against my flushed cheek. "If you did something while influenced by whatever the hell that stone evokes in us, I'd hate that."

"But I've already crossed one line," I say. "A place I never intended to go."

"Just now?" he asks, wary again.

"Days ago." I close my eyes.

"With Grayson? Were you more to each other before... the incident?" I shake my head. "By allowing the hybrid out?"

I open my eyes and look back into his steel ones to see the self I know will reflect in them. They're stormy, Rowan's pupils dilated by the desire still between us, but they don't obscure the truth: I share how he feels. "I have certain overwhelming feelings for you, Rowan. Love? I'm unsure, as the emotion is such an abstract concept. But overwhelming equals frightening."

Laughter bursts from him, and then he holds a palm over his mouth when I frown. "Sorry. Love isn't something that ever makes sense, Violet. It just *is*."

"Precisely. Abstract. Undefinable. When you kiss me, magic isn't the only thing that flows through, and you've created feelings that are more than a bond. However, I can't define them."

"Define? Okay." Rowan takes my cheeks in both hands. "This is what I mean when I say, 'I love you'. I'm never away from you, because you're always with me, whether it's the lingering warmth your touch creates, or a memory of your kiss that distracts me from the world. Sometimes, I miss you to the point I ache, everything in knots, as if you took a part I need back." His throat bobs. "I can't bear the thought of you not in my life, and you half-destroyed me when the bond blew us apart. I expected to be angry with you, but felt sick for days because you shut me out." He studies my face. "Is any of that familiar?"

I stare, the words illogical yet logical too. "Some. I had considered a stomach flu or unhealed heart damage from my fight with the fence post, but your interpretation makes sense." I frown. "Line most certainly crossed—it appears I love you."

"Violet, you're hilarious." He kisses me softly.

I place fingers on his lips, as my tangled mind attempts to make sense of the nonsensical. "The world I've lived in since I stepped outside my parents' estate confuses me, and when I'm with you, that new world makes sense. You anchor me here, and without you, I'm lost." I pause. "Although you can be irritating and frustrating, and *then* I'd rather not be around you."

"Naturally, you'd need to qualify your words with something blunt. Well, I still find you unbearably superior and rude and don't miss you quite as much sometimes," he says matter of factly. "And I also think you're beautiful and uh... desirable."

I tap my lips. "Yes. You did miss the desire for sex in your explanation of 'love'."

"Oh..." His eyes grow wide. "Right."

"I see more in your thoughts than you realize, Rowan," I inform him. "Accidentally. I don't pry. Mind you, the inevitably of that situation grows closer."

He stares, then splutters a laugh. "Man, Violet. You sound extremely unenthusiastic about going further. But I respect what you do or don't want."

"But you also struggle with the idea I may not?"

"Mmm. Especially after moments like that." He cups a cheek in one hand, kissing me in that slow way that doesn't tickle or irritate, but instead pushes me closer to that inevitable moment. "Or that," he whispers.

I lick the taste of him from my lips, grateful his blood barely touched me from the graze. "Now we've established that we each have loveable qualities that redeem each other's faults, what do we do next?"

Rowan chuckles. "You're back to analyzing so easily. I don't know. You're in charge—as ever."

"Oh, I know what we do next, but not tonight." Rowan opens his mouth, but I interrupt and point beneath the dresser at the stone no longer glowing. "I mean, what do we do about *that*?"

CHAPTER 7

GRAYSON

THE TOWN RESIDENTS pay less attention to me and don't judge as much as students at the academy. You'd think following years of stories and movies about vampires, people would've continued to avoid us once the supernatural world revealed itself. Instead, the macabre fascination that humans have with vampires, especially hemia, continues. I can't blame the academy kids for their distrust of me personally, especially the witches, considering the mistakes I've made.

I'm pissed that some accused me of joining in with the group of drunk humans and hemia at the Spring Ball afterparty, and resulting injuries. At the library, Holly's face clearly told me that she heard the rumors about 'Grayson up to his old tricks', but I couldn't read Violet's expression or thoughts. Maybe that's a reason I've avoided Violet since then—I don't want to hear Violet say that she doesn't believe me?

She's in the cafe with Leif and Rowan and I pause before I enter the human-filled establishment in town, watching them through the floor to ceiling windows. Two long bench seats run either side of the cafe tables creating booths, and Violet sits with the guys in one. Leif's opposite, listening intently to Violet, and Rowan's beside her, their bodies touching in a way I'd never expect possible.

Am I jealous? Maybe. Not of Rowan, but at the naturalness that's grown between them. They've the bonded witch synchronicity in how they move more fluidly, anticipating each other's movements in a way that unites them more. I doubt they're conscious of this—bonded witches rarely notice.

But the girl who has my heart in a vice is more than a witch and both she and Rowan come from families where the mothers' have more than one partner. Naturally that'll continue. A shifter for Violet, like Eloise? Well, half-shifter. I smile to myself—at how Leif's hand's close to where Violet's rests on the table beside her coffee cup, everything he feels for her obvious to anybody who watches them.

Leif may be the one starry-eyed, but a similar closeness grows between them too. The night of the Spring Ball, Leif definitely received a warmer welcome from Violet compared to the day *I* returned to the academy.

I swipe at my cheek, pushing away a strand that the wind stole from hair tied loosely back. The pair aren't a threat to Violet, but I am. That's why the two guys are closer to her. Rowan looked at me oddly when I said this to him and he reminded me about how I lost against her at the warehouse, as if I ever need reminding. But I don't mean physically. Rowan and Leif pushed through her walls, but Violet still easily remains in control of herself around the pair.

Me? I threaten that control, and so she keeps the barrier between us as impenetrable as Rowan's shadows can be.

I step aside as two guys leave the café, barely registering me. Why did Violet choose to meet here? This is the epicenter of the town's human teens' social scene—in the daytime anyway, since a lot our age head to the pub in the evenings. There're several groups I recognize inside, some who nod or greet me as I wander into the cafe to meet my own friends.

Violet's gaze slides straight to mine as the breeze following me through the door causes my scent to reach her first. Violet can't suppress her quickening heart—a heart that beats with my blood, something that'll never change whatever happens between us in the future.

She tied back her hair today, revealing her slender neck, and the baggy black sweater swallows Violet's figure, only slim fingers visible. Forget that I can hardly see any of her skin, it's the flicker of desire in Violet's impossibly blue eyes that's the killer, and I'm pissed at the reminder I'm nowhere near 'done'. I lied to her. I won't ever be.

"You're looking extra broody-bad-boy today," says Rowan as I slide onto the bench beside Leif, hands in my jacket pockets.

"I have a reputation to uphold," I say pointedly.

"You're attracting attention, Gray. Deliberate?" asks Leif and nods at a group of girls watching us.

"It's the leather," says Violet casually. "And the hair. The pout too."

I screw my face up at her. "Ha ha. They're probably staring at *you*."

"I like the leather," she continues. "The smell's strong to my hybrid senses. Overpowering even."

"I'm unsure how to take that comment," I reply.

"When you wear that jacket, your own scent is weaker to me."

Violet says this so casually, but my heart dives into my mouth. I'm making things easier for her? Eyes on Violet's, I shrug off the jacket and dump it beside Rowan who sits opposite from me.

Rowan looks between us. "Everything alright?"

"Is it ever?" asks Violet, and I'm unable to detect if she's referring to me or the state of the world.

"I hear you didn't get your hands on the tiara last night," I say. "What happened?"

Her expression grows poisonous, and Rowan relays their escapade to me.

"Your potion was in that room?" I ask, straightening as she takes it from a pocket. "Who has access apart from the librarian? All staff?"

"Not many," says Rowan.

Violet spins the bottle in her hands. "I bet whoever stole this is the same person who drew the runes in Wesley's room. Mrs. Lorcan or the librarian must know something."

"Why would Mrs. Lorcan take Violet's potion and risk a hybrid attacking students inside the academy?" I ask.

"Yes. The hemia cause enough problems," adds Leif. "No offense, Grayson."

I scoff at him. "Sure."

"The librarian?" Leif suggests.

"She would need a key to my room or access to one." Violet places the bottle back in a pocket.

"But Mrs. Eldridge must keep a record of everything that's stored," says Rowan.

Violet rubs her chin. "Now the potion's missing, let's see what happens."

"No, let's see what happens when Dorian finds out," I say with a smile.

"The theft wasn't a student prank," says Rowan.

"Did you take a look around the secret room at anything else?" asks Leif.

Oddly, Rowan averts his gaze and Violet glances at Leif.

"No. We weren't in the room long enough before Mrs. Eldridge arrived and accused us of planning to steal the tiara," says Rowan.

"Uh. Which you were," I say.

"And failed!" Violet says. "I bet Mrs. Eldridge stole the tiara. I shall report her to Mrs. Lorcan."

"And tell her we broke into the warded room?" asks Rowan.

"Maybe Dorian will help?" suggests Leif. "When are you next seeing him?"

"Not until tomorrow. Can you believe he's 'too busy' when an incident like this occurred inside the academy?" she asks indignantly.

I chuckle. "Dorian won't give a crap about a drunk human's hallucinations."

"You know that is *not* what happened," Violet snaps. "The tiara has significance."

"Grayson's kind of right, Violet," says Leif. His little finger brushes against hers and Violet doesn't snatch her hand away or scowl. Huh. "Dorian's focused on finding Grayson's uncle and the missing shifter."

"Can you not use Josef's and my names as connected?" I say through clenched teeth.

"Has he contacted you?" asks Violet.

"Oh yeah, we caught up for a chat and a coffee," I reply. "Family get-together."

"When?" Violet's brow creases. "Did he hurt you?"

With a scoff, I scratch a cheek and pick up the menu.

"What's wrong with you today?" Rowan asks me.

"Nothing," I mutter.

"Did he hurt you?" presses Violet.

I almost feel guilty at my jibe, especially when I see concern in her expression. "Sarcasm, Violet."

"You *haven't* seen Josef?" she asks.

I sigh. "No. Fortunately."

"That conversation was most unhelpful, Grayson. You have to tell us if he contacts you," she says sternly.

"No summons yet," I reply. "Josef knows I'm avoiding him. Y'know, after he impaled me into a wall, and I almost bled to death. Puts a damper on our relationship."

Violet slants her head. "I echo Rowan—what is wrong with you today?"

"I can't joke about this bullshit?" I ask. "And there's nothing *wrong* with me."

"You're lying," she says.

"Since when did you become empathetic?" I ask. "Learning to identify 'vibes' are you?"

"Good grief, Grayson." Violet folds her hands on her lap.

"Dude," says Rowan. "Does the attitude come with the jacket?"

"I took that off."

"But not the attitude," he replies.

"Did something go wrong at the party?" asks Leif.

"Huh?"

"Like, someone got hurt and you're in trouble because—"

"What the fuck?" I snarl but avoid looking at Violet.

"Stop," says Violet firmly. To me? All of us?

Yeah, I'm in a pissed mood because I'm constantly on edge these days. Sometimes I feel they don't a hundred percent 'get' the threat to my life from Josef. He watched me pick my side, but the side I chose is led by a man who hates me purely for my name. Oh, and probably because I want my hands on his daughter, and he thinks I want her blood.

The three don't treat me differently and it's strange to be part of a group after years staying disconnected, but I still feel like an outsider. Rowan and Leif's friendship goes back years, and they're satellites around Violet. I'm more distant. *She's* more distant. I can't understand how Violet can return to acting as if we're friends and there's nothing more between us. And it is acting—a performance I can see through. What's weird is, she's less sharp-tongued with me than before, as if that'll make up for holding me at arm's length.

So, yeah, I'm in a bad mood and couldn't care less about tiaras and dumb human girls. Dorian needs to find Josef before my uncle finds *me*.

"Is Dorian looking further into the witches who live on the property where the renovations are happening?" asks Rowan.

"Because I am. The connection doesn't end just because the witches we saw at the place are out of the picture. The elderly couple can't be completely clueless."

"Unless the witches used promise of work as a way to lure shifters. They'll stop 'renovating' now the group are aware Dorian's onto them?" suggests Leif.

"I think Rowan's correct. We need to know if the renovations have stopped or continued, and who's in charge or working on them if they have," says Violet. "That should be easy enough to find out."

"Yeah, Dorian will be onto that," I say.

"Maybe ask what's happening when you see him later, Violet?" suggests Rowan.

I sit up in alert. "Dorian only wants to see Violet, right?"

I'm pissed when Rowan chuckles. "Don't stress. Violet's asked to see him alone."

Violet flicks her tongue against her top teeth. "Adam Woodlake is still in custody and refuses to say anything, but that won't last. Dorian will really go hard at him."

"Yeah, I bet," I mutter. "He'll wish he'd died at the warehouse with his buddy Grant."

"My father should hand the witch over to the shifter elders and let *them* deal with the bastards. Keep his hands clean. That would help Dorian's attempts to bring shifters closer."

Whoa. Okay.

"Isn't Ethan dealing with the shifter politics?" asks Leif.

Violet moves to squeeze his hand. What has happened to this girl? "If the elders want to see you, I'll be there. And my father won't allow anybody to push another person into a life they don't want."

"Surely they're more interested in the necromancers killing their kind?" I retort. "Not Leif."

"The shifters think *I'm* their kind," says Leif through clenched teeth. "You know that."

Yes, but I don't know enough, obviously. I haven't spent as

much time around Leif as Rowan, or spoken to him a lot, despite our circle around Violet. I'm aware he tried to leave the academy and local area but thought that was due to trouble with Viggo, not people further up the chain. I'd ask more, but their reaction already shuts down questions.

Subject change required.

"Why are we here?" I ask. "This isn't your usual choice of hang out, Violet."

"She's hoping to see Kai," says Rowan.

"I am not," she protests. "I'm merely observing the current state of social affairs amongst the town residents."

"And listening in on their conversations?" suggests Leif.

"No."

"Don't lie, Violet," says Rowan and earns himself a slicing look from her. "You've wanted to see Kai since the night at the warehouse."

"I'm told to keep away from him." She rubs a finger across her lips. "But as I'm attempting to integrate myself into the world, I may inadvertently come across Kai in the wild."

I chuckle. "I'm sure Kai's told to keep away from you too," I say.

"Pointless anyway." Violet waves a hand at a table across the room. "Kai's under house arrest again. The story is, Sawyer's mad about the warehouse fight with shifters. The truth? He's obviously worried for Kai's safety and this time Kai's listening. That man has not told my father the whole truth, which is an idiotic decision."

"You overheard that?" I ask, and she nods.

"There was also a brief discussion around Kai's version of events and how the witches attacked us, but he fled the moment attention diverted to me and Rowan. Most unhelpful since he witnessed none of Josef's actions."

"Uh. I'd say helpful because running saved his life," I comment.

"Has anybody in the café mentioned shifters?" asks Leif and his jaw sets hard.

Violet straightens. "The girl with the short blonde hair at the table to the far right is in a relationship with a shifter. Apparently, shifters are not allowed into town still—elders' command rather than the town banning them. Due to this, the girl's and shifter's romantic trysts are infrequent, and this has led to some dissatisfaction. She's spent much of the last ten minutes looking at a boy she attends school with. And him at her." She sips her juice. "The fickleness of humans continues to astound me."

"Yeah, that'd be the end of their relationship. A shifter wouldn't share a girl," I say. "Too possessive."

"Share? She's not a tasty morsel," says Violet, then slants her head. "And by that comment, are you implying I'm 'shared'."

"No, but you're a tasty—" Leif stops and glares at Rowan. "What was the kick for? Violet would know I'm joking."

No response from Violet, who's now fixated on me. "Grayson?"

I shrug, refusing to answer, but man I would've loved Leif to finish his sentence and watch Violet's response.

"Is this opinion one you all *share*?" Violet continues.

"You didn't eat the cake I bought," interrupts Rowan and points at a chocolate icing-smothered slice in front of her. *Nice swerve, Rowan.*

"I'm not hungry."

Rowan lowers his voice, but can't hide his words from me. "You're not eating enough. I'm worried."

"Do I look hungry?"

"No, but—"

"Stop whispering," says Leif and pokes Violet's hand.

I flick my tongue against a canine. Violet's losing her appetite? Perhaps there's more hemia in the vampire hybrid side than she accepts, and I don't just mean my blood. I'm headed towards hemia maturity and a dislike for food—is Violet experiencing the same? Which adds another question. Are Dorian and Eloise blood drinkers, despite denying they ever do?

I sink back and push away the menu. "We met here purely to eavesdrop on boring human lives?"

"How else am I to keep up with current affairs and consider risks to their 'boring lives'?" asks Violet.

"Your curly-haired, over-exuberant roommate?" I suggest. "Isn't she part of the 'gang' now?"

"I don't want Holly involved," she replies. "Another reason to meet off campus—she's with Chase this afternoon and therefore won't see us."

I chuckle. "She'll be pissed."

"Better pissed than dead," comments Violet. "Why look at me in that way? We all know there's a risk to Holly if she's connected to me. I should spend less time with her, not more, now there's no Spring Ball organization."

"Whoa," mumbles Leif.

Rowan pulls on his lip but says nothing.

"What's your next move?" I ask.

"Dorian will investigate the incident. He'll come to the academy and retrieve the tiara," says Violet simply. "And question the librarian and Mrs. Lorcan."

"You sound confident," I comment. "I still reckon he won't bother. The tiara showed nothing when his people and you studied the thing before the human wore it."

"That is exactly the point," says Violet. "*Everything* has energy holding snapshots of the past. The tiara had none because they're blocked and now they may not be. Without finding those snapshots, Dorian has a piece missing from his investigations. I am certain he'll take back the item and we shall break the spell."

"And the stolen potion?" asks Rowan.

"Oh, yes. I'm sure that will be of great interest to him and my mother." Violet smiles. "Mrs. Eldridge will soon wish she hadn't interfered last night."

CHAPTER 8

ROWAN

I'M NOT surprised that Mrs. Lorcan summons me and Violet to her office today, but I am surprised that the librarian isn't present— or Dorian.

Although *the tiara* is, placed in the center of the headmistress's desk, beside a pile of books, the spiked silver object jeweled with oval amethyst gems unmistakable. Violet's barely in the room before she darts over and reaches out, but I catch her hand before inclining my head to the left.

The mantle surrounding the fireplace fascinated me when I arrived as a young kid—I'd seen gargoyles on human buildings, but her ugly carved creatures, watchful either side of the fire, look like deformed cats. Even though we're well into spring, the warm weather doesn't extend inside the academy's thick stone walls. Humans especially whine about the cold and lack of heating; I'm just surprised a vampire even *has* a fire.

Today, the ugly carvings aren't the most unusual thing by the fireplace. There's a man partially out of sight due to the open door, as silent and watchful as the gargoyles. He's around my grandfather's age, with thinning white hair and dressed in a dark-gray suit, reflecting the show of prestige and wealth many seem to think a tailored suit gives them. Just look at Sawyer and Josef. Always in their suits.

The man's cologne smells strongly of fennel and aniseed, but that isn't enough to drown out his magic aura as he regards us through sharp green eyes.

I dart a look around the room. Definitely nobody else but us.

"My tiara's no longer 'secured', I see," says Violet coolly.

"*Your* tiara?" The man's plummy voice holds a haughty disdain, one of someone who commands respect from most. Hopefully Violet figures this should include her. "I've come to retrieve my family's possession."

"Oh?" asks Violet. "And what family would you be?"

"I am Cornelius Whitegrove."

Both my brows raise. Two witch families lead the Circle—Whitegrove and Summerdown. They're not important in the witch magic hierarchy but are famed for hanging onto and building their wealth, hence their position in the Circle. I've never met anybody from either family—my parents only bother with those whose magic interests them.

"It would seem you lied, Violet," says Mrs. Lorcan. "The tiara is not a Thornbrook or Blackwood possession."

"I would like to know where you stole the item from," continues Whitegrove. "Because I need to know who originally stole this from *me*."

The room spins for a moment as if I'm on the edge of passing out until Violet grabs my fingers and her magic pulls up a wall to protect my mind. "Please keep out of my friend's mind. That's illegal, *Mr. Whitegrove*."

"As is theft."

"Me and Violet researched the tiara and never found any record of the item—no images and definitely nothing linked to your name," I put in.

Whitegrove looks down his narrow nose at me. "Rowan

Willowbrook?" I nod, but the edge to his tone unsettles me. "I could show you family albums, as I have Mrs. Lorcan." He steps forward to pass Violet, but she doesn't move, arms behind her back as she studies him. "Excuse me, young lady."

Violet snatches the tiara before he can. "What's the spell attached that hurt the human girl?"

Whitegrove's jaw hardens, and he scratches a cheek with neatly manicured fingers. "As with many witch heirlooms, the item is enchanted to prevent interference. *Pretty and expensive* items attract the magpie-like humans, and we ensured the tiara would repel them."

"Repel? Sienna thought the tiara had bound itself to her head," I retort. "I'd say that's quite the opposite."

He flicks a look at me. "The girl is unlikely to touch the tiara again, and neither would her human friends. Therefore, yes, repelled."

I look to Violet. Do we mention the other events that night? Mrs. Lorcan likely told him about the blood smeared words and the 'possession'. If not, social media did.

"Rather an extreme spell," says Violet. "Sienna's traumatized."

"The magic taps into the human's psyche, causing odd behavior." Whitegrove slices a look at Violet. "But evidently doesn't affect hybrids. Hand over my belonging."

"Have you seen proof of ownership, Mrs. Lorcan?" asks Violet. "Because I do believe my father should take this tiara, not a random witch."

"Random?" His jaw sets tight. "The tiara belongs to the Whitegroves. I'd like to take the item back to safety and away from any more attempted thefts."

"Dorian had no reports this was stolen," says Violet. "Therefore, I don't believe you."

He blows air into his cheeks. "The item disappeared almost thirty years ago."

"But Dorian's council holds a record of all artifacts missing and spends time tracking them down," I say. I'm half-inclined to believe the tiara *is* Whitegrove, but don't believe his story about protective curses. "They would've identified the 'Whitegrove tiara'."

"Unless you never reported this heirloom missing?" suggests Violet. "Now why would that be?"

"Sometimes, it's disadvantageous if another witch family knows one has misplaced a powerful item." Whitegrove holds out a broad hand, showing the Circle signet featuring an eye with six lines resembling eyelashes. "Give me the tiara. Now."

Violet holds the tiara behind her back.

"Violet. Please do as Mr. Whitegrove says." Mrs. Lorcan sidles around from behind the desk and my scalp prickles.

Has he threatened the headmistress? Mind control? Not one person mentioned this tiara belonging to the Whitegroves—or is missing—yet suddenly he steps forward with a claim and the headmistress just hands the tiara to him?

"Your father is welcome to contact me regarding the item and discuss the matter, but if he's inspected the tiara in the past, he knows there's nothing sinister."

"Mmm hmm," says Violet, tiara still behind her back. She's itching to ask about the name. The bloody message. The people in the photograph. "And you've no inkling who stole this from you?"

"Where did you find the tiara?" he bats back.

Violet smiles sweetly. "Where are you taking the tiara now?"

"Somewhere safe. Away from humans. Witches." He pauses. "Nosey hybrids."

"Did you hear about the recent murders in this locality?" she asks him, and I swear he's about to grab Violet and swipe the tiara from her hands. "Or do you hold any interest in home renovations?"

"What?" He frowns. "Oh. Yes, I know stupid witches were caught after failed experiments with shifters, but no, I don't personally redecorate my house, and can't see the relevance."

Failed experiment? How much does he know—the

necromancy? Because there's a bloody big coincidence that the thief hid this at Sawyer's place.

"Did you *know* the witches concerned?" continues Violet.

"I could reprimand you for asking impertinent questions, but that would no doubt increase your obvious suspicion of me." His lip curls. "I have no connections to the culprits."

"Or the victims, or intended victim?"

Mr. Whitegrove sighs heavily and turns to Mrs. Lorcan. "Inform the girl she needs to hand over my stolen possession and that if she has any questions, tell her father to direct them via my attorney."

She straightens. "Josef Petrescu, by any chance?"

The witch chokes. "I like to stay under the radar, not center myself. I have absolutely no dealings with any vampires. My business remains witch and human focused."

"Violet," Mrs. Lorcan interrupts. "Mr. Whitegrove is head of a respected witch family."

"I am aware. I researched the Circle and recognize his name." Violet tips her chin. "A family name without the tiniest misdemeanor attached for over a hundred years."

"Then you'll know that your father's council has no dealings with me either. I have no reason to vex him—my life and business operate perfectly under his governance. Now humans accept us, that's also a boon to my business. I don't wish for a change in that status quo."

Violet's teeth grind as she looks at me, and I shrug. "You're lying. An incident has occurred, and Dorian does not appreciate interference in his investigations. He will look for you and the tiara, and if you don't cooperate with my father, this won't end well for you."

I'm taken aback when the guy snatches the tiara from Violet's hands, his nostrils flaring. "You are an insolent, rude girl who is most certainly her father's daughter. If Dorian wants peace amongst the witches, or aid in digging deeper into that society, he will cooperate with *me*."

Whoa. Talk about mood change—even for someone triggered by Violet's attitude, that's impressive.

Violet's hands dangle at her side as she regards him unblinkingly. "Evidently, you haven't met my father yet. I wish you the best once you do."

The seething and nostril flaring continues. "Your father is welcome to contact me or my attorney any time, but he has no right to keep this from me. I have proof the tiara belongs to the Whitegroves. Your headmistress can deal with your behavior. Both of you."

"Where will you keep the tiara?" asks Mrs. Lorcan. "If any long term effects on the human appear, the item will need examining further."

"There will be no long term effects," he says tersely.

"Is Christopher Sawyer a business associate of yours?" interrupts Violet.

His lips press together. "That man? No. If he were, don't you think Dorian Blackwood would've questioned me? That human might think himself king of the town, but he's a little fish in his stagnant little pond. Whatever trouble that man has with witches, I'm not part of that."

Violet's eyes slide back to the tiara, then to his clear eyes. "Did any other jewelry items 'disappear' around the time the tiara did?"

I'm suspicious of the length of time before he responds. "No. Why? Do you have a collection of stolen witch artifacts?"

Violet purses her lips and shakes her head, but Mrs. Lorcan looks at her with uncomfortable distrust. Then me. I look back impassively.

The accusation against her and Grayson. Does she think Sawyer's missing jewelry item could be connected?

"To answer your question, the tiara will be located on my estate and fully warded."

"I want to see that happen," says Violet.

"You want to visit my home? I don't think so. The tiara could go missing again."

"I already suspect it will," says Violet through clenched teeth, watching as Whitegrove places the tiara in a leather satchel. "And if it does, you'll find yourself under suspicion. If I were under suspicion by Dorian Blackwood, I'd worry."

Whitegrove gives her a tight smile. "The person who stole this is the one who should worry."

"Is that a threat, Mr. Whitegrove?" she asks.

"Like I said, someone stole the tiara thirty years ago. You are eighteen, I believe." He fastens the satchel.

I keep an eye on Violet as Whitegrove says his goodbyes to Mrs. Lorcan, completely disregarding us further. Will Violet snatch the satchel and run? Even she wouldn't be that stupid. I hope.

But Violet won't be happy until she has her crown again.

"You are a stupid woman." *Oh, crap.* Violet turns on Mrs. Lorcan the moment the door clicks closed. "Has he mind-controlled you?"

"Violet Blackwood," she says sharply. "If you speak to me in that manner, I won't call your father, I'll simply send you from Thornwood. The man identified the item when it was displayed across social media, and approached me with proof the tiara is Whitegrove."

"Don't you care that one of your pupils suffered an injury? That a human daubed their blood over the mirror and claimed she was somebody else?" she snaps.

"In my opinion, the tiara should be with the rightful owner."

"You didn't consult my father!" she shouts. "How dare you!"

"Violet. Stop," I whisper and try to take her hand.

"I don't want the thing in my academy," she says icily. "Mr. Whitegrove showed family photos and records of the tiara. That is enough."

Violet chokes on her own saliva. "Well, *that's* suspicious. As if you *know* something about the tiara. And the missing—" She stops herself.

Mrs. Lorcan takes a steadying breath, but there's no mistaking her agitation—with Violet's behavior or her accusations? "Just who do you think you are, Violet? I want nothing more to do with this and will not listen to your impudent allegations. If your father has concerns, he can deal directly with the witch." She stalks to the door. "I suggest you leave before this unpleasantness deepens."

"In case I discover the truth!"

"Violet," I say through clenched teeth. "Let's go. If you're expelled, that won't help."

The pointedness of Mrs. Lorcan's look could cut glass as she opens the door. "Some gratitude that I allowed you to see what happened to the tiara would be welcome."

With an unmistakable derisive look and noise, Violet marches past. I give a hesitant smile and follow. Violet may not have snatched the tiara from Whitegrove's hands, or the bag from his shoulder, but she's moving quicker than normal along the hallway towards the building's exit.

Towards the witch who stole her tiara.

Through all this, one thing echoes in my mind. Nobody's mentioned the missing stone. However irritated I am that this witch took the tiara, I'm flooded with relief that my stone's going nowhere. Nobody knows we visited the secret room, apart from Mrs. Eldridge. And if she visited in order to take the tiara, she either changed her mind or failed.

I'm aware of the influence the stone has on my magic, but the possessiveness, and the magic triggered the other night isn't anything I've experienced before. At first, I felt the stone wanted my magic and for Violet to keep her hands off, but then the Blackwood magic within me triggered something stranger. Why would a magical item make bonded witches fight?

I've used the stone before, many times, bolstering my magic when I required the strongest spells against bullying assholes or simply to show people not to screw around with me. Somehow, Mrs. Lorcan heard a rumor I'd assaulted Wes, which I denied, and he had no memory about, but the academy took the stone. I'd never hidden that I had the item, proudly displaying the stone on my desk. Theft didn't worry me; the symbol of Willowbrook potency wouldn't help anybody else.

I reached an agreement with Violet that Leif should take the item. Violet wanted to give the stone to Dorian, and I had to fight against a complete freak out about the stone leaving the academy. Instead, I calmly told her that Leif understands what the stone is as he's witnessed the magic that it can prompt in me, and that if asked he would keep the stone out of my hands.

At least if Leif has the item, I'm assured that no other witch would touch it. Violet's still wary—she hates anything that might cause her to lose control. The influence on her mind causing such a response worried her more than me, although Violet's *other* response isn't something that left my mind in a hurry. In true Violet style, she hasn't mentioned the thoughts and emotions she shared with me, and I expect she'll think telling me once is enough.

I never thought I'd hear Violet Blackwood admit she loves me —even if her version is confused and confusing. But doesn't everybody have their own definition?

As I follow, I shake away thoughts of our hands on each other before my mind disappears on a new tangent.

CHAPTER 9

VIOLET

How dare she. How *dare* she. I fumble to take my phone from a pocket and call Dorian as I rush along the hallway, following the witch's distinctive magic. No answer from Dorian. One eye on the direction I'm walking, and another on my phone, I send a message.

Why won't Dorian take this situation with the tiara seriously?

I slow my pace as Whitegrove's figure comes into view. He's paused in the entrance hall beneath the academy crest rather than walked straight out of the door with his ill-gotten gain. He's standing with a tall, much younger looking man with neat brown hair. Mr. Woodside. As they speak, Whitegrove pats the satchel. I'm looking at the back of his head rather than his face, but I can see Mr. Woodside's.

What's odd isn't the teacher's expression but that he doesn't *have* one, standing stiffly, arms by his sides as he listens to the elder witch.

They know each other.

Mr. Woodside's the one person at the dance who commented on the tiara—beside the unfortunate human girls.

"Don't follow him." Rowan appears beside me where I rest a shoulder against the wall, watching the one-sided exchange between the witches from a corner.

"I'm not. I'm observing. Look." I point at the pair. "A connection to the tiara within the academy. Mr. Woodside is acquainted with Whitegrove—following an exchange of greetings and questions about each other's wellbeing, he asked the reason for Whitegrove's visit, and the man told him."

Rowan rests beside me and shakes hair from his face. "A connection to Whitegrove and the Circle maybe, but that's a tenuous link to the tiara."

I throw him a look. "Any link, however tenuous, requires investigation."

Their conversation ends, and Whitegrove walks towards the academy exit. "Don't follow him," says Rowan again.

I slant my head and regard Mr. Woodside as he watches the other witch leave, remaining still, fixated on the door long after it closes behind Whitegrove. The teacher always struck me as one who pays little attention to others, lost in his books even in class, yet he chose to speak to Whitegrove. Their conversation suggested they hadn't spoken for a number of years, but the exchange was brief.

Mr. Woodside straightens, and with one last glance at the exit to the academy, he strides away.

Has Dorian investigated Mr. Woodside or Whitegrove thoroughly? Because he must.

I won't follow Whitegrove, but I *will* follow this man. "This way," I say to Rowan.

"Where are we going?" he asks. "I know you're keen to look into Whitegrove, but we're headed to lessons this morning, right?"

"What class do we have?" I ask as I wander away.

"Geography."

"How pointless."

Rowan catches up. "Regardless, if you want to snoop on students and teachers, you'll need to attend lessons," he reminds me. "Especially if you're discouraging Holly's involvement."

"Selective lessons, yes. Pointless ones, no."

I continue to stealth after the teacher. Mr. Woodside reaches the library and I smile to myself as I reach our meeting place and sanctuary. Our frequent visits mean there's nothing unusual here. As I push open one swinging door too quickly, Mrs. Eldridge looks up, face sour as the wood hits the wall.

"We have more important matters than trips to fields or whatever the academy's organizing. Whitegrove spoke such *rubbish* about curses and the enchantment. What about the girl in the photograph?" I demand. "And the caginess as to why he never reported the item stolen?"

Again, the librarian glares at us as my voice rises. This is also her fault—if she hadn't interfered, I would've found the tiara and Whitegrove wouldn't take his 'heirloom'.

"It is plausible that the tiara has a defensive curse," Rowan replies with caution, and I hiss air between my teeth.

"Secrets," I half-growl.

"Which we'll discover, but wait until you speak to Dorian."

"I would like to see what Mr. Woodside does following his encounter. Why is he here and not walking to class?"

The library's half-vacant as usual and we pause on the lower level rather than rushing up to our meeting spot. Two guys sit at a bank of computers, blazers hooked over chairs behind, another at a desk chewing on a pen as he makes notes from a modern human textbook. This part of the library is filled with the pointless books that Holly often has piled on her own desk and bed beside a plethora of other items, but rarely looks at.

Mrs. Eldridge stops her glaring, her attention switching to Mr. Woodside standing opposite the long, curved reception desk she spends most of her time behind reading. I can't imagine she has much more to do. Oh, apart from stealing potions maybe?

I'm about to pass for a more secluded spot between shelves when I notice Mr. Woodside's fingers gripping the wood and his stance is stiff. Then Mrs. Eldridge places a hand on his, shaking her head but not speaking. He pulls his away.

I gesture at Rowan to stay where he is and be quiet, which results in an eye roll. I side-step behind a shelf adorned with physics books and peek out, training my hearing on their conversation.

"I needed the... it. Why did you allow the item out of that room?" he asks.

"I can't override Mrs. Lorcan," she says quietly.

"Yes, you can. You're responsible for the artifacts held in the academy." I can hear everything, but his voice rises enough that someone with normal senses could too.

"I am responsible for keeping items secured and out of people's reach," she retorts. "But I don't have the final say on what happens to each one."

"I saw him. Whitegrove. Why was he at the academy?" urges Mr. Woodside.

"To collect the tiara."

The teacher's grip on the wood loosens and he goes ramrod straight. "There's evidence in that item. The bloody Circle will lock the thing away after interfering with *any* chance someone can get past the enchantment."

"Julius. He has a legitimate claim. Keep looking into your own ideas. You never expected the tiara to resurface anyway."

Right. This man isn't leaving until he's aware I'm here. I stride over.

Mr. Woodside pivots to face us as Rowan joins me and flicks a look at us before he takes on a 'teacher face'. *Yes, I did hear what you said.* "Not prepared for class, Ms. Blackwood?"

His eyes might pierce souls, but they don't touch mine. "I could ask you the same."

"I'm not teaching this morning."

"Are you unwell?"

He frowns. "No."

"Only you look a little red-faced and sweaty." I look at Rowan. "Don't you think?"

"Your concern is touching, Ms. Blackwood, but no. I don't teach on Monday mornings and spend my time away from any bothersome students."

"If I'm bothersome, why would you want me in your class?" I ask.

"You took that rather personally."

"Not a fan of your job?" I must double-check with Rowan how long Mr. Woodside taught at Thornbrook.

"And how's my star pupil?" he asks Rowan, who visibly cringes before Mr. Woodside chuckles. "Are you here to hide and 'study'?"

"Yes," I reply.

"Detective work or actual study?" he continues.

I'm itching to ask about the tiara. I'm Thornwood's newest detective, but I'm slowly learning not to throw myself in headfirst. For now, indicating I heard his conversation with the librarian is enough.

"Study. We do so in the library as there's little privacy in an academy filled with *bothersome students*."

"The pains of residential schools." He shakes his head. "Anyway, as Mrs. Eldridge can't provide the book I need, I'll be on my way."

"What book?" I ask as innocently as possible.

Not a muscle in his face moves. "The Count of Monte Cristo. But apparently the library is short on classic literature." Mr. Woodside nods at me. "Perhaps I'll see you in class this afternoon?"

"Undoubtedly," I say.

He gives me one more long look, taps the desk twice, and leaves.

The librarian turns away, and I glare at the back of her head. "Anything to add?"

She glances over her shoulder. "About?"

"Last night and the tiara."

Slowly, she turns and sits in the office chair behind her desk. "I never took the item."

"I know. Why didn't you report us?" She blinks slowly at me. "Or were you not supposed to be in that room, as I suspected?"

"Where's the inventory of the confiscated items?" asks Rowan and leans on the reception desk.

"I don't know."

"If you're employed as the custodian, why can't you override Mrs. Lorcan?" I ask, continuing our rapid fire interrogation.

Her mouth parts. "Were you listening to my conversation with Julius?"

"If you knew more about this tiara, what have you hidden from us?" I demand. "We asked if there were any records or photos, you said no, and suddenly a witch appears to take the tiara!"

"I wasn't expecting Mr. Whitegrove," she says, green eyes clear.

"Why does Mr. Woodside want the tiara?"

Again, she blinks. "You misheard."

"I highly doubt I did. I can clearly hear a conversation between two male students across the library who are discussing their night at the Spring Ball party in lurid detail. This means I had no trouble hearing yours." I pause. "What is this 'evidence' Mr. Woodside claims is attached to the tiara?"

She shrugs. "Like you, he's concerned about the tiara's effect on the student and thinks the tiara should be investigated."

"Why?" I shoot back.

"Because he's a teacher and part of his role is to protect and care for his students."

"Ha. He wants the tiara. Is that why you went to the room? To retrieve the item for him?" I say.

"Why would I do that?" she retorts.

"An excellent question to which I shall find the answer." I tap my fingertips on the wood. "As I will also find why Mr. Woodside wants this item. Is he a member of the Circle?" Her eyes go wide. Hmm. "Are you?"

"No, they're not," mutters Rowan. "We have all their names from Dorian."

Mrs. Eldridge nods and gestures at Rowan. "What's *your* obsession with this tiara, Violet?" she asks. "You've never explained. Worried someone will find evidence of your spell cast on Sienna unless your father takes it?"

"I know who Madison is."

The woman attempts to maintain a neutral expression, but her pupils dilate. "Oh, really? Has Sienna's story become more outlandish?"

"I know who Madison is," I repeat, watching for more tells. "I wore the tiara too, remember, and I'm piecing together what happened."

She flicks a look to Rowan. "Did you find anything interesting in the room last night?" I suck air between my teeth at her dismissing me. "I expect Mrs. Lorcan would check the inventory list if I tell her I caught a pupil breaking into the place."

No response.

"Well, I suppose I'd best prepare for class," I say.

As I turn away, Mrs. Eldridge speaks. "Violet. If the tiara had any significance, your father's council would be all over it."

I pivot back to face her. "Oh, he will be. Once I inform him what I know about Madison."

Rowan walks alongside me as I stalk from the library. Other students wander along the hallways outside towards the classrooms, some more enthusiastically than others. I pause and step close to the wall by the library door.

"You don't know anything about Madison," says Rowan. "Why did you say that?"

"No, but Mrs. Eldridge does." I push my tongue against my top teeth. "And I'd lay bets she's on the phone to Mr. Woodside right now."

CHAPTER 10

ROWAN

WE HANG BACK after class to speak to Mr. Woodside following a lesson where one of the human's experiments exploded, and the acid burned holes in Sara's uniform. Sara accused the witch girls beside her of using a spell, and the witches claimed prejudice, forcing Mr. Woodside to referee their spat.

Violet's attendance is pointless, instead of paying attention she *drew* attention with the number of times Mr. Woodside told her to put her phone down.

I swear the last pupil is barely out the door before Violet strides over to where Mr. Woodside gathers up student papers on his desk. I'm on the verge of interrupting, but Violet instantly puts her unsubtle detective skills into practice.

"I'd like to speak to you," she says.

He doesn't look at her, shuffling the papers then reaching for his black bag. "About Madison?" Violet's silenced, whatever rehearsed words due to leave her mouth cut dead. "Andrea told me you mentioned her name and that you seemed insistent I'd know something." He looks up.

"And who is Madison?" she asks.

"You tell me."

"If I knew the answer, I wouldn't ask."

"So, you lied to Mrs. Eldridge?"

"Yes. Who is Madison?"

With a quiet sigh, Mr. Woodside pushes papers into his bag.

"Are you part of the Circle? What evidence is attached to the tiara that they're trying to hide?" demands Violet.

I join Mr. Woodside in the sighing and nudge her. "Subtlety?"

"Since when did *that* ever work? If you want the truth from people, directness often catches them out." She folds her arms over her chest. "Well?"

"I agree with Rowan. Your investigative technique could use some work." He places his hands on top of the bag. "I am not part of the Circle."

"And the tiara? What do you know about that?"

I'm shocked—I warned Violet that Mr. Woodside would never talk to her and definitely not admit any connection to the tiara. Yet, straightaway he calls her bluff. The man could send us away claiming he's no idea what we're talking about, but instead Mr. Woodside stands and allows Violet's volley of questions to hit him.

"Violet, sit down," I say and pull a chair from beneath a desk. "Let me speak."

Mr. Woodside looks between us, watching where I touch Violet on the arm to encourage her to sit. "You're bonded. That's crazy. She isn't—"

"Normal?" suggests Violet.

"Isn't a true witch. But yes, not normal either." He slides onto the desk to sit too. "Now I'm intrigued."

"How can you tell we're bonded?" I ask. "Most people can't unless they know us well."

"Your energy. My mind magic operates on a more transcendent level. That's my expertise—no mysterious earthquakes at student memorials from my magic." He raises a brow at me.

"Good grief! Who's Madison?" interrupts Violet.

Mr. Woodside smiles. "I thought Rowan was speaking."

"I'm expecting you to disappear as soon as you get the chance. Rowan's too slow."

He regards her. "I'm aware you heard my conversation in the library, but I'm unsure what you hope to gain from accosting me."

She holds his gaze. "You want the tiara. I also want the tiara. If that desire is for the same reason, we should help each other."

"And what's your reason?"

"Because I think a crime was committed against a girl named Madison and would like to solve said crime."

He laughs softly. "And you think I committed this crime?"

"No, but I believe you can help us solve what happened. I think you know something."

Mr. Woodside falls silent again, looking between us. I exchange a glance with Violet. Maybe the man's reason for wanting the tiara *would* persuade him to speak to us—if Violet treads carefully enough.

"What's *your* connection to the tiara, Violet?" he asks.

"Perhaps we could exchange information?" she suggests.

Again silence. Mr. Woodside takes his bag and stands. My hope the teacher had information he'd share drains away as he glances to the classroom door.

"Don't leave," I say. "Please talk to us."

He pauses and sets his bag back on the desk. "I might consider an exchange of information, but I don't take kindly to demanding teenage girls."

"What do you want to know, and what will you offer in return?" continues Violet.

I close my eyes in despair, but Mr. Woodside's eyes shine. "You have your hands full dealing with her as a bond, Rowan," he comments and shakes his head. "But as I appreciate directness, even bordering on insolence, here's the deal. Tell me where you found the tiara and I will tell you why I'm interested in the item and why I think Whitegrove took the tiara back."

"Back? The tiara *does* belong to them?" I ask.

"To Whitegrove? Yes, I believe so."

"Then he killed Madison," interjects Violet. "Was she a pupil here? We're looking for missing records and we *will* discover who she is and what happened."

"She might not be dead. Where did you find the tiara?" he repeats.

Violet stands again and pulls something from her blazer pocket. She holds the photograph from the trunk in front of Mr. Woodside's face. "The same place I found this. Is the girl Madison?"

There's barely a flicker of emotion or recognition in his expression, but just briefly, surprise registers in his eyes. I hadn't noticed the strength of the magic around him until it slips for a split-second. No wonder I couldn't find even the edge of his mental barrier.

"Is she?" pushes Violet.

"I'm confused why you won't tell us," I say. "By our reckoning, this photo is from thirty years ago and you're thirty-one. You can't be involved."

"Investigated me, have you?" he asks.

"Naturally," replies Violet.

His lips purse. "Exchange of information. Where did you find the tiara, Violet?"

"In a location connected to the Sawyer family," I interrupt and give a curt nod to Violet—we agreed to reveal this, but no more.

"*Sawyer*? A human stole a witch artifact and managed to hide it for thirty years? Seems unlikely."

"We can't be sure how long the tiara and photo were at the location. Could've been placed there recently," I say.

"Sawyer," repeats Mr. Woodside. "That makes no sense."

"*Obviously* there's a witch connection," says Violet, "but

there're no links between the ones who killed the shifters and the Circle."

"Are you sure about that?" he asks.

"As sure as we can be without infiltrating the coven," says Violet.

"Yes. Well. Entry into the Circle isn't easy, and I hardly think you're capable of sneaking anywhere, Violet," he says disparagingly.

"Exchange your information," she says stiffly. "Why do you want the tiara? What's your connection?"

He rubs his lips for a moment and again glances at the door. I'm about to again ask him to stay when he speaks. "Because my sister wore the tiara the night she disappeared, and it's the key to finding where she is. The answer will be attached to Madison's imprint on the tiara."

"Your *sister*?" blurts Violet.

Mr. Woodside crosses his arms. "I hoped I'd find the answer by coming to the academy, since we're on the grounds of the last place Madison was seen. I almost gave up that hope until I saw you in the tiara and recognized it."

"And are you telling me you've investigated the academy and not located her body in the vicinity?" asks Violet.

"Madison might not be dead," says Mr. Woodside.

"All signs point to deceased," replies Violet. "Missing for thirty years? Tiaras 'possessed' by ghosts? Madison wore the tiara the night she died."

"Violet," I say in exasperation. Doesn't she understand how lucky we are that he's even telling us all this?

"What? I should offer false hope and platitudes?" she asks.

Her brow pinches as I again silently communicate that the exuberance she displays when finding a way forward in her detective work isn't always suitable—and in this case, downright unhelpful.

Violet blinks as she recognizes the look. "I'm sorry for your loss, Mr. Woodside."

Oh, god. Could she sound any less sincere? "Madison might not have passed away," I say, one eye on the flush faced teacher.

"Why doesn't anybody else know who Madison is?" Violet asks and I almost groan at her immediate jump back into her rapid fire interrogation. "If Madison went missing, there'd be a record—however long ago."

"To most, she isn't missing. The story is: Madison left and never contacted anyone again because she doesn't want to speak to her family." Mr. Woodside shakes his head. "I couldn't believe she'd never contact her baby brother again. Then I discovered Madison went missing on the night of the dance, which contradicts her 'moving out'."

"So the story is that her family disowned her?" asks Violet.

"No. The other way around. Madison claimed she was too good for our family, but that doesn't make sense to me."

"How could you know if you were a baby?" she asks.

"I've investigated this longer than you, Violet," he says coolly.

"Do you know the guy in the photograph?" I ask. "Were they both students at the academy?"

"I don't recognize him from any other photos I've seen."

"And what do you think the Circle connection is?" Violet presses. "Do you think a member of the Circle killed her? Whitegrove?"

"I don't know, but in the last photos of Madison owned by our family, she's wearing the tiara and that dress." He taps the photo. "This guy isn't in a single one but mysteriously in the one with the hidden tiara. He's too young to be Cornelius Whitegrove, but he's either connected to Whitegrove or to the Circle."

"His son, maybe?" suggests Violet.

"He doesn't have one," I tell her. "I checked everybody, remember?"

"Then a nephew? A friend's son? I always knew powerful witches must be involved—that someone covered up the disappearance."

"The tiara knows," says Violet firmly. "The block against psychometry needs breaking."

"We don't have the tiara," I remind her.

"I will retrieve the item. I'll tell Dorian about Madison and—"

"No!" interrupts Mr. Woodside. "I've kept this investigation secret from the day I arrived here. I've always known the place has answers, but it's impossible to get into the academy unless you're employed. I trained to teach purely to gain entry, and nobody can know who I am. If they realize I'm investigating Madison's disappearance, I might 'disappear'. Someone important is involved, or her disappearance wouldn't be covered up like this."

"How can nobody know? Don't you have the same name?" I ask.

"My mother remarried a few years after Madison 'left' and I took the name too. The name you're looking for is Madison Riverborn."

"And she was definitely a pupil here?" asks Violet.

"Yes. But good luck in finding any records or photographs of anything before the Confederacy fell. God knows, I've tried for years. Spent hours scouring the grounds for signs of her energy too. Nothing."

"Can you find us anything that belonged to her?" I ask him. "Show us more photos? There must be clues. If you have a piece of jewelry, I could get some clear images from psychometry."

"But only items Madison wore that night would reveal the truth," he says.

Violet nods solemnly. "I will re-possess the tiara, and ensure we find your sister's body, and who killed her. Or at least who killed Madison if we can't find any of her body parts."

"Violet! Omigod." I shake my head. "Sorry, Mr. Woodside. She didn't mean to sound heartless."

Violet presses her lips together. She once claimed to be, but I know Violet has a much bigger heart than she ever noticed or admitted. Including a part that now belongs to me, which was beyond comprehension until recently.

"I'm Julius—I'd rather you used my first name when discussing this and me, as you no doubt will. Less people will know who you're talking about if they overhear." He rests his gaze on Violet. "I very much hope you don't find my sister's body and find her alive, but I'm a realist."

"And will you share your research with us?" asks Rowan. "If you've investigated the disappearance for years, you must have clues."

"You'll need to," puts in Violet.

Julius chews on the edge of his lip. "We'll meet again, more privately, and I'll show you what I've collected, but not today."

"When?" she asks sharply.

He gives her a long look. "When you've spoken to Dorian and kept your promise not to say anything about me."

She nods. "Understood."

"Now, excuse me. I have to go." He looks between us, worry in his expression—regret that he's told us all this?

But he had to. If not now, at some point. The tiara's appearance and disappearance pulled him towards a new lead in his sister's disappearance. If the man spent his life searching and failing, he'd grasp at anything to help.

Mr. Woodside may not want Dorian to know his name, but he does know that Violet's connection is his new hope.

CHAPTER 11

VIOLET

DORIAN TAPS his fingers on his desk, eyes trained on the bookshelf behind me, thoughts elsewhere. Is he even listening to me?

"You won't help me get the tiara back?" I ask tersely.

"No. My people already investigated the item and there's nothing significant."

"Apart from I found it at Sawyer's factory?"

"Violet. There's no hint of energy from the witches involved in the murders or Sawyer around that tiara. I *am* looking at Rowan's photos of the papers found with the tiara, which make little sense as of yet."

"You need to look at the tiara again, Dorian!" I retort.

"And I said, I have more important matters," Dorian replies through clenched teeth. "Now you bring me news that someone important in the academy may be responsible for stealing and hiding your potion. *That* is another concern and requires immediate investigation."

"But I need this tia—"

"Violet," he interrupts, sighing out the word. "Whatever that

81

tiara's story, there's no link to the much bigger issues at hand. Perhaps a tragic death did occur over thirty years ago, and maybe someone linked to the Sawyer family was involved, but chasing after something with no proof, but a mind-addled human isn't important at all. What *is* important is the issues between shifters and humans—and the explosion once the elders discover what the witches have done."

"Didn't the witches 'mind-controlling' shifters to kill already detonate the bomb beneath the shaky bridge between the two?" I ask.

"Yes, hence my focus on avoiding a war by treading carefully around the necromancy issue and finding the culprits, not tenuous links between jewelry and a girl's possible murder."

Why won't Julius Woodside allow us to explain? I understand the fear for his safety, but at least if he spoke to Dorian, my father might at least divert some attention that way.

"Whitegrove is a Circle leader. If I'm to investigate this *without* your help, I require a membership for the Circle."

"I have nothing to do with that organization," he replies, turning his glacial eyes to mine.

"That's a lie." Those eyes narrow. "You must have somebody 'on the inside' otherwise you would never discount them as quickly regarding the town deaths and necromancy."

"Yes, Violet. And the whole point of having someone 'on the inside' involves not alerting anybody to that fact." He leans back in his expensive leather chair and places his bare feet on the desk. "Sometimes life's easier if you give others the illusion they've autonomy. Bored, rich witches defrauding humans amuses rather than concerns me."

I clench my teeth as the frustration washes over me. "Why won't you help?"

"Fine. Perhaps your witch could apply for membership?" asks Dorian, mouth partly curved in amusement.

"They take applications?" I frown. Rowan never told me this.

"With a recommendation. I'll see what I can do."

THORNWOOD ACADEMY: LIVE TO TELL

"By asking your 'insider'?" I arch a brow.

Dorian takes a coin from the table and flicks it in the air, repeatedly, an odd habit he's had as long as I remember. "But you can't send Rowan in to steal from them, and Whitegrove is astute enough to know he might. They have rules and deal with transgressions unpleasantly, I hear."

I step forward and catch the coin as it descends back towards Dorian's hand. "The Circle 'deal with' people and 'unpleasantly'? Yet still you don't see a connection!"

He holds his palm out for the coin. "The fact of the matter is, Violet, I don't care. People murder each other all the time. They go missing. Does this affect me? No. You? Also no, so I don't know why you're wasting your time."

I straighten my shoulders and drop the coin into his palm. "To solve what happened."

Dorian's eyes turn to the ceiling. "Didn't you heal properly from your encounter with the fencepost?" He looks at me and chuckles at the confusion. "Violet Blackwood and her bleeding heart."

"Is it wrong that I want justice?" I snap. "That I believe people should be treated fairly?"

He chokes a laugh. "Well, it isn't very 'you'. You're already tangled in enough lives. You lay yourself open to problems if they don't behave as you expect or wish. Betrayals. Disappointment." He slams down the coin, "Anger, Violet, and we both know the issues that could cause. In this family, we only care about each other. Life and the world isn't fair. Nothing you can do will change that."

"Yet Ethan and Zeke spend all that time creating change with the shifters?" I retort.

"That's not justice and fairness. That's self-preservation." He pulls his legs from the table and swings around in his chair. "Everything I do is for us."

"Including killing shifters?" I blurt.

Dorian's body tenses into an unnatural stillness. "Who accused me of killing a shifter?"

"Nobody. I'm talking about Oz."

He scoffs. "Violet. Oz wasn't a shifter. He was a construct. I'd class my actions as putting Oz out of his misery."

"And Leif?" I ask, my blood icing at Dorian's attitude and admittance. "Were you tempted to 'put him out of his misery' that night?"

"Ah. So, the boy saw." Dorian slants his head. "Don't make me regret leaving him alive. I doubt the shifters would approve of my actions and I wouldn't want them to know."

"Exactly!" I hiss.

Dorian stands and looks down at me, hands in pockets. I noticed his presence less when living with the man, the energy encompassing him and everybody Dorian's close to was natural to me. Since spending time away, his sheer physical and magical aura hits me more when I'm in a room with him.

Worse, I sense the sharp edges of malevolence I once welcomed within myself.

"I never intended to kill Leif because he wasn't a threat to us," he says evenly.

"Isn't," I correct.

"*Wasn't,*" he repeats. "Sure, Ethan wants to help him out because he likes interfering, but Leif means nothing to me, Violet."

I swallow hard. "Leif means something to *me*. You will *never* harm him, Dorian."

For an unnerving amount of time, he stares at me before turning away. "I'll speak to my friend in the Circle. Your mother would like a chat before dinner. Such a shame you didn't bring your friends this time."

"Because you won't have the opportunity to interrogate and intimidate the guys?" I ask. "And no way would Grayson come here, even if I asked."

He returns an impassive look. "You still speak to him?"

"We're friends."

"'Friends'," he mutters darkly. "I'm putting everything into tracking down the kid's uncle. You'd better hope Grayson isn't back in the family fold."

My eyes go wide. "Josef almost killed Grayson and left him to bleed out!"

"And if Grayson wants to avoid worse, he might do as he's told next time. Have you considered *that*?"

"You'll never trust him, will you?" I retort.

He shrugs. "Trust is a valuable commodity that I rarely spend."

I look through the window behind at the pine trees that stand like sentinels at the edge of the driveway. "Speaking of trust, has Ethan had any luck with the elders?"

"He spoke with them a couple of days ago, but didn't get far. Roderick—the main guy—wants to meet Leif and asked Ethan to organize a meeting."

"What? No."

He slants his head. "Leif can't say no, Violet."

"Yes, he can."

"No, he can't. We'll get nowhere with solving why and how witches targeted shifters unless the elders cooperate. If Leif's what we need to get a meeting with the elders, that's what we're doing. You told me Leif wanted our help?"

"Not by delivering him to them!"

Dorian sighs. "Ethan won't 'deliver' Leif. Do you think your father would hand someone over to a situation and people they hate? To somewhere Leif would lose his free will? Look at our history, Violet."

No. But still, what if the elders *take* Leif?

"Oh, and speaking of situations and people they hate, we're invited to attend Sawyer's little birthday soiree this weekend. Guests of honor due to saving his life." He pulls a face. "Perhaps continue your tiara investigations there?"

He looks at me pointedly and doesn't need to say the words: 'because I'm not interested'.

"Kai's birthday?" I straighten. "We're invited? How wonderful."

Dorian half-smiles. "Yes. Should be an interesting evening."

"Not for the wrong reasons, I hope."

The normal Violet Blackwood would protest against attending a social gathering, but this one offers many possibilities for furthering the investigation Dorian refuses to help with.

"Now. Is that all? I'm busy with an *actual* investigation."

I swallow down how pissed I am at his dismissive attitude, especially towards Leif. "When I discover the truth, and that the tiara and death links to everything happening, I expect an apology from you for not listening or helping, Dorian," I say through clenched teeth.

"Yes, sweetest girl," he says in such a patronizing tone that I'm tempted to smack him across the head with a bolt of magic, regardless of the repercussions.

"Okay. What about the renovated house where the witches recruited the shifters? Any further with investigating that?" I ask.

"I've personally interviewed the elderly witch owners," says Dorian. "Their minds weren't hard to penetrate and I'm 99% sure they're not involved. They'd subdivided the land and sold the part with the old cottage to developers. The pair know Grant Underhill who worked as a construction manager before Josef killed him, but they weren't close to the witch. They're genuinely shocked about him using 'mind control' on his contractors, "

"Construction manager for who?" Violet asks.

"Again, I've located the development company, and I'm looking for any contacts and employees within the organization who may be significant. It's a small operation, so shouldn't be difficult." He shrugs. "Witches flipping houses for a good profit. Popular area of town."

"And the house?" I ask. "Have you thoroughly inspected the interior?"

He gives a tight smile. "You constantly question my peoples' ability to investigate criminal matters."

"Naturally, since I'm the one who's better at it."

Dorian barks a laugh. "Perhaps you should focus on the Mystery of the Cursed Tiara and channel your 'expertise' that way."

"And keep out of your business, I presume."

He merely smiles.

"Well, I suppose I'll have to spend more time with the three guys in my life." The smile drops. "Especially as it seems they need my protection against threats to *their* lives."

"Another reason to keep away from the investigations surrounding the shifters and necromancers."

I stalk to his desk and pick up his favorite coin. "That's not what I think threatens their lives, Dorian. Is it?"

Neither of us speak for a moment. Even a chuckle at my veiled accusation would help, but Dorian does nothing. I pocket the coin and leave him before he says anything else that irritates or worries me.

As I walk away, my head swims with thoughts and fears for Leif and Grayson. And Rowan? Surely Dorian would never touch my bonded witch. I moisten my lips and prepare to meet my mother.

I no longer believe I'm more Dorian than Eloise.

CHAPTER 12

VIOLET

DESPITE SPRING gradually giving way to summer, the breeze moves briskly across the grounds of the Scottish estate and through the pine trees I stared at earlier. I walk with Eloise along a route I've taken many times over the years, along a path created by footsteps through the woods over time, and towards the stream that runs along the back of the property.

The guys once queried my solitary childhood, claiming my parents deliberately kept me separate without any opportunity to become part of the world if I'd wanted to. This isn't the case—I've always enjoyed solitude, happy within my own company and headspace. Why did I need anything else? My family cared for and nurtured me, and I had all the space and time I wanted to hone my magic.

We reach the place the stream runs over larger stones creating a small waterfall, somewhere I loved to visit, but not to splash and wade in the cool spring water. I'd practice magic alone for hours, safe and happy. The ground remains scorched from the fires I repeatedly lit—once Ethan taught me to do so far enough from the trees and our home to keep everybody safe.

Eloise would spend time with me, teaching Thornwood spells and explaining how I'd inherited her Trinity Witch magic—the ability to use all three major branches. Elemental, mind, and the darker necromancy. I'd accidentally discovered and utilized all three before growing old enough to understand and control what I'd done. Before I did, I burned rooms, created parents with headaches, and (as Holly pointed out) had a collection of woodland animals worthy of a Disney princess.

But there's another side to my magic that's rarely mentioned, never performed by either Eloise or Dorian, and I'd no interest in. The Blackwood shadows. I love the destructive nature of fire as much as the re-creation of a half-life with necromancy, the two far removed from each other. Apart from the mice incident at the human school, I haven't used a necromancy spell for many years, and Eloise continually avoids aiding me in practicing. She once admitted painful memories of her parents forcing her to practice magic she never understood, a puppet performing for other families.

Eloise told me about the day her parents killed the family dog in order to force her necromancy, a horror my childish brain couldn't comprehend.

Necromancy landed Eloise in Ravenhold and as I grew older, I gradually understood why she avoids that side of herself. Necromancy brought her nothing but trouble and unhappiness— threatened her own life. The practice doesn't match Eloise's innately good nature, and she worried about my obsession.

Unfortunately, as with most teens, the more my parents denied me something, the more I wanted it, and the imperfect necromancy skills frustrated me. My family can prevent me interfering with life and death, but can't stop my inherent connection and fascination with the magic. Only now that I've relationships with mortal people can I understand why the practice is feared and outlawed. How naïve was I to believe Dorian had all necromancers under watch and control?

Eloise stands beside me as I perch on a rock that overlooks a small waterfall bouncing across the pebbles, the spray creating rainbows.

"I bet your guys are happy you left them behind," she says and smiles.

"Immensely." I take a smooth pebble and drop it over the edge of the waterfall. "Dorian won't help me take the tiara back from Whitegrove. Can you persuade him?"

"Violet. Your father's facing much more pressing matters—events surrounding the murders, and the delicate issue of necromancy and the shifters, hold more importance than a minor incident at a school dance." She holds a hand up as I open my mouth to protest. "Priorities, Violet. Don't you want to help Leif? Surely his welfare's more urgent than a mysterious object that we've already examined and found nothing significant."

"Are these Dorian's words?" I ask her.

"Merely logic, sweetest."

"Has Dorian told you what happened to Oz?" I meet her eyes, but there's no flicker of anything I can read. "If you *do* know, you'll understand why I'm worried about my friends' safety."

"Dorian would never harm anybody you care about unless they're a threat to you."

"Directly or indirectly?" I slant my head. "Because arguably, they all are. Dorian needs to stop his obsessive focus on Grayson."

"But that distracts him from Rowan, who possesses less skill at coping with your father's behavior." She looks down at me. "Dorian knows about the shadows. He saw the result at the warehouse. You can *not* encourage this in Rowan—your father doesn't meddle with that magic and neither do I. This is a part of your witch heritage you shouldn't share."

I chew my lip. If I told her the shadows come naturally to Rowan with little prompting from me, I'd cause a greater issue and put him under more threat. How can I *not* allow or encourage the magic that would keep my mortal, bonded witch safe? As long as that magic stays away from the stone.

"Would Rowan be able to practice necromancy too?" I ask.

"No. But shadows must lie within Rowan, however dormant, for you to induce them." She shakes her head. "Don't risk his mind. Rowan's life is more fragile than yours."

But they keep him safe.

"Fragile, Eloise?" I again try to fathom her look, and she reads mine. "Are you suggesting Rowan will die?"

"You know the answer to that. Please be aware that Dorian took a risk when he gave me his hybrid blood, Violet. It could've killed me."

"And you would've died *without* his blood."

She crouches down. "Is this something you've considered? Discussed with Rowan?" I shake my head. "Violet. Ethan and Zeke are mortal, and we all accept that."

"Yet Dorian wouldn't accept you were."

"Dorian only accepts the world inside his own parameters."

I sigh. "Why are we having this conversation? Rowan and I never have. I've no desire to interfere with his life or end of such."

"Mmm." She stands again. "Then take care not to put his life in Dorian's spotlight. Stop the shadows, Violet."

I'd expected more conversation about Grayson and how Petrescu blood now beats through my heart. Warnings not to give Grayson mine. Has Eloise awareness about the difference between the pair—that Grayson would avoid taking my blood, but that Rowan wants my magic?

"You don't need to worry. I have Rowan under control." Eloise splutters at me. "What?"

"His infatuation? That isn't control. You can *not* control people, Violet. Not without taking their minds or reanimating them. Even your father realizes controlling others is impossible."

Infatuation. *Bond.* Or is that another definition of love I can't fathom?

"Dorian manages quite well using intimidation and the odd

maiming," I reply. "But that isn't something I intend to do to Rowan."

"How intimate are you?" she asks casually.

"Mother..." I warn. "Since when have I craved intimacy of any kind?"

"Since you met a guy you care about and are attracted to? Or rather, *guys*."

"I'm unsure what's worse. Discussion about giving Rowan immortality or giving him *me*," I mutter.

"You don't understand, do you? Intimacy between bonded witches is different."

"Good grief," I say and stand. "Allow me to navigate the progress of my relationship with Rowan at my own pace and in my own way. Why is everybody obsessed by physical relationships?"

She laughs. "Your fathers would be happy to hear that *you're* not—especially if the physical extends to Grayson."

"I've told you why I won't touch him again." Eloise sighs at me and I swiftly veer her away from the topic. "And Leif? Do share your concerns about him and me, because I'm sure you have some."

"My concerns are *for* Leif, Violet. Don't play with his emotions."

"Excuse me?" I retort, and step back. "I am nothing but up front with Leif. With any of the guys. I will not suddenly stop speaking my mind in order to hide what I think and feel for fear I'll hurt someone's feelings. I care about and will help Leif in any and every way I can. Now can we please cease this conversation?"

With a small smile, she cups my cheek. "Perhaps you don't realize how much you've changed. You certainly don't understand how far you've yet to go."

She places her lips on my forehead. Alarmed, I stumble back. "Please, let's be done with this, Eloise. I'd like to return to the academy now and continue my investigations that Dorian refuses to help with. A total waste of time coming here."

"Oh? Visiting your loving parents is a waste of time?" She fights a smile. "Mere weeks ago, you threatened to leave Thornwood for home if we sent you there. Now you can't wait to return."

I chew on my lip, unsure what to say. Eloise is right. I've changed—I don't only want to return to the academy, but to my friends as much as the detective work. To the guys.

"I'm joining Ethan when Leif visits the elders with him."

Eloise's brow tugs together. "Is that sensible?"

"Solidarity with someone I care about who's already been through enough?" I ask pointedly.

"Alright but please don't ruin your father's hard work in gaining their trust." She taps her lips. "Keep this shut."

"Unless I feel something needs to be said," I reply.

"Violet..."

I wrinkle my nose. "I understand. Don't insult the elders."

As long as they don't insult me or threaten Leif because if they do, my mouth will be very open.

Eloise holds my cheeks in her soft hands. "To be safe, I've added a little something extra to your potion to prevent unwanted incidents."

"In case I attack Grayson again?" I smile. "Thank you."

She smiles too. "I can't do anything to change your attraction to Grayson's blood. I've added an extra ingredient in case your relationship with Rowan 'navigates' into new territory." I gawk, speechless. "Or Leif. Preferably *not* Grayson."

Finally, I overcome my struggle for words. "Are you saying you've added something to repel me from sexual relationships *as well* as blood?"

Eloise bursts into laughter. "Now, I could see your fathers requesting that if it were possible, but no. We can't allow you to make the same mistake as Dorian and I."

The same mistake... "You added a contraceptive to the potion? When?"

"To the one you're taking with you today. Violet, if you tell me you've had no thoughts of sex with any of these guys, I'd accuse you of lies."

Heat fires my cheeks and I hope she sees this as anger, not a memory of the evening in Rowan's room and the discussion of the direction we're headed. "Conversation closed."

"Alright, but I'm here if you need to talk or want advice."

"I believe we've discussed the topic enough," I say stiffly.

As we walk back to the house, I'm deflated. I'd expected help from Dorian, for him to listen to my concerns. Then my mother decides to delve into my relationships in an uncomfortable way. I'm returning to the academy no further forward. Seems the tiara will be *my* investigation, since my narrow-sighted father doesn't want to dig deeper.

And I meant what I said—when I prove the connection to the other situation that he deems worth investigating, Dorian can apologize to me. Eloise realizes I'm not their little girl anymore, and she never mocked me for wanting to help others.

I have to hope Dorian can find us a way into the Circle, then my visit here won't be a complete waste of time.

CHAPTER 13

VIOLET

THE HOTEL SAWYER chose for his son's birthday celebrations is located on the opposite edge of town to the factory and his home. Naturally, he selected a prestigious venue found on many tourist recommendation sites as exclusive and expensive. I researched the place plus every name associated before I'd set foot inside.

The manor house once belonged to a witch family and is now named the Royal Manor Hotel. Founding witch families often see themselves as royalty, but that's going a bit far. Mind you, they had to sell the place and move on—we found no witches connected to the venue—so 'royal' or not, things didn't end well for the family.

As the manor is also a popular wedding venue, the once private grounds are now more commonly covered in marquees with guests tramping across the lawns and filling the tranquility with drunken celebrations. Sawyer chose to hold his celebrations inside. He claimed due to unpredictable weather. The truth? An outside occasion means unwanted guests can more easily sneak in from the night.

I also studied the map to ensure I'm au fait with the building's layout. The two-story hotel is divided into a wing with bedrooms for guests and several function rooms used for social or business gatherings by people who can afford the prestigious hotel's prices.

Dorian persuaded Sawyer *not* to pay for guests to stay overnight and ensure any significant ones leave at the end of the evening. My father has enough concerns about what might happen without turning the evening into a game of Cluedo—a board game Holly introduced to me and became upset that I immediately won, accusing me of mind-reading.

Granted, most guests come from either the Sawyer inner circle or Kai's friends—so a distinct lack of shifters—but one can never be too sure.

An unpleasantly cramped minibus ferries those invited from the academy, and I'm squashed between Holly and Leif, seated amongst another ten or so students. I'd considered protesting against travelling in this fashion only to be reminded that my new attempt at integration won't succeed if I stride in at my father's side.

As the unwitting savior of Sawyer's son, I'm one of several 'guests of honor' at Kai's rite of passage. Rowan and Grayson are naturally included on that dubious list, and of course Dorian for his work in extracting the truth (no doubt after a threat to extract other parts) from the witch Adam Woodlake. Well, what Sawyer believes is the truth.

Christopher Sawyer decides to host an evening of thanks for those who saved Kai's life on the night he celebrates his son's eighteenth birthday? Good grief, the man must think we're stupid. Sawyer wants Kai protected.

Holly sits with the ever-vacant Chase, one of several witches invited, including Marci, who somehow scored an invite. Although the occasion requires less casual attire, the teenagers around aren't dressed in the same stiff suits and impractical dresses as the dance. Holly's chosen what she informed me is a

96

'cocktail dress'— a long-sleeved item that stops halfway along her thighs, the pink sequined material wrapping tightly around her body.

I too searched for a 'cocktail dress', informed by my mother I needed to 'look right'. The number of options in black eased the pain, and I managed to find something in keeping with my preferred style—black with flared skirts that reach below my knee, the long lacy sleeves and high scooped neckline ensuring I've much less skin on show tonight. I refuse to use a purse and the dumb dress has no pockets, so I'm forced to improvise.

The minibus crawls along the hotel driveway that's lit by tall, old-fashioned lamplights, the gold and burgundy hotel sign illuminated by spotlights beneath.

"I do hope nobody dies tonight," I comment as I take note of the large number of vehicles in the hotel car park.

A girl seated in front glances over her shoulder and Leif nudges me. "Not the best comment, Violet."

"I'm merely stating that this event could draw attention from someone with malevolent intent," I continue.

"I'm sure Dorian will keep everybody safe," suggests Holly.

"Yes. Therefore, I hope nobody dies tonight."

Someone flicks the back of my neck, and I turn to where Rowan sits behind. He shakes his head at me but says nothing.

We're deposited directly outside the hotel lobby, and I stand back as the excited students rush forward. Holly yanks at my baggy black cardigan sleeve as she passes. "This spoils the effect, Violet."

"Perhaps I'm cold."

"You don't *get* cold," she bats back. "Why cover up such a pretty dress with a shapeless cardigan that reaches your knees?"

"Because the cardigan has pockets." I pat one where I've secured my phone.

"You do look kind of odd," comments Leif.

I tip my head back to look up at him. He's wearing slacks of a nondescript beige color and a slate blue shirt and gray tie. His black shoes shine, whereas Rowan chose sneakers despite his black pants and navy shirt—no tie.

"Then I shall meet expectations," I tell him before glancing back to the empty bus. "Where's Grayson?"

"Here."

Holly squeaks as he steps from the dim beside her, and Chase sneers. "Sneaking already, Gray?" he asks.

"He's hemia. They're quiet and barely detectable in the dark," I tell Chase.

"Yeah. As I said, *sneaking*." He nods at the vampire. "There's a dress code, mate. Where's your fancy shirt and tie?"

"I don't possess one and don't particularly care if I'm refused entry," he replies and slips hands into the back of his black jeans.

"You do. You wore one to the Spring Ball," says Chase.

Holly goes completely stiff and looks away. Those two words have become offensive around her and I'm struggling to understand why the continued upset over a minor social occasion. Rowan attempted to explain the amount of time—and herself—Holly put into organizing the occasion, but the continued sullenness seems like an excessive response to me.

Grayson shrugs and a passing girl comments, "Grayson's formal shirt probably got covered in blood at the Darwin house party."

"For fuck's sake," mutters Grayson. "I wasn't involved."

"As if anybody believes *that*," she says and turns.

The girl and her inane comments suddenly piques my interest. This is Cassie—the hysterical girl from the dance, now standing beside the *other* hysterical girl who started the 'haunted tiara' rumor. Beth?

"How is Sienna?" I ask. "Is she returning to the academy?"

"Not for the rest of term," Cassie replies, amusingly looking down her nose at me. "Who knows what a bitchy witch might do to her next?"

"At the risk of repeating myself, I have no ill will towards Sienna. We've barely interacted."

Beth scoffs. "Sure. You know what she did."

"Stole my tiara."

"*No*. What she did to upset you." Beth's eyes shine, plump pink lips pursed.

"Other than sharing my breathing space and taking my possessions, nothing upset me."

With another scoff, Beth and Cassie stalk away towards the bright and welcoming hotel entrance.

"Is Beth implying Sienna performed an action against me in an attempt to bully?" I scrape through my brain. Nothing. "Surely the runes and potion theft weren't her."

"What did Dorian say about that?" asks Rowan as he takes my hand and leads me after Holly and the other students.

"He's concerned."

"But not about the tiara, like I predicted," says Grayson.

I rub my cheek. "No. And now Julius Woodside has disappeared."

"He hasn't disappeared, Violet," puts in Leif. "He's at a training course for a couple of days."

Pausing, I turn to him. "How do you know?"

"Hey, I can keep an eye on everything happening too." Leif moves to the other side of me, and we continue walking. "A couple of teachers went."

"I do hope that's the truth and he doesn't go missing before we get more information from him," I say tersely. "I hate wasting time and I especially hate additional victims. What if Julius becomes one before we extract anything useful?"

"The only person who seems to know anything is Mrs. Eldridge," Rowan says.

"You didn't tell him about Julius?" asks Leif.

"No. What would be the point if Dorian doesn't care about a possible murder? We'd upset Julius and he won't give us any of Madison's items to work with," I reply.

"*If* he does," says Grayson.

"Oh, the man knows he's struck gold if I'm helping." The guys snort a laugh at me, and I glare. "If *we're* helping."

"How will you get the tiara back?" asks Grayson. "Don't you need that?"

"Eventually, but let's see what Julius's objects hold for us—enough to demand the tiara's return for examination," I hope.

Leif and Rowan exchange a glance. They don't believe Dorian will get involved. As Grayson wanders ahead with Rowan, I catch Leif's arm. He glances down in surprise.

"Do you still have Rowan's stone?" I ask quietly.

"Yeah. In my room. Don't stress."

"Promise me you won't give it back to Rowan."

Leif sighs. "I already promised. He hasn't asked for the stone either, okay?"

I nod. "Tell me if he does."

"Because they prompt his shadows. I know." He blows air into his cheeks and looks at the back of Rowan's head. "He's calmer since... you and him. Less obsessive about magic."

"I don't believe that's true. Rowan's innate desire to become a powerful witch hasn't ended because he met me." I watch Rowan too. "He's clearly in touch with Blackwood shadows and they can have an unwanted influence. Tell me if you think he's behaving unusually."

Leif takes my hand and squeezes. "We've watched out for each other for years, Violet. I won't help Rowan with anything that's dangerous to him or others—you've seen me deal with him."

The shifter attack. The first time I saw Rowan's shadows. My worry settles a little. Leif stopped him then.

"Well then," I say. "Let us hope the evening passes quickly and without incident. How long until we can leave?"

Leif's amusement follows me as I stomp onwards to my latest purgatory.

CHAPTER 14

VIOLET

CONSIDERING the event is a celebration of his life—and of his still having one—Kai's enthusiasm almost matches mine. He's loitering in a small lobby area between the main function rooms with Dale and a collection of his other male friends. Their low chattering stops when I step into the flock-wallpapered hallway, and Kai grips his beer bottle by the neck as I approach.

Rowan and Leif flank me, something I honestly don't need, but that's more likely designed to keep me in check. As I reach the sofa they're lounging on, Kai pulls his feet from the low table opposite and stands. He's removed his tie and unbuttoned and loosened the pale blue shirt collar. If Kai wore a jacket tonight, he's removed that too. Still, he's more dressed up than Grayson. Where did *he* go?

Despite attempts, I haven't seen Kai since the incident at the warehouse and before me stands the Kai filled with bravado rather than the one whose fear turned him into a frightened boy.

"Good evening, Kai," I say evenly.

He doesn't speak for a moment, slugging from his bottle before wiping his mouth. "What do you want?"

"That's a bit bloody rude considering Violet and Rowan saved your life," says Leif brusquely.

"What? We should be best mates now?" He gestures at me with the bottle. "Have you seen her when she's feral? She's fucking dangerous!"

"How are you?" I ask evenly. "Any more problems with shifters?"

"I don't know why Dad's sucking up to supes because you're all bad news." His blurry aura and slurred voice alert me to a familiar human state I'll see a lot tonight. Inebriation. "Especially bloody witches."

"Yet you invited some tonight," retorts Rowan.

Kai looks him up and down. "Dad wants to look 'inclusive'. I've told people for weeks that they should stay away from academy kids."

"You're the one who told Ollie to stay away from Holly?" I ask. "But then you invited academy kids to your ill-fated party?"

"Yeah, and?"

I sigh. "Hopefully tonight is a calmer affair."

From behind, one of the other guys makes a derisive noise. "With you lot here? Doubt that."

"Would you mind answering my question, Kai?" I ask, reminding myself that Leif insists politeness aids me more than demands. "Any trouble from shifters? Witches?"

"No. Because I can't leave the house and if I do..." He gestures to a guy in the corner who I hadn't paid attention to, presuming he was a party guest taking time out from festivities. After all, he's smartly dressed, masses of muscles squeezed into a suit. "Him."

"You have a bodyguard?" asks Leif and stares.

"The man may rival a shifter in physicality, but he wouldn't be a match for a supernatural attack," I say, running a gaze over the sullen-faced man.

"Guns can kill witches," he says gruffly.

Kai scowls. "Get me another beer, Rick. Violet *Blackwood* is with me. I'll be safe for five minutes." The man says nothing. "Beer for the birthday boy."

With a sour face, Rick stomps away.

"Your father thinks you're in danger from witches?" I ask.

"Supes. Always has." He jerks his chin. "The man's stupid if he thinks I'll get more involved with his business now I'm eighteen."

"Do you mean the soup business?" I ask. "Of the tinned variety, not supernatural."

"Yeah. Wants to sign Sawyer Enterprises over to me. I'm not interested in his bullshit company." He drains the bottle. "Dad literally wants me to start next week."

"Why the urgency?" asks Rowan.

Yes, why indeed?

"Do you mean your father will sign all business assets to you now that you're eighteen?" I frown. "*Everything*?"

"Yeah. Supposedly, he'll train me and work in the background, but Dad wants me as the new 'face of the business'." A guy beside him whispers and Kai chuckles. "Maybe I'll sell the place and piss off somewhere."

"I'm sure your father will include a clause preventing you from doing that," I say.

"I'm gonna piss off somewhere anyway." He slides his eyes to the door Rick walked through. "I'm not dumb. My father upset witches and there's a vampire sorting his legal shit. Someone tried to kill me. You reckon I'm hanging around? The only thing I'd sign is to take my name off everything to do with the factory and escape this bullshit."

That may be the most intelligent sentence I've heard from this human, but would Kai remain safe if he did?

And a vampire overseeing the legal aspect? Surely Josef isn't still Sawyer's attorney.

"How interesting," I say. "Your father will present legal

documents pertaining to your inheritance of the business on your eighteenth birthday. Are others aware?"

He shrugs. "Only those who need to, whatever that means."

"Sawyer kept this very quiet," says Rowan in a low voice.

I tap my lips and study Kai, particularly where his shirt's unbuttoned. "Where's your necklace?"

"Uh. You ripped that off in the factory so you could use *your* magic on me." He taps the side of his head. "Everything's making sense now. Family tradition, my arse—that necklace was for protection."

"As I informed you." I gesture. "Now, you've no protection."

"Apart from him?" he mutters, lips thin as the door opens heralding Rick with another beer.

A woman accompanies him, elegant in her gold silk dress that sweeps the floor. Gems and diamonds the size she's wearing in her ears and around her wrists shout wealth and her unlined face suggests vamp—or cosmetic enhancements. Sleek brown hair falls halfway down her back, mercilessly straightened, not a hair daring to move from its place.

"Kai, sweetheart!"

"Great, now my mother's here," he mumbles.

Cosmetic, then. Or perhaps a spell? No. Kai's mother definitely isn't a witch, a possibility I've toyed with that's dashed now that I've seen her.

She takes a step towards him, the slender woman's height enhanced further by that of the spike-heeled shoes she's wearing. The gold pumps could work as a weapon if she finds herself in a tight spot. Is Mrs. Sawyer expecting trouble?

"Oh! You must be Violet!" The woman pauses and to my horror she walks forwards with her arms outstretched. "I owe you more than you can imagine."

Is she trying to take my hands? I tuck them beneath my arms. "Owe? You've no debt to me."

"I do—my darling son!" She clasps a hand against her heart. "If it weren't for you and your friends, Kai wouldn't be here."

"If it weren't for your husband's dubious dealings with witches, Kai wouldn't be under threat," I reply, on the verge of mentioning the runes from her bedroom.

I believe she's attempting to frown at me—hard to tell. "Christopher does not involve himself in 'dubious' behavior. He stands for honesty and integrity."

"Uh huh," says Rowan beneath his breath.

"Why do you think witches wanted to kill your son, Mrs. Sawyer?" I ask bluntly.

She regards me for a moment, then turns away. "Kai, darling. Your father wants to see you alone."

"What for?" he asks suspiciously and takes his fresh bottle from Rick.

Mrs. Sawyer pouts and reaches out for the drink. "I do hope you're not drinking a lot this evening. Your father won't be happy if you embarrass him. After the DUI, you're not supposed to drink in public."

"It's my fucking birthday and legal now!" he snaps.

Now, I'm known for back chatting Dorian often but never with disrespectful language like his. Mrs. Sawyer's cheeks flush. "Do not speak to me like that, Kai," she says coldly.

"And there was no DUI!" He jabs a finger at me and the guys. "*They* did something."

I tense. This is not the direction I'd like the conversation to take. Next they'll mention the lodge.

"And Dad isn't parading me around as his little heir," Kai continues, then looks over his shoulder at his silent friends. "Come on. Let's find a bar. The place has several."

"Kai Sawyer," says his mother in warning. "You'll do no such thing."

"What? You going to ask *him* to drag me to Dad?" Kai jerks his chin at a cautious looking Rick. "I bet that'd embarrass him more than me having a few too many drinks."

"You do as your father tells you!" Mrs. Sawyer's voice rises.

"I don't believe that's likely," I interrupt. "From my observations, Kai rarely does."

Her brown eyes flash in my direction. "This doesn't concern you."

"Death threats against Kai by witches and attacks on—and by —shifters? I'm well and truly in the middle of all that," I say.

"This is a family matter," she says through clenched teeth.

"Yeah, fuck this," says her son.

My inadvertently distracting his mother allows Kai to walk away. Some would pursue and accost their child to pull them into submission, but despite her flaring anger, Mrs. Sawyer watches them move along the hallway—away from the function room— through wider eyes.

"Rick. Follow them," she says.

"In case he's attacked?" I ask.

"No. In case Kai leaves."

I straighten. "Oh. Then I agree. Rick should follow him. An attack is more likely to occur away from the hotel grounds."

But the bodyguard's already at Kai's heels.

Muttering beneath her breath, Mrs. Sawyer turns back towards the door.

"Excuse me?" I call. "I have a question."

Leif laughs quietly. "Of course, you do."

The woman pivots, face harassed. "I've more important things to do than chat to you. Kai could ruin his father's night!"

"Did you retrieve your stolen jewelry?" I ask.

She places a hand over the diamonds and emeralds strung across her chest. "Stolen?"

"The item that went missing from the safe at Kai's illicit house party," I say.

"I don't know the specifics about that," she says.

"Oh? I do, since your husband accused me and Grayson Petrescu of the theft."

The hassled look grows as she darts a look between the doors to the function room and me. "I need to find my husband and solve our family matter."

Without a goodbye, the woman stalks away in her impressively dangerous heels.

Hmm.

"Well, then," I say and wander to the sofa Kai and his friends occupied earlier. "That was an enlightening meeting."

Rowan flops down next to me. "You reckon witches tried to kill Kai before he turned eighteen to stop this transfer?"

"That's obvious," says Leif and squeezes into the adjacent armchair. "But wouldn't shifters be the ones who wanted to stop another human getting rights to the lands?"

"They have their own rights," I say. "Kai wouldn't own the shifter's part of the land."

"As far as we know," says Rowan. He takes my hand and plays his fingers along the back. "Sawyer hasn't disclosed everything to Dorian. Your father knows nothing about this sudden inheritance, or that Sawyer has a 'vampire lawyer', and his big-mouthed son just dropped him in shit."

I still his fingers by placing mine over them. "Most certainly. But Sawyer invited Dorian, so he isn't hiding the situation anymore."

"Yeah, we all know Sawyer's sucking up to Dorian for protection." Leif moistens his lips. "What if he's expecting an attack?"

"Oh, joy," I say. "More public bloodshed."

"What about those papers you found in the box?" asks Leif. "Has Dorian found anything from them?"

Rowan rubs the back of his neck. "So, about that..."

I snap my head around. "What?"

"I only photographed one side of the papers. We don't have all the information, according to Dorian's legal people."

"What?" I blink at him. "That's extremely remiss of you."

"Legal papers aren't usually double-sided," he retorts. "And we were in a hurry!"

"What information *do* we have?"

"Half," says Leif and smirks as Rowan punches his arm.

"Speak to Dorian?" suggests Rowan. "I don't speak legalese."

"What's that? A witch language? Do you think the deeds were in code to trick people?" I straighten.

Leif chuckles. "You could argue legalese is a coded language that tricks people."

"Well, is it or not?" I snap my head between the two.

"Legal jargon, Violet. A *lot* of legal jargon," says Rowan.

"But only half," puts in Leif again.

"Why is that funny?" I snap. "Because half a story is never funny!"

If only we'd taken those papers along with the tiara on the night of the attack. The box disappeared from the location hidden beneath the factory floor before the papers could be retrieved by investigators. Josef removed the box? Or somebody else we never saw also present that night?

Leif presses his large palms to his thighs and stands. "We're at a party. Can we get a drink now?"

"But—"

"But unless you intend to leave for more sleuthing, there's nothing more we can do," says Rowan.

"You don't want to miss the evening entertainment," adds Leif.

I allow Rowan to help me to my feet. "Entertainment? There was the man playing music through a machine. Is there more? Not another band, I hope."

"I heard there'll be fireworks later," Leif says.

"There're witches here. He could've saved money and asked them for a light show," I comment. "Like Holly planned for the Spring..." She isn't here for me to remind her of the occasion, but I still feel I'm speaking the unmentionable.

"Nah. Well, yeah, I mean fireworks once Sawyer finds Kai," says Leif.

"They're responsible for the fireworks? And you're not

concerned someone may sabotage them?" I ask. "I did consider supernatural threats, but not threats created by items used for entertainment purposes that could maim them."

Rowan shakes his head. "No. When *Sawyer* explodes at Kai for being a naughty boy."

"Then why not just say that?" I ask. "I've enough to worry about without considering other dangers or deciphering nuances."

"Drink?" asks Leif.

I hesitate. "Perhaps I should make some notes or follow Kai."

"C'mon, Violet. You haven't scouted the whole venue yet *or* identified every guest. Surely you want the opportunity to gather more names and information?"

Leif does have a very good point.

CHAPTER 15

VIOLET

LEIF AND ROWAN conclude I never drink alcohol merely because I refused in the past. I do, in moderation, partly because I don't like the taste of most varieties and also because the intoxicating properties don't affect me. Witch potions and herbs? Yes. Distilled beverages? No.

I stand at the small bar situated between two of the function rooms, and while Leif and Rowan acquire drinks, I'm on the lookout for Grayson. I haven't seen him since we arrived. Was he ejected for failing to meet the dress code as Chase predicted?

Sawyer plans for Kai to sign legal contracts publicly at the party. *Legal.* Sawyer wouldn't invite Josef. Not with Dorian as another guest. Surely. Is the guy still his attorney? I wouldn't be surprised. After all, he supposedly helped save Kai that night in the warehouse.

No. Josef wouldn't be dumb enough to come tonight. The bastard's in hiding and this wouldn't be the best place to reappear. Even if the human detectives are prepared to let their doubts go, Dorian won't.

"I'll be right back," I say to Rowan and point towards one of the rooms. "I want to find Grayson. Just in case Josef is around."

He nods and turns away before he misses the bartender's attention.

The first room I look into contains quiet and adults, with a small podium towards the back beside a table with a cake. Much of the hotel has been restored to original Edwardian fashion that I've seen in other witch houses. Whereas my parents' home holds a dark and cluttered Victorian aesthetic, the polished floors and light-colored walls open the room.

There're modern touches amongst the mahogany furniture and ornate cornices, such as the round table my bored father sits at. He looks odd on a chair with silver ribbons tied around and runs his thumb around the rim of a glass of whiskey—his drink of choice, always. Eloise stands nearby talking to an elderly lady who bears a resemblance to Kai's mother.

I almost stay to watch and listen to Sawyer and his wife's agitated conversation, but they're only speaking about Kai's behavior. I almost feel sorry for the guy. Instead, I pass several groups clustered together holding glasses of wine or beer bottles like Kai's. Most are human and one or two definitely startle as I walk by, even without touching them. Must be my 'vibe' that Holly informs me repels people. Charming.

The second room contains the man playing the music—a DJ, apparently, and I suppose better than being subjected to a band like at 'the event that shall not be named'. Although he's rather too excited by his unusual task and appears desperate for attention from those gathered.

I cover my ears as I pass one of the monstrous speakers he brought to the party.

Teens dance in a space cleared of tables, and wine splashes from glasses onto the floor as I watch. Hmm. I'm not sticking around to face accusations when the idiotic kids break their necks from slipping on their own mess.

I flick a look around the darkened room, easily making out

those who the witches or humans wouldn't see. Where the last room filled with calm—if you discount the Sawyers—this one contains chaotic energy fueled by the now recognizable mix of alcohol and hormones.

No Grayson, but Holly's standing with Chase in a corner. At least, I think it's Holly since she's against the wall partly squashed by him. I march over and interrupt their little tryst, noting Chase's untucked shirt, and his mussed hair that Holly's gripping.

"Have you seen Grayson?" I ask loudly.

Chase goes entirely still, then withdraws from Holly, throwing me a look. She leans against the wall, breathless and pink-cheeked, and she adjusts her dress.

Good grief.

"No," she says crossly. "Violet..."

"'Violet what'?" I point at the side of her dress. "The zipper appears to have slipped."

Rubbing her lips together, Holly tugs at the zipper and a silent communication comprising of head gestures and mouthed words between her and Chase then follows.

Chase walks away.

"Why do you do that in public?" I ask and wrinkle my nose. "It's rather off-putting."

"Nobody asked you to watch." Holly smoothes her hair. "We were only kissing."

"Mmm." I flourish a hand. "Anyway. Grayson. Have you seen him?"

"At the bar earlier. Where did you go?"

"To speak to Kai."

She splutters. "I bet he loved that."

"No. He didn't. But Kai isn't having a 'happy birthday'."

"Oh, dear." Holly plays with her newly attached pink nails.

"If you see Grayson, inform him that I'm searching for him." I make to walk away. If he isn't here, I want out of this cacophony, stat.

"Violet."

"I know that look. What have I done?" I ask. "I'll locate and return Chase to you if my interruption bothers you that much, but it's not as if you rarely see each other."

"I have a favor to ask."

"A favor?" Another *quid pro quo* request, sacred words to those I've met at the academy. Always a 'favor' rather than random acts of kindness. "I wasn't aware I languished in 'favor debt'."

Holly half-smiles. "I'll owe you one in return."

"No. Keeping track confuses me."

"Returning favors are not set in stone, Violet."

"Yet it's an unspoken rule." I shake my head. "Proceed. What favor?"

"We share a room, right?"

"An obvious statement. Although often you're a third person in Marci's room."

"Chase shares a room. Most humans do."

"Yes. Why the discussion about accommodation arrangements?" I straighten. "Did you want me to leave the room?"

"Yes." I gape at her. "No. I mean, yes."

"You want a different roommate, as teachers once suggested?" How odd that her comment nauseates me.

Holly sighs and tugs on her bottom lip. "No, Violet. Would you stay somewhere else? Just for tonight?"

"Why?"

"Violet!" Holly lifts her eyes to the ceiling. "Your inability to read nuances is frustrating."

"Your vocabulary is improving. My influence?" I ask.

She looks at me with the frustration she mentioned. "I want Chase to spend the night in our room."

"And you need the other bed?"

Holly chokes. "Seriously, Violet? I don't believe you're that naive."

Oh. I suppress a retch, now queasy for other reasons. "You

want Chase in your bed and privacy. Holly. He's a horrible person."

"I like him. A lot."

"And I don't believe you've good judgement around attractive males."

"You agree he's hot?" She giggles.

"And that judgement appears further impaired by alcohol consumption, Holly." I slant my head. "Why not stay at the hotel?"

"Because Mrs. Lorcan's paranoid and wants a head count when we board the bus back to the academy. You were there when she warned us not to go anywhere." Holly purses her lip. "Like we're a bunch of middle-schoolers."

"To be fair, the student body often behave like they are."

"Well?"

I'm reminded of the day we met when I considered whether Holly was a golden retriever shifter as those are certainly what I've heard Rowan call 'puppy dog' eyes. He often uses the phrase when referring to Leif, which earns him a smack around the head from his friend.

"Will you?" she asks

"And where do *I* go?"

"Rowan has his own room." The expectant look grows. "And Grayson, but I sense there's something weird going on there."

"Mmm."

Only a select few know about my frenzied blood-drinking, and Holly isn't one of them. If she knew, I'd definitely lose her as a roommate—the girl would interpret the incident as evidence I tear my friends' throats should I be inclined.

"'Mmm' something weird or 'mmm' yes you will?" she asks. "Are you worried about getting into trouble? People do this all the time."

I sigh. "How can I answer you?"

"What do you mean? Yes or no is the answer." She drags a

hand through her curls. "Violet. You're really hard work sometimes. We'd ask Chase's roommate but uh... we've asked him too many times."

"Holly. Were you actually at Marci's or not the nights you stayed away?"

"Are you shocked, Violet? That was *your* presumption."

I cross my arms. "I can't give you an answer until I've asked Rowan, can I?"

Holly gawks at me as if I slapped her, then she snorts, that snort becoming laughter as she holds a hand over her mouth.

I clench my teeth. "You say I'm hard work? Well, your often unexplained and unfathomable amusement is hard work for *me*. Or is this the alcohol?"

Holly shakes her head and pulls her hand away, but the hilarity hasn't left. "Did you seriously just say that?"

"Unexplained and unfathomable amusement?"

"No, Violet. That you'd need to ask Rowan first."

I frown. "Well, it would be inconsiderate of me to use his bed without asking."

"I'm sure you've used his bed before."

"I've never had the need. I always sleep in my own."

Holly rubs her clammy cheek. "I swear you're deliberately teasing me."

Am I? Partially. But I don't know if Rowan *would* be happy for me to stay with him. He's never asked before and by all accounts Chase asked Holly many times. Rowan slept in my bed by default rather than planning due to his inability to stay awake in the early hours, but I never joined him.

Yet something I'm increasingly aware of remains tucked away in the recesses of my mind—denial. I can't deny that mine and Rowan's shared desire hasn't already led to unusual behavior for me. Touching and kissing. Sharing emotions. But more? I'm happy for Rowan to remain hesitant because however many times I tell myself bonded witches can't hurt each other, and that a loss of mental control won't lead to lust-induced violence against him, doubt nags.

But doubt about *that* doubt nags too.

I'm not worried I'll hurt Rowan; I'm worried if I give all of myself to somebody I'll lose who I am once and for all.

CHAPTER 16

GRAYSON

WHY INVITE ME? I may've lured away the shifter attacking Kai, but I spent most of the time impaled against a wall—hardly heroic. Sawyer continues to suck up to Dorian, hence inviting Violet and Rowan. What am I? Part of the package? I snort to myself, now scouting for the bar. Fine. I'll enjoy some of the free beers, then leave.

Most people stand in groups chatting while enjoying their drinks, others help themselves from the glasses of wine and champagne lined up on the bar. Sawyer allowing free flowing alcohol for their son's party filled with teens? Legal or not, that's not the best combination.

Violet had only set one foot in the hotel before her attention switched. She's intent on finding Kai and clues and didn't notice when I hung back as she spoke to Kai, then left, bored. Now I wish I had stayed with them, because however much I embrace my loner reputation, I'm singled out more tonight. If I'd worn a suit, that would've helped blend in. Ha ha. As if. I only wore one to the Spring Ball because Violet expected me *not* to.

I lean over a shorter guy who's standing at the bar and reach for one of the beers beside glasses of champagne. My arm brushes his and the guy jerks, snapping his head around. Human and from the academy because he immediately turns his back and guides away the girl he's with. I only glimpse the back of her head, where she piled her honey-blonde hair on top. Could be anybody, not necessarily someone I've had contact with before.

I knew him though—weaselly faced guy who hung around the edge of Wes's circle. Not central enough that I've encountered him on my old patrol nights, but close enough he avoids me. I wonder who leads the human ape gang now?

Do I actually care?

With a sigh, I take a long drink from the bottle and turn to rest against the metal bar. Maybe I should look for the others, but that would involve subjecting myself to Violet. Each time I see her more relaxed around Rowan and Leif, her smiles for them are like a knife twisted in my heart. Violet does smile at me too, but only after hesitating—and from a distance.

Am I making things too easy for Violet while struggling myself? I want her to deal with the situation by being *in* the situation. Denial's easy for Violet when I'm rarely around, and my head's a mess of indecision. Keep away or place myself in a position where Violet's forced to confront the reality of 'us' that I saw in her room the day I returned to the academy?

"Hi, Grayson." A female voice snaps me out of my Violet obsessing, and I look down at the girl who approached me.

"Oh. Hey, Marci."

"You look lost," she says, and I frown. "Violet lost one of her entourage."

My brow tugs tighter. "You might've noticed that I'm not always with the group."

"Mmm. Not quite accepted?" She smiles. "Could you pass me a glass?" Marci points behind me. "Not often there's free champagne on offer."

"Well, Sawyer's kid's eighteenth. Only the best." I take a fizzing glass and pass it to Marci.

She sips, looking every inch the person who'd drink champagne daily—black cocktail dress and make-up that transformed her from pretty witch to elegant woman. "Are you and Violet together?"

"No. I'm alone. As you can see."

"No." She tucks a strand of hair behind an ear. "*Together* together."

"Not currently," I say stiffly and look the other way.

"Oh. You *were*?" she asks. "Surprises me she manages a relationship with anybody."

I look back to the witch, who continues to delicately sip at her drink. What's happening here? Has Marci told Holly the story about Violet's attack? Violet assured me she hasn't shared the full facts with Holly, but who knows? Violet's changes might bring her closer to female friends too.

"How's Violet's business suddenly yours?" I ask.

"Whoa. Okay. I'm surprised things lasted this long with Rowan. How are they getting along?" She takes a bigger gulp of the champagne.

A new theory pushes away the creeping suspicion Marci's hitting on me. "Why? Are you jealous?"

"Violet isn't good for him."

"Good for him or good *enough* for him?" I ask, then set down the half-empty bottle. "I'm not gossiping with you about my friends' relationship. It's weird."

"Rowan's dangerous. So is she. That's all I mean." Marci drains her glass and hands it to me. "I'll have another."

Wow. "You sure?"

"Like I said, free champagne."

As I locate and pass Marci another glass, I attempt to tune out of her presence, uncomfortable by both the conversation and her proximity. The witch blood temptation isn't what worries me—I don't want the flashbacks to Josef's 'treatment' should my senses home in on her. I'm not attracted to the girl, but she's a witch and the race's blood scent naturally affects me.

"Where are your friends?" I ask pointedly when Marci doesn't move.

"Dancing in the Sterling Room." Her lips press together. "Tonight reminds me of the Spring Ball apart from *this* event's actually happening." She gulps the wine. "I failed an assignment because I put too much time into organizing the dance. Now my parents are pissed and I've nothing to show for all that work I put in."

"Right." I rub the back of my neck. Marci never speaks to me, especially not since the incident where I put a witch girl in the hospital, and now she's burbling shit I have no interest in. "Uh. I'm sure you'll catch up with your grades."

"And did you know the asshole cheated on me?" she continues. "*At* the Spring Ball. With a vamp."

The asshole? Oh. That human she dates. I'd hoped Jon might appear and take Marci away but that's now unlikely. Crap. Where are her friends? Any of them? I saw Holly earlier, but she's with *her* asshole.

"Jon thinks I don't know, but I *know*. Nothing gets past me." This time, Marci swaps her empty glass for a full one without my assistance.

"I hope you dumped the guy," I say and edge to the side as she presses against me while reaching for the glass.

Her lips curve into a smile. "Humans shouldn't screw with witches."

"What have you done?" I ask sharply.

"Nothing." Marci's smile grows. "Yet."

I pull myself tall and look down at her. "Nothing Violet can be accused of doing," I warn.

"Violet's untouchable. But then you know that don't you?" She snickers. "Is she the first witch who didn't fall for your hemia seduction?"

Irritation flares. "How many glasses of wine have you had?

Because you need to stop before you start saying shit that'll upset people."

Eyes firmly fixed on mine; Marci drinks the whole glass in several gulps then slams the glass down. "Six."

"Right. We need to find your friends. I'm not dealing with this," I say. I know where girls hang out or at least go to eventually. Bathrooms. "Come on. We'll locate your friends and then I can find mine."

I stride across the carpet, glancing back over my shoulder to ensure Marci's following. She is. Unsteadily. Why did she accost me? Yeah, we've the Holly connection now since I'm in Violet's detective gang, but I am not the right guy to whine at with her girlie bullshit.

I reach the double doors and glance left and right. Which way to the bathrooms? With any luck, some of Marci's friends will be in the hallway outside. I swear beneath my breath—I'm advised not to go near witches; chaperoning drunk ones isn't sensible.

"This way," she says.

Marci trips over an imaginary bump on the carpet and grabs my upper arm to steady herself. A slow feeling of dread slithers in but Marci drops her grip once she's fully upright.

I slow my pace and hang back, watching Marci as she walks ahead along the hallway. With any luck, nobody will think we're together. But where the hell is she going?

"Marci!" I hiss as she disappears around a corner. No reply. I groan and follow.

The hallway ends at the rear of the hotel. Through the long windows, security lights show tables set up for outdoor dining on a wide patio, set ready for tomorrow's breakfast guests but now used by partygoers. Marci pushes open one of the glass doors and chatter filters back through towards me.

"Marci!" a girl calls out.

Good. Friends of hers.

Someone seizes me around the back of the neck and forcibly

shoves me out of sight into a side room. My face almost hits the wall as a familiar presence bears down on me.

"Didn't I teach you anything, Grayson?" hisses a voice in my ear. "How long until you learn your lesson?"

My stomach leadens.

The dumb bastard Sawyer hasn't found himself a better, less murderous attorney.

CHAPTER 17

GRAYSON

I CLENCH MY JAW HARD, focusing on dampening down the immediate gut-wrenching fear from the man now pressing my face into the wall.

"You're extremely lucky that I'm here in a professional capacity today," he says, the sweetness of his breath another reminder of unpleasant pasts.

"Why?" I grit out.

"I can't walk into the party covered in blood. That would give everybody the wrong impression." Josef squeezes my neck tight, then pushes as he releases. I turn, pulling myself from the wall and side-stepping.

He stands opposite me, hands in his trouser pockets.

My muscles seize, acid filling my mouth. I last saw the slick-haired, hard-faced vamp when he skewered me, while watching with the same arrogant twist to his lips, emerald eyes retreating into the darkness that enveloped me. He can't touch me here. Josef has a reputation to uphold and that includes *detracting* from his status as a hemia vamp, not reminding everybody.

At least I bloody hope so.

"Aren't you worried about walking into this place?" I ask.

"Why? There's no arrest warrant for me. The humans happily allowed me to leave that night." He smiles the radiant, false one he uses on everyone he's capable of influencing.

"With the help of illegal skills," I retort, and tap the side of my head. He sneers. "And I'm not talking about the human threat to you."

The one thing that's holding me together right now— Dorian's here. Violet. Rowan. No way will Josef walk out of here tonight unless it's to a cell.

Josef slants his head. "Are you referring to the Blackwoods? I've no concerns about them."

"Then you're a fucking idiot," I sneer back. Josef lashes out and my cheek stings as sharp nails scratch across the skin, the attack over in a blurred second.

I remain still, face neutral, not touching the welling blood as I stare into Josef's blackening hemia eyes. He tuts and examines his nails. "Now look what you made me do. If I've blood on my clothes, I'll be extremely displeased."

"What was that? Didn't you just say you can't hurt me?" I say evenly and wipe my fingertips across my bloodied cheek.

"I said no such thing. Only that I can't deal with you in the manner you deserve right *now*. Stalking witches for their blood. Disgusting." His tone mocks me; Josef knows that isn't what he saw.

"You won't hurt me badly tonight?" I continue. "Whatever I do?"

His eyes narrow, giving his angular face a more sinister look, even without the hemia shift. "Why? What have you done?"

I drop my gaze to his silk tie, navy woven with silver, perfectly straight against the white shirt beneath his unbuttoned jacket. Then I look him dead in the eye and smear my bloodied fingers across his shirt. Even though I smirk at the streaks of blood across his chest, I'm as sick as when he held me to the wall. I've taken a risk—he'll either maintain his professional facade or pummel me here and now.

I've never once retaliated against Josef, usually because he had his back-up heavies with him, and this might be a mild, childish hit back, but will be the first of many if he tries to harm me again. Because if wiping blood on Josef's shirt is enough to silence the guy and freeze his responses, maybe hurting him badly will be easier than I'd expect.

"I'll find you before the night ends, Grayson," he growls in warning as I move by him, tensing in case he lashes out.

I slide my eyes towards him, our heads close. "That's if Dorian doesn't deal with you first."

"Dorian Blackwood won't hurt me tonight," he sneers. "And if I don't find you before the night ends, I'll ensure we catch up *very* soon."

"Best clean yourself up," I say lightly and point at his shirt. "The bathrooms are further down the hallway, I believe."

If a man who knows Josef by name didn't cross our path at that moment, and force Josef to pull back on his disguise that he's an upstanding member of society, his response to my words would've been different, I'm sure.

Forced to exchange pleasantries with the man who approached, Josef allows me to walk away.

This time.

CHAPTER 18

VIOLET

CHASE RETURNS to where I stand with Holly and looks between us. Is he aware I dislike him? Since I'm perceived as disliking most people, he wouldn't notice, but I'm less tolerant of him due to his connection to Holly. Witches in general look down on other students and although Holly's firm friends with female witches, I've witnessed Chase's indifference to her when with his friends. He's happy to spend time together privately, but not so much publicly.

Unless it's in the dark.

"Violet." Someone touches my arm and I look around. Leif? "There's a problem."

His voice wavers enough that the worst leaps into my head. "Who died?"

"What?" asks Chase.

Holly's eyes go wide. "Violet?"

"Nobody," says Leif quickly, then bends to whisper. "Problem with Grayson."

Without a word to Holly and her beau, I hurry away,

following Leif. Rowan and Grayson aren't here—nothing's changed in the vicinity—still the same dancing and drinking and intimate socializing. No blood-soaked bodies decorating the floor.

"What's happening?" I ask as we emerge from the room.

Ahead, a stern-faced middle-aged man in a brown tweed suit shepherds disgruntled partygoers towards the room the adults occupy, and another with a similar expression passes me and Leif to enter the room behind. The music cuts off.

"Who died?" I repeat as the man continues to usher guests into the adjoining room.

"Nobody," says Leif. "I think."

"Then why herd everybody into one place?" I edge backwards against the wall to avoid joining the grumbling kids leaving the dancing room.

"Oh. That's for the big moment Kai's trying to avoid. Everybody has to attend." With a furtive look around, Leif tugs me in the opposite direction.

We reach the spot where we interacted with Kai and where Grayson now stands, back to me beside Rowan. Marci's slumped on a sofa, struggling to lift her head as she mumbles and gestures. Another two girls confront Grayson, one jabbing a finger at him. These girls in their pretty dresses aren't academy students; they're human friends of Kai's.

I march over. "What is—?"

He turns his head. Grayson's face. A set of slash marks run diagonally across his left cheek—an adornment that didn't afflict him earlier. His eyes meet mine, face lined with frustration. My focus shifts to the incapacitated Marci.

"He tried to attack her!" snaps the blonde girl and jabs a finger at Grayson.

"I didn't touch Marci," he says harshly.

"Everybody saw you follow her out of the room," says the other. "Then Marci staggered outside and collapsed, and you've scratch marks from when she tried to defend herself."

Grayson throws me a despairing look and shakes his head. "If I'd attacked Marci, a scratch on the face wouldn't stop me continuing," he says with quiet menace. "Where're the marks on *her*?"

"You didn't get the chance!" says the first.

"Yeah, but if I'd grabbed her or whatever, there'd be a mark."

The blonde girl's eyes narrow. "Then who scratched your face?"

He hesitates and glances at me. "Not Marci," he replies.

"When did this happen?" I demand.

"Ten minutes ago."

Then the marks aren't from a human or witch. If Marci or another girl had scratched Grayson's face, he'd begin to heal within minutes, and Marci's false ones wouldn't cut as deep as the scratches look.

"Marci's drunk and I was helping the girl find her friends," says Grayson. "Do you think I'm that stupid I'd publicly attack someone?"

"Marci." The blonde girl crouches by the incoherent witch. "You need to wake up. Tell us what Grayson did to you."

"For fuck's sake!" he says and turns away.

Leif catches his arm. "Don't leave, they'll see that as guilt, mate."

I'm distracted by Grayson's blood. Not what's smeared on his face, but awareness from his running through me. He's defensive and unintentionally intimidating, but there's something wrong. Something I can sense as easily as if Grayson was bonded to me like Rowan. Fear. Has the accusation frightened Grayson that much? There're no injuries to Marci—absolutely no evidence of an attack apart from humans jumping to a prejudiced conclusion.

"If you believe Grayson committed a crime against Marci, then go and find someone to report this to," I announce.

"Violet," says Rowan in shock. "Dorian's here."

"My father won't do anything to Grayson because he'll know the truth."

"Like he'd stop to consider the truth," retorts Grayson.

The girls continue to fuss over Marci, whose face grows more pallid beneath the perspiration.

"And what is the truth, Grayson?" I ask. "Because I don't believe you'd attack Marci."

"What are you hanging around here for?" calls a voice, and hands clap behind us. "You're supposed to be in the Stirling Room for Sawyer's presentation to Kai."

I turn to Mr. Tweed Suit, who's continuing to gather strays. He's filled with self-importance and know why. I've seen the gray-haired man in photographs while researching—another member of the town council.

Rowan and Leif immediately stand in front of the sofa to block Marci from view.

"Is Kai still here?" I ask.

"Don't turn around," Leif whispers to Grayson.

"Yes, and Sawyer doesn't like delays. Chop chop." The man claps his hands again and gestures at us.

"Are you a teacher?" I ask him.

"I was, but I'm retired now. Why do you ask?" he says.

"Because you're treating us like kindergarteners."

He looks down his nose at me. "As one of the guests of honor, I'd advise you to ensure you're in the room before Mr. Sawyer begins his speech."

Guest of honor. The idea anybody could attach such a phrase to me seems ludicrous and if Dorian hadn't insisted, this honored guest would've kept away. Human gatherings and I do not mix well. Evidently, Grayson doesn't mix well with them either.

"Excuse me," says the blonde girl, looking up from where she crouches beside Marci. "We have a problem."

I bare my teeth at her, and she shrinks back.

"Yes, and you'll have a bigger one if you don't gather with the others right now," the man says.

"But—"

"Ah! Come back!" A couple of witches attempting to sneak

past catch Mr. Tweed's attention. "Nobody leaves yet." The man continues his corralling, gathering up the stragglers, glancing back at us. "You lot. Move."

"At least he didn't hang around to see the state Marci is in," I say as he hurries away. "I take it the girl is inebriated?"

"Yes," says Grayson tersely. "I'm leaving. I have to get back to the academy."

The girls return to their fussing, and I pull Grayson to one side. "Who did that to your face?" I ask him.

"You'd better find your father," he says coolly. "Before more than a scratched cheek happens to somebody."

"Have other supes disrupted the party?" I clench my jaw. "I knew something would happen."

Grayson shakes his head. "Only one. Josef Petrescu is here."

"Sawyer really *is* stupid enough to keep Josef," Rowan mutters.

"Whoa. Okay. I'm taking Grayson back to the academy," says Leif. "The Sawyers won't miss me since I'm not a special guest like you two."

I'm unable to respond to Grayson's lightning bolt news and nod automatically as the world of happy human parties retreats. All I can picture is bloodshed.

CHAPTER 19

VIOLET

I shove past Mr. Tweed Suit and the disgruntled couple he's escorting through the door to the function room and look wildly around me. Sawyer stands on the low dais created for the occasion, below a silver and gold eighteenth birthday banner.

Kai's at a table with two older men, who also appear to favor tweed. He's red-faced and sits stiffly with his arms crossed over his chest.

But that isn't who I'm looking for.

Dorian.

He's still sitting at the table close to the front of the room, drumming his fingers on the gold tablecloth with an air of boredom, and Eloise beside him. I'm partially amused by Dorian wearing a well-cut suit; he's rarely out of his jeans and T-shirts. I bet he hates that as much as attending. Although Eloise attracts more attention than him, her hybrid-enhanced beauty causing a glow to the woman in her emerald green silk dress. I'd suggest to the human teen guys they stop staring at her before Dorian notices but I've more pressing matters.

"Where's Josef?" I ask Rowan. "Can you see the vampire anywhere?"

"No."

"What if he follows Leif and Grayson?" I ask, darting a look to the door. "We should've all left."

"Leif and Grayson will be fine. Besides, if Josef's here for 'business' he won't leave until that business is done." Rowan takes my shoulders and pivots me towards my parents.

"Dorian doesn't know Josef's here, otherwise he wouldn't calmly sit there," I say.

My father's head turns, sensing me, and he watches as we walk over. I pull out a chair and sit beside him, shoving at the annoying ribbon. Dorian's still fixated on Rowan as he sits alongside me.

"What's wrong, sweetheart?" asks Eloise. "You appear flustered."

Beside me, Dorian's fingers suddenly stop tapping and he goes completely still. "What. The. Fuck," he snarls.

I don't need to look behind me to know who Dorian focuses his blackened eyes on. Eloise's mouth parts as she follows his line of vision, and her hand immediately covers and grips Dorian's.

"Deal with this once the humans have finished their little ceremony," she says softly.

Dorian doesn't speak, and I glance over my shoulder. Josef. I'm pulled back to the last time I saw him as he goaded me towards losing control. He threatened Rowan, expecting me to unleash, but Rowan fought back with magic nobody should know about.

Beside me, Rowan rubs his lips, not looking at Josef who's standing to the side of the dais, eyes locked with Dorian.

I glance at Eloise, who shifts closer to Dorian and folds her other hand across his thigh.

"Don't worry. I won't do anything publicly," Dorian says.

I'm as aware as Dorian is that Josef heard his words, and the small curve to the vampire's lips grows.

My father takes a glass of whiskey from the table and looks away. "How interesting that Christopher Sawyer never informed me Petrescu is still his attorney."

"Sawyer's aware you're looking for Josef," I say, and Dorian nods curtly. "Promise me Josef won't walk away before you can catch him tonight."

His eyes slide to mine. "I will deal with the situation appropriately."

"Appropriate by whose standards?" I ask. "He needs stopping!"

Dorian blinks at me. "These outbursts are unlike you, Violet."

I hold back together before I blurt the reason why—fear for Grayson's safety.

"Where are your other friends?" interrupts Eloise.

"They left," I say and press my lips together. "And I am not having outbursts."

"Mmm," says Dorian and drinks.

"As the man who loses his temper and kills people, I'd say your comment is rather hypocritical."

"Violet!" says Eloise.

Someone taps on the mic at the dais and all attention turns to a smiling Sawyer and his beaming wife beside him. Mrs. Sawyer must've chosen his outfit, because the gold handkerchief artfully folded into his jacket's breast pocket matches Mrs. Sawyer's dress. He's always well-groomed, but this doesn't prevent the woman picking lint from his dark gray jacket or smoothing his tie —also gold.

"Complete overkill for a teenager's birthday party," comments Dorian.

"Kai surviving until his eighteenth birthday is both a celebration *and* miracle considering events of late," I inform him, and Rowan nudges me hard. "What?"

"Keep your voice down, Violet."

The room falls into hush in response to Sawyer's call for attention—although I believe the hush from the group of kids at the table beside us could be due to my comment. I flash them a smile. Everybody knows I'm right about Kai's life.

Rowan places his forearms on the table and leans across, voice lowered. "What if Josef attacks Kai?"

"And risk the consequences?" Dorian shakes his head. "No. Josef's playing a longer game, remember? Let's see what tonight's move entails."

"Violet. You need to remain in sight until the end of the event in case Josef hurts someone else in a similar manner to the witches' attacks," adds Eloise and sighs. "I knew tonight was a bad idea."

"And you know that I have to suck up to the bloody humans thanks to supes killing people," grumbles Dorian.

"Thank you all for joining us to celebrate my son's eighteenth birthday," announces Sawyer, his voice filling the room via unnecessary speakers. "A truly momentous occasion in his life."

"I can think of others," I mutter.

"Now, I did intend a little slideshow of Kai's life, but Sarah informed me that was 'cringe'." He laughs heartily.

"Oh, good grief," I say.

"Shush, Violet."

I stare at the back of Rowan's head. "Why do you always tell me to be quiet?"

"Somebody has to," he replies, not looking around.

I've caught Sawyer's attention, and he's displeased. With an exaggerated sigh, I look the other way. The kids ushered in here by the Tweeds crowd tables towards the rear of the room, ready to beat a hasty retreat once they can. Hopefully things remain calm between Dorian and Josef and that hasty retreat isn't a necessity.

A handful of other families sit around tables closer to the Sawyers, all human. Relatives? Friends? Witnesses to an upcoming crime? One woman with chin length black hair stares at me, so I hold her gaze until she's disconcerted enough to look away.

"Today is also a momentous occasion for the family as my son will take on an important role in Sawyer Industries." He beckons at Kai. "And I wanted everybody to witness and celebrate that too."

"You mean he wanted Dorian here to stop someone from killing Kai," I say, and Eloise frowns at me.

Well, it's true. The moment Kai explained he's joining the family business now he's eighteen—against his will or not—the reason for my parents' presence here clicked into place. Sawyer's still worried for Kai's safety and a human bodyguard wouldn't be much defense against another witch attack. Nobody would dare attack if Dorian Blackwood's at the party.

And if Josef's here in an official capacity, what's his involvement?

Lost in my deductions, mind wandering towards new theories, I miss most of Sawyer's little speech that's met with polite laughter from some. Rowan nudges me and points at the slender wineglass on the table in front of me. Confused by his gesture, I miss the toast to Kai, instead intently watching the disgruntled teen walk towards his father.

"Now you may wonder why my attorney is with me tonight," says Sawyer.

"I certainly do," says Dorian and Sawyer slides him an uneasy look.

Kai digs hands into his trouser pockets and edges away from where his father slings an arm around his shoulders.

"Kai's always known that as soon as he turns eighteen, I'll sign the whole of Sawyer Industries operations over to him and step down." Beside me, Rowan half-chokes on the wine he'd decided to finish after the toast, whereas Kai stares down at his shiny black shoes. "Now, I know what you're all thinking—I'm handing a big responsibility to someone so young. But I'll naturally be around to help out. If I can cope with my son as my boss."

A smattering of false laughter crosses the room, and Josef

smiles before reaching into the briefcase beside him. He pulls out a set of white papers and edges over to the two Sawyers.

"The sly bastard," mutters Dorian.

"Josef?" asks Eloise.

"No. Sawyer. He's removing himself from the business publicly and as soon as he can. Whatever's behind all this, Sawyer wants the handover to go ahead uninterrupted."

"Exactly," I say and nod. "My thoughts too."

"Yeah, but Kai isn't interested," says Rowan, and sits straighter.

"I don't think he'll have a choice," comments Dorian.

Josef lays the papers out onto the small lectern, and Sawyer produces a shiny silver pen from the inside of his jacket. Kai remains still. With a flourish, Sawyer signs the papers and holds the pen towards his son.

"Kai?"

No movement. Is Kai bewitched or merely drunk? Because the guy now stares across the room, disconnected from events.

"Kai, sweetheart," says Mrs. Sawyer gently, and presses her fingers to his hand.

He blinks back to reality and looks to his father, mouth set in a thin line. "No."

The word drops like a bomb into the middle of Sawyer's plans, temporarily stunning him. "We discussed this," he says and looks furtively at the now more-interested guests.

"I don't want this," he continues. "I've told you and Mum— I'm not signing anything. I've other things I want to do with my life."

Sawyer grips his son's upper arm. "You don't have to do anything," he whispers. "This is your inheritance, that's all."

"Don't you need to die for me to inherit shit?" he asks.

Rowan sucks in a breath, and I eagerly await the next response. Guests may've missed Sawyer's whisper, but everybody heard Kai.

"The business and land become yours once you turn eighteen. You know that." Sawyer gives a flat, tight smile to those gathered.

Land.

I exchange looks with Dorian again.

Seems Kai isn't the only one who 'knows that' because this points a flashing arrow at Kai and the reason for attempts on life.

"Sign the papers, sweetheart," cajoles his mother.

"You think putting me on the spot will change my mind?" he retorts and runs a hand across the top of his head. "That I'll do what you say because I wouldn't dare embarrass Dad by refusing?"

"I'm rather impressed by his level of teenage willfulness," I comment, and Rowan shushes me. Again.

Sawyer turns Kai so their backs are to the whispering guests, but he can't hide his words from mine or my parents' hearing. "Sign or you're out of this family. You're an adult—go fend for yourself."

"Yeah, Mum told me that earlier." He jerks away from his father's touch. "You must think I'm dumb. Witches tried to kill me, and if I sign that, I'll work alongside them. You don't put my head in the noose." Kai turns back. "Sawyer Industries is practically under supernatural control," he says to people. "I don't want anything to do with the business."

Interesting. I've vastly underestimated Kai Sawyer's astuteness as to the situation. Or has this recently hit home around the time the soup cans hit his head?

Sawyer's cheeks mottle pink and he throws a despairing look at Josef, whose tightly drawn expression matches Sawyer's annoyance. Josef steps forward and the second his hand touches Kai's shoulder, Dorian shoves his chair back and stands.

"I presume I'm here to stop any supernatural interference in your plans, Sawyer," Dorian says icily. "Therefore, I must remind you that mind controlling magic is not permitted and would void any contract signed."

Sawyer laughs. "As if I'd entertain such a thing."

"How else will you get me to sign?" asks Kai and sidesteps Josef. "Because I'm *not* fucking signing!"

As Kai snatches the papers from the lectern and tears at them, I gleefully watch the spectacle. Somebody's plans are as tattered as the papers Kai throws to the floor before he strides away.

"In my recent observations, most teenagers would like a car for their eighteenth birthday and not a whole business," I inform Sawyer. "I've also recently observed that teenagers are difficult to control. Did you know that the human brain doesn't develop fully until the early twenties? And that risk-taking behavior and a sense of immortality will usually triumph common sense?"

"Your input isn't required, Violet," snaps Sawyer.

"I'm merely pointing out that your plan won't succeed." I pause. "And also, that you should send your bodyguard after Kai. I'd hate to think Kai's decision may have negative consequences on his wellbeing."

Sawyer mutters something unpleasant and also strides away after his son, and I'm quietly impressed how fast Mrs. Sawyer can move in those shoes as she hurries away too.

Josef remains.

One of the other people from Kai's table rushes to the dais. "Seems that Kai has cold feet," Mr. Tweed says into the mic and gives a short laugh.

"How does podiatry enter the equation?" I ask Rowan.

"Figure of speech."

Again? "Dorian. Do you think Kai needs protecting?"

"From his angry father?" Dorian looks down at me from where he's still standing.

"No. A supe attack."

For a moment, Dorian regards me before taking and draining his glass of whiskey. "I'd like a brief word with Mr. Petrescu before he disappears, as he is inclined to do in chaotic events."

"The party's over. I suggest everybody returns to the academy in case there are repercussions," says Eloise and stands too.

"Why? You think someone will burn the hotel down with everybody inside?"

"No. But I agree. I'd rather you left the hotel in case there *is* a crime scene later," says Dorian. "Rowan. I trust that you can ensure Violet returns to her room at the academy safely?"

I scoff. "I don't need Rowan to keep me safe."

Rowan touches my arm. "Yeah, but I'd rather make sure you're alright."

"I'm not going back to my room tonight," I tell them.

"Violet, this is a fraught situation and not the time for your interference," says Eloise firmly.

"I'm not going back to my room since I'm sleeping in Rowan's bed tonight," I inform them all.

Dorian's focus on Josef snaps and he stares at us. "Excuse me, *what*?"

Holly was wrong. I should've asked Rowan first because he stares at me as if I've just suggested I'll disembowel him.

I glance at Dorian, whose expression could suggest that very fate for Rowan.

CHAPTER 20

VIOLET

Eloise smiles. "Then Rowan can ensure you return to *his* room safely."

A muscle tics in Dorian's tight jaw.

"Uh. Right." Rowan continues to look as if I'm about to push him off a ledge.

"Apologies, Rowan. I should've asked you first," I say.

"What's wrong with *your* room?" growls Dorian.

"Holly invited Chase over and requires privacy." I wave a hand. "Please focus on Josef before he leaves."

Dorian stares at me, and he's losing focus on the real issue here—Josef. I clear my throat and jab a finger at the vampire loitering on the dais. With one blacker than black look at Rowan, Dorian switches his attention.

Party guests file from the room, the students told to leave and wait in the hotel lobby. The transport organized to return guests to the academy is now due to arrive earlier than planned.

I don't move.

Josef still doesn't move either, neither does my father.

Instead, both watch each other until the last humans leave the room.

"Are you expecting me to run from you, Dorian?" Josef asks evenly as the door bangs closed. "Because I have no need; I've done nothing wrong."

"Excuse me?" I choke. "You threatened Rowan and killed a witch!"

"Violet. Let me handle this," says Dorian.

"Yes, I killed a witch in self-defense, as I explained to the lovely human detectives that night." He stays stock still as Dorian approaches him. "As for Rowan..." Josef clicks his tongue. "Attacked me with shadows. Do many *know* about your shadows, Rowan?"

"That's a lie," I growl.

"About the shadows? No. I experienced them."

"No. Rowan did not attack you." I'm out of my chair too, ignoring Rowan's attempt to stop me from joining Dorian in front of Josef.

"Violet," says Dorian in a warning tone, not looking around.

"And Grayson! You half-killed him at the warehouse."

I'm as close to Josef as I was that night and now-familiar feelings and desires stir—disgust and the impetus to attack this man. Here he is, dressed like a human, his beguiling moves practiced over more than a hundred years. Josef keeps himself firmly entrenched in the human world, but he is *not* untouchable.

The vampire lifts his head and his nostrils flare as he studies me closely. "You have Petrescu blood running through your veins, Miss Blackwood. Are you closer to my nephew than I realized?" I tense and side-glance Dorian, who somehow keeps his expression neutral. "Grayson and I had little time to talk tonight, and I'd love to catch him before I leave. Is he still here?"

"He left," I say and tip my chin. "You can't touch him."

Josef smiles. "Then I shall *catch up* with him again soon."

I swallow down another retort against Josef, struggling to push down the anger.

"You're not leaving alone tonight," says Dorian. "I want you in custody."

Josef steps forward, the man with his slicked back hair and sharp features as tall as my father. "We can't always have what we want, Dorian Blackwood."

"You've committed crimes and should be arrested and questioned," continues Dorian.

Josef slants his head. "The problem is, I don't answer to you. I will not follow the orders of an upstart who killed many, many people and overturned the Confederacy. Who killed my *cousin*— an original vampire and a respected leader."

"Corrupt leader," growls Dorian.

"How long have you walked this earth, Dorian? Less than half a century. Some of us have lived for over two hundred years and were alive at the time of the Purge—we watched humans slaughter our kind and now you expect us to walk alongside them?"

"You work as an attorney for humans," retorts Dorian, his cool demeanor heating.

"Does that mean I accept them?" he replies, voice like winter. "No."

Dorian's nose almost touches Josef's. "You're telling me that you oppose my government and the human accords?"

"That is hardly news for you, Dorian."

"Then you definitely need to come with me tonight."

He doesn't flinch. "Or what? You kill me? I don't think that'll happen, do you?" Dorian doesn't respond to Josef's mocking. "Did you honestly believe you could keep this power you stole? Fifteen years is a drop in the ocean to us. A mere pause—time to plan our retaliation."

"Who's we?" I demand, and Josef turns his eyes to me as if he'd forgotten I stood beside Dorian.

"Those who want natural order returned and the threats to our society removed." He smiles, lips pulling back to reveal his canines. "To succeed where Oskar failed."

"Not. Happening," snarls Dorian.

Josef taps him on the chest, and Dorian snatches his wrist, squeezing. "You don't have what it takes to rule, Blackwood. You're a worthy distraction to humans, with your posturing and narcissism—exactly why you can't see what's happening around you."

I can move fast, but Dorian's reflexes are beyond mine and the space where he and Josef stood empties.

"Then I remove one of the threats." Dorian's snarled voice comes from behind me. Eloise jumps to her feet in horror as she rushes to where Dorian pins Josef high against the wall, his nails longer and sharper on the hand around the vamp's throat.

"Dorian. Stop," says Eloise. "Josef Petrescu is provoking you— and he's right. We can't do anything tonight. We're in the middle of the human world and they *cannot* see this side to you."

"I can haul his fucking arse out of here and deal with him where nobody can see," growls Dorian, eyes fixed on Josef.

Josef doesn't attempt to move and remains firmly in my father's grip. "Provoke him? I have better ways to do that. I'll remove you both and your daughter from this world."

"Good luck," scoffs Dorian.

"Put him down before somebody walks in," urges Eloise.

"Do you think the witches and their Dominion friends would create a weapon but not the way to neutralize it?" sneers Josef, as Dorian drops his hold. "Your vampire parents thought they killed every witch who possessed the knowledge on how to eliminate their hybrid mistake. Actually, I hear you assisted in those deaths. Such a bad thing to teach a child to do." He smiles. "The witches died, but Oskar had that knowledge too."

"You don't. Everything owned by the Confederacy was destroyed," says Eloise stiffly.

"Oh, but we do. In time, you will pass power back to those who should rightfully rule, Dorian," he says harshly.

"I should rip your fucking heart out now."

Rowan. He's watching all this, pale-faced. From his vantage

point, Rowan will witness everything—including the transformation on Dorian's face that heralds his descent into hybrid violence.

Chaos.

Josef wants chaos. More dissent. A reason to recruit others and strike against Dorian's council.

Eloise stands poised to intervene and my heart sickens at her truth. We can't harm this creature. Not yet. And not because the evidence will splatter the walls and floor of the human hotel, but because he would be a catalyst.

Does Dorian have enough self-control right now to process this and stop himself from tearing Josef apart?

"Eloise is right," I say quietly. "Let Josef go. Now isn't the time."

Josef smiles. "A soft spot for Petrescus, Violet?"

"If this dissenting group exists," I say calmly, "killing you would be a setback, because we won't know any more about who or what you are."

"You soon will."

"Immortality doesn't mean we can't kill you," says Dorian.

"Likewise," he whispers. "Hybrids too."

Finally, Dorian takes a step back and rubs his chin. "You will never kill Violet."

"Like I said, we're returning to the natural order, Dorian Blackwood."

"And, like I said, you will never kill my daughter." He shoves Josef hard enough that he slams against the wall again.

The doors to the room open to my left and Sawyer hesitates as he's confronted by the scene.

"Ah. Just the man." Dorian becomes his pleasant self in a single breath, striding over to Sawyer with a smile on his face. He claps the man on the shoulder. "I'm sorry things didn't work out for you tonight. However, perhaps you could share with me *why* the urgency to sign everything over to Kai."

Sawyer's throat bobs, face drained of enough color that his

skin tone matches Josef's. His fear's palpable from here—Sawyer just saw the Dorian that the humans never do.

"No urgency," he says hoarsely. "Planned for years. Tradition. Happened to me."

Dorian squeezes Sawyer's shoulder tightly and the man winces. "I do hope you're not lying to me, Christopher." He leans in to whisper, "I would take care around your attorney. The profession have a bad reputation for a reason, and so do the Petrescu family."

Dorian pats Sawyer on the cheek and glances at Josef. "We will meet again *very* soon, Josef."

My jaw drops as he steps by—away from Josef. "Dorian?"

"Time for you to return to the academy, Violet. Rowan," he says in a clipped voice.

CHAPTER 21

ROWAN

How would life be if Violet Blackwood had never walked into my world? Because since she did my world isn't the one I knew. I'd only focused on a small space around me, protecting myself and Leif while searching for spells I knew I'd learn the power to use. I'd never considered the bigger world picture—I've only ever known stability in society. Was I naive to believe that things would remain the same? Of course, I expected human/supe conflict to rear up at some point, but fighting within ourselves? No. Nobody wants to repeat our violent history. Apart from some obviously do.

Before Violet, I knew little about Dorian. A distant figure whose appearance and ability to charm and deceive made him an excellent 'face of the supernatural' for humans. Although some supes have memories of the guy from before and struggle to trust him, the supes fear of Dorian hold his government in place.

I don't know much about Dorian's origins either—or I didn't until Violet told me the whole story. A hybrid created by a pact between vampires and witches to become the Dominion's weapon against the Confederacy. An uncontrollable creature and an experiment they never repeated.

When Josef told Dorian that the knowledge exists on how to kill the unkillable hybrid, my blood pumped faster, and the darkness swam across my vision. Even the hint of a thought I'd lose Violet triggers what I promised to keep hidden. Hell, the whole time I sat in that room watching the craziness unfold between the Blackwoods and Josef, the bond primed me to step in. If he so much as reached out to Violet, I'd attack.

I've subdued the bastard once and will do so again when I need.

Violet's revelation that she intended to stay with me tonight exploded that new world—until everything that happened in the room at the hotel cast a massive shadow over the future and makes one night almost insignificant.

The lobby's empty, and we step from the hotel where Holly waits by the minibus, rubbing her arms as she shivers in her thin dress, and she pulls herself straighter when she spots me and Violet.

"Why are you not inside the bus if you're cold?" Violet asks her. "I'd rather you were not in public, considering Josef Petrescu graced us with his presence tonight."

Her brow pinches. "Didn't your father arrest him?"

Violet growls. "Sore point," I put in.

"The fact of the matter is, he may have accomplices in the vicinity. Get on the bus."

"You're damn rude sometimes," retorts Holly. "I'm waiting to see what's happening tonight."

"I believe events have concluded."

"No." She flicks a look to me. "*Tonight.*" Violet shakes her head in confusion and Holly huffs. "Where are you sleeping?"

"Oh!" Violet waves a hand. "As I informed you, I should've asked Rowan first. When I mentioned the possibility, he looked rather unimpressed."

I choke. "No. I worried how Dorian would react. You're welcome to uh sleep in my bed."

How do I get the feeling this is about to go south?

"No. I'd made a presumption. I apologize." She nods at Holly. "We'll arrange something for another night, Holly."

Yep. South.

"You don't want Violet to stay with you, Rowan?" Holly looks between us in confusion.

"Apart from Rowan's reticence, Josef's appearance has unsettled me. I'd rather sleep in our room where I can keep an eye on you."

I almost laugh. *Reticence.* Violet seriously can't believe I'd say no. Or is she avoiding the situation? "Dorian has the academy under watch, Violet. Holly will be okay."

Violet gives me a stern look. "Runes and potions?"

"Right," I mutter.

"And we need to check on Grayson and Leif to ensure they're safe."

Holly takes Violet by the arm and pulls her to one side, whispering. *Thanks, Holly, but you're wasting your time.*

I climb the steps into the bus, forced to dismiss thoughts of a night with Violet. Yeah, she should've asked me first, so I could've been crystal clear that I bloody dream of spending a night with her. Frequently. Literally.

As I flop into a seat, Chase smirks at me. "Violet's staying with you tonight, huh?"

"No."

"What the fuck? Why?" He sits forward and scowls. "You scared of her or something?"

"No," I snap back, but a familiar niggle tugs at my mind.

Am I still that guy who's too understanding and puts someone else first all the time, to the point I won't speak up? I'd never pressure Violet into anything, but she's walked all over the situation without any discussion. Again.

CHAPTER 22

VIOLET

EVERYBODY APPEARED in an odd mood once we arrived at the academy. Frankly, I've become the albatross of Kai's parties, the event doomed once I appear. Holly remained annoyed at me, and Rowan disappeared into one of his distracted moods ending the evening with 'we need to talk'. Then left. Which is thoroughly confusing, as talking isn't possible if all I can see is his back.

Grayson didn't want to talk to anybody last night and sent Leif away when they returned. I messaged to check on Grayson and received a curt answer. *I'm fine.*

Me? I'm still in a bad mood several days later because I can *not* believe that Dorian walked away from Josef. I agree now is not the right time to take Josef out, but to let him walk away *completely*? I hope Dorian has a better lead on his movements than he once did.

Following our conversation at the family estate, Dorian sends people to the academy to ask questions—but not about the tiara. Witches 'interview' all staff members, with a little mind reading here and there, not disclosing exactly what they're looking for but informing staff that the matter isn't tiara related. *Thanks, Dorian. Rub my nose in it, why don't you?*

Julius returns—thankfully unscathed—from his off-campus activities and investigators speak with him too. Good. He'll know that I never mentioned him to Dorian and hopefully will trust us enough to supply the evidence we need. The man must realize that we're his best hope.

I'm curious how the conversation and mind reading went with Mrs. Lorcan and Mrs. Eldridge and whether the investigators mentioned my potion. I heard raised voices between the headmistress and the witch investigators sent to the academy, the woman insulted by the insinuation she and her academy are under suspicion. *Her* academy.

Dorian decided to interview her and Mrs. Eldridge personally and one-on-one, which I was entirely too gleeful about. They deserve the 'Dorian treatment'. Verbal, not physical. He'd reserve that for if they're found guilty of involvement.

I presume the potion wasn't mentioned, as nobody spoke to me, although I do know that the investigators visited the artifacts room with Mrs. Eldridge and took away some items in a box. Lead-lined no doubt. Dorian must be playing the academy investigation cards close to his chest.

The extremely pissed Mrs. Lorcan didn't accost and talk to me afterwards, going as far as to avoid me completely. Although I *did* see Julius with Mrs. Eldridge again. I don't a hundred percent trust either of them.

Julius agrees to sit down and tell us everything, which Rowan informs me I should be grateful for considering my lack of compassion. To me, the natural progress in the investigation should lead to Whitegrove and the Circle.

He speaks to Rowan and arranges a rendezvous for all of us in the attics inside Pendle House, which as a witch and teacher he has access to. The precariousness of attached balconies have caused trouble in the past and the attics are out of bounds— death risks aren't welcome within the academy.

Naturally, students ignore this and use the attics for various social activities, usually secret gatherings. The room also appears to be an old classroom, used as storage space. Wooden chairs are stacked three high in a row against a wall daubed with runes. A row of desks are also stacked, in pairs to block the way onto the balcony, one upturned and resting on the top of another with legs poking into the air as an extra barrier.

Without a word, I walk over to the runes and examine each one. Who knows? There's likely other covens than Marci's at the academy, and those covens could hide their dubious activities here. But they're simple runes to enhance learning. I examine every inch of the bare floorboards—nothing. Dust covers most of the room, but the only disturbances are where some have sat on the table edges or scuffed the floor with shoes.

A tall mahogany cupboard matching those in other classrooms is unlocked, and I pull open the two doors to peek inside.

Empty shelves.

Julius watches as he stands by the large bay window that looks out onto the narrow balcony which runs the length of this part of the academy. Through dirt-smeared glass, I can see the woods at the edge of the grounds.

He usually wears a tie and a fully buttoned shirt, but today he's more casual and in cargo pants rather than his black trousers. Julius is popular amongst some students, probably because he's one of the few male teachers who 'look less than a hundred years old' in Holly's words. The bothersome students he mentioned?

Rowan lifts a chair from the stack, and then another, before sitting on one. Leif pulls out, another leaving me to sit between them.

Julius frowns when he sees Leif. "I only expected the two of you," he says and rests against the wall to the left of the window.

"We work together," I announce. "There's usually a fourth but we felt you'd be outnumbered and intimidated."

"Holly?"

"Grayson," I reply.

"The hemia who attacked the witch, and she ended up in the hospital?" he asks in horror.

I sigh. "*As if* he's the only hemia student who ever accidentally injured another."

Julius appears to contemplate something and I fidget at his silence. "Thank you for not speaking to Dorian about me. Have you spoken to anyone else about this... investigation?" asks Julius. "Holly? You're close."

So far, I've kept our activities hidden from Holly. I'm in two minds—I'll upset Holly if I exclude her, but I still want her to watch over activities within the academy. I *am* increasingly concerned about my connection to a feeble human and the risk to Holly's life, especially if there may be spies in the academy linked to the witches and murders.

"No. But if we're discussing closeness to others, how intimate is your relationship with Mrs. Eldridge? Because that raises questions *why* the staff member responsible for confiscating or 'keeping safe' artifacts is involved with you. How much does she know about your investigations and your sister?"

He blinks at me. "That's rather personal. My relationship with Mrs. Eldridge is casual," he says. "And not relevant."

"She isn't relevant?" I frown. "That's unkind."

He looks away, at the runes on the wall. "Andrea's a useful person to know."

"You're using her to help with your investigations? In my experience, people don't appreciate being 'used'," I say and tuck hair behind an ear. "Or *thinking* they are."

"Yes, well, I haven't spent years of my life focused on solving my sister's disappearance to let opportunities go."

"Or murder," I say.

"Pardon?" he asks.

"Your sister's disappearance or murder." Rowan pushes at my

ankle with the toe of his shoe and gives me 'the look'. "Possible murder. She *has* been missing a long time."

I pull a notepad and pen from my bag and watch Julius expectantly.

"What are you doing?" he asks curtly.

"Violet makes notes," explains Rowan.

"No way." Julius folds his arms. "If she does, I'm saying nothing."

My face sours and I shove the book away, pulling out my phone instead. He arches a brow and I huff before placing it back in my pocket.

"Where does Madison supposedly live now?" asks Rowan. "If she 'left the family', someone must know where she went."

"Like I said, the story is Madison turned her back on us because my parents tried to stifle her magic. They argued and never spoke again." He looks at Rowan. "Families do that— especially witches."

"Why?" asks Leif.

He shrugs. "Older generations can feel threatened by younger ones holding more power. Sure, some are proud of their kids' abilities, but others… not so much."

"And can we talk to your parents?" I say. "Where do they live?"

"Dead," he says expressionlessly.

"That's rather unfortunate and not at all helpful." I bite back the frustration—I've lost my first lead in the investigation. Rowan's foot meets my leg again. "Good grief, Rowan. If I bruised like a normal person, my ankles would be permanently covered since you kick me that often."

"I'm sorry for your loss, Julius," says Rowan, and looks pointedly at me.

"Losses," I correct. "And yes, condolences. How did your parents die?"

Rowan groans. "Only tell us if you want and if it's relevant."

"No. If Julius wants our help, he must tell us absolutely everything," I retort.

He shakes his head, bemused. "My favorite color is navy blue, my favorite food is ramen, and I enjoy watching true crime documentaries."

"Excuse me?"

"Sarcasm, Violet," says Leif.

"Oh. Droll. Everything *relevant*," I say. "Although the true crime documentaries interest me."

Julius uncrosses his arms. "My father apparently died of a heart attack a couple of years back, but I hadn't seen him for a long time since he left, and my mother remarried. She died of cancer last year. If there was any foul play, the killer waited a long time to strike."

"And your parents knew nothing? Did *they* tell you the story?" asks Rowan.

"Yes. A few times. I wanted to catch them out in case anything contradicted, but the story never changed: Madison left because our parents held her back. They were strict." He links his fingers together in front of him. "Dad didn't like speaking about her and Mum would get upset if I hinted she might be dead. She never took down any family photos in the house and she always believed Madison would return."

"And you've no photos of the guy in the photograph I showed you?" I ask. He shakes his head. "Did your parents ever mention boyfriends?"

"If Madison had one, she never told them."

"Strict?" asks Leif.

"Maybe."

"Or *maybe* Madison didn't want them to know who the guy was. Or is. *He* might be alive, and we need to find him too," I say. "Is Mrs. Eldridge lying that she has no records from the Confederacy days?"

"As far as I know, that's the truth. Isn't your father more likely to have those?"

"Almost nothing survived." I sigh. "And what do *you* have? Where's the evidence you promised? Show us." His eyes narrow. "Please."

Rowan sits forward, elbows on his knees and hands beneath his chin. "Will you trust us and share everything you've uncovered?"

Julius looks at me for much longer than many do before leaning down to unfasten a leather satchel. He pulls out a small notebook decorated with cat and rainbow stickers, an A4 brown envelope, and a manila file. Silently, he places them on the table closest to him.

"Madison's diary. Photos she took." He takes the envelope and tips out the photos, along with a small rectangular item. "A USB with the recordings of Madison and friends that I found on her old laptop. Mum left everything in her room like a shrine— part of her certainty Madison would come back. Mum moved to a new house five years ago and only then did I get the chance to take her things."

"A *youess* what?" I scratch my chin.

"USB," says Rowan. "They're not used much anymore. Do you have the laptop, Julius?"

"No. A lot of Madison's stuff was 'lost' in the house move." He places the photos on the table and Leif picks them up. "Her diary doesn't have much information apart from day to day teen things."

"Boyfriends?" asks Rowan.

"She does mention guys, but only by a single initial letter."

I hold my hand out for the diary. "Which initial in the most recent entries?"

"D. Obviously that doesn't narrow things down a lot." He scratches his head. "She writes a lot in code. Not *actual* code, but almost everything is initials—locations, other people, etcetera."

"May I take the diary?" I ask him and he tenses. "To study. I promise to return the book to you."

"Study the words or the psychic energy?" he asks.

"Both," says Rowan.

"I've tried psychometry a lot of times. Either Madison 'locked' the diary's energy with magic or somebody else did. I suspect Madison, since I found the diary hidden at the back of her dresser, behind the drawers."

Like the tiara?

"Then we find a spell to unlock the diary," I say simply.

Julius hands me the book and there's no tangible magic attached to the smooth cover and raised stickers, so I pass the diary to Rowan. He curls his fingers tighter than I did and closes his eyes, the way he did when finding the Ursa cap at Wesley's crime scene. Then he opens them again and shakes his head. My spirits dip but did I expect him to instantly find a memory on a blocked item? No.

"Have you deciphered any of the places Madison mentioned?" asks Rowan.

"Only the obvious ones like the academy, names of local cafes, stores. She mentions visiting R a lot, but I can't figure out if that's a local place or another person's name."

"Can I see the photos?" I ask Leif and he leans across to hand them to me. Teenage girl involved in teenage behavior—lots of 'selfies' with friends in indoor and outdoor locations. I tap an image of Madison with two girls, both who've long, dark brown hair, one slightly shorter than the other. "Did you identify either of these girls? They appear in a lot of the pictures."

"That's Christine and Annabelle. I met Christine. Annabelle wouldn't speak to me or tell me where she lives, but we did exchange emails. Neither have any idea where Madison went, but Annabelle told me she's sure Madison died. The three were close and it makes no sense that Madison would never speak to them again. I asked about guys and Christine said Madison was popular. Both women claimed not to know her date the night of the dance."

I scoff. "Somebody's hiding something."

"I'm perfectly aware of that," says Julius snippily.

"No photos *at all* of the guy in the formal photo?" asks Rowan again.

"None. But you're welcome to watch any footage on that USB. I've watched again since you showed me the picture, and can't see him, but he could be on there, even if just in the background," Julius says. "No computers in the academy have USB ports. Can any of you find one that does?"

"Rowan," I say. "He's an expert. Knows how to interfere with surveillance footage, break computer systems, and—"

"I'll pretend that I never heard that," interrupts Julius.

"If you've put so much time into this, why haven't you found the killer yet?" I ask.

The most telling part of his reply? That he doesn't protest his sister might be alive. "The answer to *that* question appeared a few days ago and took the tiara—the person responsible for her disappearance must be connected to the Circle. I'd always suspected this, but I'm not important or skilled enough to gain entry so that was a dead end." He gestures at me. "The guy in your photograph? Circle connected, I'm positive."

I blow air into my cheeks and tap the diary. "Rowan can gain entry into the Circle."

"What?" he asks sharply.

"You're from an important family and you're one of the best witches of your generation. Of course, they'll allow you in," I say blithely. "Dorian can help."

"And if I don't want to?" he retorts.

"You don't apply to be in the Circle," says Julius. "You're selected and invited."

"Yeah, the coven know I'm connected to you and they're not bloody stupid," continues Rowan tersely. "Violet. I am *not* joining the Circle." I open my mouth to protest. "Not happening. Not up for discussion. Understood?" I rub my cheek as he gives me a hard look. "*Promise* me you won't do anything."

Has Dorian said anything to his 'inside man' yet? I

understand Rowan's concerns, but we *need* to get into the society. I'll speak to Dorian. "Alright."

"And before you say anything, no, we are not sneaking into their headquarters," Rowan adds.

"*Obviously*," I retort, "Since we don't know the location."

"Good," says Leif.

"Why did you think the Circle was connected before the tiara and Whitegrove appeared?" asks Rowan.

He shrugs. "The name came up in my sleuthing and it made sense to me that someone with influence covered up what really happened. And as soon as I saw that tiara in the academy, I knew there would be answers because Madison wore the item the night she disappeared. I honestly never expected the tiara would come to light, so this is a sign!" His face lights up. "And a big one— seems Whitegrove gave me an answer. *If* the tiara belongs to his family, that guy in the photo could be a son. Nephew. Someone important."

"Was Madison a member of the Circle?" I ask.

"Not a member—she was too young." He wrinkles his nose. "But somehow she was involved with them. The guy in the photo? He's a good start. Find him."

"Are you still in touch with Madison's two friends? Or at least the one who would speak to you?"

Julius takes the photos from Leif. "I haven't spoken to the women for years, but I'll try and contact them now we have a new person to identify."

"I think the best bet is the USB footage," says Leif. "How much is on there?"

"Couple of hours," Julius replies, and his mouth turns down. "I only watched quickly. I can't cope with seeing my sister and knowing I'll probably never see her again."

"I delegate you the task of watching the footage," I say to Rowan.

"Why me?"

"I am not subjecting myself to two hours of teenage girl inanity. If you spot anything relevant, *then* I'll take a look."

Rowan blows air into his cheeks. "I can't do anything before I've tracked down a laptop that has a USB port."

"And I shall find relevant entries in the diary."

Julius chews on a thumbnail. "I really am trusting you not to say anything," he says quietly. "Remember, I don't want anybody to know who I am or that I'm investigating this."

"Whereas I most certainly *do* want people to know." I grin. "I want whoever's involved to worry because Violet Blackwood is on the case, and she *always* wins."

CHAPTER 23

VIOLET

I'VE an odd sensation in my chest this evening that I can't explain, somewhere between heartburn and fluttering palpitations. I must ask Dorian if that's a side-effect from a damaged heart—he's died several times and would know.

But the discomfort grows as the night continues, a scraping pain from my chest dragging into my stomach. I've experienced this before when worried about my friends, but I've no concerns tonight. Leif and Rowan are together looking over the footage, leaving me to look through the diary, and Grayson...*Grayson*.

I haven't seen him today, too distracted to realize.

No, I don't see him every day, this isn't unusual. Nothing to worry about.

I attempt to settle—nobody's under threat and my investigations are progressing nicely. Or they were because however many times I read over a page of Madison's blue handwriting; nothing sticks.

A sudden need for fresher air and the cool evening on my skin pulls me from my room and out of Darwin House. Sometimes my skin itches with the desire to get away from warmth, but this time a prickling runs across my scalp, all the way along my spine to my toes.

Something's wrong and my thoughts go to Rowan and the bond.

I text Rowan.

> how's your evening?

what do you need?

What?

> nothing just thinking of you both

aww sweet Violet 😊

Good grief. Not the pictures again.

> I feel sick

charming

> no before your unnecessarily saccharin response I worried you were hurt

I'm fine maybe you're missing me? Heart sick?

> Yes I am having palpitations

when you think of me? 😜

> Rowan stop being ludicrous is Leif ok?

yes are you? want me to come over?

> no continue with your task

😂 👍

I do wish he wouldn't communicate with such inane drawings.

I tuck my phone away. Rowan and Leif are fine, but something's wrong. My mind goes to Grayson again as I wander from Darwin House towards the academy building, absentmindedly taking a circuit of the cloisters. Nothing in the environment pulls me anywhere and I don't see or sense him; I must be imagining things. Too much obsessing about 'cursed' tiaras and murders.

A cloud passes across the almost full moon, casting shadows across the lit cloisters. Somebody moves within those shadows, and I pull myself taller. Grayson no longer walks the place at night. Since Wesley's demise, attacks on supes by humans ceased, partly because without Wesley and his immunity to trouble the humans would face reprisals.

And the academy is now under total supernatural control.

A figure wends through the dim, keeping close to the wall, and I'm assaulted by the strange lurching in my stomach again. Maybe somebody *is* up to no good. I slant my head as I move across the lawns, not bothering to hide myself. I hear nothing apart from light footsteps, but am aware of blood.

Grayson's blood.

I'm arrested by the scent and, although not as potent as the night in the factory, it's enough to evoke the choking memory of that blood in my mouth. Surely Grayson knows I'm close by too? So why run from me?

I watch for Grayson to walk into the academy, preparing to follow and talk to him, but instead, he veers past the entrance. My mouth goes dry. Does Grayson have something to hide? He's continued the nighttime walks, something we advised him against, but I understand his desire to get away from the stifling academy and student distrust.

Grayson was pissed the evening I followed—the stalker complaining about stalking as he confronted me outside the café he visited. I'd watched him drink a soda alone and read a book—

I'm unsure if the location or book reading struck me as the weirdest. Why's he spending time in human haunts?

Is it wrong that I followed because I wanted to reassure myself he isn't meeting Josef? *Or* humans for blood? If I'd told Grayson *that*, he would've been more than pissed at me.

As with that night by the cafe, I'm drawn to follow Grayson, feet moving without thinking as I stick to the dim myself. He approaches a building I've never once entered nor have any intention of such.

The sports hall.

I draw a firm, thick black line through team participation of any kind, therefore have no requirement to join Holly and Marci, and their netball team. I argued with the academy that my hybrid strength would give me an unfair advantage in any manner of sporting competition. Besides, I would've refused to attend, even if they had insisted.

The closer I get to Grayson, the more aware I become that his movements are 'off'. As usual, he's walking at a higher speed than humans and witches, but not with his usual tall, straight-shouldered arrogance.

The closer I get to him, the stronger his blood scent.

My eyes drop to the lawns I'm crossing, but there's no blood trail. Yet I'm unconsciously following blood from *somewhere. On* Grayson? Fear for him surges and floods my whole body, and the desire to catch him becomes a painful aching in my chest. When I round the corner, I finally know why I've felt this all evening.

Grayson smacks a shoulder against the rear exit door, swearing, and a wave of pain washes towards me. The dim from a nearby security light reveals how disheveled he is, hair falling around his face and blood on his hands. Panic rising, I cross to Grayson and slam my boot into the door to help.

Grayson stumbles, steadying himself on the frame as he mutters again, revealing skinned knuckles, and the face he turns my way is streaked with blood.

"Where did you come from?" he mutters.

"You didn't sense me?"

Grayson touches his temples. "I hurt my head. Not too focused right now."

He plunges through the door, and I follow, my nausea and disgust growing with each second.

This *must* be Josef's work.

"Shut the door," he says through gritted teeth and stumbles onwards.

I do as Grayson says and follow. He supports himself on the wall and moves into a different part of the modern building. I *did* enter the sports hall once at the human school and this place shares the same unpleasant odors of stale perspiration and pine-scented cleaning products.

"What's happening, Grayson?" I ask, easily catching up to him.

He manages to break through another door and lurches into a room with a row of metal lockers, where he sinks onto a bench opposite, beside some sports clothing items discarded by students.

"I'm taking time out before I go back to the academy," he says and examines his lacerated knuckles.

I hate that I do this, and hope Grayson doesn't notice, but I subtly sniff. I'm desensitized to human and witch blood, but can still detect the smell.

"Ha! You think I've attacked someone." Grayson pulls at his T-shirt and drags it over his head before throwing the item at me. "Take a closer look."

I catch the soft, warm material in surprise. The only blood soaking this item smells like his, and I swallow hard. *His blood.* But this time *I'm* different—this time the hemia isn't rising inside me. I toss the T-shirt back to Grayson, avoiding looking at the streaks on his chest.

Or how unusually perfect his muscles are.

"I won't attack you," I say.

"Likewise." Grayson sinks back, head against the breezeblock wall, hand trembling as he untangles hair with his fingers.

"Have you lost a lot of blood?"

"Not as much as last time." His eyes fix on mine.

Last time. The warehouse. "Josef?" I ask, voice hushed unnecessarily.

"Yeah. He found me." Grayson swipes a hand across his forehead. "Along with his lovely friends."

"I *did* tell you that your nighttime excursions were unwise. Now look what's occurred."

"No sympathy? How surprising," he says in derision. "So what if I refuse to live my life in fear of him? My choice."

"I mean that in a concerned way, Grayson," I retort. "Did Josef follow? Is he here?" I ask and spin around. I never sensed anybody, but Josef's an original hemia vamp and they have sneaking silently down to an art form.

Josef will regret the decision if he has followed—if I manage not to maim him, I'll take the bastard to my father.

"Nah. Josef wouldn't dare come onto the academy grounds. Dorian's watching the place, you know that." He jerks his chin. "Which is why I'm not walking into the building covered in blood."

"Where did Josef find you?"

"Town outskirts. His people who followed me the last few days told him."

"On your evening walks?" I ask and swallow down my irritation that he never listened to us. Is Grayson really that stubborn he'd risk attack over safety? "Visits to town?"

"You're still following too?" He arches a brow.

"No. I see you leave campus." But I should've.

"Uh huh." Grayson drags a hand through his hair, and I increasingly wish he'd put his shirt back on. This semi-nakedness doesn't help with my denial that I'm attracted to him. "Just spying then?"

"No, I—"

"Or you think I'm looking for human blood? You *do* believe I was involved with the hemia 'private party' that night," he says stiffly.

Our gazes lock. "Initially, I had doubts. Now, no."

"You believed I'd taken part in a blood orgy with a group of drunk humans and hemia?" His tone is dead. "I see what you continue to think of me."

"I don't think you *do* see." I approach. "Grayson, at first, you neither confirmed nor denied your involvement. Holly claimed you wanted to make me jealous."

"Holly knows nothing," mutters Grayson, and rubs a hand across his forehead.

He's still bleeding. "Where are the bathrooms?" I ask, and he looks at me oddly before gesturing to his left.

Locating paper towels, I wet them beneath the steel faucet and walk back to Grayson. "Here." He looks at the towels as if I'm offering him a dead animal. "Clean the blood."

"I'd make a comment about you licking it off me, but I won't," he says weakly.

"Yet you just did." I sit and take his arm, frowning at how deep the gashes are.

At the warehouse, my emerging hemia homed in on his blood because the substance covered the surroundings. I was torn between searching for and helping Grayson, or staying away in case I lost control. Despite already being close to losing 'Violet' after becoming feral around Josef, the moment I sense Grayson was injured I wanted to help, not hurt him.

I *had* control at the warehouse until Grayson refused to stop his starved attack on me, the guy blinded by his primal state and survival instinct. Already riled by the attack on Rowan and mess I'd walked away from, I became lost in a cloud of his blood scent.

The hybrid turned on Grayson in response, and I can't shake the guilt I behaved like his uncle.

When I read his mind outside the lodge, I saw the past horrific injuries Josef gave Grayson, and the moment I saw him pushing at the sports hall door tonight, the possibility Grayson could be in such a state again punched a hole deep in my chest.

The ache from earlier spread right through to the soul that urges me towards sharing myself with him—my life, body, and blood. The events of that evening at the warehouse didn't pull us apart. Instead, I took the first step towards yielding to this deep seated attraction and need for each other—I took part of *Grayson* when I took his blood into me.

Violet the Hybrid would've finished him; Violet Blackwood cared. I claim that I'm scared I'll hurt Grayson again—or worse. But fear I'll kill him isn't the problem at all. That night, I halfway created a blood bond and now obsessive thoughts worsen if I'm around him.

Not obsession about his blood. I want Grayson to take *my* blood.

I don't stay away because I'm scared I'll end his life in a frenzy, but because I've unique blood. If I share, I might kill Grayson and I'd lose him.

Or worse, sharing my blood with Grayson could create another like me and then I'd definitely lose him. Dorian wouldn't allow a Petrescu with hybrid blood to walk in this world.

I've given my heart to Rowan, and I'm guarding the same from Grayson.

CHAPTER 24

VIOLET

I PLACE the paper towel on Grayson's forearm, and he startles as if I'm bathing him in acid. "Bloody hell, Violet. Are you feeling okay?"

"You're not," I say quietly. Caring gesture? Partially, but the more contact I have with Grayson, the better I'll learn to control myself around him.

A voice whispers 'liar'.

"I'm fine. I'll clean up and rest. Wanted to wash some of the blood off before parading around the academy." He laughs to himself, the sound quiet and hollow.

"I know you're not fine, Grayson," I whisper, and fold the towel to dab at his knuckles. "I'll always know when you're not 'fine'."

"Stay out of my mind," he warns. "I'm respecting your boundaries, you respect mine."

"Good grief." I pause and place the bloodied towel on my lap. "I do not invade my friends' heads. Grayson, I know you're not fine currently, just as I knew you weren't okay the night we spoke in my room."

"I'm that transparent?" He takes the towel and starts dabbing at his bloodied nose. "Nice self-control, by the way."

"I've repeatedly told you that I care for you, Grayson, and that the endearment prevents me attacking you." He ignores me and continues wiping his face. "I struggle when I'm around you because something's changed."

"What do you mean?"

I meet his eyes. "Since I took your blood, I've a connection to your emotions. All evening, I experienced something odd that made no sense—dread. I'm rarely worried for my own safety, but fear for my life took hold even though nothing threatened me. Now I'm with you, that's stronger. *You're* the one with fear for your life."

Grayson's mouth parts as he stares at me. "You feel me in your blood... my blood?"

"Now yours mingles with mine? I suspect so, which is rather inconvenient. I've enough issues dealing with my own emotions without being burdened with another's."

"Whoa." His long fingers lace through mine.

"Another reason to keep away from you, I suppose." Yet I remain connected to him, not pulling my hand away.

"I can see how that'd make you really pissed."

"Oh, yes. I'm extremely angry right now. Deep, deep down, not at the surface ready to explode," I add when worry crosses his face. "You're hurting, frightened, and you feel helpless."

Grayson's jaw goes rigid, and he pulls away his fingers, turning his face to one side. "I'm not helpless. Or frightened. I can deal with shit." He looks back. "I've *dealt* with this shit for years."

"Alone. You can't do this on your own anymore."

He scoffs. "Violet Blackwood telling me that dealing with things 'alone' isn't the correct way?"

"Am I alone anymore, Grayson?"

Grayson stares ahead again and his hands bunch on his knees. "No."

"And neither are you," I say quietly. "You have three friends who'll help. I've told you for weeks that I intend to help you and if that includes killing Josef, I will." His eyes go wide. "Actually, forget that. I'm killing him, whatever. He threatens a lot in my life."

"Way to sound like your father."

"Josef wants to kill you." I don't need Grayson's blood beating through my heart to experience his spike of that fear I'm speaking about. "Josef wants to kill you due to your actions at the warehouse. You betrayed him by not doing what he demanded."

Grayson turns back to me, and I touch his injured cheek, accepting and not rejecting the surge of affection that comes from within him. From within myself.

"Josef wants to kill me because I betrayed him, but not at the warehouse. He knows that I love you and would never harm you—that he could never persuade me to hurt Dorian's precious child, who he wants killed." His throat moves, eyes shining. "And Josef's correct. I've protected you and I would again, down to my very last breath. Until he stops my heart for good."

"He won't get the chance," I say quietly. "I already gave Josef one. No more."

Grayson's shoulders slump. "I'm lucky I escaped with a warning tonight. The bastard said he'll 'catch up properly' soon."

"You don't know where Josef is now? Where he's living?" He shakes his head. "Then we need Dorian's help."

Grayson gives a bitter laugh. "Oh yeah, Dorian's all for helping me."

"No. Listen. Dorian wants to find Josef, and if Josef wants to find you, that's my father's chance. Dorian will use anything and anyone he can in order to get what he wants. Doesn't matter if he likes the person or not."

"Every time you tell me more about Dorian, the worse this

becomes. I'd hoped you'd tell me the man has redeeming qualities."

I smile. "A select few. He believes everything he does is for the greater good—or at least that's what he tells himself. Dorian's a narcissistic sociopath."

Grayson chokes. "I hope you've never said that to his face. And again, that comment isn't reassuring."

I decide in that moment not to tell Grayson about Oz's fate. I've learned enough to know telling Grayson that Dorian kills any threats to me isn't smart. "Eloise provides some balance. As do Ethan and Zeke."

"Hmm." He doesn't sound convinced. "Then I pity whoever's behind this plot against him."

We lapse into silence as Grayson rubs a scratch on the back of his hand with a thumb. The wounds are starting to heal but there's still copious amounts of blood. Silently, I head back to the bathroom and return with more paper towels.

I've avoided something he said.

Loves me.

"I thought a lot about what you said that time in my room— how you're 'done'." I hold the damp towel towards him. "You meant me."

Grayson sighs and takes hold, looking forward, silent again. "As if I ever could be, especially now we've this blood bond."

But that isn't *all* we have. I denied my feelings for Grayson long before that night, already confused by my emerging emotional responses to Rowan. And I've continuously denied the draw to Grayson as anything but his blood. Grayson undeniably shares that pull—he constantly reminds me that he doesn't desire my blood, therefore the way he looks at me is a different type of craving.

I sit beside Grayson again, his solid thigh against mine, and he pushes hair from my face. I don't move or protest, and this odd craving for Grayson's touch when I'm close to him contradicts everything I once knew about myself.

How many times have I looked at Grayson and imagined he *did* kiss me that morning in Holly's closet—or the many times afterwards? How often has my skin tingled at the idea of his long fingers stroking me?

That response to Grayson came before I attacked him. Grayson's appeal isn't his blood.

"You also said we've moved beyond worrying what I might do if I kissed you," I say quietly.

"Yeah."

"I think maybe if we *had* kissed before that night at the warehouse, I wouldn't doubt myself as much. Because I did consider kissing you many times." He turns his head, but his expression remains blank. "I don't want you to stay away from me, Grayson. Something's missing when you do."

"Not nice being closed out, huh?" he asks softly.

I stand and look down. "Grayson. I am informing you that I'd like to kiss you." No change to his expression, although there's a definite confused change to his expression. "But I understand— you're 'done'."

Grayson stands too and cups the back of my head, warm fingers pressing against my scalp, as he rests his forehead against mine. "I don't want to stay away from you either, Violet, but I need to know what you want from me."

"To kiss you. Weren't you listening?"

"Why? To prove to yourself you're not a monster?" Grayson's head remains against mine, his words a whisper against my lips, setting a tingling in my blood.

"Grayson, I thought you might drop your constant need to talk about things. If you confirm you would not like me to kiss you, I will back away."

Grayson's face remains close, his breath against my mouth, fingers still in my hair. I can hear his blood, smell what's on his clothes and running beneath his skin, but all that bothers me is how near his mouth is to mine, and how I can't breathe properly.

Then suddenly I understand what Grayson's doing by *not* kissing me.

He's waiting.

I tip my head, curl a hand around his neck to pull him closer and touch my lips to Grayson's, briefly the way he did to me in my room. His hand tightens around my head, and Grayson circles his other arm around my waist to pull me closer.

"If you are considering my proposal, I don't like soft kisses," I inform him, our mouths almost touching again.

"Not a problem."

His mouth hits mine, my breath knocked away as my back slams hard against the lockers several meters behind, the crash echoing around the empty changing rooms. Grayson kisses me exactly as I imagined he would—uncontrolled and with a desperate hunger. I grip Grayson's hair and return his bruising kiss, our tongues exploring each other's mouths. He growls low in his throat and pins me against the locker with his hips, eager lips still moving against mine.

Grayson pushes his hand beneath my sweater, sweeping his fingers lightly along my lower back. His hands don't wander further but hold me tightly, as if I might fall if he lets go. I crave more of that touch, to hold my hands against his skin too, and my blood runs hotter at the thought.

Then I lose sight of who I am completely.

I slide my hands across his naked chest, down to the tight abs before digging my nails into the muscles of his lower back. I can't move, lost in the harsh, heady kiss. My legs weaken and if I wasn't held against the locker by his body, I'd be a heap on the floor.

Good grief, Violet.

I catch a breath as he pauses and tips my chin, eyes bright. "Was that hard enough?"

"Yes. But don't dent the locker next time." I shiver as his thumb skims my bottom lip.

"I did?" He pulls me forward and frowns at the small dent. "Um. Sorry."

"You didn't hurt me," I say and touch the metal. "Hardly anything. Not body shaped."

He chuckles. "I bet the other dents in the lockers aren't from things like this."

I hold his face in both hands. "Grayson. I promise to keep you safe. I won't lose you unless you choose to walk away."

He smiles and rubs my cheek with the back of his fingers. "I promise the same. Even without the blood bond—I don't need that. I never *want* your blood, Violet."

I swallow down the desire to tell him I want the opposite. "That's sensible if you value your bodily integrity. Dorian will find accepting what you mean to me difficult enough."

His eyes go wide. "Can we not tell him?"

"Grayson. He isn't stupid. Dorian already knows how I feel about you and has since the day I stood between the pair of you at my family's home." I bite my bottom lip. "I very much hope I won't need to do that again."

"Well, if I can avoid Dorian as much as possible, that would help. I'm not keen to see him anytime soon."

"We need to see him as soon as possible. As long as Josef is out there, you're not safe. I don't ever want to see you beaten and bloodied again."

"Yet you want me to spend time with Dorian? Sounds contradictory." He draws me to him again. "Especially when I tell him I'm in love with his daughter."

"Love really does make people choose unwise actions," I comment. "One step at a time, Grayson."

With a smile, he nudges my nose with his. "Did you seriously think I wouldn't kiss you when every single time I see you that's exactly what I imagine?"

"And again, an example of how people's contradictory natures confuse me. Are you not 'done'?"

"Violet, I haven't even started yet," he whispers, echoing his words from the night his lips first met mine.

Grayson kisses me again, his mouth's warm touch moving from tentative to firm as I eagerly respond, pressing myself into him again. Grayson's grip on my waist tightens and he slides his hand into my hair.

But Grayson doesn't dent the locker this time.

CHAPTER 25

ROWAN

I MAKE another note of timestamps in the footage from the USB ready to show Violet, hoping she's deciphered something useful in the diary to help. I'd expected Violet to come over last night and inspect my work, but just me and Leif worked through everything. Her message asking if we're both okay almost had me rushing over, but when she later responded she's fine, I backed off.

Violet wasn't wrong about the mundanity of this girl's life. Many of the clips are Madison and the same two girls who Julius mentioned, camera often focused on their three faces, with wherever they visited in the background—malls, classrooms at their academy, and evenings out where the alcohol fueled the giggling further.

Seems Madison downloaded everything from a phone— Julius never found that. She would have had it with her at the dance, I suppose, so no footage from that night.

Although there aren't any dates attached, the changes in

season as the clips progress tell me the footage covers a couple of years in Madison's life. There's a guy named Archie in some of the earlier clips, who seems close to Madison, but he disappears after a few months. A failed relationship that's too old to link to the murder? I note timestamps of the places he's clearly visible anyway.

Madison and her two friends are tight knit—exclusive but not in a bitchy way. They're witches who keep to themselves, a mini-coven and a trio who are in every part of each other's lives. If Madison is as powerful as Julius and his family claim, there's no evidence, even in the classroom footage, because she isn't studious. But as I know, showing everybody how potent your magic is isn't always the best idea.

Somebody rounds the bookshelves that act as our barrier against the academy, and I look up, ready to speak.

Mrs. Eldridge, carrying a stack of large books held against the green sweater embroidered with leaves that she often wears. I stand, offering to help her but she refuses.

The comfortable relationship we've built over the years due to my often hiding and studying in the library left us the moment we met in the artifacts room. The woman who's helped me locate books and information kept something important from me, even when I specifically asked.

And *she* doesn't usually approach *me*.

"Rowan," she says evenly, not dropping her new officiousness.

"Hello, Mrs. Eldridge," I reply with stiff politeness.

The librarian places the books on the desk with a thud. "I hear that Julius spoke to you about his sister."

Oh? How much has Julius told his 'useful person to know'. "He has. Do you have anything to add that could help us?" I point at the books.

"These? They're just books I'm shelving. Human." She turns them to show the spines. Literary books bound in black leather.

"Do you know anything that could help us?" I repeat. "How involved are you in his research?"

And with *him*. She's older than Julius—not that I'm judging—but too young to match Madison's age and place her at the academy around the same time.

"Julius told me about Madison, as people do when they discuss things if they're in a relationship."

"And he told you his suspicions?" She presses her lips together. "You're connected to the tiara. Were you stealing it for Julius? Or someone else?" I continue.

"Nobody stole the tiara from that room, obviously, since the item was returned to Whitegrove the next day."

I study her for signs that'd help me, but it's impossible to tell her opinion on any of this conversation. No expression change or fidgeting.

"Speaking of stealing, I know you took your family's stone from the room that night," she says in a quiet voice. "And I'd rather not report you for the theft."

"Theft?" I ignore the prickling anxiety at her accusation. "What about the theft of Violet's potion?"

"What on earth does that mean?"

"Someone took her potion and placed it in the artifacts room," I say pointedly.

"I'm not responsible for the items; I merely keep records. There're often potions confiscated."

"But this wasn't confiscated. Somebody took the potion from her room."

Mrs. Eldridge either has a poker face or she's telling the truth. "This isn't a discussion about other items. I've no interest in Violet's hidden illegal potions."

Does she not know what the bottle contained?

"Who has access to the room?"

"All teachers," she replies.

Great—wait until Violet hears *that*.

"Why were you there that night?" I ask. "Inventory check?"

She arches a brow. "I don't need to answer your questions."

If Mrs. Eldridge didn't plan to take the tiara, was she protecting the item? Knew Violet would try to take the tiara before Mr. Whitegrove repossessed it?

She gives me a long look, the silence becoming uncomfortable. "As I said, I keep inventory records. I know you took back your family's stone, which was confiscated for a reason, Rowan."

I shrug.

"If the academy discovers you've a powerful magical item in your possession again—one that you stole from an out of bounds room—there'd be consequences." She tips her chin. "Such as expulsion."

Leaning back in my chair, I cross my arms. "Why mention this now? We met in that room days ago, and you've told nobody."

Her voice lowers and becomes urgent. "Leave Julius and his crazy crusade alone. His obsession is twisting his mind and ruining his life. I've spent months helping him move on because nothing he does will bring back Madison. Your little gang fueling his paranoia doesn't help."

"Paranoia? You know there's more to his sister's disappearance. The tiara she wore holds powerful magic—a curse, even."

"Julius had calmed down, but seeing that tiara triggered him again," she says stiffly. "As for 'curses', the Circle ward their items against human interference. Now your girlfriend wants to turn the situation into something sinister because she loves a good mystery to deflect attention from herself."

I stare at the thin-lipped woman. "If you know about Julius's 'crazy crusade' then you'll know he has other evidence."

"Diaries and video clips? I've seen some." She shakes her head. "That's a lot of information about Madison's life, so why hasn't he found anything yet?"

Because he never had the photo of the guy who's the missing link.

Julius hasn't told her.

"Leave the poor man alone," she continues.

"Seems suspicious that you're telling us to stop investigating."

"I care about him," she says tersely. "Stop this or I'll inform Mrs. Lorcan about the rules you broke."

"Report me. I don't care," I challenge.

"You want to leave Thornwood and never return?"

"For taking something that belongs to my family? Hardly a major crime."

"Rowan. Your family's aware how power-hungry you are and that the stone caused you trouble once before. The family name would come into disrepute if you're out of control."

"That's ridiculous," I retort. "I'm not intending to use the stone for illegal purposes." Not anymore. Not now I've Violet.

"And what if somebody's looking for an excuse to remove you from Thornwood?" she asks.

My head snaps back. "Who? You?"

"You're a powerful witch bonded to Violet Blackwood." I open my mouth to protest. "You've not told many people, but the staff know."

"And what's happening at the academy that's threatened by my presence?" I arch a brow.

"Don't cause trouble for yourself, Rowan."

"Well, if there's something dodgy happening inside the academy, there's no way I'm returning that stone." I close the laptop lid.

"Then don't get distracted by tiaras and missing girls from thirty years ago." Mrs. Eldridge takes the books and hugs them to her chest again before adding sternly, "Leave Julius alone."

As she turns to leave, the librarian almost bumps into someone rounding the bookshelf towards us. Violet. The two pause to regard each other but neither speak before Mrs. Eldridge strides away, head high.

"Did she have new information?" asks Violet curtly and walks over.

"Not exactly. But I do." I pat the chair beside me, and Violet sits. "How are you? What happened last night? You seemed worried when you messaged me." I stroke hair from her face, using any excuse to touch and steal a kiss.

She rubs her lips together—better than wiping the kiss away like she once would've—and pauses. "Grayson happened."

"Oh. Can you be more specific? Is he alright?"

"Josef and his associates assaulted Grayson. I found him and helped." She sighs and side glances me. "The blood thing, Rowan. That's definitely true."

Violet told me her suspicions about the effect Grayson's blood has on her, but I never accepted her denial that this brings them closer. She cares and their mutual attraction obviously causes issues for the pair.

"Grayson was a mess," she says.

I swallow. "What did Josef do? As bad as the warehouse?"

"No, but that isn't what I mean. Emotionally a mess—and I felt every one of those emotions."

My eyes widen. "Whoa. That's..."

"Unhelpful? Yes. I've enough issues understanding my own without fathoming his too."

"Right. So you left him alone because you couldn't cope with that?" I ask cautiously.

"No. I kissed him."

"Am I supposed to look surprised?" I say with a smirk. "About time. Now you can deal with things instead of pretending he doesn't affect you."

"Hmm." She purses her lips. "Anyway. Relay to me what Mrs. Eldridge said." I chuckle, then do as she asks, and Violet eyes me silently for a moment. "Have you touched the stone again, Rowan?"

"No. Don't you trust me?"

"I do. Otherwise, I'd ask the same question every day. Have I asked? No."

"Leif can confirm I haven't asked for the stone since the night I took it, alright?"

"Good." She pauses. "I have a question for you about Leif."

"All your complications with guys," I tease. "Who would've thought this would ever happen?"

"Certainly not me," she says snippily. "And this isn't about 'complications'."

"What's the Leif problem?" I ask.

"Not a problem. A question. What does Leif enjoy?"

"Um." I scratch my head. "In what respect?"

"Teenage activities. Leif activities. Something I could do with him." She pauses. "I'd buy him a gift to reciprocate his but have no clue what he likes."

"Leif likes walking?" I suggest.

"Walking? How is that an interesting activity? It's an everyday necessity."

"No. Walking in the countryside. He'd often disappear on his own for hours or did until recently, when things started to get bad with the shifters." I tap the laptop lid. "Not sure if it's his shifter side or if he's just a guy who likes scenery. I went with him a couple of times, but it was exhausting and boring."

"Walking." Violet frowns.

"Yeah. And he'd be safe if you were with him. I know that's why he's avoided going recently." I nod. "Go hiking with him. He'd like the time alone with you. Would be good to talk?"

"Talk?" Her brows tug. "Leif doesn't talk. Much."

"Maybe he's never sure what to say?" I suggest. "You offend him more easily than you realize."

"Yes. I've gathered that Leif's more sensitive than his physical size would suggest." She nods. "Very well. I shall take Leif for a walk."

I splutter. "Omigod Violet. You make him sound like a dog."

"I shall ask him once we've finished this morning's

discussions. I hope you've found something to share because the diary has yielded nothing thus far."

"Ah yes. That." I smile and flip open the laptop. Violet pulls out her phone. "Making notes?"

Violet shakes her head. "I'm looking for somewhere to walk. Are there popular places that others choose to wander aimlessly there and back again?"

CHAPTER 26

VIOLET

IN THE EARLY DAYS, I'd sit in the library with these three guys solely focused on any information we'd gleaned and how together we could solve the murders. I'd never considered that my choice in doing so unwittingly brought me closer to them. The only way I could've avoided the emotional connection and their physical appeal was to do what I originally intended—leave Thornwood as soon as possible.

But I couldn't. Suddenly other people's lives were real—and linked to mine. A bond that I denied was placed on top of a growing desire to be around Rowan, I had a constant and confusing physical response to Grayson, and a draw to Leif that kept him on my mind every day he wasn't here. Even as realization dawned, I still planned my escape, not ready to face that change in me.

Now, as Rowan's slender fingers slide over the laptop mouse pad, locating the footage, I stare at his profile and the fluttering begins in my chest again. Leif sits on the edge of the table, feet on the chair beside me as he leans across to watch Rowan. Although we're not touching, Leif's movement scatters his scent, reminding me of the time we did touch and kiss.

And Grayson. He arrives as Rowan begins talking. I wasn't sure Grayson would join us today—his decision's usually based on what mood he's in. This morning, the mood radiating from him is a world away from that of the bloodied hemia I kissed. He's calmer, those captivating eyes immediately on me when he arrives, a hint of a smile tugging at his lips. And although his blood scent reaches me before he does, this time when Grayson approaches I've no desire for that part of him.

Grayson looks down at me for a second before stroking an escaped strand of hair from my face, fingers lingering. My heart jumps out of rhythm, convinced he's about to kiss me, but his smile solidifies, and he stands behind so he can watch Rowan too. Hairs lift on my neck at his proximity.

Good grief. Was our kiss a bad idea?

Leif arches a brow at me but says nothing.

"Glad to see you're intact after last night, Grayson," says Rowan casually, focus remaining on his laptop.

"I merely kissed him and did not aim for any vein or artery," I retort.

Rowan looks up, amusement glinting in his eyes. "Intact after encountering his *uncle*, Violet. But thanks for the update."

"Oh."

Rowan smirks, and Leif laughs too.

"Josef knows better than to seriously harm Grayson," I reply.

"You think?" he says from behind me, sarcasm edging his tone.

"Can you take this as the sign to stop skulking alone?" asks Rowan. "Next time you see the guy, we should be with you."

"Learned my lesson. I'm not going anywhere alone again."

"Yes. You should've listened to me in the first place," I say, turning to look at him.

"I wanted Josef to know I'm not scared of him," he says icily.

"Bravado trumps common sense yet again." I turn away from

him. "We're here to discuss Rowan's findings. Rowan, tell them about your encounter with Mrs. Eldridge just now."

"Huh," says Grayson once Rowan's finished. "Sus."

"Absolutely," I say. "I shall inform Julius about what happened."

"Perhaps don't," says Leif. "Back off a little. We don't want to upset Mrs. Eldridge—we can't lose Rowan."

Grayson nods. "And we should be selective about what we share if Mrs. Eldridge is his confidante."

"Yeah, I want to know Mrs. Eldridge's deal," says Rowan. "Why would she threaten me and tell us to back off unless she knows more?"

"Unless she's telling the truth—the tiara pulled up stuff that's messing with Julius's head too much and affecting their relationship?" suggests Leif.

"I don't buy that," says Grayson, and Rowan adds his agreement.

"Dorian looked into all the teachers' pasts, remember?" said Leif. "That would include the librarian."

"We shall deal with her later. What have you found on the tapes?" I say.

"Me and Rowan went through everything last night while you were..." Leif smirks at me. "Busy."

"And?" asks Grayson. "Did you find anything?"

"Some footage with the guy from the photo, but only ever in the background."

Rowan plays a clip: girls eating lunch together while the one filming—presumably Madison—pans the camera around the cafe, extolling the virtues of the pies.

"Here." Rowan pauses the clip and taps the screen. "The table across the cafe. I swear that's him."

Pulling the laptop around to me, I zoom in. "Maybe."

"Yes. Because he's wearing the same jacket in another part." Rowan fast-forwards the clip and begins playing again. "Keep watching for him."

This time Madison's outdoors at night, in an area not dissimilar to that of the town fire night, apart from instead of trees circling the attendees, cars are parked around. Lit headlights point to kids sitting on camping chairs or car hoods, music blaring. The central brightness prevents me from seeing much of the surrounding area, including a few kids standing in the dark. We've no clue where they are, only that there's no other light source and dirt and stones cover uneven ground.

Madison's friends sit on a checkered blanket, opposite the camera, which occasionally moves around the party. The friend with the shorter hair holds out a liquor bottle.

"No thanks. I have to watch that you get home okay," says Madison from behind the camera.

"I'm fine!"

"Uh huh. You've already drunk too much."

I blow air into my cheeks. "Scintillating. A group of teens drinking."

"That's Annabelle," I say. "And the other's Christine."

"Just don't open your big mouth," says Christine, and takes a swig from the bottle. "Telling him you're a witch when humans are already suspicious about the academy? Bad idea."

"Meh. Humans often call themselves witches. I'll wear a pentagram next time we get together." She snickers. "Show him an interesting spell or two."

"Good grief," I mutter.

"We can't all date witch royalty," says Christine.

"I prefer vamps," says Annabelle.

"Shush!" says Madison.

"How is this banal conversation relevant?" I ask Rowan.

"Wait. Watch."

Drunk Annabelle leans forward. "You know Sergei's dating a human?"

"What the hell?" exclaims Madison. "That's worse than us. What happens when he pushes her into blood play?"

Annabelle taps the side of her head. "Mind magic."

"If he doesn't seriously injure her!" hisses Madison. "Sergei's asking for trouble."

Christine scoffs. "Like he's the only one playing with fire, huh, Maddy?"

"There," says Rowan, and pauses again. "The guy's face is clearer because he's stepped into the car headlights—and that's definitely the green jacket from the cafe. Look at the silver emblem on the chest."

"Is he human? The witches are with humans," says Grayson.

Rowan shrugs and Leif says, "He's never in any of the clips from the academy."

"Hmm." I watch as Rowan winds the footage forward slightly. "Look carefully."

I blink. "At the girls dancing in a drunken fashion while everybody mocks them?"

Quite honestly, I'm embarrassed on their behalf. Annabelle can barely stand, gripping onto Christine's navy blue cardigan sleeve with one hand and waving a liquor bottle around in her other. She stumbles in her heavy boots and a girl in sneakers yells when Annabelle stomps on her by accident. They're singing along to the music. Badly. Others dance too, and one abruptly pauses.

"Is she *vomiting*?" I ask in horror. "Please. I can't watch any more of this spectacle."

"Behind them. Look. Madison isn't filming. She's talking to the guy. Look behind the girls dancing. I've watched enough of this to know what Madison looks like," says Rowan.

The girl who wore the tiara in the photo stands close to the guy Rowan identified, with a blanket wrapped around her shoulders, opposite him. She tugs at his tightly crossed arms, agitated. He steps back, instead putting hands in his jacket pockets and replies. They've drawn attention from a group beside them who stare—the pair must be arguing loudly. I can't pick up the conversation, thanks to the music that her drunk friends are dancing to and the poor recording.

"There's no way to know what they're saying," says Grayson.

"Yeah, but he's pissed about something," says Leif.

I peer. "Where is this place? Do you recognize it?"

"Too dark," says Leif. "Though it could be a parking area outside town."

"Like where?" I ask.

"Dunno. There're a few tourist stops around, especially at the edge of the National Park."

"Rowan. You need to look closer for clues about the surroundings," I inform him.

He pauses the footage. "I don't know if you noticed, but it's dark, Violet," he says sarcastically.

"What about her diary? She might mention the place," says Leif.

I chew my lip. "I haven't gotten far with deciphering that." My gaze switches to Grayson. *Oh, how things have changed.* I left behind my investigative duties because a sickening dread that something had happened to Grayson distracted me. I lost focus. Rowan frowns at me, then looks up at Grayson but says nothing.

"Is there anything else relevant in the footage?" I ask.

"Like you said, boring teen stuff and gossip," says Rowan.

"Who's playing with fire?" asks Grayson. "That sounded directed at Madison."

"You think Madison's an elemental witch whose spell activities are drawing attention?" I ask and straighten. "That somebody reprimanded her for that?"

"Uh. No. It's a phrase—like Madison's choice of guy is as sensible as a human dating a vampire," says Leif.

"Which was a crazy idea back then," says Grayson. "Consequences for the vamp wouldn't be pleasant if he did... vamp things to her. Playing with fire in a literal sense because that's where he'd end up if she died."

I shake my head. "Madison's relationship threatened her. Is that what the girl meant?"

"If she was definitely talking about Madison, yeah," says Rowan.

"Then who's the *guy*?" I ask in frustration. "His name is never mentioned? Not once?"

Rowan's mouth tips at the corners. "Oh, they mention a lot of guys' names. I wrote a list. See if any match the initials in the diary." He slants his head. "Once you find *time* to study the pages."

I ignore the pointed comment. "Ask Julius if he knows the location. If he does, I want to visit."

"What for? To look for a body?" jokes Leif.

"Certainly not. Madison's body could be in any number of locations, and I do not have the skills to detect cadavers. That's more a shifter thing."

His smile drops. "Are you seriously suggesting I could sniff out a dead body?"

"No. But now you mention it..." I purse my lips and Leif scowls. "We track down Christine and Annabelle too."

"I'll take another look at the footage and see if I can figure out where they are," says Leif. "I know the local area well."

"Oh. Yes. We could take a walk sometime," I say and smile at him. "Just you and me."

"Uh. Why?" His expression becomes a mixture of confusion and, for some reason, worry. "What did I do?"

"Do?"

Grayson snorts a laugh. "Sounds like Leif thinks you've sinister motives for taking him into the middle of nowhere alone."

I blink. "Good grief. Is he right, Leif?"

"No. It's just..." He pushes curls from his eyes. "A weird request."

"Yeah. Violet's dates tend to be weird requests," puts in Rowan and chuckles.

Leif's eyes widen. "Date?"

"Your enthusiasm at my suggestion appears lacking, Leif," I say. "Is this due to my request to spend time alone with you or the location?"

"Location." Rowan snickers again. "A date to a possible murder site."

"The place might *not* be a crime scene," I retort. "And we shall go in the daytime and enjoy the view."

Leif stares at me as if I've suggested an evening at the morgue. "View?"

"Rowan." I look at him. "Were you lying to me about Leif enjoying walks and looking at scenery?"

"I am completely confused," says Leif.

"Do you, or do you not, enjoy walks in the countryside?" I ask, becoming exasperated.

"Yeah. Not recently though." He chews his lip. "Avoiding being alone outside."

"I would like some time alone with you and this is a perfect synergy between fun and investigation." By now, Rowan's pink-cheeked from suppressing laughter and Grayson watches with new amusement too. "Quite frankly, I don't understand the hilarity."

Leif stands as I do and places a large palm on the side of my head. "Don't listen to them. A day out with you sounds perfect. Crime scene or not."

I nod, thin lipped. "Thank you, Leif. I shall ensure we have fun. Perhaps soon, after our meeting with the elders in a couple of days?"

Every muscle in Leif's body goes rigid and he dips his head to obscure his eyes further. "Yeah, I'll see how I feel."

"Ethan and I will protect you," I say. "And hopefully impress upon the elders that you will not join them."

"Mmm." He rubs his nose.

"Any luck getting a response from Annabelle or Christine?" I ask.

"Give me a chance," sighs Rowan. "I emailed to the addresses Julius gave me but haven't heard back yet."

"And did you impress upon them how important their contacting us is?" I continue.

"Yes, Violet," he says wearily.

"Perhaps I should contact them?"

"Ha. No way. You're even blunter when you write," he says. "I explained about the tiara and photograph, and that we had a good chance at finding the truth since your father's helping."

"Apart from he isn't," I put in. "You lied."

Rowan shrugs. "Dorian will help eventually."

"Yeah, sure," says Grayson.

"Let's not mention anything to Dorian yet," I say. "I want to solve this and have him eat his words."

CHAPTER 27

LEIF

ONE LOOK at Ethan and I've a better idea why few mess with Violet's half-dragon father. This guy dwarves the Ursa elders—in fact, any elders I've met. Zeke's big, but this guy is built like the mountains that overlook the home he shares with Violet and her family.

I often obscure my eyes behind hair to avoid people immediately seeing the telltale sign of my half-shifter state, but I can't see Ethan's at all, just his strong jaw and a smattering of black scales at the edge of graying t-shirt neckline. Still, I'm pretty sure he's staring at me in the same calculating way as Violet's other fathers.

Dorian freaked me out, Zeke made me uneasy, but this man coils a different fear in my stomach.

Ethan breaks his presumed gaze at me and his face splits into a smile, at odds with his aura. "Hello, baby girl." Violet snarls at him as she struggles to escape his hug. "Eloise told me you let people hug you these days."

"Perhaps if you did not refer to me as baby girl."

He gives a throaty laugh. Doesn't Violet realize she'll always be their baby girl? "How about Mia? She would sit on my lap and read books."

"Ethan. Good grief," she snaps.

He shakes hair from his face and looks at me. "When she wasn't climbing onto the roof or setting fire to the place."

The amusement that had risen at his banter sticks in my throat. His eyes aren't human—they're reptilian. "I can imagine her doing that," I say and force a light tone.

"Ethan developed more dragon traits over the years," says Violet as if she's used to this reaction to him. "Most mids don't but..."

The Confederacy attempted to trigger this mid into a dragon to use in a war.

Swallowing, I nod.

"You don't have many shifter traits, Leif." Ethan's Scottish accent is thick, voice a rough contrast to Dorian's smoothly articulated tone. "Or do you have ones I can't see?"

"Leif's bigger than anybody else at the academy," says Violet. "His height's unusual."

"Mmm." He looks directly at me. "Violet told me she thinks you've Tigris blood. Did your father look anything like Zeke?"

"I don't remember my father clearly," I mumble.

I glance at the scales on his hand at the edge of the thick black jacket. I'd worried that Ethan would want us to meet in private and grill me about Violet, but the guy with dragon eyes and visible scales wouldn't spend much time in human circles, especially a town on edge about shifters.

Instead, we meet inside the academy, in one of the classrooms towards the back of the building, during class time. Is Ethan avoiding people seeing him? He's the face of supe society that bothers humans the most—a mid with more 'supernatural features' than a witch or a vampire's everyday appearance.

"Will Dorian join us today?" asks Violet and my surroundings come into focus for the first time since I saw Ethan standing in the room. "I need to speak to him about Josef."

"Dorian? No. I've spoken to the elders a couple of times and have built a small bridge that I don't want the man smashing to pieces before I've gotten any further." He pauses. "What about Josef? Have you seen him?"

"He attacked Grayson. Although I'm aware Dorian dislikes Grayson, any appearance by the man needs investigating."

Ethan nods. "Yeah. I'll let you speak to Dorian about that. I don't want to listen to another rant about Petrescus."

"Very well. Have you broached the subject of necromancy with the shifters?" asks Violet blithely—the question I'm too frightened to ask.

"Yes," he says softly. "The news did not sit well with the elders, and some don't believe me."

"Sit well? I bet that's an understatement," she replies. "Do they know where Trent is? Any suspicions who may be responsible?"

Ethan shakes his head. "I have to tread carefully, Violet. The actions of a few witches against shifters has set back their trust a hell of a lot."

"But the elders need to discuss this. If there's anybody within the settlement who's connected to the necromancers—or whoever's behind all this—you need to know. Dorian needs to question them!"

Ethan lowers himself onto the edge of the teacher's desk. "I'm concerned whether I should take you with us if your 'personality' might make the meeting difficult."

Violet clamps her lips together and shakes her head. She's insistent that we involved her. I wasn't sure I wanted Violet to walk into the shifter's settlement with us, although now I've met Ethan I'm more than certain she's safe.

"Violet wants to gather more clues," I say jokingly. "She won't risk speaking out of turn."

Ethan barks a laugh. "Do you know my daughter or not?"

"I'm not accompanying you for clues. I want to be with you to ensure you walk away again, and that the elders assure Ethan you'll remain free."

"Violet. The elders want to speak to Leif about what he remembers."

A sharp spike of panic hits me. I met Roderick once, when in that cell. Once he'd finished demanding answers about my connection to the deaths, he told me that 'the people you belong with' will stop anything happening to me.

Yeah, he was right. Roderick meant shifters, but Violet and Rowan—and Grayson—are the ones I belong with. *They're* who'll help. Violet's small hand curls around my fingers and perspiration beads along my back as I cautiously meet Ethan's eyes. He drops a look to where I hold his daughter's hand and then regards me.

"Is the witch okay with this?" He switches his look to Violet.

"This?" she asks.

"You and Leif. You're bonded to Rowan."

"'The witch' has a name. Rowan." Ethan arches a brow. "Is Rowan okay with me caring about his best friend?"

"There's more than 'caring' here, Violet. Hell, you just freaked out about me hugging you, and you're holding a guy's hand." Irritation edges his tone and the idea that I might walk away without upsetting Ethan evaporates. "Eloise mentioned your unusual choices, but I thought she must've imagined that."

"I mean, we're mostly just friends," I blurt out, picturing him breaking my face if he thinks I've done more than hold his daughter's hand.

Ethan suppresses his amusement. "Calm down. Eloise already had words with me about my little girl growing up."

Violet chokes. "Little girl? Stop!"

"And the Petrescu is out of the picture now?" he continues.

"I said, can we stop," retorts Violet.

I slide a look to her. She'll easily deny any closeness to

Grayson in front of Ethan because she did such a good job of denying this to herself for weeks.

He folds his arms across his chest, and I uncomfortably watch how his large muscles flex. "I hope he's worth the aggravation, Violet."

"Excuse me? I'm offended on Leif's behalf."

Ethan's dragon eyes fix on Violet. "I've no issues with Leif or Rowan. I'm concerned what'll happen if this Petrescu guy *isn't* off the scene. How do you know Josef attacked Grayson if you stay away from the guy?"

The pair are silent long enough that my skin goosebumps at what might happen next.

"Dorian's Petrescu obsession is unhealthy," she says eventually. "And how did this become about him?"

"You'll discover that once your lives become tied that you're bound, Violet. All of you. Choose wisely."

"But isn't that the point, Ethan?" she says coolly. "I'm not choosing."

CHAPTER 28

VIOLET

I'VE NEVER MET or socialized with any shifters beside Ethan and Zeke, and as I sit in the meeting room, I'm struck by how I'm pulled into yet another unfamiliar world due to my life melding with another's.

Leif's importance to me is a bigger reason for my being here than any investigation into the deaths and necromancy. I'm told I should count myself lucky the attendees allowed me to join them in sitting at the carved meeting table. I perch on the matching oak bench alongside Ethan, between him and Leif. Leif's hand stays in mine beneath the table, and I've assured him he'll walk away with Ethan and I after the meeting, with a guarantee from shifters to leave him alone.

The elder I clashed with at the station doesn't smile at me—or anybody—and the atmosphere clouds with distrust and animosity. At least one of the men present, a shifter with a shaved head called Theo, greets Ethan with a smile, the pair relaxed enough with each other that they must be familiar. Is he here as referee? Because he sits slightly further back from the two elders and hasn't said a word.

Due to the murders, Ethan and Zeke's attempts to broker peace has become more than persuading elders they can't just 'collect' anybody with shifter blood to bolster their community. The Ursas have lost people, and their relationship with the town is in tatters. Ethan suggested Sawyer join our visit to present at least an illusion of unity, but the elders refused.

The rather un-charming elder I met at the station the night authorities arrested Leif leads the meeting. Moments into discussions, he leans forward, massive forearms on the table as he fixes his feral eyes on me over everybody else. "What happened to Viggo?"

I consider my words carefully. "Soup tins and shelves."

"You knew this, Roderick," says Ethan.

"And the necromancy?" he asks, ignoring Ethan. "Why let Viggo die?"

"You wanted me to reanimate him?" I ask, eyes wide.

"No." He leans further forward. "I'm asking, if you used your foul magic on other shifters why not him?"

"We've spoken about that," says Ethan evenly, but there's a growl to his tone. "Violet wasn't involved. Neither was her mother."

"We've no proof the witches used necromancy," says the shifter beside him, the pony-tailed guy I encountered at the police station. "More likely mind control."

"Which is why you need to find Trent," I butt in. "To see his true state. Proof!"

"Trent's a possible danger to others," says Ethan. "If the necromancer controlling Trent is still out there, who knows what might happen."

"Trent has gone," says Roderick stiffly.

"Do you mean he left?" I ask. "Do you know where?"

He regards me again. "Gone."

Leif's hand tightens around mine. "You killed him?" I ask. "What a stupid move."

"Violet..." warns Ethan.

"But if the shifters did kill him, they made a mistake. Trent was our link to the necromancers." I look to my father then back to Roderick. "What if there're more shifters turned into constructs inside your settlement and you're unaware? You need to check everybody."

The pony-tailed shifter, Roderick's apparent right hand man, sneers. "Yeah. The Blackwood wants his witches in here interfering with our minds. Not happening."

"No. In order to search for more constructs, not interfere with minds, Deacon. We don't know how deeply this goes," says Ethan. "If more shifters kill, the problems you face will worsen."

"Are you implying I can't control my people?" snarls Roderick.

"The shifters wouldn't be *your* people anymore, that's the point," I say.

"Violet, you're supposed to keep out of this," warns Ethan. Sealing my lips, I cross my arms and sit straighter. "Look, we're trying to help, not interfere. You know that's always my aim."

"We don't need help," says Deacon.

"You do!" I blurt again. "Look at how the trouble between you and the town has gotten worse."

Deacon shifts to whisper something to Roderick, and the pair look at each other, something passing between them.

"You want to help?" asks Roderick, re-focusing on us. "Find the other deeds."

Ethan slants his head. "What other deeds?"

"The ones signed by the four original elders and witches hundreds of years ago. The deeds that prove we own this land and aren't tenants."

"I'm not aware of any deeds, Roderick," says Ethan.

"Because they're missing. Years ago, our people had no concept of 'owning' but along come witches who claim *they* owned the whole area, including our land. To keep the peace, the elders and witches agreed *this* part of the land could remain ours and created a deed."

"Then the land does belong to you?" I ask. "I'm confused."

"No. When the witches sold to the Sawyers, they added *our* land to *their* land's deeds. The original documents were supposed to be held by the Confederacy, but nobody could find them. How convenient because without those deeds, we had no claim to our land. The greedy bastard witches sold the whole lot and pocketed the money."

Ethan frowns, listening intently as he raps his fingers on the table. "The humans didn't take your land? The witches did?"

"They both have! We were forced to negotiate with the humans to allow us to stay on land we'd lived on for hundreds of years. Before humans and witches even settled here. Sawyer's grandfather and then father agreed, and we signed a contract. Then *this* Sawyer changed the contract—we pay rent on the land or leave, which we do because we have no choice. The whole area technically belongs to the Sawyers, and we have no rights."

"That's wrong," I interrupt. "How can this all happen?"

"There's a lot bloody wrong here, girl." Roderick jerks his chin at Ethan. "We're not the only packs forced to pay rent on land that was originally ours because we had no understanding of legal shit."

"And we've said that Dorian's council will recognize any original contracts from before the Reveal. That includes the one where the land belongs to you."

"Yeah, like I said, find the deeds with *our* names on, if they still exist. Because the only ones in existence claim Sawyer owns the land, and we're tenants."

I've no real understanding how contracts work, but I'm sure ones involving supes aren't as straightforward as human deeds of land. Dorian ensured that all shifters who had a claim on land anywhere could keep it *if* they cooperated with the accords between supes and humans. Begrudgingly, shifters do, in return for the council leaving them alone to govern themselves.

But Dorian can't interfere as easily in a situation between humans and shifters. He's no right to take land off Sawyer if human documents prove he owns it.

"And there're contracts drawn up for this agreement between you and Sawyer?" asks Ethan.

"Yes. Legally binding under human law. And a huge fucking problem. One, if Sawyer sells the land, the sale will be with 'vacant possession', and we're out. Two, if the shifter bloodlines who live here end we're out anyway, as the rights to the land are for our packs only."

"That is the most ridiculous agreement I have ever heard," I say.

Ethan clears his throat. "Violet."

Roderick sneers. "Witches help Sawyer. We know that now. They don't help humans unless there's something in it for them. What's Sawyer's 'payment' for protecting the family? They're sneaky bastards and Sawyer's an idiot. If witches are involved—there's something about this land *they* want, and they've orchestrated all this to get the land back."

"Wrong," says Ethan gently. "The witches threatened Kai. Why would Sawyer work with witches who'd do that?"

"Are you stupid?" sneers Roderick and I tense, side-glancing my father. Ethan controls his temper but doesn't take well to insults. "If a shifter killed Kai, that'd *help* the witches' plans to get us out. How could we stay on Sawyer's land if one of us killed his son?"

"*You're* stupid," I retort. "Why would Sawyer put his son at risk?"

"The witches have a hold over him. Best you find out what before the kid dies," says Deacon. "Probably want to end his family line," says Roderick. "And like I said, if shifters kill Kai of course he'd bloody evict us straightaway."

"What's so special about the land that witches want it?" I ask.

Roderick's face blackens. "The witches want to wipe out our society—they tried once before, you know that."

"That's rather dramatic and paranoid," I say. "The witches want the land, it seems. Getting rid of shifters is a side-effect."

"Excuse me?" snarls Deacon.

"Sawyer wouldn't be involved in something that'd threaten his only son," says Ethan.

"*His only son*, huh?" Deacon gives Ethan a tight smile.

"What does that mean?" Leif finally speaks. He's smaller in here, not only physically, but the environment engulfs everything about him, his fear and confusion bringing up a wall I recognize from the day I died.

"The Sawyers have another child?" asks Ethan, and frowns. "No. We'd know this."

"Yes," I add. "That's a fairly obvious part of any investigation into the man and his family."

"Not his wife's kid."

"Then who's this alleged child?" asks Ethan.

"I reckon a witch since they're trying to off Kai." Roderick shows his large teeth.

"Look at the contract to see who's set to inherit the land from Christopher Sawyer," says Roderick gruffly. "His firstborn. If the firstborn dies, the next in the family line takes over. He has no other kids 'officially'. I reckon the witches have one waiting in the wings. If *witches* get hold of this land, there's no way we could stay."

"This can't be true," says Ethan. "We would know."

"Someone might be keeping his secrets for a price," puts in another. "Won't look good if the perfect man who stands for human morality and earns respect from the town has kids all over the place. He had a reputation."

Blackmail?

Roderick looks to his colleagues, who nod. "I'm only telling you this so you can look in the right direction. Your friend Sawyer likely has more than one kid by different mothers."

"Why have you never told us all this?" demands Ethan. "Explain."

"Because we don't want attention drawing to the fact we know. When those deeds come back to us—which they will—heirs from the elders who signed will take back this land. Permanently. You think it's a coincidence Rory, Trent, and Viggo have gone? They're descendants. Now we're left with one to protect our legacy. Our land." He jabs a finger at Leif. "The kid's father was a descendent of an elder who signed." Leif's whole body goes rigid. "We need his bloodline, even half-blood. They've already taken out the others!"

Viggo. Rory. Trent.

Targets.

"Then why didn't the witches kill Leif the night Wesley died?" I ask, and Leif chokes.

"The witches don't know who Leif is yet. They're positive the packs wouldn't allow an important heir to wander around unprotected, or allow others to attack him," says Roderick. "There're a few half-shifters around, like there are witches with human blood diluting their legacies; Leif isn't unusual."

"Well," I snap. "They'll know soon, especially now you've planted this in Leif's mind!"

"You asked for the truth," growls back Roderick and jerks his chin at Leif. "See why we want you back now? You're not safe out there and needed here."

"I'm not a shifter," he says weakly. "I've no signs of shifting. At all. I would by now."

"Still got our blood, boy," he says gruffly. "Still an heir."

"No." Leif shakes his head. "No," he repeats. "I've nothing to do with this. I don't *want* anything to do with this. None of this situation is my life. That's what we came here to say." He looks wildly at Ethan. "Right?"

"Elder blood changes that, Leif," says Ethan. "Things aren't as simple now, but I'll do everything I can."

"No." Leif slides from the bench and stands. "My life isn't here or with any shifter. I've a human life."

"You'll have *no* life once the witches discover who you are," sneers Roderick. "Is that what you want?"

I look up to Leif as his hand slips from mine, the same sick feeling washing over me as I can see on his pale face. "I'm sorry, but none of this is true or makes sense," I retort and stand. "These are stories."

"I hear you pride yourself as a detective as well as a necromancer," says Deacon. "Looks like you've a lot to find."

Ethan stands and places both hands on the table. "You have this all wrong about Sawyer and Leif. Dorian's council would know. There's no secret kid."

"Like they knew about these necromancers you claim exist?" asks Roderick. "You come here offering to help. To keep us safe. Negotiate with the town. Our future lies with heirs, just as Sawyer's does. You return Leif to us, for everybody's sake."

I'm scrambling to catch up to what's happening when Ethan slams a hand on the table, silencing everybody—including quiet voices outside the door to the shifter's meeting room.

"You do not threaten Leif into giving up the life he knows to fulfill something that has nothing to do with him." My father's dragon eyes flare brighter green. "Leif has a choice. A will of his own. Regardless of who his father is, Leif belongs where he chooses."

Roderick scoffs at Ethan. "And now you understand why we never let outsiders into our society. You don't understand anything about us. Leif is our blood."

Ethan's voice lowers to a tone that raises hairs on my arms. I've memories of what simmers beneath. "I understand plenty. We made accords. We're trying to help you. And I am perfectly aware of how it feels to be forced into a life never asked for. To have my choices removed. One reason we came today is to tell you to leave Leif be. For you to see how reluctant he is to be part of your world."

"I want to speak for myself," says Leif almost inaudibly.

All eyes in the room turn to the guy who's suddenly a greater focus than he wanted or expected to become.

"I don't know what's true and what isn't, but I can't be a part of your society. This isn't the one I know. You say I'm under threat? Shifters have threatened and beaten me for years. Humans have bullied me. Witches want to join in? Yeah. Well. I'm damned if I do or damned if I don't." His voice wavers, just for a beat. "I'll risk life without your protection, thanks."

"We can offer you a future, Leif. Outside, in their world, you'll die," says the elder. There's no concern in his tone, only anger.

"No, he won't," I say as softly as Leif spoke. "Leif will be safe as long as he's with me."

The elder sneers. "And what does a shifter matter to you? A half-shifter at that."

"What an odd question to ask the daughter of Eloise Thornbrook," I say coolly. "Leif is an important part of my life."

"Your life? Which one? Hidden by your daddy on his estate to keep you safe, or now pretending you're so damn important in this town?" he mocks.

"Leif is an important part of my life, and you are a—".

"Violet." Ethan's voice filters through the gathering darkness as a part of me wants to get this man in the same chokehold he could take Leif in.

Ethan's palm rests on my head for a moment, jerking me away from the vitriol about to spill from my mouth. *Don't make this worse.* But how can things be any worse for Leif right now?

My jaw sets hard, and I stand. Leif attempts to catch my hand as I move from my spot, walking slowly around the table until I'm inches away from the elder shifter. Our eyes meet in challenge, but I'm not afraid of him. Everywhere I turn, people threaten and bully the people I care about. Twist other peoples' lives for their own gains.

"Again, what does a half-shifter matter to you, little girl?"

I snarl, teeth sharpening, each heartbeat hammering home what's happening—Leif is one step closer to becoming theirs. "Leif protects me; I protect him. He belongs with me. You do not touch or interfere in the life of a Blackwood's consort."

CHAPTER 29

VIOLET

DID LEIF HAVE ANY IDEA? Did his mother lie to him or were the *elders* words a lie?

I stand across the driveway from Ethan's black SUV, outside the front of the academy, Leif still in the passenger seat and staring forward. He's barely spoken since his speech to the elders. Back when the police arrested him, I worried how Leif coped with the accusations and treatment, but I now see how. He disappears into the place in his mind where he keeps himself safe.

Rowan does the same thing—barriers they snatch hold of and pull down against the world, ones created *by* that world.

Like the walls I too created against a world I never understood.

"What do I do, Ethan?" I ask him. "I don't know how to help. How can I stop Leif from hurting?"

Ethan takes a hand from his jacket pocket and touches the back of mine lightly with his coarse fingers. "Dorian would never listen to me when I told him how much like your mother you are."

"You mean because I've decided to take consorts?"

Ethan's mouth curves at one corner. "Ah. That. I meant caring, but yes. Maybe you should've mentioned the consort part to Leif first. I don't think the comment helped with his messed up life today."

"What?" I look back to the silent Leif, hating how big the knot is in my stomach.

"Violet. Someone told Leif he's an elder's son with a legacy to uphold that he wants no part of. Someone else informed the world that he belongs to her."

"I did not mean that," I retort. "Leif doesn't 'belong' to me. That's the whole point—he gets to make choices."

"Like the choice to be a consort?"

"Stop saying that word," I grumble. "I used the term because I didn't think Roderick would understand anything different."

"Do you love Leif?" he asks simply.

"Excuse me?"

"Simple question."

"In my experiences and observations over the last weeks, 'love' is not a simple question, answer, or anything in between."

"Mmm hmm." Ethan slants his head. "When Dorian discovers what you did and said today, I don't think he'll be happy."

"I *think* he'll be more interested in the allegations surrounding Sawyer, witches, and secret children. This somehow links to Sawyer's desperation to pass the land onto Kai."

"Maybe, but you've brought Leif into your family with your words today. *Our* family." I blink at him. "Leif's under all of our protection now—is that your reasoning? Your new desire for justice and keeping 'good people' safe?"

The SUV door slams closed and Leif walks to where we're close to the edge of the parking area, midway between the vehicle and the building. He's pale, mouth turned down and nods at Ethan.

"Thanks for taking me. For trying," he says to Ethan.

"Yeah, sorry, mate. There's a lot to dig through from all that, but we'll do what we can, okay?"

Leif nods, and the hug I give him comes from instinct. Although Leif rests his chin on the top of my head, his embrace isn't as tight as usual. Because Ethan's with us?

"I'd like to see Rowan," Leif says and moves away.

"That's a good plan." I smile, hoping to brighten his mood even just a little. "Class has finished—if Rowan went and isn't researching again. Should we try the library?"

Leif's throat bobs. "On my own. He's the person I need to talk to, Violet."

"Oh." Everything sinks, from my shoulders to my stomach. "And I'm not invited?"

He glances behind me at Ethan and then strokes my cheek. "Rowan knows what to say and what not to say. He's my best mate. Rowan understands me."

"Unlike me," I say stiffly.

Leif lowers his voice. "What you said to the elder. That's confusing. And... sometimes you say things that aren't helpful. I can't deal with that side of you right now."

My mouth goes completely dry. "You don't want to be around me."

He sighs. "I can't deal with your intensity at the moment, Violet. You'll want to talk about everything we've learned today for your investigations, and I can't think straight. I'll talk things through with Rowan and see you later and talk about the investigation?"

Ethan places a hand on my shoulder and leans down. "The guy's in shock. Don't take this personally," he whispers.

"I never take things personally," I say stiffly, but something inside me breaks apart—as if Leif pulled at my heart and it snapped through my ribs.

Leif's barely listening, but he hugs me again, briefly, but tighter this time. With another thanks to Ethan, and Ethan promising to contact him soon, he wanders away.

What do I do?

Leif's comments that I'd insist we discuss what we learned rings true, but I'd wanted to help *him* first. Somehow.

Therefore, I'm left with the only way I know how.

Gather information that puts me back in control.

THE VIOLETS in the small vase are already wilted, and I stare at them. They're soft to touch as I use magic to make them flourish again, amused with myself, as I was when I fixed Holly's tomato plants. The proud and vocal necromancer never goes further than flora these days.

I pause. With all the distractions, I've stopped nagging Eloise when she plans to teach me to strengthen and control necromancy. My morbid curiosity about how a reanimated individual would behave came from a girl who never saw anything apart from black and white—mostly pitch black. I couldn't see the issue since the person got to live a second life with their self and memories intact. Despite my semi-joke about Wesley, I'd no desire for control of another. Now, all I can see is the dependence the creature would have on a necromancer, as close a tie as a bond. Closer.

"You okay, Vi?" asks Holly and my teeth grind.

She insists on shortening my name, something she sees as a term of endearment brought about by our closer friendship. This reduction of people to one-syllable appears rife amongst the student body, but I don't partake. Holly would hear the disdain if I replied, *Yes, Hol.*

"What are you thinking about? You're quiet," she continues.

"Necromancy," I say without looking away from the violets.

"Is that what you're studying on your phone?" she asks lightly.

I swivel my desk chair. "Do you honestly believe there're 'how to raise the dead' instructions on the internet?"

"No. That was a joke." She tears a strip of strawberry licorice between her teeth. "Did you have anybody in mind?"

"Leif."

The licorice jams in Holly's throat and she chokes so hard I'm on the verge of walking over and slamming my hand on her back. I haven't figured out how delicate she is and don't want to break Holly's ribs, and so wait. She spits the licorice into her hand.

Gross.

"Does Leif know?" she asks, eyes watering.

"I'm not sure he realizes I think about him."

"Oh!" Holly wipes at her eyes and her shoulders sag. "I meant, did you have anybody in mind for the necromancy."

"Good grief, Holly. No. I am not considering Leif's death and reanimation." Especially since that was a real fear for him in the midst of the Rory and Wesley investigation.

"He'd like that you're thinking about him," says Holly and washes down the remaining stuck candy with a water from a bottle.

"Mmm." I check my phone in case any of the guys messaged me.

"Or not? Did you upset him? Violet, you have to keep practicing."

"Practicing what?"

"Not to be as blunt—consider how your words affect people more. I mean, Leif and the guys understand—so do I—but sometimes you're too much." She's cautious and holds out her packet of candy to me.

I shake my head. "Leif made me painfully aware of all this."

She sighs. "What *did* you say?"

"Nothing. The meeting with the elders did not go well, and he preferred Rowan's company to mine afterwards," I say stiffly.

"What happened?"

"I'd rather not say. Leif's business."

"Ah. So that's where they were going," says Holly. "Rowan and Leif headed off campus earlier."

"What?" I straighten and swallow down 'without me'. "Not to confront anybody I hope."

"Pub, probably." She smiles. "Officially, we're not supposed to, but we're eighteen. It's legal."

"To drink? But Leif wanted to talk to Rowan. I don't think alcohol will help the situation at all." I purse my lips.

"Are you upset because you wanted to go?"

I tense but ignore her question. "And this is common behavior for Leif and Rowan should one of them need emotional support?" I ask.

"Drinking?" She shrugs. "Ever heard the phrase 'drowning your sorrows'?"

"Drowning?" A sudden image of Rowan holding Leif under water floods across my mind. "Please tell me that's not a literal solution to life's problems because it would be permanent."

Holly laughs. "No, Violet. So, what *were* you thinking about?"

I place down my phone and look at the violets again. "Gifts."

"Huh?"

"From me to Leif. I've decided to reciprocate his gift giving."

"Oh. I did wonder if that's his love language," she says and gestures between the flowers and toy dog.

"His what now?" I frown.

"Love language? Like, everybody's different in what makes them feel extra special. Gifts. Touch. Acts of service."

I snap my head back. "What is this ridiculousness? Isn't love a complicated abstract already before adding in more layers?"

"I'm guessing yours isn't touch." She smiles wryly. "Acts of service, hands down."

"You're making little sense, Holly. Do you have a gift suggestion or not?"

"I don't know Leif well." She pauses. "What about a magic talisman?"

"He has one, remember?"

"I don't know then. Something special."

"Maybe I could win him something. I shall take him to the

arcade. Although I'm unsure I'd share his expertise at working the claw machine."

I take hold of the dog and stroke a fluffy ear. I genuinely did not understand Leif's actions in presenting this to me. Everything that occurred at the bowling alley confused and overwhelmed me, and I'd never found myself in a situation where someone would randomly gift me an item. I didn't *not* like the gesture, but as usual my confusion came across as ingratitude because my focus lay elsewhere.

"Maybe give him your time?" suggests Holly.

"I don't possess a watch."

She chuckles. "No. Spend time with him. Alone."

I purse my lips. Leif most certainly didn't want to spend time alone with me today—or even time with me and Rowan. But this *is* similar to Rowan's suggestion. Perhaps if Leif forgives me, we can still take that walk to the possible crime scene. "And that would be enough?"

"Well..." She smirks and I ignore what I know she's hinting at.

"Thank you for the assistance."

Holly continues to chew her candy, the sound setting my teeth on edge. "Have you stopped your investigations into the tiara?"

"Why?"

"Or have you met to discuss things without me?" She pulls the licorice between her teeth until it snaps, her look challenging me.

"Did you have new information to share?" I sit straighter.

"No, but I can talk to the people you can't and find information you need."

Spending life with a closed expression and attitude helps immensely in situations like this. "Dorian doesn't want to investigate the tiara."

"Since when would that stop you?" She narrows her eyes. "You're excluding me."

"Only excluding information given by a third party who doesn't wish to be identified."

Huffing, she sinks back on the bed. "So, yes?"

"I'm confused why the sudden interest when not long ago you constantly worried someone might kill you."

"I know but—"

"Someone might kill you, Holly."

"Who?"

I shrug. "If I knew, I'd kill them first."

Holly chuckles, but that cuts dead when I don't smile. "Okay. I see the problem now."

I don't think she does.

CHAPTER 30

VIOLET

HOLLY LEAVES to spend time with Chase, and since then, I've remained in the room, confused what to do next. At least Rowan messaged to tell me Leif's okay but did not elaborate—now I understand Rowan's frustration when I do the same. Rowan must be aware of everything that eventuated today, but intimated nothing in his brief message.

I'm nauseous and can't stop picturing the strain on Leif's face when we sat with the elders and afterwards. The strange feeling that Leif left me with when he walked away earlier won't leave.

Rejection.

Leif rejected me, and the girl who would once have never cared doesn't know how to deal with this. Do I go to Leif? Explain why I said what I did to the elders? Leif doesn't understand how big a deal it is that I told people he's my consort. I'm left with two conclusions: Leif has no interest in being 'one of' the guys in my life or he hates that I reduced him to that word.

But old-fashioned people require old-fashioned concepts and

simply telling the elders that I loved and cared for Leif would wash right over them.

Love.

Again, that abstract concept I'm struggling to unravel and understand. If I didn't have such a level of affection for Leif, I would never insist on interfering. I'd never care that I might've upset him—or feel this sickness when he left me.

I've spent a life surrounded by love, for me and within my whole family, and understand there're different versions. *That's* what confuses me. The fondness I've developed for Holly that has me on the verge of doing... something to remove Chase from her life is love on some level. My understanding of the emotion also tells me he most certainly doesn't love her. Despite his name, Holly's the one pursuing Chase for his attention. He only spends time with her when it suits him, but Holly refuses to see this. That mismatch of emotions heralds disaster on a greater scale than when Ollie tossed her aside.

Rowan and Leif are similar to Dorian and my other fathers—they don't have a physical love for each other, that's abundantly clear, but each would step in to protect the other without a thought and have done many times.

Naturally, I've researched the definition of love and that's only confused me more, but one element stands out. The very thing that makes me 'their' Violet rather than the one who never belonged to anybody—I'm invested in each of the guys' safety and happiness. In their lives.

Physical love? That's a deeper connection 'their Violet' has yet to explore fully, but one that's prompted another change. If I didn't love these guys, I'd never crave their attentions. Because I'm growing aware that I do want more. The comfort in Leif's hugs, and how his scent draws me to wanting more of his warmth. The naturalness of Rowan's touch and how his gentleness can give way to a desire he manages to hold back —for now.

And Grayson.

That frozen moment in my room when his lips touched mine, when the simmering need I deny almost unleashed. And when everything *did* unleash and led to damaged lockers and a new understanding between us. Grayson looks at me in a rawer way than Leif or Rowan, either because he can't—or doesn't want to —hide the need burning behind his emerald eyes.

I blow air into my cheeks and almost slap myself around the head. Focus on something I *can* find a solution for and fit everything neatly into place once I do.

The tiara. Madison. These are facts to find and solve. Solve emotions? That's never going to happen.

A knock on the door drags me from my musings over the tiara in an attempt to tune out the day. I glance at my phone. 10PM.

I should've expected the person who I open the door to.

Leif.

He looks no different to earlier in dress or the tension in his demeanor, but his cheeks are redder, and alcohol mingles with the air around him. "Hello, Leif." I look behind. "Is Rowan not with you?"

Leif rubs a cheek. "He told me to come talk to you on my own."

I step forward and sniff. "Are you intoxicated?"

"I had a couple of beers but no." Leif shoves hair from where it covers his eyes. They're duller but not awash with alcohol as I've seen in people before. "Rowan wouldn't let me near you if I was."

"Hmm." I flick my tongue against my top teeth. "I thought you didn't want to be around me because I'm 'difficult'."

He sighs and shoves hands into his black jacket pockets. "Is Holly here?"

"Why? Do you wish to talk to her?"

This time he rolls his eyes. "No, Violet. Are you not listening, as usual?"

"I never told her what happened today," I inform him and step back to allow him into the room.

"Which part? Where elders told me who I am or when you

told them I'm your consort?" he asks, following me and closing the door.

I turn to him. "Neither."

"Why did you say that I'm your consort?" he blurts. "I don't understand."

Why is my heart banging in my chest again? "Because I didn't know how else to impress on the elders that they couldn't keep you."

Leif regards me through now half-hidden eyes and silently moves to sit on my desk chair. "You've never told me what you actually think and feel for me, Violet, so excuse me if discovering I'm your consort was a bloody big surprise."

He's terser than earlier and the nausea I'd suppressed swirls in my belly again as the emotion returns. *Rejection.* "I apologize if I spoke out of turn."

"What?" His brow pinches. "No. You don't speak *enough*, Violet."

"Some would argue the opposite."

"All I'm saying is, it would be good to know what you think and what this 'consort' thing actually means to you *before* you spoke." He rubs a hand across his mouth. "Rowan told me about witch society and their often weird family set-ups, but you're not part of that society."

I remain standing across the room from Leif. How has my admitting to the world what he means to me created such a gulf? Leif picks up a pen from the desk and starts twirling it in his hands, no longer looking at me.

"And thus, Rowan will have told you that you can reject me." His head snaps up. "Which you did, and I shall accept that. But the rejection won't stop me caring for and helping you."

"What do you mean?"

I take a deep breath. "When you said that you'd rather not be around me and walked away... that hurt."

"Hurt?"

"Why say the word as if I'm incapable of experiencing hurt?" I say indignantly. "I am sorry that I say and do things that cause you distress, but I never do so deliberately."

"Because you're upfront and honest, huh?" he asks.

"Yes."

With a small laugh, Leif pulls himself to his feet and sets the pen down before moving back towards me. Perhaps because two of my fathers are oversized men, I don't always notice how Leif physically dwarfs me, but there's a shift in dynamics here that for once emphasizes this difference.

"Upfront and honest when you choose to be." Leif looks down. "Does Rowan know how you feel about *him*? Have you told him?"

I blink. "Considering our level of physical intimacy, yes."

"Rowan doesn't have to guess what you're thinking? Attempt to read little signs and hope he doesn't have them wrong?" he continues.

My eyes go wide at the familiarity of the situation. Once-over, Rowan did need to guess, until the day he refused to any longer. "Do my actions not tell you how I feel, Leif?"

"Well, yeah, today definitely did." He laughs to himself. "But before? No. You talk about rejection, but I can't even get close enough *for* rejection. You're unreadable."

"You want verbal reassurance that I have deep enough feelings for you to justify the position I've put you in?"

"Violet. I just want you to be straight with me. Drop the winding, confusing sentences and tell me." When I don't respond, Leif cups my cheek and tips my face. "Sometimes I feel like an idiot chasing something I'll never get. That I'm making things worse for myself for not stepping back, but this... I'm so bloody confused, Violet."

"Do you mean me?" I ask quietly.

He takes a shaky breath. "Nobody ever affected me the way you do. I can't stop thinking about you all the time. Literally. You're the last thing on my mind before I go to sleep and you're there the moment I wake up. But I'm going crazy trying to figure you out." Leif swipes a thumb across my lips. "I kissed you and you said that was okay, but then nothing else happened. I presumed your bond with Rowan meant you'd made your choice."

"Choice? Are Rowan and I a couple wrapped up in each other who exclude others due to our relationship?" I shake my head.

"I guess not," he mumbles.

"You'd like me to explain? You're on my mind too, Leif. Every time I think about somebody forcing you into something you don't want, I feel sick. I couldn't understand why, but today everything sharpened into focus—I don't want to lose you. Those days the humans locked you away, ask Rowan how I behaved. I hated that you must've felt scared and helpless, and I *hated* that I couldn't do anything. I wanted to—I would've walked into that station and taken you somewhere safe in a heartbeat."

"That wouldn't have been sensible," says Leif.

"Exactly!" I take Leif's hand, my slender fingers tiny against his. "How I feel defied logic. And then when you were free and didn't come to the academy... I worried that I upset you by *not* helping. Me. The person who never worries about what others think."

"I would've been upset if you *had*," he says quietly. "You know how protective I am of you. You talk about illogical? *That* is. You've no need for my protection at all."

"True, but I've grown to understand the inherent desire to protect that comes with strong feelings for another."

"Winding sentences, Violet," he warns.

"I possess the same feelings for you as I do for Rowan. Mostly."

"Mostly," he replies, his voice flat. "What's missing?"

"You don't occasionally infuriate me."

Leif smirks. "I know from Rowan's complaining that's mutual, Violet."

"Oh, I'm perfectly aware it is mutual." I gesture at him. "But you're rather a closed person too, Leif, and I'm not in the habit of pushing to know people's thoughts."

"Apart from when investigating crimes?" he teases.

I touch his cheek. "Yet you're also the most open in a confusing way. Your odd gestures, and past admissions that you care despite my withholding affection."

"Do you mean the gifts?"

"Holly informed me this is your love language, a concept that adds more ludicrousness to the human attempt to define everything they can't explain."

"Oh. That bullshit." He chuckles. "I like giving gifts. It's fun to see peoples' reactions."

"I want to bestow a gift on you, Leif. What would you like?"

He blinks at me. "Why?"

"Do I buy flowers as an apology like you did?"

"Um. If you like, but that's not typical for a girl."

"Am I typical?"

His huge palms close over my cheeks. "Violet. I don't need an apology. I want you to tell me how you feel in your crystal clear, no holds barred Violet way."

"I care deeply for you and want you in my life," I say through squashed cheeks. "A few weeks ago, I intended to utilize my friendship with you for mutual benefit—I clear my name, Rowan gets help with his spell, and you escape the threat to your future. Then I would leave Thornwood and all of you."

"And now?"

"All our lives and emotions are tangled together. The pull towards you when you're missing confused me and as the days passed, I realized that would never change. I'm not easy or straightforward, even if I'm forthright, and I aggravate people."

"Aggravate is a bit strong. Frustrate on a lot of levels, maybe." He sighs and strokes my hair. "Are we acquaintances, friends, or more? That's all I need to hear."

CHAPTER 31

VIOLET

FRIENDS OR MORE. That intangible and unexplainable spark of need that accompanies my desire for Leif's presence. He kissed me at the dance and apologized, but seeing him after many days apart had already lit up my evening and distracted me from the matter at hand. If only he knew that the moment I saw his figure in the doorway at the dance, I'd almost walked up to and placed my lips on his, hugged him tight, but instead wanted answers first.

"Would the Violet Blackwood you first met ever tell someone she had a consort?" I ask.

"I hate the word."

"Oh. Then instead, should I tell people we're much more than friends and that I love you? That I'll always protect you and that includes against elders who want your life?"

His fingers tighten on my face. "You love me?" he asks, almost inaudibly.

"I am struggling to define the word, but know I have tangible emotions for you. So, yes, love by some definition. Yours, I hope."

He shakes his head. "As straight an answer as I'm likely to get. More than as a friend?"

"I don't desire my friends, Leif." His softened eyes now widen in surprise. "I would not sit here all afternoon and evening thinking of you as obsessively as the tiara, nor would I hurt because you walked away."

Leif splutters and drops my face, shaking his head as he steps back. "Nobody compared me to an item of jewelry before."

I reach out to curl my hand around the jewelry *he* wears; the pendant that keeps him safe. The metal's warm, his skin soft over taut muscle. No, I don't need Leif's protection, but in his arms I feel oddly safe.

Oddly a few things.

I shove him in the chest until he stumbles further from me, and his mouth turns down. "You say one thing and do another."

After another light shove, the back of Leif's knees hit my bed, forcing him to sit. As I clamber onto his lap, straddling his wide hips, he takes a sharp breath. Leif shares the fever-like heat my fathers do—another tell he has the shifter blood he doesn't want, his body hot against mine.

The first time Leif took hold and engulfed me, dragging me away from the shifters at the memorial service, the power in him took me by surprise. Nothing I couldn't fight off, but Leif arrested me when he wrapped me in his arms, and I couldn't move.

For the first time ever, I'd yielded to somebody who touched me. I never noticed, but that was the point something clicked between us, as if magnets snapping together. I had no experience of or explanation for this until he began to feature more in my thoughts. My desire for justice and fairness for this big guy switched direction and became a different desire.

Only at the moment he walked into the academy after staying away for days did I realize my fondness for Leif ran much, much deeper.

Our difference in size has never been more apparent than now. The hands holding my waist are twice the size of the slender ones I place on his bulging shoulder muscles, his thighs twice the width of mine. And the power I never register, constrained by his gentleness around me, has never been more evident than what surrounds him now.

I'd never be vulnerable around Leif—only my heart, as I discovered today—but this massive guy protects me. Leif keeps me safe by protecting me from myself, a phrase I once couldn't understand. He's level-headed and calm; a protective barrier between me and my darker, angrier side.

Leif needs to tip his face to look at me and hair falls from his eyes. I rub the back of my fingers against his stubbled cheek and he catches my fingers to kiss the tips.

"I would never say you're my consort if I didn't hold deep feelings for you, Leif," I say quietly and drape my hands across his shoulders, bending my head, lips almost touching his.

His heavier breaths mingle with mine and he pushes my long hair from my face, rough fingertips grazing heat on my cheek.

"You have my permission to kiss me, so no need for flowers tomorrow."

He half-laughs. "Good."

"But do not grab my backside this time."

"That's tempting when you're sitting on me like this," he says hoarsely, fingers digging into my waist, "but understood."

"And—" I begin, but Leif's mouth meets mine, silencing me with a hard kiss, hands sliding upwards to hold the back of my head.

This is the kiss Leif wanted to give me the night of the dance, mouth moving against mine in a possessive way that sends now familiar tingles dancing across my skin. He parts my lips with his tongue, holding the back of my neck gently as he deepens the kiss, and I slip my hands into his curls.

Pressing myself against him, I kiss Leif in a way I avoided for too long. Too long because the first time I ever did, I finally understood why people do such a thing. This expression of love and desire comes from a closeness on a different level to friendship. Each time this happens I fall further into those desires.

And Leif most certainly sends that odd, burning need into my blood as our kiss becomes deeper, neither of us pulling away for air. He tastes vaguely of beer, and his hair tickles my face, but the kiss wipes away any irritation.

Leif often wipes away what irritates me, and I'd happily stay here with him for the rest of the evening.

"Ah. Alright. Did you want me to go?" asks a voice and I startle, looking back to where Holly stands, back against the closed door, with a 'gotcha' look on her face.

My face smarts, as do my lips as I look at her. "I don't require a room to myself with Leif. We're merely communicating what's not been done so before."

"In a very non-verbal way?" she says and giggles.

Giggles.

I place a hand on Leif's chest, his heart thumping against my palm beneath his shirt, then swing my legs to climb from him. He doesn't move at all, only to pull his hand from my hair when he sees Holly. I've evidently kissed him into silence.

"Everybody knows how Leif feels about you," she says. "Took you long enough to notice."

Smirking to herself, Holly wanders into the room and flops onto her bed, looking up at the sloped ceiling.

"I did notice. I'm just unaccustomed and ill-equipped to communicate my own feelings."

"Kissing works," says Leif hoarsely and stands. "And Holly probably saved me from pushing you away again."

"Pushing you away? The hold on me and the strength of that kiss had no hint you intended to do that."

His hands circle my waist and Leif lifts me from the floor, surprising me enough that I grip his shoulders rather than shove him. "In case it's not clear, I love you, Violet Blackwood," he whispers. "And partly in a way that might result in a painful reaction from you."

225

"The physical desires that are evidently clear?" He loosens his arms and I slide back down his body, then raise a brow at his uncomfortable glance at Holly.

Leif presses fingers to my lips. "I lied when I told you a smile is as good as a kiss from you. Because that was one hell of a kiss."

Did Holly just quietly squee? This situation is no longer comfortable with a third person present.

Leif tucks my hair behind an ear. "I should probably leave."

"Why? Is Rowan waiting for a report?" I ask.

He looks at me curiously. "No. But I have the answer I came to you for."

"I want a report," announces Holly and I suck on my teeth as she giggles. "And I'm tired. You should leave, Leif."

Tired? I may be the one known for interrogation, but I'm fully expecting one from my roommate. Leif kisses my cheek, having heard my protests about public displays before, and understands Holly counts as the public to me.

"I'll see you tomorrow," he says and looks up. "Bye, Holly."

"Sorry to interrupt, Leif."

He shakes his head but says nothing.

The moment the door closes, Holly's sitting up, cross-legged on her bed, hugging a sequined cushion.

"What is that look for?" I ask.

"It's so cute!" she enthuses, and my look darkens enough to tone her down. "Oh, but Leif is such a sweetheart."

I frown. "Did you want Leif's attentions?"

"No! I'm very happy with Chase's attention."

"Hmm. When that suits him."

Her smile grows coy. "*All* his attention."

"Stop," I say firmly and hold up a hand, palm out. "I've informed you in the past that I am not the correct individual to discuss your activities with."

I sit on my bed too, still aware of my racing heart, Leif's earthy scent covering me. I smooth my hair and Holly watches.

"If you ever want to talk to somebody about guys, you can speak to me. Three must be a lot to deal with."

"I don't 'deal with' all three guys at the same time."

Holly's cheeks—weirdly—turn vaguely pink. "I meant their different personalities and how to deal with guys in general."

"Yes. Why? What do you think *I* meant?"

"You know."

"No, I do not know, or I wouldn't ask." Holly mouths 'sex' at me. I think. "What?"

She sighs heavily. "Alright. I know you'd never kissed anybody before you came to Thornwood and thought you might want advice."

"Are you suggesting I've no concept of intimate relationships?" I ask. "There's a biologically simplicity—part A fits into slot B. Don't allow unwanted reproduction."

Holly's eyes go wide. "Intimacy is more than the biology, Violet. There's the emotion and talking things through."

"Oh, yes. The two things I excel in," I say with a hint of sarcasm. "As Leif made clear tonight. Holly, I am perfectly capable and happy to navigate this myself."

She nods and falls silent.

"Why are you looking at me like that?" I ask as a smile snakes across her face.

"Part A. That's funny, Violet. Sounds like assembling flat-pack furniture."

"Haven't we established I don't wish to speak about this?"

"And you have uh... experience of part A?" she continues rather impertinently and coyly. "I mean, not tonight, obviously, since I walked in and—"

"Good grief, Holly!"

Since when did we become girls who shared such privacy? But... if I speak to Holly about 'guy things', she'll come to me for help once Chase hurts her. *That* I do want.

She looks at me expectantly. "Isn't part A a prominent part of relationships, particularly around our age group?"

She laughs again. "That didn't answer my question."

"I believe I did."

Holly's eyes widen at my arched brow. "Alright. I'll shut up."

"Good."

"Though I like your analogy."

"Thank you." I pause. "Why?"

"Have you ever asked a guy to assemble furniture, Violet?"

"That is an insane question that you know the answer to."

"They never follow the instructions and just dive right in."

"What instructions?"

Whatever Holly's talking about makes no sense to me, but apparently it's hilarious to her.

"Nothing." I look at her in surprise as she sits on the bed beside me, but fortunately doesn't take my hand. "As long as you have the 'being safe' part covered."

"I have a potion for that."

"I don't mean safe from you attacking one of the guys."

"Yes, Holly, I am aware what safety you mean."

"And consent," she adds.

I scoff at her. "How would you rate the survival chances of somebody who did not acquire my consent?"

"Fair point."

"Could we please direct our 'girl talk' in a different direction, Holly? Did you have an enjoyable evening?" I pause and hastily add. "But if that evening was intimate, perhaps don't answer."

As often happens, I lose track of Holly's breakdown of her day as my thoughts drift elsewhere.

Straight back to *my* day.

Life lurched in a new direction for me again, but this time I've pulled somebody with me. Leif understands with crystal clarity how I feel about him, but will that be enough to keep him safe?

CHAPTER 32

I'm wary how Leif will respond to me the next day, and if Rowan might want to discuss the situation. He does—but only to tell me Leif *doesn't* want to talk about the what's happening with the elders any further. Until Ethan communicates events to Dorian, and he subtly—or unsubtly—investigates, Leif wants the subject dropped.

The elders gave their word that they'll leave Leif alone until Ethan explores the issues further, but I'm suspicious how far this 'word' goes. The relationship between shifters and Dorian's council is shaky at best, and now his daughter interfered with talk of consorts.

However, Ethan has a stronger hand—he and Dorian can find the deeds and uncover more secrets behind the apparent witch and human plot to rid Sawyer's land of shifters. The elders chosen solution would be violence, which hasn't worked so far.

The papers we found with the tiara and photographed—the 'half' legible ones—*must* be the shifters' missing deeds. The box disappeared from the location hidden beneath the factory floor before it could be retrieved. Josef removed the box before the investigators looked? Or somebody else we never saw that night?

Either way, the deeds may be out there. Nobody destroyed them yet, so hopefully there's a reason and they stay intact.

But what if Dorian does find the documents? Will that drag Leif further into the situation we're trying to pull him out of? Dorian showed me the current land documentation at the academy the day he interrupted the meeting. They're signed by the now deceased Grant Underhill and Josef Petrescu. How interesting that Josef killed the witch who countersigned a document that gives his client the rights to the land *and* to collect rent. At the warehouse, Adam mentioned a 'double cross' by Josef. This?

My father has a lot of investigation ahead. We all do.

The cryptic comment from the elders that Trent is 'gone' may not necessarily mean he's dead. And what if other shifters are now constructs? If witches exist who're practicing unauthorized magic and killing, Dorian won't appear in control of his world at all. What if they move on to attacking humans next? Add in Josef's clearly stated intent that he'll overthrow Dorian, and my father needs to be extra careful what information to reveal to the world and where to target his efforts.

Does anybody else in Josef's group know that the vampire informed Dorian of their plans and who exactly *is* in the group against Dorian? The witches who killed? Interrogating Adam never established a connection between Josef, the killers, or necromancers, but the Petrescu holds a lot of power both physically and mentally that he could be using over them.

I turn my attention to the other issue—Madison and the tiara. They're related to all this somehow, otherwise why would the box of magic items exist beneath floorboards in a human's factory?

I caught up with Leif briefly this morning, and we arrange to meet for breakfast but as I refuse to spend time in the cafeteria, I agree to meet him and the others on the lawns. Rowan arranged to speak with Julius to pass on selective information about our investigation, but that isn't what's at the forefront of my mind.

Leif's future.

Grayson arrives before Leif and sits on the lawn beside me, where I give him an account of yesterday's events. He's quiet at first, before lying back on the grass and staring into the sky.

The *'here comes summer' disgustingly cloudless* sky.

"That sucks. Poor guy."

"You sound as empathetic as I can fail to be. Nothing will happen to Leif," I say firmly.

"Ah. Yes." Grayson rolls onto his side and props his head up on a hand, elbow on the grass. "Consort, huh?"

I didn't relay the last part of the day in detail, only that Leif and I had straightened out our misunderstandings on the issue. "Don't say that to his face. I'm unsure Leif likes the word."

"Mmm." A smile plays on Grayson's lips, and he flops onto his back again. "Leif's lucky he has your father in his corner."

Unlike Grayson. "What do you think about the shifter's theory that Sawyer has other offspring?" I ask.

"Possibly. But well-hidden, and ones he doesn't know about, otherwise Dorian's people investigating would know."

"I think it's a fanciful theory. If witches had a spare heir and wanted to kill Kai, why wait until now? They must've had years to act," I say.

"Don't witches protect Sawyer's family from supes too? Maybe they have a bargain?"

Hmm. "I do not enjoy the extra complications."

He turns his head. "Have you spoken to Dorian about all this?"

"Briefly. Dorian will demand more information from Sawyer about his panicked insistence that Kai takes on the land and business the day he turned eighteen. This relates to the contract with the elders, the missing deeds, and the witches and deaths."

"But how?" asks Grayson. "What's significant about Kai turning eighteen?"

"I'm unsure. The elders mentioned heirs but nothing age specific."

"Yeah, then sounds to me like a bargain with a time limit," says Grayson.

Leif's distinctive figure strides across the lawn from the entrance that leads to the cafeteria. "Don't mention all this in front of Leif," I whisper to Grayson.

"Sure." Grayson looks back to the sky.

I smile when I spot the three takeaway coffee cups Leif's carrying in a cardboard tray, and Grayson sits up as Leif places the cups down. The tension wound inside Leif has lessened, but there's an edge to his smile—Leif, but not quite Leif.

But whatever thoughts and worries cloud his eyes dissipate as he strokes my hair and smiles. His large fingers link with mine as he sits close.

"Three coffees?" I ask him.

"Rowan isn't coming, right?" he asks with a frown. "Didn't I get enough?"

"Oh. Uh. One's for me?" asks Grayson. "I don't drink coffee."

"Right. Forgot." Leif takes one and passes the cup to me.

"S'okay. Not like we spent much time together before Violet."

I sip the coffee and watch them. I really have pulled these guys into each other's lives.

"Tell me, Leif, how do I gain entry to Violet's Consort Club?" asks Grayson.

I splutter coffee and it showers the side of his cheek. "I do not have a consort club and please be more sensitive."

"Sounds better than harem," suggests Grayson.

"Good grief," I mutter and glance at Leif, who drinks, not responding. I'm irritated by Grayson; Leif doesn't need a reminder of the *other* side of yesterday. "Sorry about Grayson." Leif shrugs and shifts away slightly to delve into his backpack for a paper wrapped sandwich.

Kneeling, Grayson shuffles towards me and places a hand to

either side of where I'm sitting. "Did Leif have to do anything special to achieve consort status?" he asks quietly.

I spot the teasing glint in his eyes, his gaze dropping to my lips momentarily. "If you'd like me to arrange a meeting with Dorian to introduce you as my consort, just ask," I say casually.

Grayson runs his tongue along his bottom lip, not reacting with the recoil I expected. "You're saying I *am* in the club?"

We haven't spent time alone together since the night Josef attacked him, but the kiss replays in my mind now that Grayson fills the space around us, sharpening all my senses. My pulse ramps up—is that Grayson's blood in me recognizing him, or mine wanting to be part of Grayson?

Or the intense attraction that dents lockers?

"What club?" asks Rowan.

I look away from Grayson to where Rowan stands, gripping the handle of his black rucksack harder than normal. He's paler, a hassled crease to his brow. Grayson quietly chuckles and moves away, lying back on the lawn.

"The Violet Blackwood Consort Club," says Leif, and I slap his thigh hard enough for everybody to hear. He pouts and rubs his leg. "Good thing I don't injure easily."

"Don't encourage Grayson. I do not have a club."

"But you have consorts."

"I thought you didn't like that word." I narrow my eyes at him.

He leans forward. "You can call me whatever you want if you kiss me like you did last night, Violet."

My mouth parts at his bluntness, but I'm happy he isn't the broken guy who walked away from me and Ethan. "You may regret that permission."

Leif's smile dimples and my heart fills with warmth rather than the chill of last night's rejection. My attempt to fix something with talk of consorts and belonging together backfired at first but forced something very necessary. Honesty. I'm yet another step away from a place I'd created inside myself. One where I believed I was safe, with the solitude I preferred.

Solitude I *did* prefer until these people gradually snuck into my life and now take up space in my heart and mind.

"Consort club." Rowan sits beside me. "Funny." But he doesn't sound amused or suggest his own membership.

"You look like you need a coffee," says Leif and hands him Grayson's.

"Thanks."

I touch his fingers. "Everything okay, Rowan?"

His spare hand curls around my knee. "Yes and no."

"Did you speak to Julius?" I ask.

Rowan nods and pulls a face when he drinks. "Ugh. Milk?" With a sigh, Leif swaps his cup with Rowan's. "I did see Julius. There wasn't much to tell him as we agreed, although we might have some more information soon. I heard back from Annabelle. One of two interesting communications for me this morning."

Progress? A familiar rush of excitement runs through. "Please tell me she's identified the guy."

"No. But Annabelle has something to give Dorian to help the investigation—if I keep her name out of it." He side glances me. "My lie that he's involved helped."

"Maybe the information will be enough to *force* Dorian to get involved. Did she say anything else? What did this information consist of?"

Rowan shakes his head. "Annabelle wanted my number and will send a message to meet me somewhere. Then she'll hand over what she has. Annabelle wouldn't say anymore over email."

"She really doesn't want anybody to know," comments Leif. "This must be good information."

"Well, you can't go alone," I tell Rowan.

"Why not? Annabelle specifically said only me."

"You're not that dumb, Rowan," retorts Grayson.

Rowan wrinkles his nose. "I don't have a time and place yet anyway. And Annabelle might change her mind."

"I'll take another look through the diary and find some of the initials and places. We can ask her about them too," I reply, emphasizing we.

"And Julius? Have you told him?" asks Leif.

"No, otherwise he'd want to involve himself. Even if Mrs. Eldridge *was* subtly threatening us, she's right about his mental state. Julius messages me all the time for updates and today he was weird. Lost his shit when I told him we didn't have more information and accused me of lying."

"By omission, yes," I say, "but if he's in a delicate mental state, it's best we remain selective about what we tell him."

"You know who else we need to speak to," says Leif through a mouthful of the wrap he bought. "Sawyer."

"Dorian has that covered."

"And Kai. Has anybody seen him since his birthday?" asks Rowan.

"Holly saw him at the movies a couple of days ago. Intact," I reply.

"You're still using her to investigate?" asks Grayson.

"Excuse me, but I am not 'using' her. I explained to Holly that remaining involved in our meetings may endanger her life. All I did was express interest in Kai's welfare and received the update from my curly-haired newshound."

Leif splutters. "You have such a way with words when describing people."

"Yeah, like consort." Grayson smirks again as my lips purse. "Does Dorian know?"

"I have a lot to speak to Dorian about and you should come with me. He needs to know what happened to you, Grayson. That could help us track your uncle down."

Grayson's smirk slips away. "You want me to meet up with Dorian?"

"No point in delaying the inevitable," says Leif.

"Yeah, but whatever 'the inevitable' is worries me," he mutters.

"Grayson. Dorian won't hurt you if you're helpful in looking for Josef. We spoke about this." He mutters his doubt. I look to Rowan. "And I want to check in with Dorian about the Circle. He has someone on the inside who could help with information about Whitegrove. He'll know who the man's connected to."

Rowan's expression shifts and he sits straighter. "You spoke to Dorian about the Circle?"

"Yes."

His cheeks redden and he roughly unzips his bag, then pulls something from inside. Rowan slaps a cream envelope with an embossed black border onto the lawn and pushes his hands into his hair again. "This is your doing?"

I gesture at the envelope. "What's that? More evidence?"

"No, Violet," he says tersely. "That's my invite to join the Circle. I told you; I don't want any involvement with them."

"You told me that *after* I spoke to Dorian." His face grows redder. "You could decline politely," I suggest.

Rowan grabs the envelope and throws it at me, which I catch in surprise. "Nobody declines a Circle invite. They have a grip over witch and human professional society through their network. I'd never get a decent job."

"Oh."

"Yeah, 'oh'," he mimics. Leif and Grayson glance at each other as the error of my behavior hits me. Rowan stands. "I guess the girl who'd walk over others to get what she wants hasn't left us yet. Thanks a fucking bunch, Violet."

My mouth goes dry as he grabs his bag before striding away.

Leaving the envelope on the lawn.

"Well, then," says Grayson. "How are you going to fix this one, Violet?"

An identical feeling to when Leif rejected me after the shifter visit drops into my stomach, joined by a second sicker feeling. Guilt.

But I never intended for this to happen.

"I don't know, but I will," I say.

CHAPTER 33

VIOLET

I'VE LEARNED ENOUGH about people to know that I screwed up badly. Perhaps I should've told Dorian to hold off. Maybe I believed Rowan would change his mind. And to be frank, as Dorian hasn't mentioned the Circle since our meeting, I thought he'd failed. Therefore, the request I'd made to Dorian dropped from my mind as I considered other angles to gain entry into the Circle.

In truth, I forgot.

If I explain this to Rowan, will he understand that I didn't deliberately override him?

Rowan doesn't answer my messages and so I return to the diary and throw myself back into investigative mode. The very mode that created this problem. I'll find Rowan later. Allow him to calm down, and then apologize—something that will shock him, if nothing else. And I'll speak to Dorian in order to fix the situation and arrange to rescind the invite, because there must be a solution.

I pull out Madeleine's diary and set about numbing my mind.

The diary matches the video clips for banality. Page after page describing lessons, days out, evenings out, boys Madison wants to date, boys she dates, gossip. *So much* gossip.

I compare Rowan's list, and many of the guys' names match initials in the diary. More people to investigate? There's one initial that doesn't match any of the names Rowan found: X. Names beginning with that particular letter would be unusual and easy to find—unless X is the ultimate code to hide a person?

The outdoor gatherings happen at a place initialed RK. Madison meets X at BH or occasionally inside J. Frustratingly vague. There're pages where she's scrawled through the words with a thick black marker—or someone else did, since we can't discount another found the diary before Julius. Even he could've defaced the book; we can't rule him out.

Madison details her plans for the dance over several pages, including a sketch of her dress, but no mention of a tiara. Or a date.

The most frustrating part? The last page of the diary is missing altogether. I wait until the end of the day, and corner Julius outside a classroom after lessons, demanding to know if he altered the diary in any way.

Remembering Rowan's comments about Julius's upset earlier, I gave him the list of names we'd matched to show we'd identified some of her male partners but didn't elaborate about the guy she argued with. His disappointment we'd found nothing new is palpable, but I give him no more information than we'd agreed, and he fortunately doesn't react to me as he did Rowan.

Julius believes X is a code and not a name. He doesn't know the location of the gatherings and apparently the two friends he contacted refused to tell him, claiming they never went to any. An obvious lie. I casually ask about Sergei, and if Julius knows whether the vamp and girl both survived the relationship.

He hasn't a clue about them.

Pre-Reveal, supes were banned from telling humans about our world—did that lead to Madison's demise because she broke the rule? The girls did spend time with humans. Was one Sawyer? I've researched Christopher's age, and he's old enough to match Madison's at the time.

Is he X? Or is that the mysterious guy she argued with?

A frustrated Julius told me he'd 'considered all this' and that unless I found my way into the Circle or closer to Whitegrove, I'd never find answers.

To which my mind switched straight back to Rowan. I made my excuses and left to find him.

Rowan isn't in his room or with Leif, so I have a keen idea where he may be—especially since the ominously dark clouds that threatened the day now pour rain over the academy grounds, adding an extra delight to the evening gloom.

I stride across the sodden lawns, expecting to find Rowan in the same place as the night he conjured the storm, and hinted at how potent his magic is. There's nobody in the space where Rowan stood that evening, and the prickling energy that forewarns lightning isn't in the air.

What if he's using shadows and not elemental magic?

I continue on, hoping I don't pick up on that Blackwood magic. As I pass the greenhouse, a witch light flares in the space between the glass-walled building and the shed, hovering a few inches above Rowan's hand.

Highlighting an arm wrapped with shadow.

The nausea that's followed me all day grows. *No, Rowan.*

"No cerise pink coat tonight?" I ask, harking back to the last time we met here and how something sparked.

A black jacket hood shrouds his face, and Rowan doesn't move or speak, wisps moving around his fingertips, his thick, dark magic swallowing the air.

The Rowan I met in the pink coat teased me and attempted to place himself as superior in the situation, succeeding in riling me as we verbally sparred. That Rowan smirked, but from what I can see of Rowan's face tonight, his dark expression is set in stone.

"Will you speak to me, or should I leave?" I ask.

"How did you know where to find me?" he asks flatly.

"I didn't, but last time you were pissed with me, and it rained, I found you on the edge of the playing fields. I was headed that way." I nod at him. "I thought you agreed not to use the shadows."

"And I thought we'd moved on," he says icily.

"Excuse me?" I ask as he closes the space between us, the shadows around him cooling the air further.

"I thought we'd moved past you trying to take control of my life and stomping all over my opinions and decisions."

The Circle invitation.

"We have. I've looked for you all day, Rowan. I need to talk to you."

The eyes that look down at me from beneath the hood spark silver as with his storm. "Why? For more help with your sleuthing? Are we back there again too? Using me?"

I hold his angry gaze. "To apologize."

He scoffs. "As if yours are ever sincere."

"That's highly unfair, Rowan," I retort. "If I understand that my behavior upset somebody, I apologize and mean it."

"Upset?" He leans forward, damp face closer to mine. "I damn well told you I didn't want to join the Circle and you orchestrated for the exact opposite to happen."

"I did not orchestrate anything. I asked Dorian *before* you told me."

"And did you then tell him *not* to?"

I drop my gaze. "No."

A damp hand seizes my chin and tips my face up. "What? You expected me to go along with your plans like a good boy? Accept your choice? Didn't it occur to you how angry I might get by not *getting* the choice?"

His fingers are bone cold, the shadows icy. "I made a mistake by forgetting to tell Dorian to stop, Rowan. I didn't consider the consequences."

"And what if I tell you this is the last straw for me?" His

fingers squash my cheeks. "That I now want to stay far, far away from you, Violet Blackwood."

My heart lurches. "The bond would make that difficult."

"But not impossible."

The last time I saw this much shadow around Rowan, he attacked Josef. I'm not concerned he'll attack *me,* but I'm worried that they're manifesting this strongly. There's a peculiar smell whenever shadows grow thick—sweet and heady, not the acrid scent you'd expect. Rowan no longer smells like himself. He *isn't* himself.

"I'll fix this," I whisper.

"Fix what? My unwanted invitation or the fact you've betrayed a promise to me?" he says hoarsely. "You put solving the murder of a complete stranger over what I want."

"I'm sorry, Rowan," I repeat. "I can't change what I did but—"

"You won't do it again?" He releases my face and steps back, looking down at his shadowed hands. "Perhaps I should thank you. I have what I wanted the last time we met here. I needed Blackwood help for a spell to protect myself, and now I have that."

My chest grows tighter. "You promised not to encourage the shadows, Rowan."

"Yeah, well, that was before I needed to protect myself from a powerful coven." He shakes his head. "If Whitegrove is involved in *anything* and suspects I'm your little spy, I'm dead."

"The Circle aren't dangerous."

"Oh? Secret societies led by powerful witches would never hurt anybody?" He scoffs. "Especially one protecting a secret."

"I'd never let anybody hurt you, Rowan," I say and reach out. "And I don't want you to hurt yourself because of my actions."

Rowan turns away and stomps towards the edge of the shed, forcing me to chase after him as he walks into the greenhouse, witch light guiding his way. I step into the earthy-smelling structure, navigating piled bags of soil as he moves around the benches covered in tiny pots of seedlings.

"I followed an idea that appeared logical to me. Then I forgot to stop something I put into action," I say. "I'm still learning."

"You had the chance to call Dorian off!"

"I didn't think!"

He spins back around. "Always the fucking excuses, *sweet Violet*." I back up, knocking into a bench behind as he approaches again. "If you don't see me as an equal, this between us won't work."

"You are equal," I say, "but you're also not. Because——"

"Because what?" he shouts. "Because I'm not a special hybrid?"

"Yes!"

He staggers back and yanks his hood down, giving me a clear view of his derision.

"You're equal in every other way, but you're..."

"What?" he snaps.

Mortal.

My heart dives into my mouth. What have I done?

"What am I?" he shouts.

"You can die, and I forget that!" I shout back. "I forget that you're not the same as me because so much of you *is*. I never considered the danger for you."

"And what will you do, Violet?" he asks coolly. "When I die."

"You won't die. I'll keep you safe," I say urgently. "You won't step foot inside the Circle. I promise. I'll fix this."

"No." I gasp as he grabs my shoulders and yanks me to him. "*When I die*. Next week. Next month. Decades from now. What then? Are you going to make *that* decision for me too?"

"Rowan. This is insane. This isn't you."

"But it is, Violet." He grabs my jacket and tugs me closer still. He's red-faced, skin and clothes wet from the rain as he was last time, but Rowan's beyond the witch creating storms that night.

I can blame the shadows for his behavior, but the reality is I'm looking at the Rowan he told me existed before we bonded. The

242

one whose magic Leif needed to interfere with and stop Rowan from going too far.

My magic found this dark Rowan and encouraged him.

"You've thrown me into a dangerous situation. *I'm* choosing how to deal with this. If I need my darkness, I'll use it. The shadows worked against Josef Petrescu. They'll work against mortal witches."

I swallow hard. "Rowan, please."

The rain soaked through his hood and dampened his hair, which he shakes from his face as he stares at me. "I chose to hold back because of you. Partly because you still frightened me, and I worried about the consequences if I overstepped the mark. I once told you that we'd be strong together and tonight, I realized the opposite. You've weakened me."

"Your magic doesn't look weak to me."

"No. You weakened *me*." My hips press into the bench as he edges closer and brings the darkness with him. "I won't be him anymore, Violet."

His damp chest presses against my soaked sweater, as he places palms on the bench either side of me. "Is this really about the Circle?" I ask, breaths quickening, this different Rowan unsettling me to the point of fear. Not for myself—fear that I'll need to retaliate and hurt him.

"Your actions are the catalyst. I've had enough of the obsessed Rowan who thinks of you before himself all the time." He holds his face closer. "Why should I deny what I am and what I can do?"

My throat bobs. "I never asked or expected you to."

Rowan scoffs again, then slides a hand along my face, fingers spread across my cheek as he holds the back of my head. "Do you feel the difference, Violet?"

Too much. The power around Rowan flares as he touches me, and my heart shudders as my magic courses to his fingertips.

"I want your darkness, Violet. I want you to accept mine." His lips touch my mouth as he says the words, and I can taste that shadowed place, the danger running between us. Rowan's restraint has filled a pool of darkness inside him, and I've smashed through the wall of the dam holding that magic in.

Like meets like.

I'm capable of pushing Rowan away, fighting as we did before, but there's a delicious attraction to his power, the magic from his fingertips tripping along my skin. Through my blood. My bones. My very soul.

The physical ache that Rowan's touch causes has never been satisfied, and right now that ache overwhelms me. Sexual desire for Rowan is another 'something' to deal with, and I'd put his restraint down to awkwardness. I'd welcomed the avoidance and held back too, even after our conversation in his room.

The Rowan whose body touches mine now, the furious desire in his eyes as his magic pulses between us, isn't that guy. Yes, Rowan has kissed me in a way that brought me to the heady center of where our magic converges and pulled me towards tasting the power he suppresses, and I've loved those moments more than the gentler ones.

But we've always stopped.

"Will you accept who I am?" he says, voice harsh. "That I'll go as far with my magic as *I* want. Because I'm not holding back from you anymore, Violet."

His other hand moves to press fingers into the small of my back, nudging my knees apart until he's between them. Our breaths mingle as he waits for my answer, stroking a cheek with his thumb.

"You're not only talking about magic, are you?" I say and move my face closer, the charged space between our lips shrinking. "Are you, Rowan?"

He mutters something under his breath and grips my hair with his other hand, tugs my head back, and kisses me the way I like. His lips are firm, frustration pouring from him, as he delves his tongue deeper into my mouth. Rowan presses me against the bench, and I steady myself with a hand behind, knocking seedlings to the floor.

Rowan's face is damp against mine, and he tastes of the shadows that wind us together, his kiss and touch harsher than ever. I can't move from the grip on my hair, shocked at how I don't care because I want to dig into the place that holds the real Rowan and sink myself deep.

My hair winds further around Rowan's hand, a demand not to move, and as his damp body warms mine, his magic isn't what fills my veins. The white-hot heat that burns through is the desire I shy away from, even though I want him.

That aching desire overtakes me, but as soon as I put my hands on Rowan, he pauses, breathing against my mouth, saying nothing. He releases my hair and my scalp tingles to match my lips.

Sucking in a breath, Rowan pushes himself away from the bench again and wipes water from his face. I reach out. "Rowan."

He stares at my mouth, quiet, listening to my breathing. Then he makes to walk away.

"Rowan!" I snatch his arm, touching the shadows clouding around.

Rowan looks down at my hand, then slowly his eyes meet mine. "The night of Kai's eighteenth. Do you know how fucking rejected I felt? How pissed I was at myself for not telling you that I wanted you to stay the night? You didn't even speak to me about it."

"I avoided discussing the situation," I admit.

"Why? We were closer. Hell, we even went on dates recently. Spent time together and actually enjoyed ourselves. I wouldn't have pressured you but at least we could've *talked* about it. We've been alone enough for you to know I'd never do anything you didn't want. I get that you're not normal about all this relationship shit, but did you never consider I'd be happy just to have you there, with me? To sleep with you—hold you, wake up with you beside me?"

"And do you really think that's all that would've occurred?" I ask stiffly.

245

Rowan steps forward again. "Yeah. Actually, I did, because you're not interested in anything else. Which I respect. That's why I'm walking away now."

I push wet hair from my face too. "Perhaps we need to discuss the subject now. I feel there are still misunderstandings."

He drags fingers through his hair as he looks at me. "I'm not in the mood for talking. I'm too pissed with you right now."

But pissed isn't the energy coming from him—or me.

With a shake of his head, Rowan drags his arm from my hold and walks away.

CHAPTER 34

Broken.

I stare at a ceramic pot and the seedling struggling through the earth, seconds away from picking up the item and throwing it to the ground besides the ones that fell. Throwing them all to the ground.

I've broken a promise. I've broken us.

I've broken Rowan.

Tipping back my head, I take in a lungful of the damp, earthy air and focus on staying calm. At every turn, I face assault. I'm attacked by emotions each day, fighting not against but to understand them. To allow myself to experience and work through the effect they have. Dorian insists staying dead inside helps. I can't do that, and my inability to control the changes that I deny are happening makes everything worse.

I dig my fingers into a bag of soil, cool and dry as I squeeze, heart banging in my chest. Why can't I understand the world better? See things as more than black or white? I didn't deliberately ignore Rowan, but the importance skimmed over my head. And when Dorian never mentioned the Circle again, I dropped the plan.

I've broken something fragile, and the consequences could spread far if I don't fix this.

Wiping the dirt onto my damp sweater, I shoot back across the lawns towards the academy, ignoring curious looks as I trail water behind me walking along the main hallways. Rowan left his own muddy footsteps and I follow them towards Pendle House. To his room.

I knock on Rowan's door with a damp fist.

Nothing.

"Rowan," I call, calmly.

No response.

He's definitely in there, and Rowan will know that I'm aware. I place a hand on the wood, ready to absorb and identify any magic, bracing myself for the possibility he's taken things further with his shadows. But there's nothing apart from the faint barrier that repels people he doesn't want to visit him. One that would never affect me.

"Don't you want to hear Violet Blackwood tell you she was wrong?"

The door swings open as Rowan yanks at it. "You already did. And apologized. Such an honor."

With a huff, I slam a palm into his chest, and he stumbles back. I turn and carefully, quietly, close the door, before looking to him again. No shadows, just a pissed looking, tired guy, his towel-dried hair wilder than usual. He's no longer wearing his sodden jacket and replaced his T-shirt with a dry one.

"What do you want?" he asks tersely.

"To sleep in your bed."

Rowan's jaw slackens, and I suspect that wasn't on his list of expected responses. "What?"

"To sleep in your bed," I repeat.

He continues to stare. "Violet. I shouldn't have said what I did about the night of Kai's birthday. I realize how crap that sounded now."

"No. I'm glad you did." I move closer.

"Then this isn't kissing me to stop an argument," he says, eyes darker again. "What you've done... The problem isn't only about the Circle, but how you continue to treat me like an extension of yourself."

I walk towards Rowan who freezes as if the non-existent shadows were here and holding him.

"And in response to your question earlier, I accept your darkness, but as long as I see you using shadows, I will never share mine."

A familiar energy shudders through Rowan, his eyes switching to those darker ones I've begun to recognize. "You're coming to me when I'm shadowed, Violet. That's pulled you to me."

I place a hand on his chest, Rowan's heart beating faster against my palm. "No, I'm coming to you because I want you to hear this. You are not just someone I use. I do not only see you as my bonded witch, and I hate that you hold back who you are. From the first day, what's in you recognized what's in me. And I saw him tonight. The one you hide. The Rowan that Violet wants. The equal." I tiptoe to meet him eye to eye. "You want all of me? To take the risk from what our union would mean? Here I am. I want the same but if I share all of myself with you, this will change everything."

"Yeah. That's normally what happens," he says, voice hoarser.

"I don't think normal applies here. You're bonded to a hybrid, and we've already experienced the intensity that happens when our magic joins. We don't know what might happen if *we* join."

My body presses to his, sweater soaking his fresh T-shirt. "Not what I expected, Violet," he says quietly, smoothing wet hair from my face. His eyes glint, the steel blue darkening, but not due to magic.

"I met a different guy in the greenhouse."

"And you're a very different girl, sweet Violet."

"Then maybe you should kiss me before I change my mind."

His restraint trembles through his fingers against my cheek. "You know I love you, Violet, but are you sure you—"

I grab Rowan's hair and pull his head towards mine, close my mouth around his and kiss him, smothering his words. Rowan draws me closer to him, and his lips move against mine, until he tenses and his warm breath hovers against my mouth as he stops.

In frustration, I tug his lip between my teeth and bite, careful not to break the skin. He winces and makes a sound low in his throat before thrusting his tongue into my mouth. Lips hardening into a devouring kiss to match the one in the greenhouse, Rowan keeps a tight hold and backs me against his door.

Rowan's kiss sends lightning dancing down my spine, electrifying every nerve in a storm of sensation that overwhelms me as his lean body presses against mine.

Something inside urges me to do this, to unite the last part of myself with him. But this isn't the shadows whispering. This is me. I'm at the edge of a chasm I've stared across many times with Rowan, too scared to jump. If I missed and fell, how much would I lose? And if I reach the other side, what am I leaving behind?

If I take this step with Rowan, the consequences won't only change what's between us on a physical and romantic level. The bond will tighten to the point that my need to protect will take a different turn: I could never let death take Rowan away from me and I could never die with him.

CHAPTER 35

LEIF

I LEARNED to shut down shortly after Dad died. At four years old, I'd no understanding of grief stages and spent a hell of a lot of time in denial. He worked away several months of the year, so I pretended Dad took a longer trip than usual. Mum never remarried and struggled, so as I grew older I misguidedly tried to be the adult to look after her, hiding behind the responsibility this gave me. Mum then struggled a second time because she'd allowed this to happen. I'm not a talker, but Mum forced me to therapy sessions with her and I kinda understand now. I also made sure I talked a lot so I could end the sessions as soon as possible.

The meeting with the elders pulled me back into the tsunami I'd weathered as a young kid, my reality taken from me as I'm drowned until everything's numb. Rowan told me to speak to Mum, but I can't face that. I'm scared the numbness will break and become accusations and anger, but more than that, I'm frightened that Mum can't tell me the elders are wrong.

I don't remember Dad well, only that he seemed like a giant

compared to Mum and that when he hugged me, I lost all my breath. I do remember the love in the house and also the whispered conversations that stopped the moment my parents saw me. I've always known Dad was a shifter but not what type —he didn't say much about that side of himself, neither did Mum after he passed. Was he Tigris? An elder?

I'm not the only half-shifter in the world, just like there're plenty of half-witches, but when I hit my teen years, I began to panic. I'd lived a human life and didn't want to shift. I researched and spoke to people to reach a conclusion—human hybrid shifters don't take on their parent's form.

Then why did I sense changes a couple of years ago? I'm physically stronger despite not playing sport or working out, and my eyes switched to the amber color I try to hide. In my early days at Thornwood, I blended in, average kid in every way, but as soon as I hit sixteen, everyone saw I'm 'different'. The bullying stopped at the academy but began in town—from shifters, and later by elders.

That's when years of Rowan and me protecting each other stepped up a notch and he swore he'd find a spell to get me away. Far, far away, and magically protected.

But the physical changes aren't all that's different; Violet pointed out something else. I can influence Rowan when he loses himself to the darker side he pursues to protect himself. I sense how Rowan feels sometimes, I know when he's going downhill, but that could be eight years as best friends. Now, I wish she'd never mentioned Tigris abilities match what I experience, because that awareness around Rowan is evidence to support the elders' claims.

And now more niggles—Dad worked as a nurse, but why did that take him away from us when he could find a job at the local hospital? When old enough to understand, Mum told me he left the pack behind as the elders couldn't accept their relationship, which was not a unique situation either. Had he not broken all connections and that's where Dad went for weeks at a time? My Dad, the Tigris elder.

What the fuck do I do? Even thinking about the situation tightens my chest and leaks fear into my veins. The elders won't let this go— I'm lucky they let *me* go. For now. I want to believe that Ethan can help, and that solving this confusing mess about deeds and ownership might change the situation. So that's what I'll hang onto.

That and this 'consort' thing. Sure, Rowan explained how the situation is normal to witch society, but I'm not a witch. Violet's revelation blew apart my theory that she kept a distance between us *because* I'm not a witch, or a full supe.

At least the revelations opened up other truths—Violet finally putting into words how she feels about me. Opening up. She still can't see the irony—the most outspoken, no-nonsense girl couldn't tell me until I forced her to. Or did she honestly think I just 'knew'?

I'd reached the point that I decided to give up on Violet and her inability to understand how I felt, or for her to at least explain what was between us. I couldn't deal with the confusion or see-saw of emotions. But I also couldn't stay away.

Now? I know the love I have for Violet isn't misplaced. The unexpected and mind-blowing kisses aren't what I needed from Violet. The truth I'd hoped for but never really expected, her explaining how she cared about me, that she *thought* about me meant more.

Who am I kidding? I've replayed those moments in her room a thousand times in my mind. I'd tasted her lips once before, a move I thought would push her away forever, but to *really* kiss Violet... that's something else.

Every touch and taste intensified Violet's power over me, but in a way I never expected. My world smashed apart earlier that day, but with Violet I didn't care that I'm standing in the ruins of my old life, only that she was with me, in my arms.

There's no witch bond. No mutual desire for blood. But I've

found a place in her heart, and she'll always be a part of mine. I shake my head at myself. Violet isn't the only one who scoffed at romantic words, and I never understood how people could think or say these things.

But then I've never opened up enough to love anybody. That's the bond we have.

My stomach churns as I sit in the half-empty academy cafeteria, not touching the fries and energy drink that I bought myself for lunch. Nobody speaks to me apart from a quick hello, and the room fills with chatter from students around tables, which I filter out.

I've avoided time alone since the revelations, not wanting thoughts to seep through in the quiet moments like this, but today I can't find Rowan or Violet. Now, I'm worried. Rowan lost his shit big time yesterday, refused to speak to me most of the day, which the moody git does sometimes.

I'm suspicious why he visited my room briefly, saying little, but wandering around, edgy. Rowan wasn't pacing—the guy wants his stone back, because the moment I implied that's the reason for his visit Rowan abruptly left.

That's concerning.

Can Rowan and Violet hurt each other? I'm learning more each day about Violet's 'state' and how a powerful witch like Rowan can match her unless she's an unleashed hybrid, where her two sides joined together can overwhelm anybody. What if Rowan managed a spell she couldn't resist *before* she could defend herself? Because he's met her magic with magic of his own before and not lost against the hybrid.

If they fought, one or both might get hurt and unless Rowan's feeding his darker magic, I'd lay bets one hundred percent that the guy would lose. But they're bonded, right? The pair can't intentionally harm each other.

I laugh to myself. There I go again, protective Leif, worrying about the delicate girl he loves, who's anything but fragile.

Someone takes the seat opposite me at the table, and Rowan

reaches out to steal one of my fries. I slant my head. He's in uniform, different from the pale guy and his black mood from yesterday, although he looks tired.

"I've tried to contact you all morning," I say. "Where were you?"

He eats, then reaches for a second fry. "Phone was off."

"And Violet?" I scan what I can see of him outside of his uniform. No visible injuries. "Have you seen her?"

Rowan lifts his eyes to mine. "Yeah."

"Vague. Everything okay? You talked things through with Violet?" I scratch my cheek. "You don't look as mad today."

"Yeah."

I pull the plate back so he can't reach my lunch when he attempts to take more. "Is everything okay?" I repeat.

"Violet apologized. Explained. Violet made a mistake, but she understands why I reacted the way I did."

"Because when you lose your shit, magic takes over?" I look at him pointedly. "Your brain stops functioning and you turn into an unreasonable asshole."

His mouth drops open. "Wow. That's harsh."

I eat a fry. "But true."

Rowan looks around the cafeteria, then lowers his voice. "I was straight with her about a few things."

"You *did* fight," I say and groan.

"And resolved some issues." He pulls on his bottom lip. "I've hidden part of myself from Violet."

"That, I know," I reply. "The side that came looking for the Willowbrook stone last night?"

His steel eyes don't leave mine. "Or rather, Violet couldn't see that side because she's too caught up in herself. I've tried to explain several times what I am, and she's finally listened."

"How? What the hell did you do to her?"

I've explained Rowan's past to Violet before, and his ambitions, but the spell we searched for hasn't interested him lately, which unsettles me. Rowan might've found something else that he's hiding from Violet, created by her. He *is* attracted to dark things—obviously.

"We did fight, but we didn't hurt each other." He pauses. "I also told her how I felt about the Kai's party 'thing'."

Ah. That. The story he shared at the pub the other night, about Violet's decision not to stay with him overnight. I joked she'd probably have told him to sleep on the floor anyway, but he ignored me. Rowan always rambles after a few beers and at least his griping distracted me from my hellish day. In the end, I shut him up by reminding him at least he got close enough to Violet to *feel* rejected.

But I understand. Violet never even discussed Holly's idea with him and made presumptions about his thoughts and feelings—the crux of their issues.

I'm distracted by Holly across the cafeteria. Or rather distracted by how she's walking purposefully over, head high. Without looking at me, she pivots to face Rowan. "Where's Violet?"

Rowan's mouth tightens at her accusatory tone. Holly doesn't *not* like Rowan, but as with her and Violet, Holly and Rowan are opposites. His reputation as the odd witch who few people speak to because he's dodgy doesn't help. And I bet Marci told her some stories.

"You're looking for Violet? She's in the library, I expect," he replies.

"I heard that you and Violet argued and then someone saw you in a weird mood walking around in the rain," she continues.

"According to you, I'm always in a weird mood," he replies. "Do you honestly think I could do anything to Violet? We're bonded witches. Kinda goes against that to hurt her."

"Well, you upset Violet, because she never came back to the room last night." She looks between me and Rowan. "Or is she in Scotland? Has something happened?"

"No. She was with me." Rowan leans back against the wooden seat and crosses his arms. "All night."

Holly stares in a way I can only describe as gob-smacked, something I share right now. "Where?" she whispers.

"In my room. Obviously."

His challenging look remains and if I was eating right now, I'd choke.

Holly studies him closely. "In your room?"

"Yes."

"All night?"

"All night."

Her eyes grow to the size of saucers.

Whoa. "In your bed?" I ask and he shoots me a look. "Sorry, but you have whined at me about this a few times."

"I'm not discussing last night. I'd rather Violet didn't break my face," he says.

"Well, I hope you're not discussing it with Leif."

"Again, my face looks better without a broken nose, Holly." Rowan drags a hand through his hair. "Like I said, check the library."

Holly hesitates, hovering around, as if she can't leave us in case Rowan does or says something wrong.

"Interesting," Holly says stiffly when she finally speaks.

Then walks away.

I arch a brow at Rowan. "'Resolved some issues'?"

Rowan sighs. "I'm still not discussing last night."

"Yeah, but you're not telling me that I've presumed wrong." I chuckle and shove him in the shoulder. "As if I'm going to ask sordid questions. Just hope you had a good night."

"I love her, Leif," he says earnestly. "You know that."

Yes. But... How do I broach this? "And the bond... nothing weird happened? I'm only asking because the Blackwood influence on you worries me."

Rowan rubs two fingers across his lips and doesn't reply for a moment. "How many times? I'm choosing not to say anything and being respectful to Violet."

"And?"

257

"What *happened*, Leif, is everything changed." He pauses. "Take that answer however you want."

There *is* something about Rowan today. Not the better mood, which there's a clear explanation for, but the edge to him. I've sensed this build around Rowan in the past, usually before the magic simmering beneath his calm exterior erupts. He isn't pissed with Violet anymore, so that isn't the reason. If they did sleep together in more than a 'sleep together' way, has Rowan absorbed more Blackwood darkness?

"And you?" Rowan asks. "Are you meeting with Ethan today, as planned?"

I swallow. "Nice swerve, Rowan. Yeah. Ethan wants to speak to Mum."

"You didn't want to see her," Rowan says cautiously.

"There's a lot I don't want. But I do need answers." I rub a hand down my face. "Even if I don't want to hear them."

Rowan's stiff attitude softens. "Sorry, Leif." I shrug. "We've all got your back, you know that?"

I smile. "Yeah. Since I'm a member of the consort club."

Rowan steals my last fry. "But not a full member."

We both know exactly what *that* means. He fights a smile at my stunned look—one which immediately slides from his face as he looks behind me.

"Rowan. I hope you are not discussing last night's events with Leif."

That's what wiped his smirk away. I tip my head back to look at Violet. "Afternoon, Violet."

"No, we're discussing Leif's upcoming visit to his Mum with Ethan," replies Rowan hastily.

"Did you hear from Annabelle again yet?" Violet crosses her arms, eyes darting between us in suspicion.

"Meeting arranged. Tomorrow. Will you be back by then, Leif?" asks Rowan.

"Probably not."

"Violet Blackwood!" Holly's voice carries across the room as the curly-haired, flushed girl marches up to Violet, lips pursed.

"Ugh. Not again." Rowan stands. "I need a coffee. Violet?"

But she's not listening, instead Violet is in an odd eyeballing standoff with Holly. Holly breaks the gaze to watch Rowan walk to the long counter and join the queueing students. "I had no idea where you were last night, and I worried." She meets Violet's eyes again.

"I was with Rowan. Building furniture. Now, if you'll excuse me, I'd like my coffee."

Huh? Doing what, now?

What's odder—her response to Holly or that she takes hold of Rowan's hand and doesn't respond negatively when he kisses the top of her head.

"Violet's changed," says Holly, half to herself.

"Yeah. Everything's changed." I crack open my can and take a long drink. "Everything."

CHAPTER 36

VIOLET

Everything's changed, but no longer broken.

The world remains a confusing place, as do people, but the four I've met and allowed myself to trust do help. Rowan, Grayson, Leif, and Holly—infinitely patient and good people. They're helping me decipher the code that is this world—pause and think before speaking, attempt empathy when appropriate. Think of others 'feelings'. Although, I can *not* drop my opinion that if people can't communicate how they feel in a direct, verbal way, they can't blame me for responding inappropriately.

Therefore, I continue to say the wrong thing, especially to strangers, and unless I become a mute that's unlikely to change. Social cues escape me too, and I will never understand why people speak in riddles or expect me to read nuances.

I'm still Violet Blackwood, half-vampire, half-witch, but now with a fondness for four people who've shown me I'm not dead inside. Just a little dark around the edges.

Like Rowan is. He worries me. Leif mentioned his temper and I've seen this in increasing intensity, notably two days ago. I accept what Rowan is now—that we're bonded and alike, but *not* the same. Those similarities scare me too, but I finally understood the need to replace the shadows I give him with myself instead, and to show Rowan how I can't hide from *any* part of what I am.

And to be frank, the curiosity and increasing frustration saw me walk into the arms and bed of the guy I love. *Love.* At least that's not a minefield now we've reached an informal agreement of what constitutes our individual understanding of the emotion. Although, Rowan did comment that I'm overthinking still, based on that sentence alone.

Holly's correct that intimate matters are more than parts joining, but I already knew that. If I didn't possess the emotional intimacy with Rowan, regardless of a witch bond, I would never want to jump that chasm. We'd had some more minor intimate moments before last night and only now do I understand what Rowan meant about not holding back anymore. He was *not* only talking about magic.

The guy who had part of me, and sees the Violet nobody else has so far, now has all of me.

Things aren't easy for the others. Leif remains in limbo, unsure whether he'll need to run as he planned the first time we spoke. He's still with Ethan at his mother's, something my father will find uncomfortable, as she's human and they're intimidated by his appearance.

I spoke to Leif last night, and he flatly told me the elders weren't lying. Leif's father was a Tigris elder, but she knew nothing about the deeds or land. His father shielded her from shifters once he made the decision to leave. Again, that odd tugging sensation in my chest grew along with an itching need to fix this.

And Grayson. He spends each day wondering when Josef will catch up with him again. When. Not if. I've nothing to say that can reassure him because I won't lie. Still, I'm an apparent distraction to the guy, who's not letting me forget that for a moment. The emotions of his I sense are stronger than before, as is the physical longing, not helped by the blood inside me wanting to join with his.

He's truthful about not wanting the full blood-bond, but when Dorian discovers our tryst, will he believe Grayson? Highly doubtful.

Dorian. Today we'll gather evidence that I can present to Dorian and query how *his* investigation is progressing. From the start, I've felt a certainty in the core of me that the tiara links into the puzzle somewhere. And activities in the academy? Is that linked to Josef's group, the tiara, or the necromancer witches? Because I'm not entirely sure the two factions are working together, which could either help or hinder Dorian.

Please let today and our rendezvous with Annabelle bring us a step forward.

I sit on the park bench beside Rowan, beneath the boughs of an oak tree and scrutinize the faces of passers-by—a little too intently because one or two of the joggers speed up and an elderly couple pick up their clipped white poodle and veer away.

Our legs touch and Rowan holds my hand, and there's a strange calmness about him I've never sensed before. Quite the opposite to how he usually is—and a world away from the guy who flipped out in the greenhouse last night. The pull to him became tighter, the invisible thread holding us together shorter. For once, magic never entered the equation.

"How clandestine," I comment to Rowan and gesture at our unusual meeting place.

"And public," he reminds me, then points at a large pond nearby where I've absentmindedly watched ducks attract children's attention. "Maybe we should've brought bread?"

I blink. Mind reading? "Bread is actually harmful to ducks and feeding them the foodstuff should be discouraged."

"Um. Okay." He shakes his head. "I bet you never fed ducks in a human park as a kid. Far too normal."

A small girl whose mother grabs her arm as she veers too

close to the water triggers an odd memory. "I did. At least once, but I caused trouble and Ethan carried me away from the scene."

"Necromancy?" he asks, not as quietly as he should.

"Not on those particular ducks, no. I left the reanimated ones on the island when we left."

"Right." Rowan elongates the word and takes my hand. "I can't imagine you feeding ducks."

"I didn't. I tried to steal them."

A laugh bursts from him. "Steal? Best you don't approach these ones."

"I believe I may be conspicuous if I did, and Annabelle evidently desires the opposite."

A woman walking alone catches my attention. Most who've passed without a dog or pushchair attached to their hands were joggers, and few travelled alone. This slender woman walks, even though dressed in sports gear—tight black leggings and a snug blue and black jacket, a baseball cap pulled low on her face, and sunglasses.

"Somebody doesn't want recognizing," I say and point. She halts when she spots us, standing stock still at the edge of the graveled path that runs between the benches and pond, before pulling a phone from a jacket pocket and turning her back on us.

Rowan's own phone sounds with a message alert and he looks down. "I told you Annabelle wouldn't like you coming with me."

> we're supposed to meet alone

I sigh and take the phone from Rowan

> you're both safer with me here

Annabelle now stands beside a group of mothers watching their offspring, her attire aiding her with blending in.

why? who followed?

who knows?

"That's not helpful, Violet." Rowan takes the phone.

"Is Grayson nearby?" I ask.

"Yeah, he's at the trees at the edge of the park." Rowan points. "Well, in a tree."

"Which won't look odd in the slightest to anybody who sees him," I mutter.

"Nobody will. He's a predator, remember?" I meet Rowan's eyes, surprised how pointed the comment is. "Grayson stays hidden until he's ready."

Another message appears.

I'll leave what I have in the trash can by the car park

no, we want to talk to you

I jump to my feet as Rowan types the message, ready to pursue Annabelle as she hurries away.

"You should've stayed hidden too, Violet," says Rowan tersely. "Come on."

"I don't like climbing trees," I inform him as I follow.

We tail Annabelle at a short distance, and I dart a look around in case she's worrying for a valid reason, and a supe followed. Did she choose to wear joggers for a fast getaway? "What type of witch is Annabelle?" I ask Rowan.

"I never asked. She can't be practicing, or I would know the name." Our shoes scuff across the gravel as we speed up, although I'm careful not to reach my personal speed.

Besides the railings surrounding the car park, food packaging and plastic bottles fill a tall metal trash can to the brim. As Annabelle passes, she pulls something from inside her jacket and drops it on the top without pausing, then begins to jog towards the cars.

"Annabelle can't leave!" I protest. "Grab whatever she left in the trash, and I'll stop her!"

I'm perfectly aware my appearance doesn't help in my decision to pursue Annabelle—the weird looking Goth girl stalking the ordinary human mum. Rowan's equally aware and catches me by the arm before I get far, the pair of us positioned between two family size cars with a view to our mark.

"No way will Annabelle talk to you if you accost her, Violet. Something obviously worries her. Don't make things worse." I remain at Rowan's side and rest against the red car as Annabelle approaches a silver minivan favored by humans who have a collection of offspring. I could easily pull away and chase Annabelle, but grit my teeth and accept Rowan's decision.

"What did Annabelle leave in the trash?" I ask.

Rowan holds an A4 brown envelope in his hand, and he guides me away with his other, back towards the bench. Annabelle's already driving towards the car park exit, and I'm itching to follow the car containing someone filled with information. But, as I promised him, I consider Rowan's opinions on what to do. I understand—Annabelle's scared of someone, or something related to the tiara murder.

We walk back to where Grayson now sits on the back of the bench, his boots on the seat, watching the ducks. His head turns before any normal person would know someone approached, but he doesn't move or speak until we reach him.

"Where is she?" he asks, eyes going to the envelope.

"Violet scared her away."

Grayson's eyes roll. "Violet... what did you say to her?"

"Nothing! I never had the chance," I retort.

He takes a slow look the length of me. "Next time you insist on meeting scared witnesses in public, borrow Holly's clothes again?"

"I am not physically overbearing, and hardly imposing to humans," I reply.

"Yeah, but the black and your accompanying death stares don't help the aura you give off to people. Annabelle—or those watching her—would know straightaway who you are."

"Too late now anyway," I grumble and take the envelope from Rowan. "Annabelle left and we don't know where she lives. Rowan can't find an address."

"Yet," he puts in. "At least we have something. Hopefully."

Grayson slants his head. "I took a look at Annabelle's car. There're two stickers in the rear window. One for a local soccer team and one for a school. She also has a clipboard on the front seat. And a pile of those things that kids wear over their shirts when playing sport. I reckon she's involved with the team."

My mouth parts. "I'm impressed with your detective skills, Grayson. You're improving."

"Yeah. Nobody lost any internal organs," says Rowan. "Good improvement." Grayson scowls at him.

Ignoring them, I sit on the bench and tip the contents of the envelope onto my lap. Torn pages with lines and writing that match Madison's diary, and one piece of paper folded into a small square, which I unfold.

This isn't over until I say, Maddy. You don't get to screw around with me, then kick me aside for that pathetic asshole. I took care of you because I love you. I don't understand why you accused me of suffocating you, when all I wanted to do was keep you safe. You stopped answering your phone, and I worried, that's why I followed. I apologized for what I did and swore that would never happen again, but you won't speak to me. Now you're avoiding me. After everything I've done for you, you're an ungrateful bitch. I'm warning you that if you stay with him and humiliate me there'll be consequences.
I'll be at the dance on Saturday and you will be too—wearing what I gave you.

You don't want me to keep you safe anymore? Fine, but if you don't stop this, you'll need keeping safe from me. I've told you what I could do to you if you try to leave me.
Yours forever, V

I raise both brows and shove the paper at Rowan. "Well, he sounds like a thoroughly unpleasant individual. Exactly the type of male who deserves to be castrated."

Rowan frowns as he reads. "This is incriminating to whoever V is, if he's still around."

"Show me." Grayson holds out a hand and as he takes in the letter, I pull out the missing page from the diary.

If you have this, Vik won.
Hopefully I stopped the worst.
I warded the jewelry because I know he'll try to destroy it. He can't. Please, please keep your promise not to tell anyone what you know. THEY will come after you too. THEY will protect him and I don't want anybody else to die. Just wait. One day someone will find what I wore and know what happened. Vik can't hide forever. The whole fucking family needs taking down and I wish I could be there to see that happen.
I love you both, M

Rowan goes completely still and his hand shakes slightly as he takes the scrawled page from me.

"Is X actually Vik?" I ask him. "Is there a Vik Whitegrove? Or in the Circle? I bet he gave her the Whitegrove tiara to wear!"

"There was never a V referenced in her diary or the name used even once on the video clips. I'll go back through Circle records, but I don't recognize the name and it's not a typical one. "

"We have a name though!" I take a steady breath. "I know you don't like my normal response to unpleasant findings, but this is amazing."

Rowan chokes. "Not really. Someone likely connected to a

senior Circle member might've killed a girl, and they covered this up for years."

"And they won't get away with murder any longer," I say in triumph.

"Won't they?" Rowan shakes his head. "You told me Dorian doesn't care about random murders from thirty years ago. If this isn't linked to whoever's plotting against Dorian, or to Sawyer and necromancers, he won't do anything, Violet."

"But that's wrong," I blurt.

"Haven't you always said Dorian Blackwood lives by his own definitions of right and wrong?" says Grayson quietly.

I shove the papers at Rowan and grit my teeth.

"Exactly," says Rowan. "The famous Blackwood justice."

I smile slowly at him. "And I'm a Blackwood and capable of dealing justice of my own, with or without my father. The world already knows that."

CHAPTER 37

GRAYSON

"I STILL BELIEVE LOITERING around the clubhouse is as conspicuous as standing on the side-lines." Violet gestures across the tarmac space between the playing fields a few hundred meters away and the wooden bench where we sit and wait for Rowan.

Rowan made a pointed comment how 'a couple of weird Goth kids' hanging around a kid's soccer training match would look strange, to which I retorted better that than they know I'm a blood-drinking vampire.

But it makes sense to keep Violet out of view after Annabelle's freak out earlier.

Rowan stands beside a group of parents who're enthusiastically cheering on their kids as they play. They're young—pre-teen—and a mix of boys and girls, some in red bibs over their shirts, others in blue. He's out of Annabelle's sight, the pony tailed woman now without her baseball cap and with a whistle around her neck that she uses for the fourth time.

Violet cringes. "If somebody blew a whistle at me, I'd punch them."

"Yeah, the tone isn't great on our hearing sensitivity."

"Neither is the human spawns' combined cacophony," she remarks.

I frown as I unpick her words. "You mean the soccer players?"

"High pitched shrieking voices and too much shouting." She wrinkles her nose and gestures at the kids enjoying their day beneath a cloudless sky. "Worse than the hospital. Let's hope this excursion is worth our time and Annabelle speaks to us."

"Mmm."

"And that she confirms Vik is the witch concerned and elaborates who he is and the events hinted at in the letter," she continues.

"Right."

She turns to look at me. "Are you paying attention, Grayson?"

No. I'm suffering from constant replays of Violet's lips against mine, how the girl who wouldn't let me near pressed herself to my naked chest, surrounding me with her blood scent as I tasted the sweetness I've craved.

But best I don't say that.

I barely touched Violet's skin but still discovered the hard-edged girl is impossibly soft on the outside; softer than anyone I've touched before. My obsession with Violet took over my life too much before, and I'm a fully crazed fanatic now.

"Are you listening, Grayson?" she repeats.

I stare at her lips. "Mostly."

"I do recognize that look, by the way," she tells me. "I'm learning male body language extremely well."

Unable to resist, I slide my long fingers across her cheek to cup the back of Violet's head and move my face closer to those tempting lips. "Kiss me."

"Good grief." Her small hand comes between us and not-so-lightly pushes at my chest. "I will *not* be one of those girls who subject others to public displays of physical desire."

I run my finger along Violet's nose. "Although I'm

disappointed, I do like that you mentioned physical desire. Maybe a less public display later?"

Violet's eyes slide ever so briefly to my lips. "Meaning?"

"Alone."

"Depends how busy I am," she says. "Now stop distracting me."

I splutter in amusement, but what else did I expect from hitting on Violet when she's mid-investigation mode?

"Look." Violet points at where Annabelle strides towards Rowan, barely pausing but clearly speaking to him as she continues walking away from the soccer pitch, Rowan at her heels.

"I'll get the water," she shouts over her shoulder and heads towards the opposite end of the building we're loitering outside.

Rowan wanders after her, and Violet's on her feet in a heartbeat.

Sidling along the wall, we find and pass through an open door into a small office-like room with a kitchen attached, where notices are attached to cream painted brick. The smell of rubbery balls and stale sweat isn't the nicest, but something's worse—we can't see Annabelle.

As I'm the last to enter, the door slams behind me and I spin back around. Annabelle leans against the wood, looking between the three of us with undisguised fury.

"Are you trying to get me killed?" she snaps, her accent clipped and refined, unlike the local one.

"By who?" asks Violet. "Vik? Or is he dead?"

Her brown eyes go wide. "Wow."

"Speak to us about Madison and Vik and we'll leave," says Violet.

Annabelle steps forward, the woman tall enough to look down on Violet. "No. *You* leave. Now. I've handed over what I have."

Violet's lips thin at her response. "I shall leave when I'm ready."

The woman's eyes narrow before she turns to go—not that she gets far since the door handle becomes too hot to touch. I look between Violet and Rowan. Which one did that? Annabelle swears and rubs the palm of her right hand with the other thumb.

"Speak to us about Madison and Vik and *you* can leave," corrects Violet.

Annabelle glares at each of us. "I don't live in witch society anymore," she says through gritted teeth. "I want my family left out of that world. *I* want to keep things that way."

"And we shan't bother you again after today," says Violet. "If you want to catch Madison's killer, speak to us."

Annabelle leans against the door again. "I'm only doing this for Maddy because I now know that your family—" she points at Violet "—have some chance of catching the bastard."

"I will," she says. "Despite a reputation to the contrary, I'm anti-violence and murder. Well, anti-murder involving innocent people."

"Such as girls bullied by abusive, controlling assholes?" asks Annabelle, then shakes her head. "I'm sure you got that much from the letter he wrote her."

"Yes, thanks for giving the papers to us," puts in Rowan. "That helps."

As does his more diplomatic words and tone because Annabelle's riled by Violet, cheeks pinker by the second.

"What was Vik threatening to do?" asks Violet. "Is Madison dead?"

"Yes. And I'm glad she is."

Annabelle's words steal Violet's, and Rowan steps between the two in case Violet reacts badly. "Were you complicit?" he asks.

"Ha. As if I'd show you that evidence if I helped kill my best friend."

"Then why say you're happy your friend died?" asks Violet through clenched teeth.

Rowan steps to his left as Annabelle pushes him. I bloody

hope she doesn't push Violet—in any way. The woman crosses her arms and peers down.

"You're Violet Blackwood. The necromancer's daughter."

"That's a fact that rarely needs establishing."

"What do you think about necromancy, Violet? Do you practice the magic?" she continues.

I tense and exchange a look with Rowan, whose eyes dart between the pair. The guy's skilled in stepping in to interrupt Violet saying the wrong thing, but in this case we've no idea why Annabelle asked the question.

"I've only succeeded in reanimating animals," she says coolly.

"*Succeeded*. You've tried a human?"

Violet looks her dead in the eye. "Not yet."

Annabelle's mouth twists in disgust. "It's a disgusting, immoral use of magic and everyone who possesses the power has a corrupt soul. Necromancers use their abilities to further their own ends."

"My mother never has," she retorts. "And neither will I."

"I don't believe *that*," she sneers.

"How did Madison die and who killed her?" shoots back an increasingly agitated Violet. "Tell us and the door handle will become functional again."

Annabelle sucks her lips together and looks between the three of us. "Since nobody has seen Maddy since the night she disappeared, my best friend killed herself."

Again, Annabelle manages to stun Violet into silence.

"Why would she do that?" asks Rowan cautiously.

She gives him a long look. "Because Viktor Whitegrove was—or is—a necromancer. He threatened to kill Maddy himself and bring her back as his. Permanently. Maddy intended to ensure her body wouldn't be... viable."

"How?" I ask.

"She was one of the top students in potions. Created something that would poison her blood and body, and no magic would touch her."

Violet scoffs. Actually *scoffs*. "Then Madison must be alive. The sensible course of action would be to use the poison on Viktor."

Annabelle gawks at Violet. "If she'd killed him, Maddy wouldn't survive long. His family would discover what happened. His father's Cornelius Whitegrove. Circle leader."

Whoa. Violet stares. "Cornelius Whitegrove covered up a murder?"

"There's no Viktor Whitegrove on record as his son or a relative," says Rowan. "Neither is there a Whitegrove male who matches Viktor's age. I've looked into his family. Repeatedly."

Annabelle shrugs. "The family would never risk a scandal like that. There's no record of him because he 'disappeared', and they erased him from the family. The Whitegroves would know what happened—no way would Vik manage to dispose of Maddy's body on his own. I bet someone paid Maddy's parents a lot of money or used some potent mind magic."

"The Whitegroves would've killed Maddy?" I ask.

She blinks, as if finally noticing me. "Are you a hemia?"

"Yeah, why?"

"Keep away from the kids out there." She jabs a finger towards the playing fields.

My jaw slackens. "Hemia don't spend their days stalking and murdering kids—or anybody. That's racist."

She throws him a look of contempt. "Believe me, humans are less accepting of your type."

"How is the likelihood of Grayson massacring a children's soccer team relevant?" interrupts Violet.

Annabelle keeps her eyes trained on me for a moment. I've seen the look many times—distrust mixed with distaste, as if I'm a rodent that needs poisoning. "I don't trust hemia."

"Oh. So not relevant. Can we get back to Madison's ridiculous decision to poison herself?" says Violet blithely.

Something within Annabelle twists and snaps as if a glow stick, sending white magic to her fingers. "How would *you* feel if death was the only way to escape life controlled by a necromancer or his family?" She fists her hands against the magic. "You'd never understand because no male would ever attempt to control you."

"Neither could they kill me," she replies. "So, no. I don't understand."

Annabelle's mouth turns down. "Maddy split with Vik after months of him treating her like crap. She wouldn't listen to us—either he used mind magic, or she couldn't see him for what he was. A week before the dance, he attacked her, and she finally woke up to what type of guy he was. Maddy ended the relationship, but he refused to leave her alone."

"Why didn't Madison go for help? Ask authorities to involve themselves?" asks Violet.

"The world was a different place thirty years ago," says Annabelle stiffly. "The Whitegroves had too much power and influence."

"How did she know exactly when Viktor planned to kill and reanimate her?" asks Rowan cautiously. "Surely she didn't carry poison around every day."

"Maddy was future-sighted and saw the evening of the dance. I suggested we take him out ourselves first—we planned to. Only Maddy took things into her own hands because she didn't want the Whitegroves hunting me and Christine too."

"Maddy saw and told you where the death would happen?" continues Rowan.

Annabelle shakes her head. "Unless Maddy decided to change the location, after the Spring Ball he took her to the place they hung out in private. A place that belonged to friends of the Whitegroves. That's all she told us—I think she worried that we'd follow."

"Do you know where that is?" asks Rowan.

"No. Never invited. Close to town, I think."

"Then we need to find where and visit to the scene with the tiara," says Violet. "Your psychometry might be clearer."

Rowan pulls on his bottom lip but says nothing. I don't think *I'd* like to see what the tiara remembers either.

And there's the small problem that we don't *have* the tiara.

"And Viktor?" I ask. "What happened to him that night?"

"I'm not sure, but someone took the tiara when they took Maddy—that bastard probably."

Violet chews on her lip, a crease of confusion to her brow.

"Why did you never tell Madison's brother or parents any of this?" asks Rowan.

Annabelle gives him another disparaging look. "Firstly, how the hell could I tell them she took her own life, and secondly, I'm not supposed to know any of this, am I?"

"Thank you," says Rowan. "For trusting us and giving us the papers."

She shakes her head. "Nobody knows I had those things of Maddy's."

"If he's out there, I will find the witch," she says solemnly.

"And kill the bastard?" she shoots back.

My heart jerks as she pauses before replying. Never a good sign.

"I believe the favored idiom in this case is 'death would be too good for him.'" Violet smiles sweetly. "Well, immediate death anyway." She looks at Rowan. "I'm building quite a list, aren't I?"

Annabelle chews on her lip as if biting back words. She sighs. "The reason you can't find him, Rowan? He doesn't call himself Viktor anymore."

"But you know his name? The one he uses now?" urges Violet.

Annabelle runs her tongue along her top teeth. "Yes."

"Why didn't you say?" she protests.

"Fear for my life?" she replies sarcastically.

"And?"

"And if I give you his name, can you promise me that Dorian Blackwood will find and arrest him for what he's done? *Deal* with him?"

Violet doesn't respond for a few moments. Dorian told her he wasn't interested, but will this change his mind? I hope for Annabelle's sake that it does.

"Yes."

"How can I be sure?" Annabelle asks.

"Because my father is looking for a necromancer," she says quietly.

"What? What's the bastard done?" She drags a hand down her face. "I should've come forward before, but you have to understand I'm scared. I am only doing this now because Dorian can catch him."

"Do you believe somebody may know you intended to meet Rowan?" asks Violet.

"Are you being watched because you're digging into things you shouldn't?" she replies.

"Undoubtedly."

"Then whoever watches you will see me too. Now do you understand why I wanted to keep away? You could've put me in danger now."

"Realistically, you did that yourself by agreeing to meet and hand over the evidence you have."

I close my eyes in despair at Violet's Violet-ness.

"And I said, I expect you to find justice for Maddy. Her body. *Him*."

The bloodied words: *this isn't over until he is,*

Violet lifts her chin. "Only somebody connected to the crimes would follow or threaten you. In those circumstances, I've no qualms in using my less *pleasant* side to deal with the person concerned."

"Neither does he," says Rowan, and points at me.

"And Viktor?" asks Annabelle.

"I will also ensure you're protected—and yes, we'll catch him," says Violet. "What's his name? Please."

Annabelle closes her eyes for a moment. "Joe Smith."

"But that isn't even a witch name," says Violet.

"And a ridiculously common human one," says Rowan. "Smart guy."

"Because he doesn't live as a witch anymore—not publicly, anyway. He lives in the city, but I don't know anything else. I've kept my distance."

"How would you know this is him if the Whitegroves managed to hide Viktor from everybody else?" I ask.

She scowls at me. "He'd already used the name to hide his identity when he screwed around with humans." She pauses. "He had fake ID. A few of us did. I knew Vik's 'other' name from Maddy telling me, so I looked for him."

"To challenge him?" asks Rowan in surprise.

"And get myself killed? No. But I wanted to know if he's alive. Stupid idea because it just upset me more, and I knew I couldn't do anything without proof." Annabelle's mouth turns down.

"We'll find proof," says Violet. "And him."

"You don't know what his profession is?" asks Rowan. "What type of witch was he—officially, since nobody admitted necromancy back then?"

"Mind magic. Add in necromancy and he's the perfect rotten combination," says Annabelle. "Now, let me go. Do not follow. And if I have a single suspicious supe arrive on my doorstep, that's on you."

With a shake of her head, Annabelle walks by me and into the kitchen behind, re-emerging with a blue bucket filled with bottles of water.

"That door handle had better work now." Violet nods. "Don't follow me out."

"One more thing," asks Rowan and her face sours again.

"What?" she snaps.

"Who's the other guy? The letter read as if Madison had a new relationship."

"I don't know," she says. "And that's the truth. Maddy hid him from everybody, but obviously Vik saw them together when stalking her."

"Do you think Viktor killed this person too?" asks Violet.

Annabelle fixes her with a look. "I don't know."

"Do you think he was human?" continues Violet. "Her secret lover?"

"Possibly. We hung out with humans."

"Then what if Viktor *didn't* do this?" I suggest. "What if Madison broke the rules and told the human what she was and about the hidden world? People died for that."

"Vik did this," says Annabelle tersely. "As I said, I'm leaving. Do *not* follow."

Annabelle has her hands full with the water for the kids, so I open the door for her. The woman doesn't thank me for my gentlemanly gesture and gives me that same look as earlier. Does she have a bad history with hemia?

"Sawyer," says Violet as the door clicks closed. "He's the secret lover."

"That's a long shot," says Rowan.

"Are you kidding me? We found the tiara hidden under floorboards in the man's office!"

I tap my lips. "I agree with Violet. There's a link, especially if the witches targeting shifters and Kai are necromancers."

"You think *he's* the one behind the shifter deaths?" asks Rowan.

"Kai said Sawyer hates witches, even though he associates with them. Maybe Madison is the reason why?" I suggest. "Someone's trying to screw up Sawyer's life and if this Viktor is as bad a psycho as he seems, I'd lay bets he'd kill."

"Perhaps Dorian will listen to me now," says Violet. "We need to talk to him, and he won't be happy."

"Uh. I'll sit that one out. I don't want to be in a room with an unhappy Dorian," I say quickly. "Ever."

"Why won't he be happy?" asks Rowan. "Dorian told you he doesn't care about random deaths."

"But Dorian will care that there're people hidden from him. That a witch he discounted as harmless has a son who murdered and could be responsible for all this," says Violet. "He needs to find Joe Smith—who he is, where he is."

I don't want to say what I increasingly believe. Dorian isn't as in control as he thinks and it's only a matter of time before he loses the control he still has.

Over his world and himself.

CHAPTER 38

VIOLET

FINALLY—AND begrudgingly—Dorian listens to me, immediately setting about searching for Joe Smith, a job made difficult by Viktor deliberately choosing a ridiculously common human name. As there's no Joe Smith connected to witches, the task proves harder than we thought. I've arranged to meet Dorian tomorrow for a full debrief, which will include some smug looks from me.

Annabelle told us Viktor lives in the city, but how long ago did she discover that? What if he doesn't live there any longer?

The witch held in custody over the attack on Kai either feigns ignorance or is mentally blocked from sharing information about Viktor/Joe. We can't be a hundred percent sure Joe's involved, but there also can't be many hidden necromancers out there.

I sit with the guys in the cafe we've adopted as a meeting place, now that we want to avoid Mrs. Eldridge and the library. Rowan has his laptop and the four of us huddle around. Humans watch—what do they think we discuss when we're here? They still avoid us—and I still haven't seen Kai. A good thing that he's not walking in the world while the threat to him still exists.

I spent a little time with Leif when he returned from his mother's, again reassuring him we'd fix the situation. I'm more certain than ever that the deeds Rowan photographed must be the missing ones, so if we find who's connected to the box, we'll find those. I'm still curious why nobody destroyed them. Leverage?

Mostly, Leif hugged me and stared into nothingness, revealing little about how he felt—something I still find a little contradictory to him accusing me of the same behavior. At least he's safe from the elders for now, if they keep their promise to leave him alone while Ethan searches for the deeds.

Leif now munches on a chocolate muffin the size of my hand while Rowan drinks coffee as he contemplates his findings. Grayson and I never eat or drink anything at the cafe, which the others don't comment on. No surprises with the developing hemia, but I'm pushing away concerns why I've less appetite recently.

"How many Joe Smiths have you eliminated?" I ask, and pull out my notepad. Inside, I've a folded A4 sheet with a list of addresses, each Joe numbered. "And I don't mean literally."

"Narrowed down to five who're the right age," says Rowan.

"Good."

"Yes. But we need to be prepared that Viktor isn't any of these if he doesn't live in the city anymore," Rowan replies. "And there're a *lot* of Joe Smiths in the country as a whole."

He takes the sheet of paper from me and draws asterisks by five Joes. Crumbs from Leif's muffin fall onto the sheet, and I brush them away. "Anything significant about any of them? Please say yes."

"Ordinary people, ordinary jobs. A couple of them also have a family."

Grayson tenses beside me. "A family of victims?"

Rowan looks up. "Or ordinary humans."

282

I'm struggling with Annabelle's insight into Madison's life and death, unable to fully comprehend the girl's actions, and I gaze around at the other teens in the cafe. Is such a dynamic common in relationships?

"You okay, Violet?" asks Leif.

"I can't accept that Madison killed herself," I say stiffly, and the guys glance at each other. "Viktor must've killed her."

"He's a necromancer and a psycho," says Rowan quietly. "If you were Madison and knew he intended to take your life and create a puppet from you—"

"I'd rip his throat out," I interrupt.

"Okay, I'll rephrase that. Madison wasn't you. She chose an extreme response, but maybe that was her only way out—or Madison felt she had no choice," Rowan replies.

"But why would Viktor do this?" I protest. "If Madison didn't want a relationship with him, he should've accepted that and found a girl who did."

"Like I said, psycho," says Rowan.

My spine straightens. "Are you suggesting my father could be capable of such actions?"

"I'm sure not all psychopaths are alike," says Grayson lightly.

My hand curls around the paper. "Do you think *I'm* capable of something like this?"

"Violet. You're not a psychopath, remember?"

"No, but I'm a necromancer."

Leif leans back in his seat. "You're not capable. Violet, you'd never use necromancy to harm someone. Annabelle's wrong— not all necromancers are immoral. Look at Eloise."

But am I? I'd joked that I would've reanimated Wesley and demand he perform tricks, but did that idea come from somewhere inside? Now that I've seen the shifters and the result of necromancy, that joke's hollow. I'm increasingly confused how I feel about this side of my nature now. The desire to master the dark magic exists as an inner compulsion, rooted in curiosity and pride that I'm one of few who can. But should I stop pursuing the ability?

I finally understand Eloise's reticence. Even if you've saved a life, you've also taken one.

"Sounds like Viktor is a controlling, entitled asshole who manipulates people and refused to let Madison go from their abusive relationship. He had the added benefit of magic he could use to control Madison and ensure she couldn't ever leave him." Rowan shakes his head. "The disgust on your face proves you don't have that evil in you, Violet."

"No. I guess my darkness lies elsewhere."

"Violet, the world's full of people like Viktor," says Leif. "People are shit."

Grayson laughs softly. "Yeah."

"I don't like this world," I announce. "Sometimes, I wish I'd never left Scotland."

Rowan nudges me with an elbow. "But you wouldn't have three wonderful guys in your life or the thrill from your new occupation as a detective."

I regard him. Dorian's words—tangled lives lead to betrayal and disappointment. Anger. If I'm already filled with disgust and fury at this witch for causing a girl's death, what will happen when I see him? Rowan's an example of a potent witch influenced by unconstrained emotions. I don't use shadows, and I'm not capable of actions like Viktor's, but what if I unravel and reveal my black center too?

I could kill Viktor.

"We'll find the guy," says Leif and finishes his muffin. "Bring Julius closure."

Grayson nods at me and Rowan. "Why haven't you told Julius what you discovered from Annabelle?"

"I wanted to, but Rowan informed me that's not a good idea at present."

"The guy's mentally fragile," says Rowan. "Violet agrees."

"No. The reason I never told Julius is because he might say

something to Mrs. Eldridge, who I *still* suspect has a connection. She told Rowan to back off, remember?"

"And to save Julius from having a major breakdown?" asks Grayson.

"No. I imagine he'll have one anyway, so that's best delayed. He could reveal too much." I tap the table. "Perhaps if we find Madison's body—even a bone or two—that could help?"

Rowan stares. "How?"

"Julius will have part of his sister back, therefore his breakdown may not be as intense."

"Yeah, I think you've a way to go yet before you learn about people, Violet," says Leif.

I huff when I recognize the look they're all giving me—the one where I prompt them to remember the Violet who needs to work on her empathy.

"Tell me about the Joes."

Rowan outlines what he knows about each one and they shoot down my suggestion to follow them all for a couple of days. By the end of the discussion, we're left with two likely possibilities—one Joe, who lives with his wife and young daughter in a suburb at the edge of the city and another who lives alone. The family could be a cover—Rowan already checked them out: the daughter attends a local school, and neither she nor the mother are registered supes.

"I'd like to get close enough to ensure the woman and/or child aren't the result of a spell," I say. "That would help."

"What are these Joes' jobs?" asks Leif.

"Loner Guy's an electrician and Family Guy works in an office. Accountancy."

"And are either wealthy?" I ask. Rowan shakes his head. "You have addresses we can visit?"

"Violet..." he warns. "We pass this to Dorian."

My jaw clenches. Following his dismissal of the case, I'm pissed he's taking over. I've visions of dragging the witch to justice myself, while Dorian apologizes to me for ignoring my requests.

"And Whitegrove's movements?" I ask, swerving the subject, but about to broach one that I don't want to. "Any Circle activity?"

Pink dots appear on Rowan's cheeks and the atmosphere shifts. "They don't meet frequently."

"Business trips? Holidays?" I ask. "We need to get into the Whitegroves' house."

"You can't steal the tiara, Violet, we discussed this," says Grayson.

I shrug. "No, I want to look inside the place."

Again, a familiar reaction. Silent non-agreement.

Huffing, I tap the paper. "I don't care whether you help or not, I'm looking into the Joes, starting with the accountant and his family." The quiet continues. "Don't worry, I won't stalk them in the middle of the night. Perhaps a visit to his place of work? The man must have an office or some such premises."

Leif's shoulders relax slightly. "Good. I worried you planned to loiter outside the kid's school."

I smile, neither confirming nor denying.

CHAPTER 39

VIOLET

INSTEAD OF ATTENDING lessons the next day, I sneak away to the library to look for witch history books, specifically ones pertaining to the Circle. Rowan's continuing his own research and I sense his growing frustration at the missing 'Joe'.

As I head back to my room, lost in plans of what I'll say to Dorian later, I don't notice Grayson until I'm almost there. He's leaning against the wall to the left of my door, engrossed in something on his phone screen. Grayson's in uniform, but without his blazer, and there're two distinctly different reactions from the two human girls walking by. One edges closer to the opposite wall, the other takes a keen interest in his presence.

"Hi, Grayson," she says, and he looks up.

Laura, the girl who 'accidentally' bled in front of me in class that day, evidently a hemia vampire fan, considering she's appraising him closely. He doesn't answer, immediately turning his head as he senses me.

Again, he doesn't speak, but he's regarding me in the way he often does. For a guy who claims he doesn't want my blood,

287

there's always a craving in that look. I glance at Laura, who also appears interested in our interaction as I approach Grayson. Does he see my warning look not to kiss me?

"What happened?" I ask him, as he touches my hand with the side of his. Yes, he saw the warning look.

"Nothing."

I stare at Laura long enough that she walks away, then I open the door to my room, and Grayson follows me in.

"You busy?" he asks as I set the books down.

"Always."

"Want to go out somewhere?"

"Out?"

"Off campus." He steps forward and runs a hand along my hair.

"Where?"

"Not the graveyard." He smiles. "Where do you go with Rowan?"

"He once took me to the movies, but I'd rather not repeat that experience. My ears and eyes bled." He gives me a disbelieving look. "Almost."

I don't think he's listening to me again, and that thought is confirmed when he holds my face and presses his lips to mine with a gentleness I don't expect. I apparently lose my mind when around Grayson since I close a hand around his neck and kiss him back. Grayson growls, and he responds with the expected fierceness, teeth almost colliding. I hear and feel his heart as ours thump in rhythm, matching the way our lives have joined in a way that's about to cause problems.

"Good afternoon, Violet," says a clipped male voice.

Like Dorian problems.

Grayson takes several steps back, and I turn to Dorian, who's loitering in the doorway. Despite the thick, malevolent energy Dorian's projecting, he's inscrutable, looking between me and Grayson.

He isn't pinning Grayson to the floor in a fit of rage as I'd expect, but is blocking Grayson's exit from the room.

"What are you doing here?" I ask.

"We're meeting to discuss developments, aren't we?" As he says the word developments, his look at Grayson becomes blacker, and I prime myself to intervene in an attack.

"Not until later this afternoon, and not here," I say. "And please do not cover the room in Grayson's blood. Holly would be most unimpressed if she finds splatters across her rug."

Dorian laughs in derision and steps inside; Grayson shuffles slightly further backwards.

"I wanted a chat with Mrs. Lorcan before we met. While in her room, I happened to see Grayson walking towards Darwin House. I thought I'd catch up with him too, as you mentioned he'd had some issues with his uncle."

"Oh, really?" I ask.

"And to see why he visited *your* house. I apparently have my answer." Dorian's eyes return to mine, dark as the ocean depths, not his glacial blue. "Why was *he* kissing you?"

"Why do individuals normally kiss?"

Grayson remains rooted to the spot, but his focus is the escape route behind Dorian now that he's moved.

"And in your room," he says harshly. "Does this happen often?"

"No. I normally kiss Rowan or Leif in this room," I bat back.

Dorian's face hardens, and he takes slow, deliberate steps towards Grayson. I'm pissed he's deliberately frightening him when there's no reason. Pausing, he looks down at Grayson. "You're fortunate you're useful to me, otherwise you'd be in a lot of pain by now. Do you understand?" he says deceptively calmly.

Grayson clears his throat and nods.

"Useful?" I ask suspiciously.

Dorian's focus remains on Grayson. "I haven't found your uncle yet. He's elusive." Grayson nods again, throat bobbing. "I'd like your help with that."

"How?" I put in.

As I did to Laura outside, Dorian keeps his eyes on Grayson until he becomes uncomfortable and fidgets, then steps back from him. "We'll talk later, Petrescu."

"Not without me present," I say. "If you haven't found Josef, what about Joe Smith? Trent? Spoken to Sawyer? Whitegrove?"

Dorian blinks away his thoughts and sits on my desk chair. "Whitegrove and the Circle are under observation until we have something more concrete. Sawyer is under our watch and isn't impressed by his witch bodyguards. We've deciphered enough of Rowan's photos to strongly suspect the missing deeds *were* in that box."

"And Kai's with his family?" Dorian nods. "Then Sawyer didn't ostracize him for refusing to sign the papers?"

"No. And Sawyer continues to insist it's a family tradition, yet seems surprisingly clueless on his ancestors' dealings with witches and contracts." Dorian scoffs. "I'm unsure whether the man is mentally affected by witches or merely a liar who'll regret withholding information from me."

"You can't touch a human," I remind him.

"Mmm." He stretches his arms behind him, hands on the bed, legs also outstretched. "He also claims not to have any illegitimate offspring, which appears to be the truth." He taps the side of his head. Mind reading. "But maybe he's unaware they exist."

"And did he know Madison or Viktor Whitegrove? He's their age."

"Again, allegedly not, but that one's a bit cloudy in his mind." He scratches his cheek. "I have people visiting the Joes that Rowan identified."

"What?" I straighten. "We can't alert him yet."

"I thought you wanted my help?" His smile is tight, and I clench my jaw. Help, not to take over. Which he will.

"What if Viktor disappears?" I ask in panic. "He's hidden for years!"

"Violet. You must understand that if the man is connected to the deaths and threat to Kai, I need him in off the streets." He sighs. "Aren't you happy you may've found the missing link?"

Yes, and you'll snap the chain. "Could we track his movements rather than turn up on his doorstep with accusations?"

Dorian pokes his tongue into a cheek. "Because you want information about this girl and the tiara first? That's secondary, Violet."

Exactly. Which is why I need answers from Viktor before Dorian gets his hands on the witch.

"Everything's connected! Like you said, the missing link. Maybe even to the academy too?" I protest.

"The academy." Dorian looks around, brow drawn in frustration. "I've discovered nobody suspicious yet and now have to interview every single student. Hundreds. Mrs. Lorcan isn't impressed." Neither, apparently, is he.

"Watch Mrs. Lorcan."

"*Yes*, Violet; that's why I'm meeting her today. I'll chip away at the woman's mind until I find something useful."

"Breaking the rules?" I ask.

"I made the rules; I'll break them if necessary." He flicks his tongue against his teeth and rests his gaze on Grayson. "Like you broke my rules by touching Violet, Petrescu."

"I believe that wasn't a rule and more of a threat to Grayson's wellbeing," I put in.

Dorian's scrutiny of Grayson doesn't waver and he gestures between us. "Okay. Here's a *rule*. That boy does not take your blood, Violet."

"I don't want to," blurts Grayson.

Silently, Dorian steps closer and looks down, at a paling Grayson. "Liar." Then he turns back to me. "There's something in your blood that would kill him, Violet."

"Because I'm hybrid? Vampire blood kills witches, not the other way around. You risked that with Eloise."

"No. Not because you're hybrid, but because you're Violet Blackwood." He frowns for a moment. "Risk it if you want, I don't care. You know I'm happy to reduce the Petrescu population."

I swallow down impertinent words that could lead to an argument and rile Dorian further—unwise when one of his targets stands in the room. Dorian's *obsessed*. And frustrated; an unsettled undercurrent running through his self-assured energy. My father hasn't tracked down the man who explicitly threatened his rule or the people Josef works with.

Has Dorian's gamble by letting Josef walk away from Kai's birthday cost him?

I glance at Grayson. Dorian 'has use' for Grayson? Exactly what I told Grayson would happen when he worried about his safety the night in the gym.

Always one to enjoy the final word, Dorian saunters from the room, and I call after him that we'll speak later but get no response.

Grayson drops onto my desk chair. "Fuck."

My phone buzzes.

"At least he knows about us now," I say, pulling the phone from my black cardigan pocket.

"Yeah, that's the reason for me saying 'fuck'."

"Mmm." I'm not listening, forgetting all irritation with Dorian as I read Rowan's message.

I've found something big

"Rowan's room. Now." I snatch Grayson's hand and drag him after me, attempting to keep myself at an allowed speed.

We head straight to Rowan. His room's in the usual disarray, an open laptop beside notes, and his face a picture of excitement.

"Joe Smith's connected to the elderly couple who live next to the reno house," he says breathlessly, and I watch as he pulls up images on his phone screen. "While you were at the library, I went back to the street because I'm convinced we've missed something. There're a few trades vans parked outside, including an electrician. JS Electrical. I looked them up—Joe Smith."

"Joe Smith is working on the development company's renovations?" I ask, glancing at the door, ready to leave. Now.

"Wow," says Leif. "You sure?"

"Yeah. And better than that, I've discovered another connection—the Brightgroves were once Circle members. They're friends with the Whitegroves. Go back years."

"Good grief!" I grab Rowan's cheeks and kiss him hard on the mouth. "You're amazing!"

Rowan smiles wryly. "The way to Violet Blackwood's heart."

"You should ask for a reward," says Leif and snickers.

"I would be careful what you say," I retort, and he holds his hands up, palms out, but his eyes glint. Shaking my head, I grab Rowan's phone and swipe across the photos he took earlier.

"Dorian's search missed something at that house," I say, "the witches are tearing the place down for a reason."

CHAPTER 40

VIOLET

A LANE RUNS BEHIND THE WITCHES' property and renovations, alongside the fields towards the nearby modern housing estate. The narrow, unlit pathway offers a route for locals on the human estate to walk into town away from the busy roads or serves as a shortcut for kids headed to the bus stop.

What would be a busy route in the daytime becomes an unlit walk from town to the outskirts, and I doubt many hop over the stile between the meadow and the street-lit boxy homes across the way.

We stealth along the lane as if walking towards the estate, but to locate the witches' property from the rear. The house isn't visible to those who walk by, due to a tall hedgerow bordering the edge of the land for privacy. The watery moonlight helps Rowan find his way and I focus on not rushing onwards even though I'm worried I might miss something.

The thick privet hedge tugs at my hair and jacket as I shove my way through the first gap that I'll fit through. As I pull a stray leaf from my sleeve, I watch Grayson and Rowan push through the hedge too. Leif finds maneuvering his bulky frame through a small gap harder. Rowan and Grayson aren't small, but their figures are leaner and Grayson in particular has a feline fluidity that helps him.

Rowan drags hair from his face and peers at where I'm partially hidden in the bush's shadowy overhang, out of the moonlight.

"You're quiet," he comments.

"Merely assessing the situation."

Pursing my lips, I stare into the inky blackness towards the misshapen building, and beyond to the house Rowan and I visited. Inside the intact house, lights glow behind curtains at an upstairs window facing us, but there're none lit on the lower floor.

"And if we detect witches—" begins Grayson.

"We call Dorian," I finish.

"Uh, no. We *leave*," says Rowan. I turn my eyes their way and say nothing.

"We call Dorian."

"And leave," he repeats with a stern look.

"Watch from a distance. Follow if necessary," adds Grayson.

"What? You're really not helping, Grayson," retorts Rowan.

"I'm not looking for witches; I'm seeking shifters or evidence of Madison." I tramp across the unkempt lawn before the conversation descends any further into an argument.

More renovation rubble fills the dumpster located at the side of the house, and I note that another wall inside has disappeared. Pausing to focus my senses a moment and trusting there're no witches in the vicinity, I step into the building. Scaffolding props up the ceiling in the center of the house and the only wall divides the open area from the gutted kitchen.

I prowl around the space, gazing upwards. Where a staircase once led to the upper floor, there's now a hole. Silently, Rowan and Grayson follow me into the building, Leif hanging back to watch the house from the edge of the bushes. We're in our darkest clothes, Grayson wearing a black beanie, but Rowan is hidden behind a hood. He holds a flashlight—no conjured witch light tonight, as we don't want spells detected. If only his eyesight could match mine and Grayson's and we could dispense with the need for artificial light.

He shines the flashlight upward to the gap left by the missing stairs. The ceiling's intact in this part of the house, as is the roof above. "What do you—Violet!"

I barely hear him as I disappear through the gap, effortlessly pulling myself up on the exposed floorboards. Crouching on hands and knees, I survey my surroundings. A bedroom perhaps? No furniture any longer, but the carpet remains and there're four marks where a bed frame may've stood. The wallpaper peels from what remains of the wall between this room and a small bathroom with lime green, dirty fixtures.

Grayson pulls himself up too, and I look down to an annoyed Rowan. "Help him," I say and walk through an empty doorframe, then stand, arms crossed, waiting for Rowan.

Rowan grumbles, brushing off his jeans as he and Grayson join me. "Anything?" he asks.

"No. Not even an attic."

Rowan tips his head and walks along the bare floorboards before pausing. "Yes, there is." He opens a small door at the end of the hallway to a short set of narrow steps. "Attic access."

"Hmm. My lack of late twentieth century architectural knowledge fails me," I say as I run a hand along the small door. We I would need to bend to get through here.

"Okay, but let— Rowan begins, but I'm through and up the steps in seconds, emerging into a dusty space.

Several cardboard boxes are piled at one end, household items protruding from inside, the room empty of everything but those and a single metal bed frame.

And something I did not expect to see.

"Look at this," I call quietly.

Rowan and his flashlight appear, Grayson close behind, and we stand beneath the sloped ceilinged.

"What the hell?" asks Rowan, voice hushed.

"Whoa." Grayson approaches the wall by the bed.

A single set of chains with manacles are attached to the exposed brick wall, and the floorboards gouged in places. Claws. I turn one eighty degrees and come face to face with a set of runes daubed on the painted ceiling.

"Rowan." He shines the flashlight at the shapes and then at the floor beneath.

"Runes here too," he says.

They're not intricate. On the floor, intersecting lines and circles create a spell circle that enhances magic, and the runes above us appear to be protective.

Protecting the room from anybody entering? I exchange a look with Rowan. He recognizes their purpose too.

Behind, the chains rattle as Grayson takes hold.

"I don't know whether to be happy or not that we haven't found a shifter," he says. "Rowan. Can you pick up any images or energy from the chains?"

"Uh. Maybe."

But he stays by the runes as I prowl around the dusty attic space. Squares mark the floor where stored items held off the dust—items since removed. There's a skylight window above, large enough for someone small to wriggle through, and the ceiling's dry walled and painted a light cream color rather than exposed beams.

"This was a room," I say. "Someone's bedroom?"

"Someone who likes chaining up guests?" asks Rowan hoarsely.

"No, I think the chains are more recent." I walk over and take hold of the cool metal. "Dorian's people went through the place carefully. The chains are newer than the bed. That's rusted; these are shiny."

Grayson crosses his arms and slowly turns full circle. "Look under the floorboards, I guess? Seems a popular hiding place for people involved with this shit."

Rowan shines his flashlight downwards. "Yeah, but most boards are already wrecked. Looks like Dorian *was* thorough."

"The man had the tiara," I say, half to myself. "He hid the box here and had to move it."

"Viktor?" asks Rowan.

"Or Whitegrove. *Somebody* connected to Madison's death. I bet Whitegrove helped his son cover up what happened," says Grayson.

Rowan's hand shakes and the beam from the flashlight wobbles. "Do you think Madison's body's here?"

"Good grief, Rowan, calm down. If someone moved the box with the tiara, I'm confident they wouldn't be stupid enough to leave a body behind."

"If she was ever here," puts in Grayson.

"Check on Leif," I say. "In case we were followed."

Grayson nods and moves towards the gap we climbed through and silently disappears back down.

"There must be a clue to *something*," I say in exasperation.

"The box was probably here," says Rowan and waves his light at where the floorboards are removed, not broken. "And I'll ignore your rude dismissal of my fears."

Crouching down, I peer into the hole, but it's smaller than the one at the factory. Would the tiara box fit in here? I place a hand inside the dark hole. Nothing. No bones either, but I don't say that to Rowan.

Standing again, I rub Rowan's arm. "I apologize for my earlier response. Are you prepared to touch the chains?"

"Do you think I really need to—someone obviously chained up shifters here. Good thing Mrs. Brightgrove is half-deaf; I bet the 'guests' weren't quiet."

"Hmm. Magically subdued, I imagine. We need another visit for tea and biscuits," I say. "Meet her husband this time."

"How? We created a dubious reason for visiting last time. We might not be so lucky twice."

I suck on my teeth. He's right. "They're friends with the Whitegroves," I say.

"And?"

"And part of the Circle."

Light blinds me as Rowan lifts it to my face. "No," he says roughly.

"Yes, they are. We established that."

"No, I will not attend a Circle meeting," he says, the coldness in his tone setting the hairs on my arms.

"I wasn't suggesting you do. I'm merely reiterating the connection." Whitegroves. Brightgroves. The similarity in names— a close enough relationship that they'd protect Viktor on the family's behalf? "I'll find a different way to figure out their connection and how to visit the Brightgroves. Lilac—or whatever her name is—was easy enough to use mind magic on, despite the deafness."

"Elizabeth. Her name."

"Uh. Okay." Rowan doesn't speak again as I crawl around the room, checking each disturbed floorboard and examining the walls. Not surprisingly for a witches' house, there's residual magic infused into those walls and floors.

But did I dismiss Rowan's theory too quickly? Was Madison's body once here?

"Sienna felt like she couldn't breathe when wearing the tiara," I say to Rowan as I stand and brush dirt from my jeans. "Do you think Viktor hid her under the floor or in the walls?"

"Don't," he says. "And no. Like you said, whoever wouldn't be stupid enough to leave a body here when the place is under investigation. Sienna's response might be the poison and how it affected Madison's heart and lungs."

"Perhaps," I say quietly, but that doesn't rule out a body hidden here in the past.

Rowan sets the flashlight on the floor and his arms wrap

around me, and I'm suddenly aware my heart beats faster. "I know you're not coping with this," he whispers.

"I believe our investigations are going well."

He pulls back and strokes a strand of hair from my face. "The way Madison died. Viktor's necromancy threat to her. It disturbs you."

I take a shaky breath. "Only because I imagine something like this happening to Holly. Before, I wouldn't've cared, but knowing a girl who's Madison's age too adds a different angle. Holly's vulnerable."

"Chase is a bit of a dick, but he's harmless," says Rowan and rubs my cheek with a thumb. "Not a great witch, either."

"No," I whisper. "Holly's vulnerable in every way because she's human. Do you think I should end our friendship?"

"What? Why?"

"In case she gets hurt." I swallow. The idea she'll die becomes more a possibility to me as the days pass. "Or worse."

"That's your decision, Violet," he says quietly. "But you'll upset Holly. She cares a lot about you."

Again, all issues that would never bother me in the past.

"Speaking of. Holly approached me today," says Rowan and rubs a cheek. "Which is odd because she rarely does."

"That's because Holly doesn't like you much."

He snorts. "Yeah. I know. She asked me if I enjoyed building furniture with you the other night. I'm confused—did you use that as an excuse when you never invited her to a meeting? Because that's a weird choice."

"Hmm. Did she giggle? And had Holly consumed alcohol?"

"Maybe? Holly said something like 'I hope you followed the instructions' and then walked away snickering."

I sigh. "She's referring to the night I stayed at yours and alluding to sexual activity between us."

"Huh?"

"We need to leave." Grayson looks up from the bottom of the narrow stairs. "There're people in the house."

"This house?" asks Rowan in alarm.

"No. A new light on in the Brightgroves' place. Leif saw car headlights too. Come on."

As silently as possible, we slip downstairs, through the gap in the floor, and back into the main part of the house. I'm pissed I haven't the chance to look through the whole building for clues, but those that existed in the dilapidated home were probably obliterated before Dorian could find them. I can only hope Rowan's correct, and Dorian's people searched thoroughly.

Rowan sucks in a huge breath as we step into the night. "That place felt... wrong."

"Agreed," says Grayson.

Leif's partially blended into the hedgerow at the rear of the property, waiting, and I slant my head, listening, but whoever arrived in the car must be inside the Brightgroves' downstairs room now lit.

As I ready myself to dart across the open space between us, he steps backwards, the bush rustling as his figure disappears. "Leif?" I whisper.

"Shit. Did somebody take him?" asks Rowan.

"Take who?" asks a voice.

Startled, I look in the moonlit space between the two houses. A male witch around Sawyer's age, close-cropped hair and a green polo shirt revealing muscular arms, stands amongst the broken brick with his arms crossed.

And Trent stands beside him.

CHAPTER 41

VIOLET

"Him," I say quickly and point at Trent. "Did somebody take *him*?"

Trent's uninjured, dressed in the same scruffy attire as the last time I saw him in human form—before he tried to tear Rowan apart. I step closer to Rowan, whose impassive face gives the witch no hint of the memory I sense sending shadowy fear through Rowan.

I'm desperate to look over at the bushes holding Leif, hoping he backed off further. The witch didn't spot him, or he wouldn't ask who I meant.

"You're trespassing," he says roughly, looking between the three of us. "What are you doing here?"

He doesn't recognize me?

The man chuckles. "Yes, Violet Blackwood, I know who you are."

Immediately, I throw a barrier up in my mind, pissed I didn't the moment I saw him. Superior mind magic skills. Trent at his side.

"And you are?" I ask.

"Joe. I hear you and your father have been bothering the Brightgroves."

Joe. Smith, presumably.

The coincidence of the pair's presence feels unsettlingly large.

"Then you'll know my father is investigating missing shifters who worked at this site." I point at Trent again.

"I ain't missing," he retorts. "Shifters keep dying—my *friends* keep dying. I'm not hanging around to die next."

"Then why not tell people where you are, Trent?" I ask.

"Rather defeats the purpose of hiding," says Joe. "Trent's living at my place temporarily. He's my new apprentice."

Grayson scoffs beneath his breath.

"Why's that funny, asshole?" growls Trent. "Think I'm not capable?"

"No, I think you're not yourself right now," I say and fix my eyes on the witch.

"Why are you here?" asks Joe sternly. "Seems an odd place to spend time on a Thursday evening."

"I agree. Why are *you* here?" asks Violet.

"We ain't trespassing. Joe and me work on site."

"Bit late for building work," says Rowan.

"Bit late to be snooping around a derelict building," Joe says in a mocking tone. "You're lucky something didn't collapse on you—I wouldn't want to explain that to authorities."

"No. I imagine you don't want to meet authorities at all, Joe," I say.

"Is that so?" He tips his chin. "I also hear you've been asking after *me*. Why? Because I'm mates with the Brightgroves? Or reporting me for dodgy electrical work?"

"Just looking for kindred spirits," I say casually. "We're a rare breed."

"Witches? Not really." He gestures at Rowan.

"Necromancers. Seems my father likes to track them down too."

He splutters. "You think I'm a necro?"

"I have many opinions on what you are," I say coolly. "Did you once live here, Joe?"

Interestingly, he shifts his hard gaze from me. "I've visited a few times. The Brightgroves are friends."

"The type of friends who'd help if there were a great need?" I suggest. "Offer sanctuary, maybe?"

"Uh. When you visit people they tend to give you a bed," he says sarcastically. "Violet *Blackwood*; tell me why you're trespassing."

"Because I believe this house is linked to the *issues* in town recently. Now, why do you have chains in the attic?" I watch for a reaction.

"*I* don't have anything. I'm just a contractor."

"And a witch who knows the family. Did you live in that house?" I ask. "After you changed your name?"

Joe crosses his arms. "Changed my name? Who do you think I am?"

"Violet," whispers Rowan.

I turn to him. "I'm not playing his games. I need to know."

"But still..."

I tip my chin at Joe. "I think you know something about Madison Riverborn's disappearance."

"I don't know a Madison. Is she another person missing from town?" he asks. "Do you know a girl called Madison, Trent?"

His feigned innocence sets my teeth on edge.

"Nah," replies Trent.

"Do human girls often go missing?" he asks.

"No. And Madison isn't a human girl. You know exactly who she is," I reply.

Joe taps his lips. "Everybody knows about the human kid murdered at the academy and the threat to that other one's life. But weren't those responsible arrested?"

"Threat to Kai by Trent because he was there?" puts in Grayson.

"I was where?" asks Trent roughly.

"At the warehouse when witches attacked Kai and Rowan."

Trent stares, mouth open in a rather stupid fashion. "I ain't been near any warehouses."

I slice a look at Joe, who smiles but doesn't join the conversation. Of course, he'd make Trent forget.

"Where are you taking Trent?" I ask.

"I'm not 'taking' him anywhere. I left some tools here earlier by mistake. Expensive ones. People scope out building sites and steal shit, and my insurance company won't cover the loss if I left tools in an unlocked place." He purses his lips. "Any power tools hidden in that jacket, Rowan? Grayson?"

He knows all our names.

"That was a rather thorough explanation," I say. "Why do you need Trent with you to do that?"

"'Cause he's helping me keep away from elders," says Trent. "They know I left and want me back. Could be waiting anywhere to grab me."

"I hear one of your closest friends has the same problem, Violet," remarks Joe, "Trent filled me in. Leif, isn't it? If he needs help, I'm happy to take him in."

I snarl, and Rowan speaks. "Quite the benevolent man. Do you take many shifters 'in'?"

Joe shrugs. "None of your business. Now, I suggest you leave before I call the police and you're arrested for trespassing."

"This isn't your land *to* claim trespassing."

"Then I'll take you to Mr. Brightgrove and ask how we deal with his intruders. He can be quite cantankerous and that wouldn't be pleasant." He arches a brow in challenge.

"I'd like to talk to you more," I say.

"We could talk another time? I'm busy tonight."

"I'm positive my father will want to speak to you too—and you, Trent. Perhaps you should come with us now?" I suggest, playing my fingers around the edge of his mind.

Blank.

Trent's mouth parts again, and Joe steps in front of him. "I do hope you're not using mind reading on Trent. That would be another complaint."

I step forward, and there's no doubt in my mind that this average man with his small green eyes is Viktor Whitegrove. Few witches hold such tangible magic, fewer still an energy that snatches oxygen. "The police want to speak to you, Trent. Perhaps you should let everybody know you're safe."

Joe makes a disparaging noise and pulls something from his back pocket. He hands a crumpled business card over. "If your father's *that* keen to speak to *me*, he'll know where I am, but just in case, here's my number."

"I advise you not to avoid Dorian," I say. "You'll evoke more suspicion."

"Suspicion of *what*?" he retorts. "Substandard workmanship?"

"I've already told you, Viktor Whitegrove," I say coolly. "A girl died. Our government's permitted to use mind magic on suspects. We'll find the truth why you've changed your identity."

"Suspects for what?" he repeats, nothing in his demeanor reacting to the name.

"A girl's disappearance."

He regards me quietly, then steps closer until he's in the personal space only my guys are allowed in, bringing with him that magic aura that sets my teeth on edge. "Is Madison a friend of yours?"

"No."

His eyes glint. "Are you worried another girl might disappear?"

Unease crawls down my spine at his laced words. "No."

He looks at Trent. "Who's the girl that Violet's friends with? I imagine the Blackwood doesn't know many people who like her."

"Don't know her name. Curly hair. Always went to fire night."

"Do you think you'd recognize this friend, Trent?" he asks, eyes on me. "If you met her?"

306

"Yeah, why?" He frowns.

But Joe smiles and my stomach turns over. "Oh, just wondering. Now, Violet. I suggest you leave before there're consequences."

Holly. He's subtly threatening her—exactly the worry I discussed with Rowan only minutes ago. I dart a look between the necromancer and his construct. Viktor knows I'm aware of who he is. What's his next move? He'll know we're looking for him.

He edges around me to face Rowan. "And I suggest you stop digging into things that might lead to unpleasant consequences."

"For you?" I put in.

Joe nods at Trent. "Head inside and find the tools, mate. I'll be right with you."

"You okay with this lot?" he asks.

"They won't touch me," Joe replies, and Trent pauses. "*Now*. I don't have all night."

The shifter straightens at his terser tone and wanders towards the house, and Joe watches before turning back to us. "I don't know what little detective game you're playing, but I'd be careful who you accuse."

"You don't know the Whitegroves?" asks Rowan. "Cornelius?"

Joe flicks him a look. "I work in a human profession, but not one that causes me to cross paths with people like them. Yeah, I've met the guy, but haven't seen him for years."

"You don't work in an occupation where you'd use your magic, *Joe*?" I ask.

"According to you, I'm a necromancer, so there isn't much call for that," he says with a chuckle. "Some witches lour our society."

"Because they're forced to?" I suggest.

He leans forward, in my face, and the dankness surrounding him touches my skin. "I suggest you leave before somebody gets hurt."

"A threat?" I don't move a muscle, holding his challenge.

"You're at a demolition site. Accidents happen." He steps back. "Now piss off back to your academy and friends."

Joe turns on his heel and marches towards the house, swallowed by the darkness as he follows Trent.

CHAPTER 42

ROWAN

VIOLET PERCHES on the wooden stile between the pathway and the fields that spread across the land between the old and new part of town, and I don't need to read her mind to know what's coming next.

"That witch brought Trent here to chain him in that attic." She gestures at the bushes a few hundred meters away, where the property sits behind.

Leif stands opposite her, hands in pockets. He'd hung back behind the bushes but listened in—I'm glad he did because, again, I know what's coming and I'll need his help.

"We need to free him," she announces.

"Uh. Or call someone?" suggests Leif. "*If* Trent is there."

Grayson splutters. "Or not look at all because Viktor will expect you to. He'll hang around."

"I'm not stupid, Grayson. I shall wait until he leaves in his van."

"And if he doesn't?" he replies.

"Then we return tomorrow with Dorian's investigators."

I shove hair from my face. "Will Dorian listen to you this time?"

"I hope so."

"What if Viktor disappears because he knows you're onto him?" asks Leif.

"What's more likely is he'll resist any investigation into his mind if caught," she says. "Annabelle said he's a strong mental magic user. If Viktor approaches Dorian and offers him the chance to look into his head, then walks away having revealed nothing, he'll think he's got away with this again. *Then*, Dorian's people can follow him. He'll slip up and we'll get proof."

"About Madison's death? Dorian isn't interested," I say.

"No. About Viktor killing and reanimating shifters. Threatening Kai who's still in danger. His connection to Sawyer."

"And threatening Holly," says Grayson quietly.

Leif tenses. "He did?"

"In a roundabout way. That's his attempt to make me back off." I nod. "We'll need to ensure we keep an eye on Holly, especially outside the academy."

"That'll be fun for you." I smirk. "Nights out with Holly and Chase. Afternoons at the mall with the girls."

She presses her lips together. "Not for long. We'll catch Viktor soon."

"Did you recognize the guy's voice from your memories of the night Wes died?" I ask Leif.

Leif's jaw hardens. "No. You know the witches screwed with my head. I might not remember."

"Can one of you stand somewhere the van and road are visible? Tell me when Viktor leaves," puts in Violet.

"This is *not* a good idea, Violet," I say.

She snaps her head around. "And what if we never see Trent again? This could be our last chance."

"Someone would notice if Joe's 'apprentice' disappeared," says Grayson.

"Nobody would give a shit," says Leif gruffly. "Trent exiled himself and nobody tried hard to get him back, despite what the guy said. Humans wouldn't care either."

Unlike Leif.

Since that day he came back from his visit to the elders, Leif's changed. Nothing I could do that afternoon pulled him from the mire he now struggles to escape. Leif still jokes around, the guy who thinks about others in a way the total opposite to Violet, but he left something behind at that place. And if the elders already have part of him, it could be easier to get the rest.

"We really can't wait," urges Violet.

"What if Viktor killed Trent already?" asks Leif flatly.

"There're too many witnesses that put him at the scene," says Violet. "Us. The Brightgroves must know he's here too."

"Yes. But your presence at another 'dead shifter' scene wouldn't look good," I tell her.

"Trent's already dead, remember?" puts in Grayson. "Why bother?"

Violet's eyes go wide. "You sound exactly like Dorian."

"Trent would've killed Rowan that night and might try again," Grayson continues. "Best he dies."

"Good grief!" Violet jumps down and taps the side of Grayson's head, hard. "Trent knows things. If his unlife ends, that information is lost."

"Ah, there's the Violet I know," he says with a half-smile.

Ignoring him, she turns back to me. "We won't all go. Viktor never saw Leif and only knows the three of us are here. Grayson can wait hidden outside the house, and Leif nearby again. Rowan, it's better that you come with me."

"Because I can't protect myself like they can?" I retort.

"What an odd thing to say. We are both aware that isn't true. No, we stay together for magical strength. I sensed Viktor is stronger than *my* witch side—like you are. If he attacks, I'd need help to stop him overcoming me before my full hybrid can take him on at full force."

"Bad idea all round, especially if you're 'full hybrid' emerges," says Leif. "Let's go."

Violet puffs air into her cheeks. "No. Don't worry. I'm not walking into that house until we're sure Viktor left. He won't hang around."

"I bloody hope you're right, Violet," I say. "Message Dorian. Tell him where you are in case we need him."

"Dorian can't travel to us using blood runes," she reminds me. "He never visited the location when his investigators did. The closest he'll get is the cafe on the edge of town."

"Still, he should know," I say.

Violet nods. "I'll message him. Grayson, can you conceal yourself somewhere closer to the Brightgroves' place and let us know when the van leaves?"

As Violet hops back onto the stile, I fold my arms over my chest and stand in front of her. "What we spoke about... if Viktor comes back and anything happens to me."

She runs her tongue along the back of her top teeth. "I'd kill him before he managed to end your life."

"Excuse me?" says Leif in shock.

"Rowan has requested I don't interfere with natural events should he die." Violet's eyes bore into me. "But you're being extremely fatalistic."

"If that witch is the one behind the plot against Kai and your father's council, and he's stayed hidden, don't underestimate him."

She hops down and takes both my hands in hers. "Then I hope he knows not to underestimate me."

CHAPTER 43

VIOLET

As we wait for Grayson, I hear the slam of the van door and start of the engine and wait impatiently for him to return and reassure Rowan and Leif that Viktor left. He takes a few minutes—Grayson pursued the van, ensuring Viktor left the area and didn't turn back. Rowan relaxes. A little.

"Joe climbed into the van alone," says Grayson. "Trent must be in the house."

Leif takes a ragged breath. The whole time Grayson watched and waited; Leif remained quiet. Everything we've witnessed feeds into his fears. The elders offered Leif protection from exactly what's happened to Trent: abuse and possible death by witches.

I promised to protect Leif, and I will. With everything I have.

"I'm not going in there," says Leif.

"No. We won't all go in. Like I said, me and Rowan will. You two stick together somewhere you can watch anybody else approach the house."

If they've the element of surprise between them, they can

subdue a witch long enough for me and Rowan to join the scene and help.

I take Grayson's arm and guide him to one side. "I hope I don't need to tell you to leave internal organs where they belong."

"And I hope I don't need to tell you to stay away from fence posts," he says quietly.

I'd hoped my unhelpful physical reaction to Grayson would calm now I'd accepted what he is to me, despite his blood in my veins. A stupid conclusion because our mingled blood rushes to the surface along with my own as he strokes my cheek with cool fingers.

"There are no fence posts, and even if there were, I'll be inside an attic."

He smiles. "I'm saying, keep away from impaling instruments."

"We've suffered enough impaling in recent days," I say.

Grayson's fingers trace my face, and he watches as they stroke my cheek. "Be careful, Violet."

Before I can pull away, he presses a hand against the back of my head and kisses me in a way that makes Leif clear his throat. Grayson's fingers linger as he speaks to Leif. "Where do we hide?"

"This way."

As the pair meld into the evening, me and Rowan edge around the house, keeping to the shadows too. We edge through the broken entrance and across the torn floor towards the hole in the ceiling. I nimbly leap up and reach down to help Rowan through.

"If he's there and chained, what do we do? Call the police?" Rowan whispers as he stands and brushes away the dust.

"I don't trust humans. They might allow shifter interference if they do. This isn't a human matter. We could take him somewhere until Dorian arrives and let Ethan take over, with the elders?" I suggest.

"Have you seen the size of Trent? Hardly easy to hide. And where do you suggest? Your room? Holly would freak out." His voice drops to a whisper as I push at the small door to the attic. "Has Dorian replied to your message yet?"

"No. I've told Dorian that if we find anything, I'll meet him in the least public place the runes can transport him too," I say.

"And you told him we found Viktor and Trent."

"Yes."

"Send another message," he hisses after me as I guide myself up the steps into the attic. "Better still, call him."

My sight immediately sharpens on the undead shifter lying on the bed, hands manacled either side by the chains, ankles cuffed to the frame. Trent's completely still and quiet. First, I panic he's *dead* dead, and secondly I'm somewhat relived that he's here and we could possibly help.

Sneaking over, I look down at Trent. He's unconscious but not in sleep—the construct barely breathing. Rowan climbs the steps behind, as silently as possible, but uncomfortably loudly to me.

"Oh, fuck," he breathes out as he emerges into the attic. "Is he...?"

"Deader than before?" I lean over and touch Trent's forehead, but he doesn't move the tiniest of muscles. "Viktor likely spelled Trent into inaction until he wants his construct's 'help'."

"And not help with installing wiring," mutters Rowan.

Rowan hasn't conjured a witch light, but the moonlight that was unhelpful outdoors now shines through the small window positioned above us onto a scene clearly horrifying Rowan.

"Dorian *has* to listen now," I say.

"I still think we should call the police," he mumbles. "Viktor isn't dumb enough to leave Trent like this when he knows you're around. He'll be back."

"Then find Leif and Grayson." I take a walk around the attic, re-examining the space for other objects in case Viktor left something else in the room.

Sending a quick text to Leif, Rowan heads back down the stairs. I should share his horror that Viktor did this to Trent, but that isn't the worst the witch has done to the guy. I'm faced with another confronting example of the spell. Right now, necromancy is less of a magic I'm proud to possess and more a disgust that I've something in common with Viktor.

My eyes go to Trent's torn shirt and my heart skips. A familiar rune adorns Trent's chest. If that's Blackwood, I've more proof Viktor's connected. Has Trent's life ended like the last victims? No —blood whooshes through his veins, slowly, as a shifters does, and there're no other visible injuries.

I quickly kneel. Apart from the runic carving, his chest is intact, and I gently turn Trent's head to one side, and then the other. Again, nothing. The edges of the rune bleed from incisions deep enough to show the shapes beneath the blood oozing around. I've seen the photos from Wesley's and Rory's investigation files, and I'm looking at exactly the same rune.

Footsteps sound on the steps again as Rowan returns. "Couldn't you find them?" I ask when I don't hear voices.

But even before he emerges, in a stuttering heartbeat, I know Rowan isn't climbing the stairs.

Viktor.

He pauses and gasps. "Violet Blackwood, what *have* you done?"

"Where's Rowan?" I ask sharply, looking behind him.

"I'd heard the rumors that you're the true killer. Your father *has* covered up your crimes," he remarks, gaze still fixed on the immobile shifter. "How long have you stalked me, looking for Trent?"

"We never knew Trent was with you. We're looking for Viktor Whitegrove. Trent was an added bonus."

Eyes on him, I focus my mind for any sign he's hurt my bonded witch, but my thoughts won't stretch from my head, a leaden barrier blocking the way.

In my head or the room?

"You're Viktor Whitegrove," I say. "Your father is Cornelius Whitegrove, and he assisted in removing you from records and memories due to a crime," I continue, as he watches me impassively. Still, no reply. "You've used necromancy on Trent—and Rory. Now you have one of them chained to a bed!"

Viktor pivots and crosses to me. The thickness of his magical aura grew since earlier, more seeping out around him, invisible but as encompassing as Rowan's shadows.

"I know you're a necromancer," I say harshly. "I sense the death in your magic."

"Like you and your mother? I guess it takes one to know one." He smiles. "What are you and your little boys hoping to achieve here?"

"Help Trent and restrain you until authorities arrive."

"He's beyond help." My teeth grind at his mocking laugh. "I see your rune on him. Won't you finish the job, Violet? After all, Trent wants to kill your beloved witch."

"Let him go," I demand.

"That's a rather stupid request," he sneers. "Me and a construct versus you? Even that's too much for a hybrid without her back up."

"You think?" I snarl. "Try me."

He laughs at me again. "I won't need to."

I jab a finger at Trent. "Why bind him? If Trent's your construct, he'll always do what you tell him. He's no danger to you."

Viktor shrugs. "What can I say? I like to be in complete control, Violet."

"By killing people and using them? That's sickening."

He leans forward and whispers, "You'll change your mind once you realize it's the only way to stay safe."

"I will never use necromancy on a person." The words fall from my mouth without a thought, and they're true. My life's ambition diminishes with each new connection I make to the world and people I meet. My curiosity, and later the desire to show how powerful and unique my magic is, doesn't fit who and what I'm becoming.

How can a necromancer ever be anything *but* the creature Viktor is, once they've taken that step?

"Then you're weak. Although it has come to my attention that your hybrid side weakens both sets of powers, Violet. You don't know who you're playing with here," he says.

"Oh, I'm very aware how Viktor Whitegrove excels in mind magic, but I'm *not* weak. Especially with my friends."

"They won't be any use." He smirks. "The shifter-in-denial who thought he'd hidden himself might be more help to *me* than you."

An icy sensation slushes my blood. "What? Have you touched Leif?"

"No need." He taps the side of his head. "His mind was easy to shatter that night. Has the guy put the pieces back together yet?"

"You're admitting you're involved in Wesley and Rory's deaths!" I say in triumph. "Viggo's. The plot against Kai."

"Yes, because you can't and won't do anything about that." He slants his head. "Did Leif find the missing pieces yet?"

"You screwed with his memories. I know that."

A sardonic smile covers his face. "No, Violet. I screwed with his *mind*."

CHAPTER 44

VIOLET

"What have you done?" I ask sharply and push past Viktor. "Where is he? Leif!" No response. I dart towards the steps. The door at the bottom is now closed. "And Rowan. Where's he?"

"Helping Leif."

"With what?" I snap.

Does this stupid witch not realize that with each moment the side that can hurt him crawls from the pit of my soul? Evidently not, since he's now standing between me and the exit.

"I'm aware you're drilling into my mind," I whisper, as pain focuses between my eyes. "But the other Violet won't be influenced because she won't listen to anybody."

"Oh, yes. *Do* invite her."

"Move," I snarl.

He leans forward. "No."

I keep my face close to his, disgusted by his dank magic touching me, but refusing to move. "That's right. You don't like girls who refuse to do what you say. Did you keep Madison here too?"

"Are you expecting a confession?" he whispers.

Play for time. Stay calm. The guys will be here soon. "I don't need one. I've evidence against you for the murder of Madison Riverborn. I'm positive if I break through the tiara's spell, we'll see exactly who you are and what you did, *Viktor.*"

"Two problems, Violet," he whispers. "One, you'll struggle to find any records because Viktor Whitegrove never existed. You'll find Joe Smith's history from birth onwards, which will back up my story and blow apart yours. And two, you won't try because you'll be in custody."

My mind clouds as I swing between allowing the hybrid out to attack this man or staying reasoned until the others arrive.

I can't kill him, but an injury or two would work.

Heavier feet climb the steps and as Leif's broad figure emerges, he lurches straight for Viktor. Without looking around, Viktor holds up a hand, palm outwards and Leif's head snaps back as if the man punched him.

"Good. You're here." He spins around to face Leif, who's holding his head with both hands, face pained. "Kill the threat to your friends."

"Violet," he says through gritted teeth and makes to grab Viktor again, but instead falls backwards, landing heavily on the broken floor.

A handful of times, Rowan spiked magic into my mind in retaliation or to shut me up, leaving me pissed that he had the strength to do so. The magic Viktor throws at me now is like a dagger through the temples and I'm temporarily blinded, suppressing a yell of pain.

Hybrid. Bring the hybrid.

White dots dance across a world harder to see and I stumble again as the knife-pain twists deeper.

"What are you doing?" snarls Leif.

"Kill the thing on the bed," he commands.

"I'm not your fucking puppet." Through the cloudy world, I

see Leif throw himself at Viktor, but he stops short, arms by his side instead of raised against him.

"No, but human and shifter minds are *ridiculously* easy to corrupt." He grabs immobile Leif's hair and yanks his head back. "You should thank me. I allowed you to walk away alive that night, but you'll do what I tell you." He tugs his head further back. "I'm in your mind, Leif. I've known exactly where you are every moment since that night. Including tonight."

Leif's mouth moves but he can't speak, and the dizziness from the stabbing in my head fades away, the dark anger moving from the heart of me into every cell. "You bastard," I growl.

I'm nauseous as I look at how the average sized, middle-aged witch can hold Leif in check with his mind—that he can stand there with just a hold on Leif's hair to control him.

The hybrid rises and bays for violence, focusing on the threat before her.

"The two original suspects found with their latest victim. Trent lacerated and a rune left on the body." Viktor smirks. "I honestly should've stepped forward before, you make things too easy, Ms. Blackwood."

"Not. Happening," I snarl, lips pulling back as the serrated hemia teeth pull at my mouth.

"Stop him from harming Trent, then." He tightens his grip on Leif's hair.

"You think you'll walk away tonight?" I growl.

"Untouched by you, maybe not. But I will. I always do." He sighs. "Your witch and vamp can't get through the door. A magical lock that'd take even your cleverer than average witch too long to break through."

I teeter on the ledge between unleashed hybrid and rational Violet. But Leif. If he loses rationality, he *could* do what Viktor says. Lacerations and a rune? The lacerations need adding to the body and that's Leif's purpose here.

"You're pathetic," I spit out. "Weak. You'd rather manipulate people than work with them? Kill a girl to be your construct because nobody would ever love you? Madison poisoned herself rather than spend another moment near you."

He blinks at me, then his face twists, anger shining in his cruel eyes. "Kill the fucking shifter, Leif. Protect Violet."

"I don't need protecting! Leif!" I shout as he unsteadily approaches Trent and looks down. Where are Grayson and Rowan? Can they really not get through the door?

He purses his lips and frowns at Leif who has his fists curled by his sides, panting as he fights his thought. "Will you just bloody shift, Leif?" he says.

Leif's eyes close, breath laboring further. "I don't. Can't."

"Fine—you're strong enough. Break his neck instead." Leif shakes his head hard, mumbling to himself. "Violet's in danger, Leif."

"I am not!" I shout. "Look at me."

If Leif turns, he'll see the changes to my face, the move towards hemia features—blacker eyes and sharp teeth. He'll witness how my nails tear into Viktor. How I'll kill him before he bends Leif to his will.

How can a witch meld necromancy and mind magic into this halfway state afflicting Leif?

"You'd do anything to protect Violet. Just fucking do it!" yells Viktor.

Leif lurches towards Trent, hands aiming for his neck, and I dart over to snatch both his arms before he can touch the shifter. "Leif! Look at me."

This is the guy who held me tight at the memorial, using his strength he usually holds back. The guy terrified he'd see blood on his hands inside his memories of Wesley's death. Scared that he's a construct.

Even killing an undead Trent would destroy Leif.

Leif attempts to take hold of me, but this isn't the memorial. I won't yield. My instinct is to claw, but with a yell, I uppercut him, needing him unconscious before he tries to fight me, and I end up causing serious damage. The punch propels Leif backwards and as he lands on boxes behind him, my heart lodges in my throat. What if I hit him too hard? Broke his neck?

I dash over and crouch down. He's whiter, eyes closed, but lips parted in shallow breaths. As I reach out to touch his head, I'm caught by the sight of my inhumanly long nails, my thoughts blending into the hybrid mist.

Who'll miss Joe Smith? The necromancer who's already dead and who constructed a new life for himself?

I'm on my feet in half a breath, shoving Viktor hard in the chest, nails tearing at his jacket. He coughs as the breath leaves his lungs. "At least solve your mystery before you kill me," he rasps. "Madison Riverborn? She didn't poison herself. I knew her plan, but Madison changed her mind."

I fist his jacket, nails scraping the edge of his neck. "She's alive?"

"A tip for the future, Violet. Until they turn, you won't discover if a construct will be fully compliant. I've made mistakes and had to kill them in the past. Quite recently, too."

"Is she alive?" I shout.

"I poisoned Madison." I almost drop my grip in disgust at his sneer. "Weak girl. *Rude* girl. The things she called me... I couldn't take the risk she'd misbehave when mine, so I forced the fucking poison down her throat." His teeth clench. "That girl ruined my life just like your father fucked up our society."

"You're part of this?" I pull Viktor forward and slam him against the wall, winding the bastard again. "The plan against Dorian. Deaths. Where's Madison's body?"

"Look at how your corrupt soul can hurt someone you love. Grayson and now Leif." He smirks, ignoring me. "Magic that we hold can never be constrained, Violet. Rowan will learn to give himself over to the wonderful gift you've handed him."

My hands shake and I jerk my head around. Leif's definitely breathing. I haven't hurt him. I only meant to subdue Leif. To stop him from ruining his life.

Viktor pulls something from his pocket and holds up a small

pen knife, then flicks open the blade. "Such an ordinary human implement that can cause so much trouble." Blood stains the tip. *The knife used for the rune.*

"That's the weapon you have? Because your magic won't stop me either." I bare my teeth close to his face, moving a hand to circle his throat.

"I see you, little hybrid, strangling the sense from Violet. You want to kill me? Go ahead, but you won't kill the roots of our crusade to get rid of your father."

You can't kill Viktor.

But he can't live.

Viktor *can't* survive and leave to hurt more people. Madison. The shifters. *Kai.* And how many more past or future?

No. You can't kill.

He'll disappear. If I let Viktor go, he's gone forever.

I suck in a breath. I'm not the hybrid arguing with Violet in my mind. *Rowan.* He's below us, trying to break Viktor's wards.

Wait, Violet.

Low snarls come from me as the hybrid tries to shove away the interfering voice.

"And do you know who's next?" he whispers, stupid enough to point the blade tip at me. "Not tonight, or when you expect, but soon."

"Kai," I spit back. "And you'll fail again."

"Trent couldn't remember her name, but *I* know who she is." The malevolence in his grin—in every ounce of evil surrounding him blinds any remnant of control, because before he says the name I've already unleashed. "Holly."

I scream in his face, baring my teeth, veins filling with furious energy. I'm unaware if the injuries the hybrid plans are memories absorbed from Dorian, or stories he's told me, but as I hold Viktor to the wall with both hands all I can see is his skull smashed open, the mess he'd leave on the wall as he slid to the ground. How *I* could be the one to take his heart and watch its final beat.

For the first time, Viktor's arrogance switches to fear, face draining of color and eyes flickering with a terror that the hybrid loves.

"Too far, Viktor," I say, calmly, and clamp my hands on either side of his head until he cringes in pain. "You've threatened my guys, who can protect themselves. But now you've threatened Holly, and I've no choice but to end your life first."

"Then you'll lose," he rasps out. "The first time you kill, you're lost, Violet Blackwood."

My arms shake as my clawed nails dig into his scalp, ignoring his desperate slicing at me with his tiny knife. A few fateful seconds is all it would take to pull him back, smack his head, and destroy the brain of a man who's a curse to this world.

I take a deep breath, relishing the terrified knowledge in Viktor's eyes that he's about to die. My father's best kills happened when he had control, when he soothed the savage and bent his hybrid to his will.

As I can.

"Dorian takes pleasure in killing, let's see if I do," I whisper.

Shards of glass splinter across the room as the window above shatters, and I'm torn away from Viktor. I scream out, guttural, furious, as Grayson holds me to him, and I slash at his hands, thrashing from side to side.

"He has to die!" I scream again.

"You made me promise not to hurt anybody because that's not the way," he pants out as he struggles to keep his grip on me. "Viktor knows things."

"Let me go!" I scream, the seething rage switching to Grayson.

I'm a dervish of arms and legs, but the Petrescu proves his point that they're superior to me physically, as Rowan and Viktor are magically.

Viktor snatches his chance and I wail, 'no' as he charges down the steps. *Rowan will be there. He'll stop him.*

As Grayson's grip loosens, I spin around and circle my hands around his neck instead. He looks up, impassive, as I throw him to the floor and kneel on his chest. "You stopped me killing Viktor and now Holly will die," I scream.

"Choking me to death won't change anything. Calm the fuck down, Violet."

I press fingers harder into his throat, eyes blurring with the tears replacing the mists of fury. This time the blood from the glass cutting Grayson doesn't affect me, the fear for Holly creating an overriding acrid scent in my nostrils.

"Surely you won't half-kill me a second time, Violet," he croaks out. "Once, okay, but twice? I'd take that personally."

Growling at his dumb words, I loosen the pressure, lean in, and half-spit the words in his face. "If Holly dies, you're dead to me."

CHAPTER 45

GRAYSON

ARE HYBRIDS DESIGNED TO CRY, or is the blood welling in Violet's eyes a result of her change? I look at the face I glimpsed before she tore into me at the warehouse and wait for another assault.

Her weight leaves me, and Violet blurs from the room. I should've restrained the psychotic hybrid, because Violet will go much, much further than when tearing into the shifter at the lodge.

But I couldn't. I'm stronger than at the warehouse and we're a closer match. She isn't the only one who could lose control if we fought. The fury Violet threw at me before she left holds me in the room. I'm not worried she'll attack me if I follow, but I don't want to aggravate her more.

I stare at the sloped roof and rub my neck. So much for staying quiet—she's screaming Viktor's name. Rowan's. I bloody hope *both* the Brightgroves are deaf.

Minutes ago, I gave up waiting for Rowan to break through Viktor's wards, acutely hearing Violet and Viktor's fight, and took the only possible route into the attic to stop her. I'd heard Viktor demand that Leif attack Trent yet Leif's the injured one. Trent's unconscious and shackled to the metal bed frame, oblivious but unharmed apart from the rune.

Leif lying in the boxes close by—what happened to him?

I rub my neck as I crawl across the floor to look closely at Leif. Purple and black bruises blossom across his neck and jaw—if he's badly injured, that's elsewhere. At first, I don't notice he's conscious, Leif's eyes are closed, but he speaks as I tentatively touch his neck.

"Is Trent alive?" His amber eyes meet mine, dulled.

"Think so. Only injury I can see is the rune." I nod at his arm. "What happened?"

Leif shakes his head. "Where're Violet and Viktor?"

"She tried to kill him, Leif. I stopped her and she's furious that I did." I swallow, bile rising in my throat. "Violet said Viktor's threatened Holly."

He falls quiet and winces as he touches his jaw. "Shit. Do you think he would?"

"Look at what Viktor has done so far in his life," I say quietly.

"We have to get back to Holly." Leif presses his palm to the wall and unsteadily stands. "Or is that where Violet went?"

"She's determined to kill Viktor." I point downwards to where scuffling and voices continue, but only Rowan's and Violet's.

With a grim face, Leif moves towards the steps and grabs the rail. "I'm going back to the academy. We all should leave before somebody appears who won't understand what happened here."

"And him?"

Trent. Leif runs a hand through his curls. "I don't know what to do. Find Rowan. Ask him."

"Not Violet?"

"She *definitely* needs out of here considering the evidence carved into Trent's chest and that she..." Leif takes a shaky breath. "Attacked me too."

My jaw slackens. "What? She did that to you?"

"Yeah. For a good reason, but this scene's incriminating. Come on."

I follow Leif down the steps, his bulk between me and whoever's at the bottom.

But I needn't worry about Violet. She's slumped on the ground, resting against the damaged wall with her head lolled to one side, bleeding slash marks on her hands. Rowan stands close by, his whole body shaking. Shadows move around him like snakes in the air, barely visible in the dark, fading into the dim.

Leif's on the ground beside her before anybody can speak, moving her head upwards and speaking her name.

"Viktor didn't do that to Violet," I say coolly to Rowan. "If he had, you'd have the bastard bound by shadows beside her—if not worse."

He swipes an arm across his face but says nothing.

"Did you hurt Violet?" asks Leif. "*What* did you do?"

"Stopped her from killing Viktor." His eyes are wide in his pale face. "Is that what she's like, Grayson? When she loses herself to... *it*. I thought she'd be feral and out of control, but Violet knew exactly what she was doing. Could still weigh up what she planned to do."

"Did she hurt you too?" asks Leif.

"Too?" Leif points at his face. "Shit. No, she didn't. I used magic against her."

"Against Violet as the *hybrid*?" I ask in shock. "What magic?"

"Shadows. Obviously. Blackwood." He swallows and glances at Violet, his eyes not staying on her long. "She gets pissed if I ever slap her mind with a spell. God knows how she'll react to this."

Leif takes Violet's hand. "I thought the hybrids were infallible."

"Nobody is, Leif. She's told you before, her hybrid halves are lethal together but can't top the most potent hemia or witches," I say. "If I'd been full strength when Violet attacked me in the warehouse, things would've ended differently."

Like tonight could've if we'd fought harder.

"How?" asks Leif through clenched teeth.

"You're saying a hybrid is vulnerable to magic?" I ask.

"To shadow," he repeats. "And only because she's created that strength in me. I could probably hold her with other spells, but she'd break them."

Rowan couldn't hear Viktor and Violet's conversation as I did. That the darkness would corrupt Rowan. Violet demands that Rowan doesn't use the shadows in case he's consumed, and he's used them again.

The guy could be a weapon against the Blackwoods. Somehow, I don't think I'm the one in the most danger from Dorian anymore.

"What have the shadows done?" I demand. He swallows hard and takes a step back. No. "Did you *kill* her, Rowan?"

"What the hell? No. I paused her breathing."

Leif stands and grabs Rowan's jacket to shove him against the wall. "You did what?"

"She's breathing now, Leif," I say. "Let him go."

"Long enough for her to lose consciousness!" he protests.

"Then why isn't she fucking moving?" snarls Leif. He yanks Rowan forward and then slams him back, and Rowan swears as his head hits the wall. "You lost your shit when she died at the lodge. How could you do this?"

"Let me go, Leif," says Rowan through clenched teeth. "Or I'll defend myself."

This is insane. All of it. I'd approach Violet, but now that I'm unsure of her state, I'm wary. Violet swore she'd never harm me again, but look what she did to Leif and threatened to do to me.

"How long until she's back with us? Because we need to get the hell out of here. Viktor might come back," I ask.

"More likely he called the police," says Leif, and his grip on Rowan slackens. "'Anonymously'."

"Whatever happens, Dorian won't be able to hide the necromancy part anymore," says Rowan and brushes at his jacket. "Whoever finds and takes Trent, Dorian won't get to him first."

"Good," says Leif.

"Why do you say that?" I ask.

"Sometimes his interference isn't great," Leif replies and looks away. Huh? "Elders won't identify him as a construct," adds Leif. "But it *is* time Dorian admits what's happening."

"And Viktor?" asks Rowan.

"I heard him confess to Violet about Madison. Even if Dorian doesn't care about that, he's clearly key to a plot against him." Rowan rubs his temples. "Who's brave enough to carry Violet out of here?"

I chuckle at him. "You did the deed; you suffer the consequences." He darts a look between me and Violet, and he stumbles slightly when I slap his shoulder. "At least her nails and teeth aren't sharp anymore."

Nobody smiles at my making light of the situation when we don't know what we're facing next. I rub my neck again as I regard the unconscious hybrid.

Holly. Academy. Now.

CHAPTER 46

VIOLET

At the lodge, the moment the post impaled my heart passed suddenly, a split second before death overcame me. This time, nothing impaled my heart, but when Rowan stopped it beating, I had time to look into his dark eyes before I lost consciousness.

He choked me with shadows, arresting me before I could catch Viktor. I couldn't fight back, and not because we're bonded, but the magic he chose. Rowan could never harm me but in his mind what he did would stop worse from happening.

I don't know what to do about the shadows. Nothing I do or say stops Rowan from using the magic when provoked. Rowan claims he doesn't call on them, but if he's truthful then that's worse—they come without him summoning the spell.

The aftereffects from the heart-stopping are milder than heart-piercing, and I blood runed myself back into mine and Holly's room the moment I regained consciousness. I've never been so relieved to hear her shriek, or happier to hear her scold me for waking her.

And equally grateful Chase wasn't in the room.

Where do we start with dealing with last night's events?

I'd left the guys at the scene to wait for Dorian, who'd been alerted. Later, he called to tell me he arrived before human authorities, and I relayed some of what happened, our conversation brief, but we came to an agreement.

I'm to leave Thornwood and bring Holly home with me, along with Leif, Rowan, and Grayson. Persuading Holly to come was harder than persuading Dorian to allow Grayson.

At least a dozen outfits lie the length of Holly's bed, a small pink trundle suitcase open and half-filled with shoes and a large make-up tote.

She's ended her protest about leaving, but the amount she's packed is overkill.

The door closes behind as I step inside, and she looks up at me. "How cold is your house? Will I need a sweater?"

"I'm happy you changed your mind."

Holly takes and folds a blue shirt from the bed, focusing hard on pressing the creases. "I'm only coming with you if you explain why."

"Because you're my best friend and I want you to see where I live. You've always been curious."

"Despite your sometimes monotone, you're such a bad liar, Violet." She places the shirt in the suitcase. "Why are you worried about me?"

"I'm always worried about you. You're rather weak physically and far too trusting. Your inclination to lose consciousness at the sight of blood also makes you vulnerable to head injuries."

Her eyes narrow. "Stop the clever talk. Who threatened my life?"

Holly doesn't often hold my look in challenge and although I'm often inscrutable, she has no need to decipher my look. The girl isn't stupid.

"Your connection to me makes the current situation

dangerous. There's an individual that my father's searching for and until he's caught, I'm worried about you."

Her eyes don't move from mine. "Has this individual threatened me directly?"

A memory of the ear-splitting pitch of past hysteria and a girl weighed down by fear rushes into my mind. "No."

She's silent for a moment. "I can't tell if that's a lie."

"My family's house is one of the safest places in the country and also rather pretty." She likes pretty, right?

"Are you worried someone inside the academy could be a bad guy?" she whispers.

"Bad guy? Holly, this isn't a movie—it's real life. Your life. Mine. Everybody's."

"But you can't die."

"Not permanently, but a short incapacitation will prevent me protecting you. And if there's a lot of blood..."

She huffs at me. "Do I have to spend time with your parents?"

"They won't hurt you. Zeke and Ethan are friendly. And Eloise. *Everybody* likes you, so will they." I chew the edge of my lip. "The guys will be with us too."

"*Your* guys. Can't I bring Chase?"

Ugh. "No way. Dorian's selective about who he allows into his home. I'm surprised he's allowing Grayson. There must be an ulterior motive."

She scratches her nose, but we avoid the 'Violet greatly dislikes Chase' conversation for once. "I'm to stay until Dorian catches this person? What if that's a long time? I can't miss too much study."

Or too much Chase.

"I'm certain Dorian will find this individual soon." I pick up a fluffy yellow sweater and hand it to Holly. "There're protective spells we can use. With Rowan, Eloise, and me, we'll create something strong."

"Like a supernatural bodyguard?" she asks. "A small hellhound?"

"Good grief, that's ridiculous," I retort, then catch the smile playing on her lips. "A talisman. A ward."

But is there anything that would ward against necromancy?

"Fine, but I want to say goodbye to Chase before we go." She pauses. "Properly."

I blow air into my cheeks and pick my phone up to check the time. "Ethan and Zeke arrive in half an hour. Meet me out front of the academy."

"Okay." She grins and takes the handle of her suitcase.

I watch her trundle through the door. Ugh, again. Maybe some time away from Chase will help—especially when he doesn't contact her, because I'm betting he won't.

Viktor's threat to Holly could be just that—a threat. Would he be stupid enough to show his face again after confessing to me? The guy thinks he's as untouchable as Josef, and as adept at staying hidden. No way will he be at the address Rowan found.

Are the hemia original and necromancer connected?

Still, keeping Holly away from harm until we do locate Viktor —because we will—makes sense. I'll find spending time at home with four other people weird when the place is my sanctuary, and I'm worried about the possibility of clashes between Dorian and the others. Grayson informed me he's locking himself in a room for the duration of our stay. I half believe him.

Hopefully only a short visit home.

Following a lot of illegal mind magic on human authorities who arrived on the scene, Dorian has Trent. With any luck, Trent's mind will be filled with images of where Viktor took or kept him, besides the house he chained him inside. Or is his construct-created mind already too blank to read? What fate does Trent face now? Dorian will need to speak to the elders along with Ethan, and Trent won't know or believe what he is. Trent can't be allowed to roam in case Viktor prompts him to act.

Dorian now has his own witches living with the Sawyers while they untangle whatever the hell these deeds and contracts are, so at least they're safe. Hopefully.

No. The only people I should worry about are my friends, and I'm doing everything possible to keep them safe.

Rowan appears as I'm stuffing clothes in my rucksack, knocking on the open door but not entering.

"Hey," he says cautiously.

The shadows linger, imperceptible to most, but they edge his energy as he steps inside. We haven't spoken since last night, and although I understand and appreciate Rowan and Grayson's decision to stop Viktor's death at my hands, Rowan's future scares me. *Rowan will learn to give himself over to the wonderful gift you've handed him.* The Willowbrook stone needs taking away from the academy; I don't think Leif guarding it will be enough.

I cross and look up, chest tightening as it did last night.

Rowan stopped a heart. A *hybrid's* heart.

"Dorian can never know," I whisper. "And you are *never* to do that to me again."

He holds my face in both hands, and I swallow as the shadows stain the magic on his fingers. "If you'd killed, I would've lost you."

"When the shadows consume this Rowan, I'll lose *you*."

Rowan takes a sharp breath. "They won't."

"But you keep succumbing." I peel his fingers from my cheek. "Please don't reach the point where we need to stop touching."

He smiles wryly. "Words I never expected Violet Blackwood to say."

"I'm serious. Part of you is obsessed by my darkness, Rowan, and that's as dangerous as if Grayson were to take my blood." I rub my cheek. "And he's the opposite. Grayson doesn't want what's inside me."

Rowan's cool lips meet mine, one palm across my cheek, fingers sliding into my hair. Rowan kisses me softly, cajoling, as he silences me with the light and love he shares, not shadows.

"If you could promise never to lose yourself to the hybrid, then I could promise to control the magic. But you can't. Not in extreme situations," he whispers, nudging his nose against mine. "Not when someone you love is threatened. So, I can't promise, Violet."

He's calm, not the furious Rowan who yelled at me for weakening him, but that doesn't change who this witch is. And that frightens me. Not because Rowan could threaten lives, but because he threatens his own.

"You forgive me for last night?" he asks.

"I am extremely uncomfortable with the decision you made, but we're not in the position to create discord between us, Rowan. I hope Leif forgives *me* because we all need to pull together now."

Rowan's face tenses. "Leif's freaked out about the hold Viktor had on him. He's happy you smacked him in the face."

I frown. "Happy may be an exaggeration."

"And Leif definitely isn't a construct?" asks Rowan warily.

"No! I told Leif at the time I looked inside his head that somebody tampered with his mind. I think Viktor needs to be close by to influence Leif." I pause. "We'll fix Leif, now we've a better idea what happened to his mind."

"I hope so, Violet. He's seriously messed up about this."

"Let me find him. Is he waiting with Grayson?"

"Yeah, Grayson's excited about his visit *Chez Blackwood*."

I frown. "I would expect the opp... Oh. You're joking."

"They're out the front. Come on." Rowan crosses to the bed and grabs my rucksack before throwing it over one shoulder.

We wander from Darwin House towards the steps leading into the academy, where Leif and Grayson wait beneath the threatening rain clouds. I spent a little time with Leif last night, mortified by what I did and profusely apologizing, but as usual he shrugged that off. Can Viktor still alter Leif's mind and if so, *how* close does he need to be?

We've a lot to talk about with Dorian and my family today.

Grayson's gaze remains on me as I walk over. He's the one guy

I haven't spoken to yet, because I've confused thoughts about what happened. I'm angry he contributed to Viktor's escape but should be relieved he stopped me from killing. Viktor's words about losing myself when I do kill still shudder through me. Yes. Grayson did the right thing, but if something happens to Holly...

And I attacked him again when I swore I never wanted to lose him.

I sit on the wall beside Leif and hug him tight, whispering to ask if he's okay and getting a nod in response. As Rowan joins us, Chase walks through the double doors and starts to hop down the steps. Asshole. Always one step ahead of Holly, as if they can't be seen as a couple. I wait for Holly and her pink suitcase to emerge. He couldn't even help her with *that*?

Holly doesn't appear.

"Where's Holly, Chase?" I ask him, now a few meters away.

He turns. "She's going on vacation with you, isn't she?"

"Yes. After her tender goodbye with *you*," I reply.

"I haven't seen Holly this morning."

I curl my fingers tighter into Leif's thigh and stare at Chase. "What?"

The utter confusion on his face adds more dark clouds, then he points at something beside the large stone pot to the left of the stairs. "She's left her suitcase. Can't be far."

No.

I look to the others, waiting for an assurance to match Chase's. Leif already strides into the academy and Rowan quizzes Chase on his movements.

Grayson sits beside me, hands buried in his jeans pockets. "Let's wait. She probably got caught up talking to someone."

I nod, but nausea burns in my stomach, pushing upwards into my throat.

But I wait.

And wait.

Ethan's car appears half an hour later.

Holly does not.

The series continues with
Thornwood Academy: Dance With Death
which will publish in 2024.

Printed in Great Britain
by Amazon